The Apparition in the Kitchen

Jana O'Brien

authorHOUSE®

AuthorHouse™
1663 Liberty Drive
Bloomington, IN 47403
www.authorhouse.com
Phone: 833-262-8899

Published by AuthorHouse 11/17/2020

ISBN: 978-1-7283-6285-4 (sc)
ISBN: 978-1-7283-6283-0 (hc)
ISBN: 978-1-7283-6284-7 (e)

Library of Congress Control Number: 2020909664

DEDICATION

This book is dedicated to my brother Michael Corey O'Brien
I hope you had the time of your life
We love you & you are here with us every single day
1970-2019

THANKS TO

Tony Sturgis, a friend since Jr. High, for continuing
to provide me with all the beautiful artwork for
The Granger's Girl Series; these books simply
wouldn't be the same without your covers!
Jemison-Van De Graaff Home in Tuscaloosa
AL (location for cover art)
Stephanie's Flowers in Tuscaloosa AL (provided flowers for cover art)
Jahnese Hobson & Carolyn Breckinridge for EVERYTHING
My family for their support & endless patience;
I couldn't do it without you.
I love you all so much.

CONTENTS

CHAPTER 1

It was quite warm in the old, dark, Greek revival plantation home on Teague Road in Liberty Creek, Virginia. It was warmer than usual for this time of year. The moon hung high over the Appalachian Mountains with sneaky clouds creeping their way across the dark night sky.

Outside the usual things were taking place; deer stepped cautiously into the pasture and cougars screamed in the hills. The horses in the paddocks picked their ears up at this sound. But the cows in their own barn paid the cougars and their screams little mind. They just stood chewing their cud, bored and unimpressed by the big cats.

The barn cats played in the yard, chasing bugs and watching the bats flying near the eaves of the stable. They frolicked with the pack of seven rabbits that came to visit almost every single night.

Inside the home the usual things were taking place; the doors were all locked tight, even though every window was left wide open. The house was dark downstairs, except for the light over the big farmhouse sink in the kitchen, and the single lamp in the hall. Warm breezes blew through the big windows, and the antique grandfather clock in the hall announced it was one o'clock in the morning. The house made pleasant settling sounds that old houses tend to make in the night. A comforting smell of old wood, old brick, and old books wafted through the wide halls. Here and there was the scent of the countryside courtesy of the open windows. It was a very pleasant night downstairs.

Upstairs the hall was lit by two antique wall sconces. The soft lighting was comforting in the massive house. The open doors at either end of the hall brought breezes through their screens. Meanwhile, many photographs of ancestors from long ago, hung on the walls, keeping an eye on things that went on. Yes, things were going on. Even in the middle of the night, something was always going on, in this house.

Faye Granger had come upstairs, and out of habit, went to the end of the hall to make her nighttime rounds. The bedroom door at the end of the hall belonged to Roy Granger, Faye's brother-in-law. But he lived across the road, now. However, this had been his bedroom since he came into the world. It would *always* be his bedroom. But since Roy was not here at the time, Faye felt no real need to check on him.

The next bedroom door belonged to Faye's son, Will Granger. In here, Will and his wife, Anne, slept soundly. This had been Will's bedroom since he was just four years old. He may have been a grown man, now, with two children, but that didn't matter.

Faye cautiously opened the door and listened. She wanted to make sure they weren't in the middle of something inappropriate before she went in. When she heard only silence, she went inside the room. She picked up a few things on the floor and pulled the quilt around Will's shoulders. She lovingly tousled his blonde hair; at this, his brow furrowed. She picked up an earring that had fallen off Anne's bedside table and set it back on the table. She smiled at her daughter-in-law. She looked around the room, and left it, quietly. She shut the door.

Faye went to her grandson's room, tucked him in snug, and made sure all was right in his cowboy-themed bedroom. She kissed the sleeping child on the head, and pulled his door to, not closing it completely.

Now, Faye went to her granddaughter's bedroom, and did the same thing. She picked up a baby doll and looked around the princess-themed bedroom. She shook her head; she didn't like the princess theme in the bedroom. She didn't think one should encourage a child to think of herself as royalty. She kissed her head full of dark brown curls, and pulled her door to, also. She skipped another room that wasn't in use.

Now, Faye made her way to the last bedroom. This bedroom at the end of the hall belonged to her and her husband, Jerry Granger. For some reason, things were different in this room. She crept quietly across the massive bedroom and looked out the French doors that opened to the balcony. She had always loved the view from this room. She picked up a few things that were out of place, and went to the edge of the huge, dark cherry, tester bed, where Jerry lay, sleeping. She smiled lovingly at him; she had never loved anything so much as she loved this man.

Faye kissed his cheek. Unlike the other kisses she had given tonight, this one was felt. A very faint smile came to Jerry's lips. She ran her fingers through his hair, causing him to smile just a little more. She left his bedside and went around to the other side of the bed. Now, she pulled back the quilt and lay beside her husband.

The temperature in the bed changed just slightly, but enough to be felt by the softly snoring man. He felt the moving of the quilt and the slight shifting of the mattress. He sighed happily in his sleep, as he felt the presence of his beloved wife. They had been dear friends for 55 years. They had been married for 41 of those years. She was with him, tonight, as she was every night.

Jerry didn't need to see her to know she was there. Sometimes he could see her. Most of the time, he saw her. But tonight, he simply felt her. Tonight, nobody saw her. But the spirit of Faye Granger had made her rounds, as she had done every night of her life, and in her death.

The Granger family was an interesting one.

Seven generations of this one family had lived in this house, Faye's grandchildren being the seventh. This house was a very special house. So many people had lived in it and had died in it. Family had passed-away quietly, in its' beds. Civil War soldiers had died, agonizingly in its' fields. This house had been referred to as one of Virginia's most haunted places. There had been stories of spirits of soldiers wandering the property. There had been stories of dearly departed family members still making regular appearances in the old house. There had been stories of many spirits on this property; these stories had been told since construction of the house began, in 1835.

By the time construction of the house began, a good deal of things had already happened in these parts. This property had been referred to as "a hot bed of paranormal activity" by ghost enthusiasts. These stories of ghosts were true. It was never understood what it was about this place that was so appealing to the deceased. Even those who had died horrific deaths in its rolling pastures, preferred to stay here. People didn't have to live here, to want to spend eternity here. There was one story of a family member who was merely visiting, in 1842. This story had become one of the most popular stories surrounding the property.

Clarissa Buchanan was a charming lady of just 20 years old. She came from a well-to-do family in western Tennessee, of Scottish descent. Her family, attempting to get her away from a certain undesirable young man who had sparked her interest, sent her to spend some "quality time" with relatives in Middleton, Virginia (a town which would later become known as Liberty Creek). Clarissa went, unwillingly, to spend time with the Grangers and Teagues in their lovely home in the Appalachian hills. They were certainly pleasant hosts, going out of their way to make sure her every want and need were met. They felt sorry for her, knowing the real reason her parents had sent her to them.

Clarissa was introduced to several local gentlemen, but none of them could hold her interest. She knew Samuel was not someone her family cared for, but she was intrigued by him. He was a fascinating man, with swarthy looks and his wild, mountain-man ways. He wasn't from one of the nicer families, and this bothered her family. In fact, nobody knew anything about his family, at all. His family was in Kentucky, as far as anyone knew.

But Samuel was in Tennessee, and Clarissa was now in Virginia. It didn't seem so far away, until she really went. Now, it seemed very far away. What made it worse, was she hadn't had time to even tell him that she was going. One day she was there, in love. The next day, she was told that in the morning, she'd be catching a stagecoach to Virginia, to spend some time with her relatives.

She and Samuel had exchanged a couple of letters, unbeknownst to her family in Tennessee, with the help of her Virginian hosts.

She had been in Virginia for almost two months, when she fell ill. She had begun writing a letter to Samuel, asking him to please come get her. They could leave together, she wrote him. They could leave together, get married, and be happy. Before she had a chance to finish her letter and mail it, she passed-away in the big tester bed she'd slept in, in the Granger-Teague home. A home in Virginia, which was meant only to be a temporary fix in attempt to stop an ill-advised romance, had become a permanent resting place for a heartbroken young lady of just 20 years old.

Samuel Perry never received his final letter from his beloved Clarissa. He waited and waited, before receiving a letter from John Hayes-Teague, giving his condolences. Samuel's sweetheart had died from influenza. Samuel, overcome with grief and guilt, for having not rescued her sooner, went to Middleton to visit the grave of his girl. He met with the Teagues and Grangers and told them he appreciated all they had done to help him keep in touch with Clarissa. He told them of their plans, to run away together and marry. He regretted he had not come for her in time. They directed him to the family burial ground; he asked to go alone. Once he found her grave, he sat down beside it, and shot himself in the head.

Since just days after Clarissa's passing, others on the property told stories of seeing her. The field hands would tell of a woman, with long black curls, in a white dress with full skirts, wandering the property at night. The help in the house would tell of seeing Miss Clarissa in the bedroom that she had slept in. She was often seen from the bedroom doorway, staring out the window. But there were times, if you stood in the front yard, and happened to look up in Clarissa's window at the right time, you'd see her looking back down at you. It was thought she had stood at this window, watching the driveway, waiting for Samuel to arrive to take her away. It wasn't long before everyone on the property had seen Clarissa's restless spirit. She was quiet, except for her habit of humming. She was active, and there was no question as to whether-or-not she was really, there. Everyone knew she was.

It was only a matter of time after Samuel killed himself that reports of seeing him began circulating, too. A figure of a man, matching the description of Samuel, was seen wandering the property any night there was a clear sky. Nobody understood the significance of the clear night sky until three years after the tragedy.

The Grangers found a letter amongst Clarissa's things. In the letter, Samuel had told her to look to the sky on any clear night. When she looked at the stars, he wanted her to think of him. He promised her that he would be looking at the same stars, thinking of her, so far away. So, they assumed that's what brought Samuel out on those clear nights.

It frustrated the family and those who worked the property. These two people were buried not two feet away from one another, and both of their ghosts wandered the property regularly, apparently grieving over not being together. This was what started the abnormal relationship between the family and their resident ghosts.

One evening, Ella Teague was walking upstairs past the bedroom Clarissa had slept in. She heard the familiar humming coming from the room. She opened the door and looked to the window. There stood Clarissa, staring out the window.

Ella spoke softly,

"Clarissa, darling. Don't you know he's looking for you? He did come for you, and he's here. You must find a way to go find him, dear. He's looking for you."

The humming stopped, and Clarissa then disappeared before Ella's eyes.

While the ladies in the house were encouraging Clarissa to go find Samuel, the field hands were trying to reason with the spirit of Samuel. They didn't like ghosts *at all*. But it was quite obvious that these two ghosts weren't going to go away. So, the field hands finally decided it just made sense to try to talk to them, and maybe hook the two back up somehow.

"Hey, Mist' Samuel! Go on in 'da big house! Your gal is in 'da house lookin' for you! She only out here *sometimes*! She *always* in 'da big house though! Go on in 'da house and get her now!"

The family, house workers, and field hands all did their best to reunite the two heartbroken spirits. Eventually, the sightings became fewer and further between. Then, something happened that, oddly, caused quite a celebration on the property.

One clear fall evening, seven years after the sightings began, two ghostly figures were spotted together near the long dirt driveway. The figures were undoubtedly Samuel and Clarissa. After that, the sad story of the two lonely ghosts became a romantic story of two lovers who had lost one another in life but had managed to find one another in death. The sightings of the ghostly couple became a regular thing on the Granger-Teague farm. The couple would still be seen, 174 years later, mostly on clear nights.

So, this house was indeed a special house. The peculiar happenings didn't happen just at this house though. They happened all over the property. Teague Road consisted of three houses and numerous outbuildings.

Karen Townsend lived across the road, about a 15-minute walk away (10 if you cut through the woods). Karen's ancestors had been among the first slaves to have worked for the grand Granger-Teague plantation. Karen's family had been living on this very road, working this very property, since construction was completed in 1837. After the war, her ancestors elected to stay on the farm, working for the families that had been good to them.

In time, the Grangers and Teagues gave Karen's great-great grandparents 20 acres across the road, to call their own. They farmed the land and built a small house for themselves; a house that would, in time, become a large farmhouse with a wrap-around porch. Well, it was almost a wrap-around porch. The porch wrapped around the front, left side, back, and half of the right side of the house. It stopped abruptly on the right side, no steps there or anything. It was speculated that they had simply run out of lumber and had never felt the need to finish the project.

Karen grew up in this house, spending her days playing with the Granger boys, Roy and his little brother, Jerry. It was a happy life, but even as children, these three knew about the spooky things that went on, on Teague Road. They had all heard the stories growing up. Every child in town had heard the stories! Karen's own house had its share of odd occurrences and bumps in the night. One of the stories was about the ghost of her great-great grandfather and his goat.

Thomas had a goat, which he used to take for walks on a lead-rope. The goat would often come up on the porch, and bleat for his owner to come out and visit with him. But his wife disliked the goat on the porch. She would go out and try to run the goat off. The goat always insisted on exiting the porch by jumping off where the porch stopped on the right side of the house. So, hearing Jerusha the goat walking around the old wooden porch was quite a common occurrence.

Jerusha died years before Thomas did, due to a tragic incident involving an area cougar. He never did quite get over losing his beloved Jerusha. Four years later, he passed-away, himself. It wasn't even a week later, those in the house were awakened in the night, by the sound of hooves and heavy boots on the porch. They went outside to investigate but found nothing. This happened every night, at just about the same time.

Finally, they sat up one night, waiting. The boys were each positioned at a different window, with a gun. The girls gathered together near the front screen door. Chester was the first to hear it. The hooves came up the back porch. The rocking chair near the steps began rocking. Then, the sound of heavy boots joined the sound of hooves, and the two sounds passed right by the window where Chester sat ... but nothing could be seen. The hooves and boots passed by every window, and the front door. The sound continued across the front of the house and turned to go down the right side. Willie sat at the bedroom window, which was located right where the porch dropped off.

Willie heard the hooves and boots approach. He heard what sounded like someone jumping off the porch into the fallen leaves. Then, he could clearly hear the sound, of something walking away, through the leaves. This sound happened every single night.

In the afterlife, Thomas and Jerusha had met up with one another, again. Upon doing so, they proceeded to take their walks together. And, to this day, if you stay up late enough at night, you can still hear the sound, of the old man and his goat, out for a moonlit stroll.

Down the road a piece and across it was the third home. This was a new house, but with a very old soul. In 1757, Thomas Sewell had a house built in these hills. It was a brick and wooden home, a comfortable sized farmhouse. In 1835, John Hayes Teague and his brother-in-law, William Granger purchased the Sewell land and the several hundred acres surrounding it. Thomas stayed on the property until he tragically took his own life, after seeing his son murdered by an Indian. Story goes, that an Indian shot Nathanial Sewell in the back with a bow and arrow, as Nathaniel drew water from the well out back.

Following these events, the Sewell house remained empty. Thomas had already lost his wife in childbirth. She and the stillborn child were buried in the family graveyard. Now, he'd lost his son. He had no desire to live. The tragic passing of Nathaniel, Thomas, and the mother and child, plus two other young children, were too many tragedies for the family. Nobody had any desire to live in a house where such sad things had happened. The story of the Indian was enough to make nobody want to live there.

The Sewell home remained empty throughout the Civil War. It became nothing more than a place for squatters and war deserters. It was exactly nine days before Lee surrendered at Appomattox, that the house caught on fire. It was decided it was likely accidental, caused by one of the aforementioned-squatters or deserters. For many years, the house was nothing more than a stone and brick foundation, with remnants of what had once been a happy home.

Then, the property got a new chance at life. The Grangers had a friend who worked for their horse farm, Jason Connelly. The Grangers and Karen had been friends with Jason's own parents all their lives. So, when Jason got married not quite two years ago, the Grangers gave Jason and his new bride, Lexi, 20 acres of the property. This elaborate wedding gift included the old, remodeled horse stable Jason was currently running, as well as the Sewell home place.

Jason and Lexi had managed to obtain the floorplans to the original Sewell home and had painstakingly rebuilt their home as an exact replica. It seemed like a good idea, at the time. Now some things were going on, that made them wonder if it'd been such a good idea, after all. Numerous unexplained things had begun happening in the Sewell-Connelly home. Sometimes, these things weren't a big deal. But other things had begun happening that made the Connelly family a bit uncomfortable. It was becoming more and more obvious that the Connelly family was not the only family there. It appeared that the Sewells had come home.

These are just a few of the stories surrounding the Granger-Teague plantation, a thriving horse farm since 1837. There were so many more. No, Faye Granger was not alone. She had the company of many others. She was grateful to them all, for she knew that these souls had helped carry this family through many trials over the past 180 years.

Faye knew that these souls had saved her shattered, heartbroken husband, following her own passing. The many nights he had come so close to giving up, loved ones that he couldn't even see had pulled him through. There was a night that her darling Jerry had sat in the bedroom, drunk and crying. He had pulled out a pistol and had gone so far as to hold it to his head. As he began to pray, he heard a soft voice, humming a tune. He suddenly felt quite cold, as he felt his hand being guided by another, to the table before him. He set the pistol down. He folded his arms on the table, laid his weary head down on them, and cried himself to sleep.

One night, in a drunken stupor, Jerry tried to go down to the cellar to retrieve more bourbon. The spirit of a concerned Union officer had no doubts that that would end disastrously. Jerry Granger could barely walk five feet across a somewhat level kitchen floor. Had Jerry tried to make it down the numerous old, steep, roughly made earthen steps that led down to the dark cellar, Jerry would have died before he reached the fifth step. The soldier shook his head and went to the cellar door, where he prevented Jerry from opening it. Jerry struggled with the door but couldn't get it open. He found nothing odd about that, in his condition. He did smell a familiar smell of pipe smoke; a smell often smelled at night, while he sat drinking alone in his quiet, empty house.

Jerry didn't realize that the spirit of this Union officer spent many nights drinking with him. This man could relate to Jerry's grief; he himself had found a love outside of Richmond. She was a pretty thing! She sang like a bird and made the best cornbread he had ever eaten! He had assured her he would return for her and make her his wife. He wanted a proper wedding he said, not one done in haste. She promised to wait.

Then, he had come by the Granger-Teague home for something so innocent! He had pulled something in his arm, badly. He had heard such kind things about this family. They had opened their home to the wounded and weary of both armies. The slaves on this property went out of their way to be courteous to even the Union army. It was for these very reasons that the Granger-Teague home had been spared when the Union army made its way across Virginia.

So, this officer was somewhat surprised by the hostility he was met with when he approached the front porch. There were several Confederate soldiers receiving medical attention on the front porch. There was a doctor and a woman assisting him. The Union officer dismounted his horse in the yard, tied his horse to the fence lining the driveway, and walked up the porch steps. He simply wanted someone to look at his arm for him, and perhaps bandage it, if there was any bandaging to be had.

Somehow, his arrival was completely misinterpreted. The Confederates got belligerent and started shouting at him. The doctor tried calming them down, but they did not listen to him. The Union officer began shouting back at them, telling them to be quiet; all he wanted was a bandage! Then, he heard a gunshot. He never even saw the gun or which of the men had shot it. But he did hear the lady scream, as he fell to his knees. He laid his hand across his bleeding chest and fell forward. He bled out all over the beautiful plaster porch.

This entire situation brought about a wave of panic. The women inside came running outside to see what had happened. They saw the dead Union officer on their front porch and started screaming. The first woman who had seen the entire thing was, by now, yelling at the Confederate soldiers. She was scolding them, and shaming them, and raising quite a lot of Hell. They glared at her and at each other. The doctor began yelling at them too. Silas, one of the field hands, saw this unfolding and felt the need to interrupt these crazy people.

"Listen! Listen, Miz Granger! Doctah! You folks needs to listen to me now! We gots to get this feller off of da porch! He's dead! We caint be seen with no dead Yankee officer man on our porch! Da Yankees will come and burnt this place 'round our heads! Don't y'all need to stop all dis hollerin! We need to put dis feller somewhere now!"

11

The soldiers, ladies, and the doctor all stopped yelling long enough to consider the wise old black man's advice.

"Alright. Yes, of course. Silas, can you move him? We ought to make you damn fools help him! Shame on you! What were you thinking? Get better and get out of here!" Elaine Teague scolded. Silas and the doctor managed to get the dead officer to the family graveyard and bury him. He was given a marker, although it did not specify who he was. The horse was stripped of anything Union related and put immediately in the stable.

However, there was still the issue of the very large blood stain that his passing had left on the front porch. The ladies scrubbed it and scrubbed it, while lecturing the soldiers. Finally, it was obvious that the stain would not come out. They feared, somehow, it'd be discovered what had happened. Elaine got an idea. She looked at the huge tub of geraniums on the porch. This tub had been here for years. She suggested they simply move the tub so that it covered the blood stain. So, the ladies got together and pulled the tub of geraniums over the blood stain. And it has been in that very same spot ever since.

Now, a century and a half later, the officer remained here at the Granger-Teague plantation. He wandered the grounds, quietly. It was a nice place to be, despite what had happened on the porch many years ago. He had become quite comfortable, here. He wandered the grounds, and the wide old halls of the house, smoking his pipe.

He had befriended the confused and lonely Jerry Granger almost immediately after Jerry's wife passed-away. Jerry was quite fond of liquor, and the officer appreciated that. Jerry would sit in the kitchen, and in his bedroom, and on the front porch, and he would drink heavily. He drank during the day, and he drank during the night. He always thought he was drinking alone, but during these days and on these nights, the officer was with Jerry. He made sure that Jerry did nothing that could cause himself any harm, and he made sure that Jerry stopped drinking while he could still walk.

It was difficult, some nights. It was odd, but Officer Johnson had begun to even love Jerry Granger, a feeling he thought he could no longer experience. He began to see this man as a dear friend, family even. Jerry was like a brother to Officer Johnson, now. He felt a need to take care of him ... and he did. Yes, Jerry Granger had no idea that he had so many friends, during those long, hard times.

In the beginning, Faye had a hard time figuring this haunting thing out. She didn't know how to help Jerry or what to do about his issues. She just crept about the house, watching, and listening. She wanted to help him through this, but she had no idea how.

In time, she did figure things out. She became stronger and more in touch with what was going on around her. Faye was as much here now, as she was before she had passed-away. And the family had come to terms with this. Those who frequently visited the home had also come to terms with this. Having Faye around was no different from having the neighbors over.

She often picked up around the house (which her daughter-in-law took offense to). She often watched the children and stalked her husband when he had his new girlfriend, Marilyn, over. She especially kept an eye on her husband and his *other* girlfriend ... his own daughter-in-law.

Faye was as much Will's mother now, as she always had been. She took care of him and was so proud of him! He'd become such a dashing, smart, God-fearing man! She could not have been any prouder of Will Granger! She was proud of his children, and she was proud of his wife, well, sort of.

Faye did love Anne. Really, she did. But it was no secret to anyone in this house (or in this town, for that matter) that something a bit abnormal was going on between Jerry and Anne. Faye had seen things, more than the others had seen, and more than Jerry and Anne would have liked for her to have seen. They knew what she knew, and they just dealt with it.

Faye already disliked her husband being romantically involved with Marilyn Beales, of all people! Marilyn had always had her eyes on Jerry, that fast piece! Even when she knew Jerry was happily married, she was after him like a duck on a June bug.

When Marilyn showed up in Liberty Creek to be the counselor at the high school, Jerry was the high school football coach. She came in with her sappy Kentucky accent, her big hair, her tight jeans, and high heels. She threw herself at Jerry. Faye saw this firsthand not two weeks after this woman had arrived!

That year Will was a freshman at the school. Jerry and Faye were at the Remember September Dance at the school. The high school dances weren't just social gatherings for the students; with so little to do in Liberty Creek, these dances were hot gatherings for pretty much everybody. It was quite common to see parents mingling among the students in the gym. And on this night, Marilyn Beales mooned all over Jerry from across the gym. Jerry knew, and he obviously ate it up. But he never left his wife's side. Jerry was just like that.

When Faye passed-away, Jerry had become a recluse, and Marilyn didn't see so much of him anymore. He'd already retired. But Anne showed up at the Granger home, and literally, saved Jerry's life. Jerry cleaned himself up again and began going to town again. That's when Marilyn became *especially* interested in Jerry Granger.

Six months after bumping into one another in town, Marilyn had been a guest at Will and Anne's wedding, and she had made it a point to reconnect with the grieving widower that night. She felt he'd been single long enough, now. It was time for him to move on. A month after the wedding, she finally got him to ask her out on a date. She was elated that the very desirable, and now available, Jerry Granger was finally in her hands.

Well, she thought he was available. Little did Marilyn realize that Jerry was still quite heavily involved with not only his quite deceased wife, but with his daughter-in-law as well. Yes, Jerry had told her upfront and early on, that he had married once. He had taken a wife, and she had been a very good wife, and he'd never take another. He wore that golden band around his finger, to this very day. He'd not divorced, he'd said. Why should he take off his wedding band?

That was all very sweet and touching, Marilyn supposed. But it would have been much sweeter and more touching if the widower's dead wife was dead and gone. No, this widower's dead wife hung out with them in Jerry's bedroom, the kitchen and living room.

And to add insult to injury, there was Anne. Anne Granger was an angel, in Jerry's eyes. She could do no wrong. She had shown up, on a bad day, and suddenly all was right with the world. Within a week, Jerry ate, smiled, laughed, danced, cleaned, worked, and rediscovered his sex drive.

Anne was a sweet, pretty thing with long brown curls tumbling down her back, eyes as green as grass, and (as much as Marilyn hated to admit it) a quite cute little five foot four inch figure with a fabulous chest. Anne was perfection, as far as Jerry was concerned. He loved her from the moment she made him that first breakfast, on that second day.

He didn't care if Will loved her, too. Jerry had loved her first. She had loved Jerry, too. She loved Jerry in so many ways, ways were that were innocent, and ways that were purely and completely inappropriate. She loved him in a way that she couldn't ever explain; Jerry never had any trouble explaining his love for her, though. He was infatuated. He loved her as a person, and he loved her sexually. He felt no shame. She was just a fascinating creature! She was sweet, cuddling, nurturing, caring, sexy, beautiful, natural and earthy, and funny. She reminded Jerry so very much of his beloved Faye, right down to her dark hair and cute little body.

Faye was frustrated by this relationship between Jerry and Anne. Marilyn was frustrated by this relationship between Jerry and Anne and Faye. Anne was frustrated by the relationship between Jerry and Marilyn, and she was frustrated by the relationship between Jerry and Faye. Faye wasn't particularly frustrated by the relationship between Jerry and Marilyn, but she did think he could have found somebody better to take her place.

But it wasn't Marilyn who had taken Faye's place. Could *anyone* ever really take her place? In some ways, it seemed so. In other ways, it seemed impossible. What it all boiled down to, was Jerry Granger was quite the ladies' man without even trying to be. He was just a nice guy, who had a habit of having things working out for him perfectly. And things were certainly looking good, as far as Jerry was concerned. He had himself three loves, each of whom loved him to pieces, even though they all knew about each other … the beautiful school counselor, the daughter-in-law, and his wife, the apparition in the kitchen.

CHAPTER 2

The next morning, Jerry didn't want to get up. His bed felt wonderful. His body was sore, for some reason. He stretched in his sleep, and it hurt. He opened his eyes, without wanting to. It took only a moment of lying there before he realized he didn't feel very well. Damn! He *just* got over a cold it seemed!

All these people! It was all these people he had to hang out with all the time! Someone was always coming down with something and passing it around like Bible scriptures on Halloween. And here it was, Sunday! He enjoyed going to church but could already tell he was not going to want to go today.

He was tired the day before but had blamed it on the events of the past week. It was a bad week. Between work, the relationship issues that had taken place on this road all week, Caleb going missing, and the fundraiser … yes, it was a long week.

So, last night, when his shoulders and back were sore, and his head was starting to ache, he just figured he needed some quiet and rest. He was glad that his girlfriend, Marilyn Beales, had a brunch to attend this morning. He usually spent Saturday night with her, in town. Then, he'd meet his family at church on Sunday morning, and go home afterwards. But when she pointed out she was going to the brunch he saw an excuse to stay home Saturday night.

They had been enjoying a day full of visiting and company at his home, on Teague Road. As late afternoon light started falling across the yard, Marilyn leaned over to Jerry.

"Hey, honey? Listen, I'm going to that brunch tomorrow. You don't seem to be feeling so hot. You wanna just stay here, tonight? I'll be going to sleep early, anyway. I'm tired, for some reason. Maybe it's just from last night. Anyway, what do you say? You wanna come back with me, or stay here? It's up to you, love."

Jerry sighed. He closed his eyes briefly. He began to look up to the sky for advice, but his neck hurt.

"You know, I'm like you. I'm tired. A lot's gone on this week. I'm thinking it just wore me out. Yeah, I guess I'll just stay here tonight. You won't mind?" he asked her. She smiled. No, she wouldn't mind. She had spent a good bit of time with this crowd over the past few days, and she was looking forward to a quiet night.

She enjoyed the time she spent with sweet Jerry. She worked at the high school all week, and on Friday night, Jerry would come to her house. He would spend Friday night at her house. On Saturday morning, they'd go visit the beautiful horse farm his family lived on. Late Saturday afternoon, they'd go back to her house in town. Sunday morning, he went to church, then home. Sometimes she went to church with him. Usually, she did her own thing. He kept several changes of clothes at her place. He kept his own collection of shampoo, body wash, cologne and such at her place, too. Yes, it was a nice arrangement.

But being in a relationship with Jerry meant being in a relationship with everyone Jerry knew. She had been an only child, growing up in a modest house outside of Lexington, Kentucky. Her mother was a legal secretary, and her father worked for the power company. Yes, it was quite different from the way Jerry and his brother had grown up. Marilyn loved this crowd of people; she really did. But she always felt just a bit out of place.

It wasn't that these people acted uppity or deserving; they were just the opposite. But the fact was this family was very well off and had been for nearly two hundred years. This didn't seem to have any influence on the way they acted, though. This was a country crowd. This was a crowd that got up at daybreak, worked horses all day, tended to gardens and cows and children, and defended their home and family with a vengeance.

17

This was the kind of place people often dreamed of living. Jerry's daughter-in-law hung clothes on the line, baked her own bread, cared for the massive Greek revival antebellum home, and hosted breakfast and lunch for numerous people five days a week. It was a pleasant life that the Grangers had.

Growing up, Jerry and Roy had lived in that house with housekeepers. Will, Jerry's son, had also grown up in this house with housekeepers. It was a lifestyle that Marilyn wasn't familiar with, and she often felt a little strange visiting this house.

The house was comfortable; it wasn't one of those old homes made to feel like a museum. It was a mix of overstuffed couches, big screen televisions, and antique cabinets. There were most of the original old pieces of furniture in this house; the only exceptions being things such as couches, recliners, and entertainment centers. Even the entertainment centers had been custom made to look exactly like antique cabinets.

Next to gorgeous antique pieces, one could often find a dishpan of Matchbox cars, or an armload of stuffed animals and dolls. Next to a century old vase on an antique end table, one could find the remote for the big screen TV. Yes, it was a relaxing mix of old and new. It was mostly old, but enough new to make it feel like home.

It wasn't the furniture that made Marilyn uncomfortable here. It was Jerry's wife. Well, she was one of the things, anyway.

Marilyn had been sweet on Jerry Granger since she had shown up to work at Liberty Creek High School almost 30 years ago. She remembered how he looked that very first day she arrived. It was the first day of school, and she was waiting in the office to talk to the principal about something. Jerry came in and smiled at her.

His dark blond hair was in-need of a trim, but he was clean shaven. His warm smile reached his blue eyes. He was chewing gum and wearing a Virginia Tech Hokies shirt. His smile got just a little bigger when he saw her.

"Well, you must be new in these parts! New folks don't happen much around here. So, when one of you shows up, it gets noticed. Jerry Granger, head football coach. Oh, and everyone's favorite staff member," he said, as he held his hand out to her. The secretary laughed.

"Favorite? Don't you mean, fastest?"

Jerry merely smiled at this comment. He winked at Marilyn.

"She's just jealous. Don't listen to her."

Marilyn smiled and shook his hand.

"Hello. It's very nice to meet you. I'm Marilyn Beales, the new guidance counselor. I heard about you. You were one of the selling points the school board used when trying to convince me to take the job. Lots of championships, huh? And quite the football star at Virginia Tech it seems. Yes, they seemed quite fond and proud of you."

Jerry blushed charmingly at this news. The blushing and genuinely embarrassed smile that crossed his face won Marilyn over immediately. He chuckled softly. He took his other hand and covered his mouth briefly. He took his hand from Marilyn's and put both hands in his front pockets.

"Well, I don't know about all *that*. I mean, yeah, I'm pretty well-known for the football thing around here. But I'd hardly consider myself to be a selling point."

"Well, *I* bought it. I'm glad I did. I'm *very* glad, after meeting you," she added.

Leon Addams, the principal, came in, then. He looked at the very beautiful woman standing in his office, looking longingly at his football coach. He sighed. If this was the new counselor, he was dreading it. Over half of the female staff already hit on Jerry. Hell, over half of the female *students* hit on Jerry. He found out that girls regularly tried out for cheerleading, not to be near their football player boyfriends but to hang out on the sidelines with Jerry. They also enjoyed the away game bus rides with him.

"Hi, Jerry. Hello, Miss Beales, is it?" Leon asked. Marilyn unwillingly pulled her gaze from Jerry.

"Yes! Yes, Marilyn Beales. How are you? You must be Leon Addams?"

"That's me, alright. Um, this is Jerry Granger, our head football coach. I'm pretty sure you've been told all that already," he added, looking at Jerry, amused.

"Yes, Mr. Granger and I have met one another," Marilyn told him, smiling at the good- looking coach. He smiled back. Leon shook his head.

"Yes, Jerry and I grew up together. Oh, and this here is our secretary, JoAnne Jeffries. Her daughter attends our school. Well, so does Jerry's son actually. He's a freshman this year, one of the new additions to our team. Like father, like son *we hope*! Eh, Jerry? Anyway, come on in my office for a moment. Let's discuss just a few things."

So, Marilyn followed Principal Addams into his office, but she couldn't stop thinking about Jerry Granger.

She continued to flirt with Jerry every day at school. He let it be known that he was married, not that that was necessary. She had already been told by several others about Jerry's wife. Faye had a fan club it seemed.

Oh, Faye was so sweet, pretty, fun and charming! Everyone loved Faye! Faye was such a hit at every school event! She had been an active parent ever since her and Jerry's son, Will, was just in kindergarten. Faye was homecoming queen, and won the beauty walk two years in a row! Faye had such a cute little figure and a great personality! Above all else, Faye had Jerry Granger. Faye had managed to hook Jerry when they were five years old, and she had managed to hang on to him ever since.

Well, that didn't slow Marilyn down (much). She continued to smile, and visit with him, at every opportunity. Whatever she happened to be carrying when she saw him approaching, would suddenly become much heavier. Then, of course, he'd offer to assist her. She made sure to sit with him in the teacher's lounge, during lunch. This was a lot of fun until the Remember September Dance.

Marilyn had been eyeing Jerry for a few weeks, by now. She offered to chaperone the dance after Jerry asked her if she'd be attending. He told her that all the teachers came to these things. He also pointed out that there wasn't a whole hell of a lot to do in Liberty Creek on a Friday night. She told him that *of course* she planned to make it to the dance!

Marilyn painstakingly selected a fabulous, deep red slip dress and black strappy heels. She rushed home Friday afternoon, showered, and put her hair up in rollers. Finally, with hair and makeup perfected, she pulled on her short crimson colored slip dress and heels. She looked at her reflection in the full-length mirror in her bedroom.

Perhaps she was overdressed for a school dance. Oh, well she didn't care. She wanted Jerry to see just how fabulous she was capable of looking.

Well, when Marilyn walked in the school gymnasium that evening, with her fabulous five- foot eight-inch figure, Jerry certainly did take notice. He wasn't the only one. Most every boy and man in the gymnasium took notice. And so did Faye.

"Who in the hell is *that*?" Faye asked Jerry, who had a rather goony look on his face.

"That's Marilyn ... I mean, it's Miss Beales."

"Miss Beales? Wait a minute. Miss Beales, *the counselor*?"

"Huh? What? Oh, yeah, the counselor," he answered, pulling his attention away from Marilyn and back to his wife. Faye looked horrified.

"*That* is no high school guidance counselor! That's *a stripper*! Who in the world hired her?"

"I don't know! Don't yell at me! It wasn't me! Besides, she's nice. The kids here like her. Jason said he likes her a whole lot."

"Jason, Jerry? Doesn't that tell you anything?"

"Well, not just Jason. Will has even gone to her office a couple of times ..."

"For *what*? He is an honor student, top of his class, popular and well-rounded. Why in the world would he have needed to have gone to her office *twice* in just three weeks?" Faye insisted.

"Oh, shit, Faye! I don't know ... maybe he's suffering from sort of over-achieving complex. I don't know why he went, and I honestly don't care. Quit judging her. You don't even know her. That's not like you," Jerry scolded her quietly.

"That woman is dressed completely inappropriately for a school dance, Jerry. She looks like she should be hanging out down at The Tavern."

"Hush, she's coming over here," Jerry scolded his nagging wife.

"Hi, Coach. Oh, is this your wife?" Marilyn asked sweetly.

"Yes, this is Faye. Faye, this is Marilyn Beales. So, you having any fun, yet?"

"Oh, yes. This is all so ... quaint. It's very sweet. I think it's great how the school dances are such a big deal around here. There's so many parents here!"

"Well, you look rather 'big city.' I guess small town functions are unfamiliar to you," Faye said.

"I look 'big city'? Well, thank you ... I think. I'm not sure ... well, I'm from Lexington. It's not hardly Chicago, but I guess it's a good-sized town. I mean, yes, it's bigger than Liberty Creek."

"Most places are!" Jerry laughed. Marilyn laughed with him. Faye smiled, but looked as if it pained her to do so.

"So, is this your first teaching job?" Faye asked.

"Well, no. I was the counselor at Holy Cross Catholic School in Lexington, but they closed. It was sudden, a scandal of sorts, I guess you could say. Put it this way, I worked on Wednesday. Thursday during third period, a student assistant brought me a letter. It called for an emergency teacher meeting after school. By Monday, I was looking for work because the school had closed."

"Wow. That was quick," Jerry remarked, eyebrows raised.

"Yeah ... it was kind of an ugly situation. Anyway, so ... here I am!"

"We're so lucky!" Faye said.

"Yes, we are! I'm going to go fetch Faye and me a drink. Can I get you anything?" Jerry offered.

"Oh, yes. Thank you so much."

As Jerry turned to walk away, he made sure he gave Faye a warning look. *Don't start shit at a school dance*, the look clearly said. She gave him a look right back. Her look said, *oh shut up.*

And that was the beginning of Marilyn's relationship with Faye. It wasn't off to a great start. Over the years, Marilyn remained attracted to Jerry, but she never did anything inappropriate. She never tried to get him to do anything that would get him in trouble with his beloved wife. She learned, quickly, that Jerry and Faye were somewhat of a town staple. She respected this, for the most part. Innocent winks, smiles, and setting her hand on his arm when speaking to him at the school were about as far as it went.

Faye did not like this woman. Faye saw her at every school event, and saw her in town, and saw her at holiday parties. She saw her at community events. Faye always acted civil to Marilyn, but she never could quite trust her. Thankfully, she did trust Jerry.

Jerry may giggle, blush, and run his hands though his hair when the girls flirted with him, but he never did anything to worry Faye. Even the few times they broke up briefly in school (once for six whole weeks) Jerry would clear it with Faye, before seeing someone else.

The first time they broke up, in third grade, he approached Faye on the playground and told her, "Joyce wants me to eat lunch with her, today." He said this hesitantly. She looked at him.

"Well, do you want to?"

"Yeah, I guess so," he shrugged, frowning thoughtfully. She shrugged back.

"Fine. Eat with her. Maybe I'll eat with Gary."

"Okay," Jerry replied. He was just about to turn and walk away when he thought about something. He looked back at Faye, his brow furrowed.

"Is he going to buy you an extra milk?" Jerry asked.

"I don't know," Faye admitted. As of right then, Gary Connelly didn't even have a clue that she was booking a lunch date with him.

Jerry fumbled in his pocket and pulled out a nickel.

"Well, here, in case he doesn't." He handed Faye the nickel and went to go play ball. Gary did pay for her milk, but Faye didn't want to hurt Jerry's feelings, so she kept the nickel, and didn't tell him. To this day, that nickel remained among Faye's keepsakes.

Every time he and Faye broke up, it pretty much happened like that. Faye always knew that she had Jerry, and Jerry always knew that he had Faye. So, no … Faye wasn't exactly worried about Jerry doing things he shouldn't with this woman. She worried about this woman trying, though.

That was how it was for the next many years. Jerry didn't leave his job coaching until just the year before Faye passed-away. He considered staying until he was official retiring age. Something told him to do it early. He had money enough, so he wasn't under any financial obligation

23

to stay at the school. He left early, with plenty in savings and retirement plans in place at the bank. At 54, he could retire with at least 30 years of teaching under his belt, which he had. A year later, he would realize what it was that told him to leave his career early. He had no doubt it was God, pushing Jerry to make the absolute most out of his last year with his wife, his best friend, his wife. Jerry had heard and made the decision to announce his final season.

This caused a lot of upset, since Jerry had taken them to countless championships. But he promised to help them find a new coach. He promised to help-out, still. He promised to stay involved to an extent.

That first year he wasn't coaching full-time, he did help-out. He even remained employed, by the school. But once Faye passed-away, any interest he had in football was gone. Any interest he had in anything was gone.

Marilyn had tried to get in touch with him numerous times following Faye's death. She had gone to the visitation, and to the funeral. She had brought Jerry food several times over the next couple of weeks. She had called to check on him many times. It wasn't long before her calls went unanswered. Her knocks on his front door went unanswered. The times she'd see him in town, her greetings went unanswered.

Nobody knew it then, but Marilyn had already begun worrying about this man. They never had anything romantic, or sexual. They never had anything inappropriate or trashy going on. Jerry had become a friend to her, a very dear friend, over the years. It was simple, and pure (for the most part). She remembered him on that horrible day. It was at the visitation, two days after Faye had passed-away. Marilyn was genuinely sad that Faye was gone. Faye may not have cared much for her, but she was always cordial and pleasant to be around.

Over the years, the tension between the two women thinned and they were even able to make jokes about Marilyn and Jerry's relationship. It was a somewhat awkward relationship the two ladies had, in the beginning. Marilyn was attracted to Jerry and she could tell that Faye knew it. Faye knew Marilyn liked Jerry, and she knew Marilyn knew that she knew it. Jerry knew that each woman knew what they knew.

All this knowledge made the whole situation rather amusing. Marilyn did wish that Faye had liked her though.

At the visitation, Jerry didn't talk to her. She walked up to Will and hugged him. She gave her condolences to Jerry's brother, Roy. She spoke with Karen, who she knew was taking care of Jerry, Will, and Roy throughout this. But when she got to Jerry, he didn't even really look at her. Well, he looked at her, but she felt that he didn't really see her.

"Jerry? Please, please let me know if you need anything. Please let me know if there is anything in the world that I can do or help-out with. You know me, Jerry. I'd do anything for you and your family. Jerry, *I am so sorry*. Jerry? I know what you must be going through. I don't understand how you feel, but I do understand how … Jerry?"

That was when she realized he wasn't even hearing her. His eyes were looking in the right direction … but right through her. She fought back the urge to cry. She had sworn she'd not cry, for him and Will. She looked at Will, who'd obviously been crying all day. Will looked back at her and just shook his head at her. It was as if he were telling her, *don't even bother*.

Marilyn thought about hugging Jerry but changed her mind. She thought about reminding him to let her know if he needed anything but changed her mind.

"I'll see you later, Coach. Okay?" her voice caught. She left him alone.

It was the beginning of something very strange.

For, whereas Elizabeth Faye Granger had passed-away, she had gone nowhere. She was there. She was watching everything that took place and listening to everything being said. Every now and then, someone would get sad, because they thought they saw her. They'd look again, and she'd be gone. They would think to themselves their mind just couldn't accept the fact that she had died.

In truth, it was Faye who couldn't accept the fact she had died.

She saw Marilyn, and there was a strange feeling of comfort. She thought to herself, there is someone who cares about Jerry! Jerry had friends; she knew this. But she knew that Marilyn cared for Jerry in a different way. It was a way that Faye hadn't been too crazy about all these years … but now? Now, she thought maybe Jerry needed that kind of care from someone.

Faye had already begun to worry about who was going to take care of her boys. Jerry and Will were going to need help through this. Karen could help, some. She knew this. But Karen had gone through so much herself here lately.

She had just come out of a brutal relationship. It had been a long, painful relationship for Karen. It had finally come to an end when Karen's husband beat her to the point she could barely walk. She managed to escape when he had gone out back. She was able to make it to her car, without even a shirt on her back. One eye had swollen completely closed, by the time she had made it to town. Then, she had to still go through the long, endless procedure to get the divorce finalized.

No, Faye didn't feel she could count on Karen to keep this crowd together. Just four days ago, Faye was checking on Karen! Karen needed someone! Oh, now Faye was *really* worried. Who was going to help Karen through all of this? Who was going to help Karen through the divorce, and now this?

Faye didn't know what to do. Karen needed someone to help her through things; she wouldn't be able to help Jerry, Will, and Roy through all of this! Marilyn, though … that was hard. Faye didn't *want* to hand Jerry over to *any* other woman, but he *was* going to need help. She knew immediately that he'd never pull through this on his own. He'd never had to do anything on his own. Jerry had always had a crowd cheering him on. Jerry had always had housekeepers and mothers and wives to take care of him.

Jerry, she realized, had been spoiled rotten. She also had to acknowledge that she had played a large part in that happening.

She knew that in his entire life, Jerry Granger had never had to wash his own clothes or cook his own supper. Jerry had never had to iron a shirt, write a grocery list, or fold a fitted sheet. She guessed he'd never even had to wash a dish. Oh, what had she done? She spent so much time taking care of him that she made him completely incapable of taking care of himself.

That very morning, Karen had come over to help the men get ready for the visitation. But it was rather like the blind leading the blind. Karen cried throughout the entire day. Will cried throughout the entire day. Roy cried and snapped at people. Jerry didn't cry. Jerry didn't talk, or smile, or hear anything anyone said.

Faye was with them all, all day long. She didn't know what to do. She couldn't do much. She couldn't do anything really. When visitors came to comfort her men and Karen, Faye found herself studying these people, hoping to spot someone who might could help them all through this. Gary Connelly was a dear, sweet soul. She loved him to pieces (after all he bought her extra milk during their brief courtship in third grade). Gary was Jerry's best friend in the world. But Gary was hardly the one to take over a family in crisis. His own ex-wife, who had been a friend of Faye's, was a strung-out drug addict in Philadelphia. He had to raise their son on his own. Whereas he'd done a relatively good job with doing that, he could never be expected to take on something like this. No, Gary couldn't be the chosen one.

Then, Faye began noticing something that mortified her. These people were all entirely too eager to help Jerry move on! Oh, this was not good. She had hoped to find someone who could ease them all through this process. She wasn't expecting to hear her very own friends telling Jerry that he'd get over it and find someone new! She wasn't even in the ground yet!

When Bess Rhone told Jerry, "Faye was a lovely, wonderful woman. She was loved by all of us, but don't despair, Jerry. You are young, and good looking, and you'll find someone else," Faye was so mad she wanted desperately to haunt that old bat! She wanted to know how to do those ghost things, right then. She wanted to know how to push her down on the ground or knock her in the back of the head. She wanted to do something scary to Bess, but she hadn't yet mastered that.

It wasn't that Faye thought these people didn't care. She knew that they cared. She knew that they really were good friends of theirs, and that they *thought* they were saying the right things. Of course, they were not going to walk up to Jerry and tell him, "It sucks about your wife dying, man. The next few years are going to feel like shit."

However, the tactic they were going for was hardly one Faye and Jerry wanted to hear. Jerry was mortified by the heartless things these people were saying to him. It was very early in the visitation that Jerry just stopped talking to them. He was noticing that, in addition to saying some really, thoughtless things, they appeared to all be reading from some script.

They all said the same things. Jerry would be fine, he'd meet someone new, and that Faye was in a better place. They said that she was loved, she was a good person, and it was such a shame. They all said that they understood. Jerry wanted to tell them they obviously *didn't* understand. Had they *really* understood, they'd have not said such stupid, stupid, thoughtless, generic funeral things.

Yes, Jerry was angry and shocked by the fact they were saying these things. But it was something said by Trish Thurman, Faye's friend from the salon that sent Jerry over the edge.

Trish held Jerry's hand and told him how very much Faye would be missed at the salon. That *one* comment made Jerry shut down. That was when he realized it was real. All of this was real, and Faye was not going to be going back to work. Faye wasn't going to come home from work. Faye was not going to make him salmon croquettes anymore, and she wasn't going to rub his forehead when he had a headache anymore. Faye wasn't going to flush the toilet when he was in the shower anymore, and she wasn't going to sit on the back porch and drink bourbon and vodka with him anymore. Faye wasn't going to make him smile anymore, or laugh anymore, and she wasn't going to make love to him ever again.

Jerry didn't talk again for four days. Four days later, when Roy was going back to Nashville, Jerry told Will to go with him. That was the first thing he'd said to his son since they buried Will's mother.

It was about 20 minutes later, after Trish ran her big mouth that Marilyn came into Mathis Funeral Home. She wore a practical, long black dress. Her dark, curly hair was pulled back into a bun. She was in awe of all the people.

The visitation had been scheduled to take place after school, so people of all ages, and local school employees could attend. All the businesses worked around schedules so that everyone would be able to at least attend the visitation. Marilyn knew that during the time the funeral was to take place the next day, all the local business had agreed to close their doors. Marilyn was touched by this gesture. She couldn't imagine the whole city of Lexington shutting down because a citizen died ... even if it was very nice, much-loved citizen.

By the time Marilyn arrived, Will's eyes were terribly blood shot and Jerry's were completely unfocused. But when Marilyn came in, she brought an odd relief for Faye.

Jerry and Will were told they should be first in the receiving line, but they both refused. They didn't want to be there, at all. They wanted to be home, not standing a matter of feet away from Faye's casket. So, it was decided that Faye's brother and his wife would be first in the line. Then, Karen and Roy. Will and Jerry would be last.

Faye's brother, Ellis, argued about the receiving line not being proper, but Roy told him to shut the Hell up or go back to his hippie pad in California. Ellis and Roy didn't speak much more, after that.

Marilyn saw Ellis and immediately saw Faye in his face; he looked just like his sister. She spoke to Ellis and his wife, Peggy politely. Then, Marilyn approached Karen, and hugged her tight. She kissed her cheek, and said, simply,

"Karen, I am so, so sorry. Let me know if there's anything I can do."

Then, Marilyn stepped over to Roy, who stood beside Karen. He looked so sad it broke her heart. She bit down hard on her lip to keep from crying. Will was next in the receiving line and she didn't want to cry. She tried so hard to not cry for Will and Jerry.

"Roy, I'm just sorry. I am so, so sorry. Really, please let me know if I can do anything for any of you. I promise, you can call on me for anything," she assured him. Roy sighed, his grey eyes filling with tears. It was the first truly sincere gesture he'd heard today, with exception of Gary Connelly Gary's son, Jason. He hugged her and kissed her cheek.

"Thank you, Marilyn; that means a lot."

Then, the worse of it came. Marilyn had dreaded talking to Will about this. Will, she knew, was a *mama's boy*. Will had been his parent's pride and joy. Will had his mother wrapped around his every finger. In return, Faye had had Will wrapped around her every finger. Marilyn had known Will since he was 14 years old; it was going to be so hard to face him.

"Will, I want you to listen to me. If you need to talk, honey, you know where to find me. But here; take my card. I wrote my cell number on the back. Really, Will. I am so sorry, and just know, sweetheart, that I'm here if you ever need to talk or just … cry," she told him, her voice breaking. Will smiled a wobbly smile. He just nodded because he didn't trust himself to talk. He put his arms around her and held her close. He hugged her hard for a moment. He pulled back, and just winked at her.

Marilyn looked at Jerry, standing beside Will. It was as if Jerry didn't even realize she was there. He was looking in the direction of the door, but he wasn't really looking at anything. She could tell he was just trying to avoid looking at anyone. She stepped up to him. Will elbowed him. Jerry's gaze settled on Marilyn's face. He may have been looking at her, but he wasn't seeing her, and she knew this.

His gorgeous blue eyes were cloudy looking; the bright light in them was gone. His hair was disheveled, as if he'd run his fingers through it numerous times that day. The corners of his usually smiling mouth were turned down. Seeing Jerry like this scared her.

"Jerry? Please, please let me know if you need anything. Please let me know if there is anything in the world that I can do or help-out with. You know me, Jerry. I'd do anything for you and your family. Jerry, *I am so sorry.* Jerry? I know what you must be going through. I don't understand how you feel, but I do understand how … Jerry?"

That was when she realized that her best friend, Jerry Granger, had not heard a word she had said. He may not have even realized she was right there, a foot in front of him. There was an urge to hug him, but she didn't. He didn't look like he wanted to be touched.

"I'll see you later, Coach. Okay?" she said softly. As she turned to leave, Will broke down in tears, again, and sat down on the step behind him. He buried his face in his hands and cried, without shame. The others gathered looked uncomfortable by Will's breakdown. Jerry didn't even look at him. Marilyn knew she was about to break down too. She had to leave quickly.

What Marilyn didn't realize was, in life, Faye had wanted her to stay away from her darling Jerry. Now, Faye had already decided that Marilyn was the one who needed to be there for Jerry. She had been the first to say just the right things, and the first to do just the right things. She had shown Faye that she'd take care of Jerry.

Faye didn't have a lot right then. She had lost her life, and she lost her capability to fix everything for her loved ones. She didn't know what to do, or *how* to do it, even if she knew what to do. She didn't know what was about to happen. She didn't know if this was temporary, her being here with her family. Did she only have today? Did she only have through the funeral? Was there a system? Were there rules to this? Would she be able to help Jerry, as she always had? Or would she have to leave him?

Faye didn't know very much. She had questions about how this dying thing worked. She hoped she'd figure it all out soon. And she really hoped that Marilyn would come back around.

CHAPTER 3

Jerry stared at the ceiling. He thought maybe he *was* okay to go to church. Maybe he could do it, if he really tried. He sighed. He flexed his fingers and made fists. The fists made his forearms hurt. He really didn't feel well enough to go to church.

But he knew, he just *knew,* if he told them that he didn't feel well enough to go, his beloved Anne would worry about him. He liked that part. But then Will would insist they *all* stay home. He said it wasn't nice to go to church when the whole family couldn't go. Jerry never did quite understand his son's reasoning. The few times he asked Will to explain it, Will just looked at him with a combination of utter astonishment and pity. That look always made Jerry feel somewhat uncomfortable. So, Jerry just quit asking.

It wasn't all so cut and paste though. Jerry, announcing he felt bad, wouldn't just result in them all staying home. It would become much more complicated than that. The day would either start with Jerry lying in bed until Anne or Will came in there to see why he wasn't up yet, or else he'd go downstairs and whine to Anne. Either way, Will would sigh heavily, shake his head sadly, and stir his face with his hands. He'd let the kids sleep in and eat his breakfast.

To begin with, Jerry hated the way Will made him feel when he was sick. It wasn't Jerry's fault that Anne made such a fuss over him when he was sick. She made just as much fuss over Will when he was sick. But Will was special. Will seldom got sick. Will had no patience for sick people. There were times Anne pleaded with Will to take a day off and get some rest. Will usually insisted he was just fine and went about his everyday routine.

Jerry couldn't do that. When he was sick, he was sick. He did what absolutely had to be done and nothing else. With so many people working the farm, Anne's attitude was there were more than enough healthy people there to make up for a sick one. She'd make Jerry stay inside with her, and he was perfectly fine with this.

Anne was the very best daughter-in-law in the whole world! She was pretty and sweet and fussed all over him. She took such good care of him every day, but especially when he was sick. She'd bring him his breakfast, lunch and his medicine. She'd check on him every 30 minutes or so. She'd bring him a cool, damp washcloth for wiping his feverish forehead. Yes, she was wonderful. She'd sit on the edge of his bed and talk to him. She'd bring him his cat, and make sure he had everything he could possibly need. If it weren't for Will acting so pissy about it, being sick would be quite fun.

Will disliked how much attention Anne paid to Jerry. Well, that wasn't entirely true. He was glad that she took such good care of his father. It gave Will a sense of security and comfort. He knew that his dad was taken care of. He knew that his father had the best of everything. He may have been widowed, but he was surrounded by people who loved him and cared about him. Will never had to worry about his father not being taken care of, when he got older. Will never had to worry that his father would be alone. Jerry was taken care of.

It was a funny relationship. In one sense, Will liked seeing his father in this situation. It was just the fact that his father seemed to eat it up! When people thought Will was mad about Anne taking care of his dad, they were just wrong. It wasn't the fact that she was taking care of him that irritated Will. It was the fact that his father would suddenly become absolutely incapable of doing anything. His father would have a fever of two degrees, but he'd act like he was on his deathbed. The thing is it wasn't about Anne; his father had *always* acted like this.

Will remembered when he was little, his father was such a baby! Once, Will and his father had both gotten sick at right about the same time. Will stayed in bed for about two hours and went to school the next day. Jerry, however, had stayed in bed for three days and looked like Hell. Even at seven years old, Will reasoned his father looked like Hell because he had stayed in bed for three days.

These days, it was Anne who encouraged this pitiful behavior of Jerry, but it used to be Will's mother who did it. Faye would act just the same way Anne did. They both patted Jerry and brought him juice and soup and worried about him. They insisted he get rest, and they brought him hot water bottles. Will saw this similarity between the two women. While the rest of their friends and family were disturbed by Anne's extreme fussing over Jerry, Will found it somewhat sweet and amusing.

Will had always loved what his parents had had; yes, even the nauseating bedside behavior his mother provided when his dad was sick. As a kid, Will would pretend to be grossed out by the way they acted toward one another, but really, he was always quite happy about it.

A few of Will's friends from school had a bad home-life. Maybe their parents were divorced … or, maybe their parents weren't but needed to be. It wasn't very common though. Liberty Creek prided themselves on the fact that there just wasn't a whole lot of bad stuff going on in that town. There had only been seven divorces in Liberty Creek since 1967. One of those had been Gary Connelly, but his wife had been a strung-out drug addict. Everybody kind of understood why he left her, and they couldn't help but agree with the route he'd taken. Another divorce had been Karen's from her abusive husband. Most people agreed with that divorce, too (well, her ex-husband's friends and family, not so much).

Will was glad he had the kind of life he had. He was glad that his parents played, teased, kissed, and danced in the kitchen. He was glad that his dad was always smiling and in a good mood. He was glad that his mom always looked at his dad with the same love-struck expression she'd carried for him since she was just five years old. Will was glad that his parents had loved each other so much. And he truly was glad that this love had found a way to defy the odds and survive even in his mother's death.

Will had gone through so many misfired relationships over the past many years. They never worked out for him. He wondered what he was doing wrong. All he wanted was what his own parents had had. Then, it hit him.

Everyone always compared him to his father. He was so much like his dad! So, Will figured if he was so much like his dad, then all he needed was to find a girl just like his mom. Then, he would have the ideal relationship that his parents had had all these years.

It was a good theory, and it worked just like he thought it would. Anyone who looked at Will and Anne Granger saw Jerry and Faye Granger all over again. Will and his wife were able to pull it off. There was just one little problem in Will's well-laid plan.

Jerry was one of the ones who saw Faye in Anne. When Anne showed up, she immediately put Jerry first. She was hired to help-out around the house, but the house came second. Jerry needed to be taken care of, and she saw this within the first 30 minutes of walking in the door.

For starters, Jerry didn't look well. He looked like a sick, tired, old man. He looked hungry; he was too thin for a man of his size. She could look at him and tell this wasn't how he used to look. When she saw photographs of him throughout the house, her suspicions proved true. He had been a dashing man, before his world fell apart. His eyes had once been bright and merry. But on her first morning there, his eyes looked hollow and sunken. Actually, he was in a good mood, that morning she met him. He had overdosed on Will's energy drinks and was on an extreme caffeine high. He was smiling, laughing, and nearly bouncing off the walls that morning.

But by afternoon, he had started quieting down. He sat still and looked around. His eyes looked nervous. He was in bed by six o'clock that night. Jerry often spent most of the day in bed, anyway. But that day, he went to bed because Roy made him.

Jerry had come downstairs, completely missed the bottom step, stumbled to the first floor and hit his mouth. The amount of blood was startling. It was so startling, that Anne went to the back door and screamed for Roy. Roy was in the middle of finishing up his work on replacing the door frame on the stable.

Roy impatiently came across the yard to see what her problem was.

"What the Hell is wrong with you? Stop yelling. What happened?" he grumbled.

"Jerry fell down the stairs and split his mouth open! There's blood *everywhere!*"

"Everywhere? By splitting his lip? What was he doing on the stairs that made him fall- down them? He's been going down those damn stairs every day of his life for 60 years. I swear, it's always something with him. Well, where is he?" Roy asked, obviously angry at this inconvenience.

"He's in the kitchen. I got him a wet towel, Roy. He was … Roy? Roy!"

Roy had walked off toward the kitchen, leaving her in the hall, trying to catch up to him.

"What did you *do?* Jerry? What'd you do?" he asked his little brother. He may have been irritable in the yard and hall, but Anne noticed something; the moment Roy walked in the kitchen, and approached Jerry, his mood softened, and he looked worried. Jerry didn't answer Roy. He just looked at Roy in anguish. He looked so very pitiful. He looked like the saddest man Roy had ever seen. Roy just shook his head.

"Aw, shit. Anne, wash the towel out. Hand it to her, brother. Give me the towel Jerry, so she can wash it out, and so I can see what you've done to yourself." Roy finally took the towel from Jerry and handed the damp, bloody dishtowel to Anne. Anne looked at it with a sneer but took it to the sink. She looked back to see what Roy was doing.

Roy had taken Jerry's head in his hands and was holding it back, so he could see it better. Jerry's full beard and mustache made it hard to see the details surrounding the wound.

"Oh, you done a job on yourself this time. I declare, Jer. Anne, grab that ice pack in the freezer. He's going to have a nasty old lip, come morning. What's the matter, brother? You look rough … well, rougher than usual. Here's the ice pack. Hold it on your mouth, man. I'm gonna go out there and try to get some more … Aw, screw it. I'm just going to finish up out there. Then, I guess I'll go ahead and make us something to eat."

Roy left a wounded Jerry at the kitchen table, and Anne did her best to tend to him. Roy soon came back inside. He made him and Jerry some canned ravioli, and even went so far as to serve it to Jerry. Anne was somewhat touched by the scene, but there was something else about it that nagged at her.

Once they finished, Roy took their bowls and put them in the sink. He rinsed them out, then turned to his brother.

"Jerry? You okay? Your mouth just looks bad. Jerry? Oh, come on and at least *act* like you fucking hear me!"

Jerry just glared at the door. He didn't want to talk to Roy. He didn't like Roy very much these days. Roy was nice and all when he came in and looked at Jerry's lip. But usually, Roy was just such an asshole to him. Jerry knew it pissed Roy off when he acted like he didn't hear him, so Jerry did this often, just to get back at Roy.

Well, sometimes, he honestly just didn't even hear him. Jerry tended to zone out a lot.

Roy closed his eyes very tight. He began breathing hard. When he opened his eyes, they looked kind of crazy, to Anne.

"Jerry, just go on to bed."

"Bed, Roy? It's not even six o'clock!" Anne protested.

"I am well-aware of the time, thank you, honey. I am tired and am just not in the best mood today. He goes to bed, and I don't have to worry about tending to him anymore. I'm going to bed, too. I'll see you in the morning, honey."

Roy shoved Jerry to get him to stand up. Jerry stood up, shoved Roy hard in the shoulder, and stomped out of the room. He said nothing to Anne. Anne was surprised that she had been hurt by this. She and Jerry had had a lot of fun that day, she thought. She liked this man.

Jerry had been her friend that day. Even when his caffeine high started dropping, he was still sweet as could be. She found herself wanting to spend time with him, so she was disappointed to learn Roy was making him go to bed. She was more disappointed though, that Jerry had not even looked back at her.

Jerry thundered all the way up the stairs; he had begun talking though. Who he was talking *to* Anne wasn't sure. But he seemed to be having a very involved conversation with whoever it was. Roy pounded his head on the wall five times.

"Hey, is he okay?" Anne asked, quietly.

"Jerry? Is Jerry okay? Hell, no. I told you, earlier … he's depressed."

"Well, he didn't so much seem depressed today. He seemed happy. But even now … is it depression? Or is he just crazy?"

"Is there a difference? Really? Yeah, he's crazy. He's got something going on. Just don't ask me what the Hell it is. You're going to see him acting weird, honey. You're going to see him doing things that you're not going to understand."

"Why don't you get him help? Why does he act that way? You said he's depressed. Why?"

"His wife died. They were best friends all their lives. She had a heart attack four years ago; nobody ever saw it coming. He fell apart after that, is all. He got worse and worse. Karen, a dear friend of ours, across the road, saw what was going on, *finally*. She called me and told me to come here and fix everything. So, here I am. It doesn't appear I've done such a great job. Will showed up this past fall. He came a few months after I did. He's a big ol' help out here, but I don't know that his heart is in it. Of course, neither is mine. But hey! It's home, right?" Roy smiled. His smile was nice. Anne felt he really should do it more often.

"But Roy? Why don't you get him help?" she repeated.

"Ehhh … it's complicated," was all he'd say. He looked at her, though. He looked as if he were thinking very hard about something. Then, his expression changed. He just looked tired.

"Look, I'm going on to bed. Will should be home any minute, though. You two can visit. You didn't get to talk to him much this afternoon, I guess. He's a nice guy, just a little neurotic."

"So, you're *seriously* going to bed?"

"Yes, I seriously *am*. I've been up since five this morning. I'm going to get my Dr. Pepper and go to my room, take my clothes off, lay down, and watch *The Waltons*."

"Fine. Go on," Anne said, already bored, just thinking about hanging out by herself. Will should be home soon, but she didn't know how long.

"I'm so glad you approve. Goodnight, honey," Roy patted Anne on the back and left.

So, Anne was on her own. She went into the hall and looked at the numerous pictures hanging on the walls. There were pictures dating back to the 1830s. There were pictures covering every decade since this house was built, it seemed. Anne managed to kill a good half hour just looking at pictures.

She came across a picture of someone she recognized; the smile alone did it. It was Roy, as a child. He looked about eight years old. Then, she saw pictures of someone else. He looked like Will, but obviously these pictures were taken long before Will's time. She saw several pictures of this fellow and Roy taken together. She realized it had to have been Jerry. She saw Jerry's and Roy's senior pictures and had to smile. What good-looking men they were! It was hard to believe Jerry was so dashing.

There were pictures of a pretty, dark haired little girl amid these pictures. There were pictures of her as she got older. They started with her baby pictures, just like Jerry's and Roy's did. Then, there were her school pictures. Then, there was a picture of her and Jerry, together. In this picture, they looked like they were about five or six years old. They appeared to be at a birthday party. Anne saw more and more pictures of this girl, as she became a teenager. Again, Jerry was with her in many of these. Finally, Anne saw her senior picture. Then, there was a wedding picture of this girl and Jerry. Anne felt a little knot in her stomach. Roy had told her that Jerry and his wife had been best friends all their lives; actually seeing this story told in photographs somehow made it different.

The pictures began to show this happy couple with a baby. Anne walked down the hall, seeing two children grow up before her eyes, marry, and have a child of their own. She watched that child grow up too. That child would become the very dashing Will Granger she had met today. There were so many pictures of so many people! Anne noticed that there were numerous pictures of black people; one family-in-particular. Anne wondered who these people were. She assumed they maybe had something to do with this house, but she couldn't imagine what. Most of these pictures were taken within what appeared the past hundred years; some seemed to be taken in the 1940s through 1970s.

One certain girl showed up in many of these pictures. It was a pretty little black girl, about Roy's and Jerry's age. There were many pictures taken of the three of them together, and several taken of her and Roy. They had obviously grown up together, as there were pictures of them, through the years. There was a picture of them together, in their high school graduation gowns. She had become a gorgeous woman, whoever she was. She had a big, beautiful smile and kind, warm eyes.

Anne finally reached the end of the wall of pictures. She had decided she'd go sit outside, on the front porch. There was nothing else to do. So, she walked toward the front door but stopped to smile at another picture. This one was hanging beside the front door. It was a large, framed portrait of Will. He wore a royal blue long-sleeved knit shirt with a white T-shirt beneath it. The blue in the shirt made his eyes look like pools of water. He was so incredibly good looking that Anne felt shy just looking at it.

She went outside and sat in the swing on the porch. A huge, giant calico cat wandered up. The cat meowed loudly and started pawing at Anne's jeans. Anne patted her lap and the cat jumped up. The weight of this cat startled Anne. She began petting the cat, and realized this cat was quite pregnant. She could even feel the kittens moving around in the mother cat's belly. It was kind of weird. This cat had so much hair that it was hard to tell she was fat.

Anne and this cat sat on the porch for about half of an hour. Anne thought about a lot of things while she sat there though.

Jerry's situation was an interesting one. She liked him (a lot). He was funny; he made her laugh. She knew that it had a lot to do with the over consumption of Will's energy drinks. But she just had a feeling that there was something special about him. He must have had a terrible time when his wife died. She wondered what he must have gone through.

Was he really, out here, all alone? How in the world could someone leave that poor man out here all by himself? What was wrong with Roy and Will? How could they have left him out here? She just didn't understand. Will had to have known his father missed his mother. She realized that whereas Will was certainly beautiful to look at, she was already somewhat angry with him. How could he have done that?

She thought about the pictures she had seen in the hall; Will was brought up in the lap of luxury. This child was obviously loved to pieces by his parents. It appeared he was their world. How could he have allowed his father to go through something so traumatic alone?

And Roy was a confusing one. Will had very little interaction at all with his father that day at lunch. However, Anne had seen quite a bit of interaction between Roy and Jerry. Anne had an idea that Roy loved Jerry a lot. She had an idea that Roy was genuinely worried about Jerry, and that he really did care about him. But Roy seemed to resent the fact that he cared about Jerry. He seemed mad about it.

Well, Anne didn't know these people yet. She just knew that there were some issues here. She decided though, that she really did kind of like these guys.

She liked Roy. He was the strong, silent type. She got the impression that he was the decision maker, the grown up around here. He was a good-looking man, but he seemed very unhappy.

Will ... well, she *really* liked Will. He was handsome and seemed rather smart. He had a way of talking that just made him sound educated. He was very articulate and well spoken. He also had a way of carrying himself that made him seem above painting houses. She hoped that he wasn't a snob though. He didn't seem like he would be.

Although she had known these men such a very short time, she already had a feeling of responsibility to these guys. All three of them seemed to be needing something. Well, she'd do what she could for them while she was here. She didn't know how long she'd be here, but she'd try to help them clean the place up. She'd try to make everyone feel a little better.

As Anne thought about these three men, Faye was observing. Who was this girl who had shown up in her kitchen? Faye didn't have the whole story on her because Anne had given her story outside to Roy. All Roy had told Jerry, was this was Anne and she needed a place to stay. She could stay with them, and help-out around the place.

Faye was unsure about this. At least Marilyn, she knew. Faye didn't like this, at all. But she had not quite mastered this haunting thing yet. She didn't know how to let her feelings be known. There had been so many times that she desperately wanted to throw things, yell, hit someone, or just say "boo," but she didn't know how. She knew that Jerry saw her sometimes; she assumed he did anyway.

Faye realized she didn't trust this girl, whoever she was. Why would she be out wandering the mountains by herself? Why would she be alone, walking up to strangers' houses, asking to live with them? Faye couldn't believe her brother-in-law! He'd apparently just move any old body in!

Faye had been in the house observing Jerry, who was (again) left alone when he really shouldn't have been. He had sliced his hand open and had used an old dust cloth to wrap around his hand. The only good thing about that was, he hadn't dusted in four years, so at least the dust cloth was relatively clean. Faye was mortified when he split his hand open. Then, she panicked when Jerry started making the noises he did when he saw the blood. Jerry never did deal with blood very well. He sounded like a wounded bear. She wondered how in the world Roy didn't hear him. She hoped that Jerry would at least have enough sense to go find Roy for assistance. But no; he just went in her pantry and dug through the drawer of rags. He sat down and impressed her with the skill he exhibited, tying the rag to his hand by himself.

She worried he was going to have a stroke, the way he was running around, like a chicken with its head cut off. He needed to sit down for a few minutes. She had always disapproved of those energy drinks. Will had started drinking those after he came home from college. His schedule was incredibly messed up; he slept odd hours and not enough hours. He didn't want to work the stable; he didn't want to work at all. He started consuming the energy drinks to stay awake, he said. Faye suggested coffee; he told her to leave him alone. It was only a matter of days later, he was adding his Red Bulls to his bourbon.

So, Faye didn't care for these energy drinks, anyway. Now, watching Jerry act like he was on something bothered her. She really wished Roy would come inside and check on him. Then, Roy finally did. Right about lunchtime, Roy came inside with a girl. She looked about Will's age, but Faye couldn't be sure. Once Jerry met her, he seemed quite fond of her.

This girl, Anne, also appeared to be somewhat of a smartass. Then Will came home for lunch. At first, Will seemed to be as wary of her as Faye was. But before he left, he was smiling at this girl, even flirting with her! Well, Faye felt these men were all being entirely too accepting of this weird girl. They just open the door and let *anybody* in here, it seemed!

Now, this strange girl sat on Faye's front porch, holding Faye's husband's cat. Even the cat seemed to be perfectly fine with this girl! Miss Priss usually required a few encounters, at least, before she let someone hold her. But she ran right up to this girl and just jumped in her lap! Faye realized that she, herself, felt somewhat betrayed. The cat was never willing to sit in Faye's lap for more than 30 seconds. Faye disliked that cat. She liked cats, but this cat had little interest in anyone except Jerry. If Jerry was anywhere in the room, the cat ignored Faye and went to Jerry. But this damn cat would sit in this girl's lap? After, what? A few hours? From that day forward, Faye had no use for Jerry's precious Miss Priss. She decided, right then, that she didn't like that old snob cat.

But Anne? Faye was curious about Anne. She was insulted that Anne had already gained the trust of this cat, who Faye had been trying to bond with for five years. But Miss Priss aside, Anne was like an invasive species. She didn't belong here, and nobody knew anything about her.

However, Faye also had to accept the fact that this girl had been incredibly kind to her addled Jerry. Nobody had any patience with Jerry. There *was* the Yankee officer who had been gunned down inhospitably on their front porch. Officer Johnson had been very patient with Jerry. His spirit spent countless hours in the kitchen with a drunken, crazy, confused Jerry.

Faye acknowledged that Jerry needed someone in his life to take care of him … someone who had not been dead for a century and a half.

So, Faye decided to take this girl, this intruder, into consideration. Obviously, Roy was okay with her. Roy was usually a somewhat practical man. If he thought she was okay enough to invite inside, then maybe she was worth giving a chance.

Jerry certainly seemed to like her. That's what really mattered to Faye. Jerry needed someone he could count on, and someone he could talk to. Faye was incredibly disappointed in Will these days. He was treating his father like a hired hand. He didn't talk to him, or visit with him, or even try to spend time with him. No, Will certainly couldn't be counted on, to be the one who'd help Jerry through all of this.

And Karen? Well, Karen was just useless these days! She had driven past this house for three years and had not noticed anything! She had stood outside and visited with Jerry, never telling him that he looked like shit, and never asking why he didn't want to invite her inside. What was wrong with her? It was a divorce, for God's sake! How long was Karen going to dwell over that jackass, Luther? It wasn't like she was even alone in the world. Faye happened to know that their good friend Gary Connelly was frequenting Karen's house at night. Faye had an issue with the fact that Gary, the police chief, was obviously on duty during several of these visits.

Faye didn't care if Karen and Gary were getting it on. She knew there was something going on, because Karen stayed with Gary when she ran away from Luther. Okay, so Gary found her that night, and took her home with him. But Karen could have gone to a friend's afterward. No, she chose to stay with Gary. And she stayed with him even days after Luther was forced to leave Karen's house. Faye knew that Gary and Karen had always been somewhat fond of one another; they'd been childhood friends, despite Karen being four years older than him and black.

Faye did have to wonder; she also knew that Karen was incredibly fond of Roy. She had discussed this with Jerry on many occasions. Jerry had told her, already, that once they hit junior high, Karen was obviously interested in Roy as something more than a friend. But whenever Jerry would tease Roy about it, Roy would just tell him he was crazy. So, Faye and Jerry knew Karen liked Roy romantically.

Oh well, Roy was in Nashville. If Karen wanted to run around with Gary, Faye guessed she could. The Karen and Gary thing continued long after Faye had passed-away. Sometimes they saw each other several times a week; sometimes weeks would go by and Faye wouldn't see Gary at Karen's at all. It seemed to be a casual arrangement that they had.

So, the people Jerry *should* have in his life really weren't there much at all. But now there was Anne. Faye observed her and Jerry all day. Then Jerry and Roy retired to their bedrooms, leaving Anne by herself downstairs. As Anne was left alone, looking at pictures on the old walls, Faye watched her. Anne wasn't *as* alone as she thought she was.

CHAPTER 4

As Jerry lay there, contemplating his next move, someone knocked on his door.

"Yeah, I'm up," he answered to the knocker. The person who was knocking opened the door. He smiled as Anne made her way into the room. She was wearing her bathrobe, and had her long brown curls pulled up in a messy bun.

"It doesn't look to me like you're up. You lazy, today?" she asked, as she walked to his beside.

"Well, I don't feel very good," he admitted.

"What's the matter?"

"I'm sore, tired … I don't know; I just don't feel good. My head feels heavy."

Anne placed her hand on Jerry's scruffy cheek, then his forehead.

"You've got a fever! Again! Oh, honey. You just got over being sick."

"Well, I didn't feel great yesterday, but I thought it was from the hectic week. It's all these people, Mama! There's always someone breathing around me. Caleb is always snotty. There's four kids and five thousand adults …"

"Are you taking your vitamins?"

"Oh, come on! Don't go on about the vitamins again. I take the damn vitamins. You know, sometimes, people just get sick."

"Well, you've just gotten sick an awful lot it seems. I can't help it, love. I worry about you. Well, I guess I'll go tell Will. Might as well, before he starts getting ready for church."

"He's going to get mad at me. He's going to act like I'm faking it, or I'm doing it on purpose, or I'm just some big wuss."

"I'll go downstairs and tell him that you were awake when I came in here and that you *do* have a fever. If he gets mad, well, I'll chill him out. You stay here. I'll bring you something. Do you feel like breakfast? Some juice or coffee? I'll be happy to bring you something when I bring your medicine up."

"Just some orange juice, I think. Oh, and maybe a bagel. Can I have a bagel?"

"Yes, Jerry. I'll bring you a bagel … and juice. Hang tight, sugar."

As Anne talked to Jerry, she looked around his room. Usually, there were things strewn around, that needed to be picked up. This morning, the bedroom seemed to be rather orderly.

"Thank you, Mama," Jerry told her lovingly. He often called her Mama; it started after James was born. Nobody thought it odd. There were other things around here that were a *lot* weirder than Jerry calling his daughter-in-law *Mama*. She kissed his feverish cheek and left the room.

Anne made her way down the massive staircase. She paused to pick up a lone Matchbox car she spotted near the landing. She finished her descent down the stairs. She stepped into the living room and dropped the car into the dishpan full of Will's old Matchbox cars. She looked around. The bright early morning sunshine came through the big, uncovered windows. Dust particles danced in the beams of light that washed over the room. It was quiet and still in here. It had that smell that Anne loved so much. It smelled like old, unexplored closets, old books, and very old wood. It smelled like history.

Anne left the room and made her way down the hall to the kitchen. This was her favorite room. In the time this house was built, it was customary to build the kitchen separate from the main house. This was done to reduce the risk of the house burning down from a kitchen fire, and it also kept the heavy kitchen smells from the main house. However, when this house was built, the two sisters who would be the ladies of the house loved to cook. Therefore, they wanted the kitchen to be included as part of the main house, which would be more convenient for them.

When Martha Granger and Ellen Teague told their husbands that they wanted the kitchen to be part of the house, their husbands frowned upon it. But the two sisters were persistent, and they got their kitchen. The only condition was, the kitchen walls had to be brick because in the event of a fire, the brick walls would help protect the rest of the house. Then the ladies said the brick was ugly inside, so they talked their husbands into putting wood up over three of the brick walls. The three white wooden slat walls with the one massive, whitewashed brick wall made the room interesting.

The kitchen was huge, with the whitewashed brick exterior walls and the three white, wooden interior walls. It had a huge, whitewashed brick fireplace, taking up the majority of the brick back wall. It still had the original cabinets and workspaces. The only thing they had really done to update this room, was add modern appliances and lighting. Even the funny, wavy panes of glass in the windows were original. The original oak flooring was somewhat uneven in places and slightly warped. The cracks between some of the boards made sweeping easy.

Faye's collection of Depression glass, three plates that had been brought to Virginia when her family immigrated here from Germany, and numerous other antique knickknacks still rested on the buffet and built in-shelving. Several framed pictures sat on the massive mantel built around the fireplace. A small stack of firewood sat on its wide hearth. The deep kitchen windowsill over the old farmhouse sink still held the three large blue Ball Mason jars that Faye had always kept flowers from the yard in. Anne kept Faye's jars filled with Faye's flowers. Yes, they'd always be Faye's jars and Faye's flowers.

The kitchen table had sat in this room, in the very same spot since the construction of the house and kitchen was completed in 1837. It was a massive table because it was originally used by the house staff. Now, it was perfect for the family and all their guests. It easily sat ten and was Anne's favorite piece of furniture. Its tabletop was constructed of four very long, wide oak boards. The boards were somewhat warped now. The cracks between them were bigger than they had been when the table was first constructed. But this imperfect piece of furniture was the heart of the home. It represented the perfectly imperfect family that had lived here for seven generations.

This kitchen was comfortable, simple, and the heart of the house. It was the setting for many sleepless nights, many heart-to-heart conversations, and even a fist fight or two. It was the setting for countless holiday gatherings, get-togethers with friends and family, and cozy meals. There were so many reasons it was where everyone gathered when they came in the house. Yes, it was Anne's favorite room. For the same reasons, it was Faye's favorite room.

The kitchen was where Faye was most frequently seen. She spent most of her time in this room when she was alive and tended to hang out here a lot in death, too.

This morning Will was staring out the window over the sink. He was holding a bottle of water and looked deep in thought.

"Boo," Anne said, sneaking up behind him. He smiled, shaking his head.

"*Boo* in this house doesn't have much effect on folks. Try it on Jason, at his place. He would love it, I'm sure."

"Lexi said her mother wants them to get someone in there to do tests. She says it's not safe for the kids to be there, if something is really going on," Anne told him.

"I know. But Jason and Lex already told me they wouldn't do anything like that. His dad told him getting some sort of ghost vanquishing out there could possibly affect what goes on here, too. Besides, it's part of this place. Jason was stressed about it; still is, I guess. Lex thinks it's neat."

"What do you think would happen if someone came out here and did something to run ghosts off from his place? Do *you* think it'd affect things here?"

The radio turned on by itself. Will and Anne both looked at it. It was on the classic rock station that the radio always stayed on. Will nodded toward the radio.

"I think there's your answer. Don't worry Mom ... we won't get any exorcists out here. Cut the radio off, baby. I dislike that song."

Anne shut the radio off; she didn't know this song. It sounded weird though. It's what her mother used to refer to as *underwater music*. Anne never quite understood why she referred to it as that. It sounded like what music would sound like if you were tripping on acid to Anne. As she turned it off though, she shook her head. Only Will would say he *disliked* a song. Anyone else would just say they didn't like the song, or it sucked.

"Listen, Boss, I just went upstairs. Your dad was up and all, but he looked bad. He said he didn't feel very well. He said his head felt heavy, and he just didn't feel well. I felt his cheek and forehead. He *is* hot, Will. Remember, he didn't feel too great yesterday. He thinks you're going to be hateful about it though."

"Hateful?" he asked, looking quite surprised.

"Yeah, you know how you get. You sigh and stir your face with your hands. You act all put out and shit. He knows you do that."

"You know what? I don't really feel so fantastic myself. It's all okay. Does he need anything?"

"I said I'd bring him some juice and a bagel. I'll run that up there with his medicine."

"Okay. Well, I already took care of the horses and cows and shit. They're turned out to pasture. I am going to go back to sleep, I think. You coming?"

"Probably. I only get up this early on Sunday because you make me. I'll be in there after I take care of your daddy."

"Okay, then. Gimme kisses, before Dad gets them all."

"Oh, stop it. If you're both sick, I don't want to kiss either of you."

Will laughed and pulled her close. He kissed her anyway. She scolded him afterward and sent him to bed. She prepared a bagel and cream cheese for Jerry, got his juice, and severe cold and flu medicine. She almost tripped over Miss Priss as she left the kitchen with the tray. The cat began yowling.

"Come with me, kitty kitty. Let's go see Daddy."

Miss Priss followed Anne up the stairs and down the upstairs hall, to Jerry's room. Miss Priss ran ahead of Anne and went inside. She went to the extra set of food and water bowls that Jerry kept in his room for her. Jerry and Miss Priss were entirely too close.

"Here's your stuff, sweetheart. And yes! I brought your vitamin."

"Hey, do any of these vitamins help with … you know?" Jerry asked.

"No, I don't know," she said, looking at him suspiciously.

"You do too. Do any help with stamina? You know, sex?"

"Sex, Jerry? Really? *No.* These kinds of vitamins help with eyes, heart health, blood pressure, immunity, and with your energy and stuff. Well, and your prostate. You're going to tell me that *you're* having a problem getting excited?" she asked, astounded. She knew firsthand, that it really didn't take much at all for Jerry Granger to get turned on.

"Noooo. I'd just like to stay excited *for longer.* Never mind," he decided, embarrassed.

"Well, did you *used* to? I mean, did you used to stay excited for longer than you do now? Maybe you should see someone, then. Maybe something is wrong with you."

"No, I didn't used to! There's nothing *wrong* with me! I just know that there's things you can take that make you go longer is all."

"Don't yell at me, you creep. You talk to me about your sex drive and I ask perfectly normal questions. Hey? Is Marilyn complaining?" Anne asked. If Marilyn was complaining about sex with Jerry, Anne would have yet another reason to dislike that woman.

"Hell, no. Just forget about it. I just wanted to know if any of your damn vitamins covered that. I didn't really expect to get into a huge discussion about my sex drive. It's fine, *really*! I just thought it'd be even more fun if I could go on longer than I always have. That's all."

"If Marilyn has any issues with your performance ..."

"Anne! Come on. She hasn't complained ... exactly."

"What do you mean, exactly? She has *indirectly*?"

"Ohhh, listen. She's just said a few things here and there, you know? It makes me feel like maybe she's used to guys who ... you know? Go longer?"

"There is *nothing* wrong with your sexual performance. If it was good enough before, it's fine now. You said nothing changed. So, obviously, it's just that sex snob Marilyn."

"Miss Beales. Call her Miss Beales, Anne. What in the Hell are y'all talking about?" Will asked from the doorway. He didn't even question why his wife would be familiar with his father's sexual performance.

"Your dad thinks he needs special vitamins to increase his ... his sexual ... what was the word?"

"Stamina. Thank you, Anne. I appreciate you discussing this with my son," Jerry said, dryly.

"Well, it's not any worse than *you*, discussing it with my *wife*. Right? What's the matter, Daddy? Miss Beales not satisfied with the service?"

"Will you two kindly leave the room now? This conversation has progressed way past where I intended for it to go. Anne buys vitamins. I simply wanted to know if there were vitamins to help with stamina. My stamina is fine; I was simply aiming to make it even better. Okay?" Jerry just wanted them to go away.

He already realized the mistake he'd made, discussing sex with Anne. To begin with, because Anne went on and on about it, he started thinking things about her. That was to begin with. But he also knew that Anne was going to hold this over Marilyn. Anne picked Marilyn apart, as it was. Ever since he let it slip that Marilyn suggested he color his graying hair Anne had an issue with her. How dare anyone suggest Jerry change anything about himself? He was absolutely gorgeous and perfect in Anne's eyes!

Faye had to agree. She was also somewhat upset that Marilyn wanted Jerry to color his hair. Faye thought Jerry was beautiful with his graying hair. He was so rugged looking with his darling goatee and tanned face that Faye truly hated that she was dead. He was so good looking that she'd give anything just to make out with him again. She thought he was handsome when he was five. She thought he was handsome when he was 15, and 30. Jerry just got better looking with every year, as far as Faye was concerned. She learned that Anne shared this opinion.

Faye wasn't quite sure how she felt about that. She supposed she was happy that Anne loved Jerry the way he was; Faye knew that Anne would never, in a million years, try to change anything about him. The love that Anne had for Jerry was much like the love Faye had had for him. This was what confused Faye (and everyone else). Faye was his wife; Anne was not. Anne was his daughter-in-law, who was very much in love with his son. There was no doubt Anne was very much in love with Will. Many people felt Will and Anne reminded them of Jerry and Faye.

Then, there were those who felt *Jerry* and Anne reminded them of Jerry and Faye. Faye had shaken her head at this situation numerous times. She didn't know what to make of it.

But this morning, Jerry, Will, and Anne all laughed the situation off. Jerry blew contagious kisses to Anne. In response, Will (who already could tell he was coming down with something, too) went to his father's bedside and kissed him all over the face, just to make him mad. Jerry kept trying to slap Will away, while trying to block his own face at the same time. He didn't do a very good job at either. Will continued to smack kisses all over his dad's face, laughing the entire time.

"Stop it, you damn fool! Quit it, boy!"

Anne left the two men kissing in the bedroom, as she made her way out of the room. She happened to glance in the standing mirror as she walked toward it. In its reflection, she thought she saw a person. As soon as she thought she saw it, it was gone. She sighed, assumed it was Faye, and left the room.

Anne may have been able to shrug it off, but the situation gave her the creeps. As she walked down the wide, old hallway, the antique wall sconces flickered on and off. Anne paused beside one and just turned it off. She went to each one of the sconces and turned them all off. As soon as she cut the last one off, all the sconces flashed quickly. Anne just sighed. It was only 6:30 in the morning, too early for ghosts.

Anne had always grown up thinking what the vast majority of people thought. Ghosts came out at night. She never put much thought into her reasoning. Ghosts weren't vampires; why should they be opposed to sunlight? Who decided, she wondered now, that ghosts were only supposed to haunt at night? The more she thought about it, the dumber that was. Where were ghosts supposedly hanging out all day?

She knew that was a bunch of bunk now. She had seen way too much since moving into this place. She knew that ghosts had no time restrictions. They came out whenever they wanted to. Anne went downstairs and cleaned up the kitchen a bit. She was still sleepy. If Will wasn't going to make her go to church today, she'd go back to sleep.

She checked on Jerry one more time, told him she was going to bed and made sure he didn't need anything first. By the time she got back into the bed, Will was sound asleep and snoring softly.

It seemed only a matter of seconds later, her cell phone was ringing. She woke up. Confused, she blindly and hurriedly answered the phone without bothering to see who it was.

"Hello?"

"The *one time* we get around to going to church, and *y'all stayed home*? Really? You never stay home, until the one time we decided to go?" Roy Granger's voice boomed through the phone. Anne sighed.

"Look, Jerry is sick. Will said even he didn't feel good. Jerry feels bad about it; he's supposed to take Miss Beales out for her birthday. But when Will says even *he* doesn't feel good enough to go, you know they must be sick."

"Well, I tried to call before church, but nobody answered. I tried calling Will, Jerry, you. After church, I tried to call the house phone again ..." he began. Anne woke up a little bit.

"Wait ... sorry for interrupting ... but after church?" she asked.

"Yeah, after church, I asked Jason if he heard anything, and he ..."

While Roy talked, Anne sat up and strained to see the clock on Will's bedside table. Her eyes flew open. It was 12:15 in the afternoon! The babies! How in the world had they slept until after noon?

"Oh, my God! Look, Dad, I gotta let you go. I'm sorry about today. I have to get up and go check on the kids ... make lunch. Will? Honey, get up," she coaxed.

"Get up? Are y'all still in the bed?" Roy asked, incredulously.

"Yes, we went back to bed after we decided to stay home. We overslept. This is going to be a mess, today. Shit!"

"Go take care of things, honey. I'll call you back in a bit."

"Okay. I love you. Bye," Anne told Roy distractedly. Her attention turned to Will.

"Will! Get up! It's after lunch! Will! Get up!"

"I don't feel good! Quit yelling at me!" he retorted. Anne thought for just a minute. Even though he knew it was after noon, Will didn't want to get up? She laid her hand on his bare arm. It was hot, very hot. She felt his neck and cheek. He didn't stir.

"Oh, Will! You've got a fever. You really are sick. Hang on, Boss. I'll be right back."

She left the bedroom and walked down to Jerry's room. Jerry was sleeping soundly. She laid her hand on his very hot forehead. Jerry was breathing heavily, and the breathing sounded kind of bad. His face looked flushed to her. He and Will had said they didn't feel well this morning, but how in the world did they both go from that to this, just six hours later? Jerry started chewing in his sleep, something he'd done since he was an infant. Anne couldn't help but smile at this. She sighed as she realized the kind of day she was looking at.

Anne left Jerry's room and went downstairs. She made her way to the big pantry. The Grangers kept somewhat of a pharmacy in here. Anne found the severe cold and flu medicine. She pulled out a dose for Will and a second dose for Jerry. She thought for just a split second, before adding a dose for herself. She might as well go ahead and take some now. She was bound to catch whatever they had.

She got the tray from the shelf, added the medicine to it, and went to get them something to drink. She added two glasses of orange juice, and two bottles of cold water. She carried all of this up the never-ending staircase. She went to Will first. He didn't want to get up to take anything, but when it was obvious that she wasn't going to go away, he sat up and popped the capsules expertly, threw back the glass of juice as if it were a shot, and drank the entire bottle of water in three swigs. He handed his wife the water bottle, thanked her with his eyes closed, and lay back down.

Anne went to Jerry and went through pretty much the same thing with him, except Jerry acted more pitiful than Will. He also had not perfected pill popping like Will the aspirin addict had. So, he didn't take his pills as gracefully as Will had. She went and got two cool, damp washcloths. She took one to each man, for his hot forehead. She went so far as to wipe their foreheads for them. She folded the rags up, leaving them on the bedside tables.

The children were both still asleep at almost one o'clock in the afternoon. Anne dreaded what this was going to mean for her tonight. She'd be alone with two wound-up toddlers and two sick, useless men. She got the kids up and dressed. She went downstairs and broke into Jerry's bourbon. She knew she'd need it before the day was over anyway.

It wasn't until after she'd taken three big swigs from the bottle that she realized she'd taken two severe cold and flu capsules. Well, shit. She wondered if there were any warnings about mixing the medicine and liquor. There probably was. Well, too late to do anything about it, now.

Anne fed the children a quick lunch. She was glad Will had already taken care of the morning chores outside. She took care of some laundry and housework, before getting ready to go check on the animals. She was getting very tired. She hated when her sleep got messed up. When Anne slept too long, it made her drowsy for the rest of the day.

James wanted to know if he and Eliza could go out back and play in the sandbox. Anne made them go with her to the stable and barn first. The stable hands were off today so they may or may not have been by to check on things. The children helped Anne tend to a few things in the stable and barn. Then, Anne absently told them they could play in the sandbox. She walked them to the playground and went inside. She knew they'd stay in the little area of the yard that Jerry had fenced off for them. Inside the white picket fence with a gate were several things to entertain little children. There was a sandbox, teeter totter, playhouse, child-sized picnic table, climbing gym, and swings.

Jerry had gone through great pains to make the backyard safe for the kids. He said when it was just Will, he didn't worry so much. Will had been fairly easy to keep an eye on when he was a child. But when Eliza was born, Jerry decided there were now three small children, with possibly more to follow. Sure enough, Teague came along. Now, Gary and Kylie were going to have a baby, who would surely visit. It was a large area and the kids loved it. Caleb was the only one who was allowed, to come and go as he pleased.

Anne was standing in the living room, feeling a little addled. The front door opened, and Roy walked in. His eyes fell on Anne.

"Hey, honey. So, what's going on?" he asked. She yawned.

"Will is sick. Jerry is sick. The kids ate, helped me with outside chores, and they're out back."

"You look like Hell, too."

"Thanks, I appreciate that," she said insincerely.

"Come here," Roy directed her. She walked to him and he laid his hand on her face.

"You're not hot."

"I know. I felt fine. I just went ahead and took some medicine before I did get sick. As much time as I spend with both of them, I figured I'd get sick eventually."

"Well, maybe it's just your sleep getting messed up," Roy decided. Due to a head injury Anne had suffered her first winter with them, Anne had to take medication and keep a very regular sleep pattern. When this sleep pattern got messed up, it affected Anne greatly.

"Yeah …"

"Sit down, Anne. I'll go get us some tea." He shoved her toward the couch, where she happily sat down. Roy went to the kitchen. He found Anne's glass on the table and got one for himself. He made two glasses of tea. He began to walk out of the kitchen when his eyes caught sight of the antique liquor cabinet near the buffet. The cabinet door was open, and the bourbon was on the little shelf. He wondered something, then decided to go ask Anne about it.

He went in the living room, to find her half asleep on the couch.

"Anne, listen to me, baby. Did Jerry drink last night?"

"What, like his booze? No, he went to bed."

"Well, did *you* or Will drink last night? You said you all slept in. Somebody got into the bourbon. It's just kind of surprising it was left out all night. That's not like y'all."

"Oh, yeah. Well, I thought about everything going on today, and it sucked. If it'd just happened tomorrow even, at least Karen and Lexi would be here. I have two sick men, and two toddlers. And Will is mean when he's sick, and Jerry is pathetic when *he's* sick. So, I decided to drink a little. I thought it'd chill me out. You know, stress and all," she explained.

"You took cold medicine and *drank bourbon,* you dumb-ass?" he asked, astounded. How could she have done something so incredibly ignorant?

"Oh, yeah, I thought about that too. But not until after I drank the bourbon. I took the medicine while I was still upstairs. By the time I drank the bourbon, I had forgotten about the medicine."

"And are you tired? Getting sleepy or anything? I mean, I can tell you're tired. Do you think it's from oversleeping or mixing booze and medicine?" he demanded loudly.

"Oh. Aw, I don't know. Don't make me think about stuff like that right now. I mean, what difference does it make why I'm sleepy? I'm still sleepy regardless."

"Because if it's from mixing those two, you will likely get even sleepier! Damn it, Anne. I thought you had more sense than that. Doing something that fucking stupid, in addition to being on your prescription? Oh, you need to be *beat.* I'll have to do that later though. For now, go take a nap. I'll stay here with the kids."

"Take a nap? I slept for 15 hours!"

"You are tired. You have problems, Anne. Did you take your pill yet? This is the exact kind of thing that screws you up! Did you take the pill?"

"The pill?" Anne asked blankly, wondering why Roy would care about something like birth control right now. Will wasn't in the mood for sex, she knew.

"Your prescription, Anne! Did you take it yet?"

"Oh, *that* pill. No, good grief! Do you have any idea how crazy things have been since you called and bitched us out?"

"Go take the pill, Anne. Right now, or else in a few more hours you won't be acting right."

Anne went to the kitchen to take her medicine. It was for her migraines. Her migraines were a big problem. They didn't just mean bad headaches for Anne. They meant confusion, mood swings, forgetfulness, loss of appetite, exhaustion, and other things. She didn't like taking these pills, but she liked the migraines even less.

Anne took her pill and sat down at the kitchen table. Her legs ached. She yawned. She stretched, while sitting there. The stretch felt so nice. She crossed her arms on the table and laid her head down on them. Anne Granger fell asleep, alone in the kitchen. Well, she thought she was alone.

Faye was there with her. When she saw Anne fall asleep at the table, Faye thought, again, that whereas she didn't understand this girl, she loved her, worried about her and cared about her. So, she went to find Roy.

Roy was in the living room, thinking about the very long day he was looking at, ahead of him. He decided he'd call Karen in a little bit. She could come help-out. While he was thinking about this, he could swear he heard his name being called from the doorway. He looked but saw nobody. He went to see if Anne had been calling him from the kitchen, even though he admitted to himself, it had sounded more like Faye's voice.

Roy entered the kitchen, and found Anne passed out at the table. He sighed heavily. He went to her and shook her shoulder. She mumbled but didn't lift her head. Finally, after much prodding, he was able to get her to stand up, but she couldn't open her eyes to walk straight. Roy finally just picked her up. He carried her to the living room and laid her down on the couch. Anne looked terrible. He covered her with the throw blanket.

"Dad?" she asked. Roy smiled. Over the past year, Anne had begun referring to him as *Dad* more and more. She'd said he felt like a father to her. So, she began referring to him as *Dad*, and he rather liked it.

"What is it, honey?"

"I'm sorry about this."

"It's okay. Just rest. Did you get around to taking your pill when you went to the kitchen? Before you fell asleep at the table?"

"Yeah. I took it. The kids are out back," Anne muttered, falling asleep again.

"I'll take care of the kids. Don't worry about them. I'm gonna call Karen to come over here in just a little bit. Now, go on and get some sleep."

Roy left a sleeping Anne on the couch. He went down the wide hall and looked out the back screen-door. The children were playing in the sandbox. When James began throwing handfuls of sand up in the air, making Eliza scream, Roy sighed. He opened the door.

"Boy! Quit doing that! You're wasting the sand and getting it in y'all's hair and everything else. Its gonna get in your eyes and its gonna hurt. Now, play nicely or get out." The children stopped and looked mildly surprised.

"Uncle Roy!" James shouted, as he abandoned the sandbox and his baby sister. He ran toward Roy. Roy came out on the porch and came down the steps to meet the child. Roy opened the gate, picked up James and cuddled him. The child laid his head against Roy's shoulder, as Roy patted his back.

"How you doing, buddy?"

"I'm tired."

"So, *you're* tired, too? Oh, no. Wait a minute. Do you feel okay?"

"Yes. No. I don't know. I'm just tired. I told Mommy and Mommy said she'd call Miss Lexi." The two-year old's vocabulary and eloquent manner of speaking was credited to Will.

Roy laid his cheek against James's cheek, and sighed with relief.

"Well, so far, I don't feel a fever. But I guess I'll keep an eye on you, just in case. Everyone coming down with something at once. That's just great. Liza? Come here, baby girl."

Roy set James down and he and James walked through the gate to the play yard. Eliza stood up carefully and toddled toward Roy with a huge smile on her face. Her brown hair was a riot of tiny ringlets. Roy couldn't help but smile at her in her tiny pink shorts and white top.

"Uncle Yory!" she called out to him, with her arms raised.

"Miss Liza! Let me see if you feel warm, sweet pea. Nope! You just feel like sunshine. I'll keep an eye on you two though. Y'all can stay out here and play. Let me go inside and call Miss Karen for a minute." Eliza first took Roy's face in her tiny little hands and turned his face, so his cheek was facing her. Very carefully and deliberately, she kissed him on his cheek four times. After each kiss, she said a word.

(Kiss) "I," (kiss) "love," (kiss) "you," (kiss)

This was a game she and Roy played. He smiled, looking into her grass-green eyes.

"I love you too." He kissed her a dozen times, sending her into a gale of laughter. He left her and James in the yard and went inside to call Karen. As soon as he stepped in the kitchen, the house phone rang. He sighed.

"Hello?"

"Will?" a woman's voice asked.

"It's Roy, Marilyn."

"Oh. Well, I tried calling Jerry's phone and I'm not getting anything."

"No, I don't guess you would; he's sick. He's probably asleep."

"Asleep? Sick? He just got over being sick. What is his deal?"

"He's around a lot of people, especially kids. It's not just Jerry anyway. Even Will and Anne are down. James doesn't know if he feels good. I'm about to call Karen to come over here and help me. I'll probably end up spending the night."

"Anne is sick too?"

"Well, she took medicine before she got sick, but then ..." Roy paused. He decided not to tell Marilyn that Anne, in panic, drank booze after taking the medicine.

"But then?" Marilyn pressed.

"Oh. Then, she just felt real tired. She took the medicine as a precaution. But it may have been too late," he fibbed. He didn't know why, but he felt a need to cover for Anne to this woman. Marilyn's feelings towards Anne were hard to read. Marilyn seemed to like her as much as she resented her.

"Well, won't the place just fall to pieces? Who's going to take care of everyone, if Anne is down, too?" Marilyn asked, sincerely but snidely.

"I just told you that I am here. I also told you that I'm calling Karen over to help me out. It won't be the first time I've taken care of this crowd." Roy was getting testy.

"Well, I guess I could come and take care of Jerry."

"Aren't you working tomorrow?"

"It's spring break."

"Oh, I see. Well, if you want to come out here ..."

"Well, you don't sound like you want me to."

"Oh, for the love of God! Can none of you women just cut the bullshit? You all sit around trying to make mountains out of molehills! I didn't say anything to imply I didn't want you out here. If you want to come out here, come out here. I will also be here, and Karen will likely be here too."

"Is it really necessary for all of us to be there? I mean, I think I can take care of Jerry on my own."

"Can you take care of Will and Anne? Would you even want to? I mean, really? Can you take care of these kids? I mean, come on, Mare," Roy pointed out. He thought (to himself) that it wasn't even likely she could take care of Jerry adequately. Jerry had always been high maintenance when he was sick. He was high maintenance even when he wasn't sick.

Anne had Jerry's needs down. Anne knew everything Jerry needed, where it was, and when he needed it. Marilyn? Well, Roy just didn't think she had it in her.

"I can take care of Jerry. Maybe you're right. I mean, if there's that many people sick, I guess it makes sense for you and Karen to hang out."

"Hang out? Yes, I'm sure that's all we'll be doing. Look, if you want to come here and help Jerry out, then feel free to, dear. I'm going to call Karen now and tell her what's going on."

"Well, wait a minute. What time would be okay for me to come?"

"Anytime. Come now. Come tonight. That is entirely up to you."

"Fine. I'll wait and come closer to dinner. I'll make him something to eat. I mean, I'd go ahead and come now. But I have to get some stuff together and all."

"Whatever, Marilyn. You don't have to explain anything. Just come out whenever."

"Alright. Well, bye, Roy."

"Goodbye, dear. See you later." Roy hung up.

Marilyn hung up too and immediately felt apprehensive. What had she gotten herself into? She did love Jerry and she really did want to take care of him if he needed it. But realistically, she knew that she'd be a nervous mess. There was just something in her that had to prove something to this crowd … even if all she proved was that she didn't have a clue what she was doing when it came to taking care of Jerry Granger.

CHAPTER 5

M arilyn had not been off the phone with Roy two minutes before her phone rang again. She saw that it was Emily, her friend from the school. She didn't feel like talking to her, but she answered it anyway.

"Hello?"

"Well, hello to you, too! What's the matter with you?"

"Huh?"

"Well, you sounded mighty testy when you answered."

"Oh, there's just some stuff going on."

"Oh, well, forget about all of it. Tonight, JoAnne is having a get together at her place, to kick off spring break. Bunch of us girls are meeting over there at about seven."

"Oh, I can't make it."

"Well, why not? It's Sunday. Isn't Jerry staying on the farm?"

"He's sick. The whole family is down ... well, most of them anyway."

"So, he's sick. He wouldn't feel like doing anything, anyway. Come on, Marilyn. It's going to be fun. Janine is going to be there, drinking. We're thinking we might be able to finally get out of her, what's going on with her and Ricky Stephens."

"I *know* what's going on with her and Ricky. They're sleeping together, but not committing. She said she doesn't want any strings attached, and neither does he. I think it's kind of sleazy, but they didn't ask me."

"Why didn't you tell me all that before?"

"It wasn't my business; Ricky works for Jerry. I don't go around talking about things like that. But since y'all were evidently going to get her trashed to get it out of her anyway, I figured I'd just spare her the hangover and publicly humiliating herself."

"How kind of you."

"Yeah. Well, anyway, I have a few things to do before I go up to Jerry's. I'm going to go help out."

"Can't Anne take care of him?" Emily asked. This question cut like a knife.

"I told you the whole family is down. That includes Anne. I'm going to go help Roy and Karen out. And what the fuck is that supposed to mean anyway? He's my boyfriend. Why should Anne take care of him when he's sick?"

"Well, because she lives with him, and according to you, she usually does take care of him," Emily answered, reasonably.

"Well, tonight, I'm taking care of him. Have fun getting trashed. Bye, Emily."

"Marilyn!"

"What?"

"I wasn't trying to make you mad! I mean, you guys have been together for a while now, and I simply never knew of you to go tend to him when he was bedridden."

Marilyn almost snapped back that, that was because he had never needed her before; he'd had Anne. But she thought it in her head, first, and the realization hurt. It was quite a blow to her self-esteem, but it was true. Jerry had never really needed Marilyn, not like that. He had Anne there to take care of his needs. She composed herself.

"Anyway, this time, I'm going over there. Yeah, Anne usually takes care of those things. But Anne is sick. If Jerry and Anne and Will are all down, it's likely just a matter of time before the kids get whatever it is that they have. I'm not going to expect Roy and Karen to deal with all of that, alone. I'm trying to be nice ... *okay?*"

"Jesus, Marilyn. Excuse me. Fine, go over there. I'll tell everyone why you couldn't make it," Emily exclaimed. Marilyn was being a jerk this afternoon. Emily figured they'd have more fun without her anyway.

Marilyn stepped out on her porch. She decided to sit down for a few minutes before getting her things together to take to Jerry's.

Liberty Creek was relatively quiet, as it tended to be on Sundays. Okay, it tended to be quiet most every day. The only difference was on Sundays, you didn't hear lawn mowers, weed eaters, the teenagers blasting music at the car wash, or things like that. Gary Connelly, former police chief and substitute preacher, made sure loud music and unnecessary noise was not a problem on Sundays. Marilyn liked Sundays. It was her quiet day. It usually meant her spending the morning alone and sometimes meeting up with friends later in the day for lunch.

Today, she had met with Carol for brunch.

She went to church sometimes. It didn't happen very often. She and Jerry usually stayed up late on Saturday nights. She didn't feel like getting up early the next day. Jerry didn't always feel like it either. But he knew he had to get up and go or else Will would bitch about it. Also, Jerry had told her that Gary made the situation awkward. It'd never do for Gary to suspect Jerry had missed church because he'd stayed up all night making out with his girlfriend.

Gary may not have been perfect, but he was a devout church goer. He'd behaved himself all these years for the most part. Right out of high school, he did get Charlotte Banks pregnant, but to redeem himself to the church, he married her immediately. His parents would have disowned him, had he not.

His family was always very, very serious about church. His ancestors founded and built the church he still attended. His own father and all his grandfathers for several generations back had preached in that little church. Gary's parents were disappointed when Gary didn't go to college to pursue theology, choosing, instead, to just go to the police academy. Gary's father pointed out he had managed to get a degree in theology in addition to going to the police academy. Gary was proud of his father but simply had no desire to study theology. Choosing to not pursue a degree in theology, in addition to getting a woman pregnant out of wedlock, didn't go over well with his family.

After Charlotte had the baby and became a drug addict, he kicked her out and raised Jason on his own. This alone redeemed Gary in the eyes of the locals. It was a mighty good, strong man to be willing to take on such a responsibility! Then, when Jason was 10 years old,

Gary became ordained. Yes, the locals admired Gary Connelly after his marriage ended. And he pretty much behaved himself ever since. Oh, he dated here and there a few times. He and Karen Townsend had a brief fling; unfortunately, she was still married at the time, so that fling didn't go over too well. But even that was somewhat dismissed. Everyone knew that Karen's husband was an asshole.

So, when Gary announced he'd be marrying the much younger Kylie Johnston, everyone was actually pretty happy for him. Nobody knew (yet) that she was expecting a baby already. They would deal with that when the time came to deal with it. Anyway, although he secretly worried about this now, this situation would also be dismissed. It was Gary. Everyone knew he was a good guy, a devoted Christian, and a fabulous father.

So, yes, Gary was highly respected in the church. Gary was the first man in his family to not preach at the church every Sunday, but he did fill in when Brother Lawson couldn't make it for whatever reason. It was for this reason Jerry didn't want Gary knowing about him skipping out on church. Gary may not have been the actual preacher, but he was close enough as far as Jerry was concerned. The fact that Gary was also Jerry's best friend just made it even more complicated.

Another preacher might would make little comments here and there about how much you were missed at Sunday services. Not Gary. Gary had no problem at all interrogating Jerry about why he wasn't at church. He wasn't subtle or kind about it. If Jerry missed church, Gary would call him, and say, "Hey, why weren't you at church, today?"

Yes, it was that direct, no beating around the bush or dropping little hints. So, Jerry made sure he went to church. Marilyn had assumed he had gone, today, but obviously, he had not.

She sat on her porch for only about ten minutes. She was stressed, now. She decided to just go ahead, go inside, pack a few overnight things, and just go on to Jerry's house.

This should have been an easy task. However, Marilyn found herself being particular about what she took. She wanted to take clothes that'd be attractive enough to make Jerry smile, yet she didn't want to take any sleepwear that would offend Faye. Yes, she really selected sleepwear based on what the resident ghost would have to say. She felt the skanky baby-dolls and teddies just wouldn't go over well. She grabbed her tasteful pajama set with the matronly floral print and sighed. After another half hour, she felt she had packed appropriately. She grabbed her bags, and made one last run around the house, checking locks and lights before she left.

Marilyn stopped by the gas station first, to get gas and to load up on some junk food to get her through the night at Jerry's. Will seldom had any junk food in the house. Anne made cakes and cookies if they wanted anything like that. Will saw no need to buy Little Debbie or Hostess. He only had Anne pick up so much junk at the store. He preferred the children not get accustomed to eating poorly. This was all very admirable, Marilyn supposed but it made snacking at the huge old house difficult.

Jerry kept a secret stash of junk food in his room. Marilyn found out from Jerry that Anne also kept a secret stash of junk food in Jerry's room. Marilyn found this amusing. Nobody wanted to get lectured by the neurotic control freak Will. So, they just did things he disapproved of behind his back. So, Marilyn knew a secret stash was okay. She'd just keep it in Jerry's room.

Marilyn walked in Lowery's and was just about to get a bag of chips when someone greeted her from behind.

"Good afternoon, Marilyn. We missed y'all in church this morning. You and Jerry make it a late night?" Gary Connelly asked her, smirking. She sighed at his insinuation. It also irritated her that she felt guilty for not going to church.

"No, Gary. Jerry's sick. He's at home. Apparently, the whole family is down, even Will. I'm on my way up there now."

"Well, when Roy and Karen were the only ones that showed up, I did wonder. So, you gonna go play nursemaid?" he asked, looking amused.

"Why is that so fucking funny to everyone?" she snapped, temporarily forgetting that Gary often served as a substitute preacher. He raised his eyebrows at her outburst.

"Well! I asked a perfectly normal question. I wasn't expecting that response! If that's how you greet friends on a Sunday afternoon, perhaps an occasional Sunday morning in the church would benefit you, Miss Beales. Give my love to the folks when you see them. Good day, dear," Gary said pleasantly, although a bit disproving. He winked and turned to leave. Marilyn was ashamed of herself now.

"Oh, come on, Gary! I'm sorry. I'm just kind of stressed out, is all. I'm sorry I yelled at you like that."

"Well, thank you for the apology. I was more offended by your use of the f word in public on a Sunday afternoon, than I was by your tone of voice. What is it you're so stressed about, doll?" he asked. He stood before her there, in front of the honey buns and pecan spins, and waited patiently. She was suddenly shy and embarrassed. Suddenly he was *Gary the Preacher*, rather than *Gary, Jerry's Friend*. He looked interested.

"Okay, look. Yes, I'm going to help-out at the house. But I wasn't really planning to. It just sort of happened. Then, once I offered, or whatever it was I did, I don't even remember what it was I said now, it was too late. I went and told Roy that I wanted to come take care of things or something. He said he and Karen would be there and they didn't need me, and it hurt my feelings, I think. I don't even know. Anyway, long story short, I offered to help take care of Jerry and them, and I don't know what the Hell to do … oh, sorry about that. But really? I don't know how to take care of sick people.

"What do I do now? I *have* to go take care of Jerry. I said I would. And jerk Roy sounded like he thought it was funny. He acted all impatient with me. But of course, he thought it was funny! He knows I can't do this kind of thing! He's not stupid. But boy! *I* sure as Hell am! Oh, sorry. Sick people, though? I don't have a clue what to do once I get there. I mean, people who are sick in the head, that kind of sick, I can handle that kind of sick. That kind of sick is interesting. But like, sneezing and coughing and throwing up and stuff? No. I can't do that," Marilyn sighed. Gary looked at her hard.

"Well, you can call and say that something came up but that's not really honest. You could call Roy and laugh it all off and tell him you weren't thinking right when you made that offer. Or you could maybe go on to the house, help-out the best way you know how, and at least be making the gesture." He smiled apologetically. He knew what he said wasn't what she wanted to hear, but he thought it was the best advice he could give her.

"Oh, fine! I'll go on to the house. I'll make an idiot out of myself. But whatever. Alright. Well, I'm going to pick up a few more things to take to eat because I know Will won't have anything fun there to eat."

"Do you want me to help you out with something? A suggestion?" Gary asked.

"Yeah, sure. What do you got?"

"Take Jerry some Cokes. He usually gets that stash of them every Saturday at the co-op you know? But since he didn't come to town this weekend, he's likely about out."

Marilyn smiled and nodded at Gary's suggestion.

"Yeah. That's a good idea. I'll grab him some. Thanks, Gary."

"No problem. Just chill out, Marilyn. They'll probably all sleep most of the time, anyway. I mean, if Will is sick, then it's gotta be pretty bad. Surely, they'll all sleep a lot. Now, I need to be on my way if your problem has been taken care of,"

"Oh, yeah, it's all good. Thanks, again. I'll just do what I can, I guess," she told him, smiling. The smile was forced because she really didn't believe she'd be able to handle this. Gary gave her a thumbs-up, and a wink. He took his purchases to the register, and Marilyn went and found Jerry some Cokes.

The drive to the Granger's was a pleasant one. The weather was beautiful. The dogwoods were all in bloom, and the wildflowers were scattered throughout the wooded hills. Marilyn turned off the main road and began the journey down a dirt road before turning onto the last dirt road, Teague Road. She was still impressed that this road featured not only a county-issued road sign but a historical marker. A good many impressive things had happened on this road, so it was decided it deserved a historical marker.

Teague Road was just that: a road. It was a dirt road that was above being paved. It had been a good old road all these years. The family took pride in this road, as they should have. It was the Grangers and Teagues who had cleared the trees to make it and had painstakingly and lovingly maintained it. It was free of potholes and shaded by the huge trees that formed a canopy over it.

Civil War battles took place on the property this road traveled through. Soldiers set up camps in its woods and fields, and Robert E. Lee himself, had slept and dined in the Granger- Teague plantation home at the end of the tree-lined drive. If you were lucky enough to be invited into the home, you would find an impressive collection of historic photographs, hanging on the walls of the back parlor. Among this collection was a photograph of General Lee standing on the front steps with his gracious hosts, John Hayes Teague and William Stanford Granger.

And, whereas no major Revolutionary War battles took place near here, it certainly saw its share of Revolutionary War soldiers, nonetheless. Soldiers en route to war, traveled through these woods and fields. Thomas Sewell, the original owner of a portion of this property, was a Revolutionary War soldier himself. His grave was in the Sewell family graveyard, beneath a tall cedar, in a fenced-off section of pasture. The history, in conjunction with the almost 200 year-old family graveyard, stately home, and countless ghost stories made this road worthy of a historical marker.

Marilyn did love this road, and she did love the beautiful houses on this road. The Granger home was, of course, the highlight of the road. But Karen's home was certainly beautiful, itself. It had a beauty that was much more modest than the Granger home. The Teague farmhouse was wooden, painted light yellow, trimmed in white, featuring huge windows, wrap-around porch, and lovely hardwood floors.

Down the road, about a 10-minute drive from Karen's, was a long dirt drive tucked into the trees. This dirt drive was pretty enough during the day, but truly terrifying at night. It led to the Sewell-Connelly home. The name was given to it, because it was the original homesite of the Thomas Sewell home. The original home burned to the ground at the end of the Civil War, but Jason and Lexi Connelly built their own home (an exact replica of the Sewell home) on the site. They even used much of the original stonework and wood that was found scattered amongst the remains of the Sewell home.

This seemed like a good idea at the time the house was being built. The Connellys would end up second guessing this decision before very long however. Whereas Jason and Lexi, and even their son, Caleb, had seen more than enough to believe the Granger home was haunted, they were surprised to learn that their own house was too. It appeared that the Connellys had done such a magnificent job at replicating the old Sewell home, that the Sewells thought it *was* home. Or at least something did.

Furniture had recently begun moving on its own, right in front of them. Lights had begun turning off and on. Doors had begun swinging open and closing. One day, Lexi was in the back yard, hanging clothes on the line when she remembered she'd put water on to boil. Upon realizing how much time had passed, she rushed up the porch steps and into the house and went to the kitchen. When Lexi got to the stove, over half of the water had boiled away. It was still steaming but no longer boiling. Lexi noticed that the burner had been turned off. Besides Teague, her youngest (who was not quite six months old), Lexi was the only one at home.

So, perhaps it was a nice ghost, who was apparently very safety conscious. Still, it wasn't something the Connellys had been prepared for. They were dealing with it though, best that they knew how.

The driveway to that house ran through the deep woods of the Appalachian hills and past century-old fencing and a few abandoned structures tucked back in the trees. There were numerous outbuildings; these creeped Marilyn out. The Grangers, Connellys and Karen all found these decaying, dilapidated buildings to be charming. In the light of day, the drive itself was pretty (the outbuildings aside), but in the night, it was like a horror movie, going down that drive.

Marilyn preferred her own little white house downtown, with its big yard, and streetlights in front, surrounded by neighbors. She had grown up in the heart of Lexington, Kentucky. Marilyn was a city girl. She supposed the country was nice enough when you were in the mood for some fresh mountain air and a horse or two. But truth was, you got that slap in the middle of town.

Liberty Creek was settled in the quaint rolling hills in southwest Virginia. Mountain air was abundant here. Liberty Creek didn't have much in Marilyn's opinion, but it did have a lot of fresh air, trees, and football trophies from the local high school.

Marilyn approached the driveway to the Granger home. She drove under the massive stone archway and down the dirt driveway. As she drove toward the house, three dogs came running up to her car, barking at her. She kept losing sight of them, as they ran around her car. She drove about two miles per hour, swearing at these stupid dogs. They saw her every single week. They knew her car. They knew her. Yet, they came running after her car, today, as if they'd never laid eyes on her. She finally parked at the side of the house.

Marilyn put her hand on the door handle and lifted it when suddenly Patton, one of the dogs, let out a howl that sent the other two dogs into an even worse fit of barking. They looked mad and hungry. Marilyn rolled her window down half-way.

"Go away! Get out of here, you damned fools! Go find a squirrel or something!"

This only got the dogs more excited, because now she was visiting with them. They barked louder and with a lot more enthusiasm. She finally picked up her phone. She called Roy. When he answered, she could hear Eliza screaming in the background.

"Hello?" he asked, rather cranky.

"Roy? The dogs won't go away."

"What are you talking about?"

"Y'alls dogs! They won't let me out the car. They keep barking at me."

"Oh, are you what they're raising hell about? For God's sake, woman. You know those stupid dogs. You see them every week. Just get out of the car and kick them out of the way."

"Well, I think they don't know me, if I'm not with Jerry,"

"They bark every time anybody pulls up here! They always act like that. They're dogs, Marilyn. They don't have that much to keep themselves entertained. Just bark back and ignore them."

"Can't you just call them or something?"

"Marilyn! Just get out of the car, already. They aren't going to do anything to you!"

Marilyn was just about to tell Roy how one of them looked like he might have rabies, when she saw Karen come around the corner of the house. She stood up on the porch and leaned against one of the large Corinthian columns. She looked amused, even pleased. She shook her head, then called out to the pack of farm dogs.

"Come on y'all! Shut yourselves up! Go on! Get the Hell out of here! Get! Patton! You and Markus get out of here! Get out of here! Granger! Shut up!" Patton and Markus, the Grangers' dogs, followed Granger (Karen's Springer Spaniel, that the Grangers had given her several Christmases' ago) back to the field they had come from. Karen smirked at Marilyn with raised eyebrows.

"You're scared of some yard dogs?" she asked, as Marilyn made her way up the steps.

"When they act like that? Yes, I am."

"These dogs aren't going to do anything to you, fool."

"Look. I've had a bad day. If you don't mind, lets drop it. I know you're used to these dogs. One of them is yours. But I'm just not that into dogs, okay?"

"Why'd you have a bad day?"

"Oh, let's just say I said something I shouldn't have."

At this, Karen broke out laughing. She got a hold of Marilyn's arm.

"Girl, you talking about offering to come help this messed up group of people? I hear you, if that's what you're talking about. I sure as shooting wouldn't spend my Sunday playing doctor to this crowd, well, if I had a choice, which I don't.

"Roy calls me on the phone and tells me, '*Woman, you need to come over here and help me out. This whole bunch is down sick, and kids are running loose and folks need to be fed and tended to, and I can't do it on my own!*' Bless his pitiful self. It's not that he can't; he ain't fool enough to try it, is all.

"Now, leave your attitude in the yard. It isn't going to be welcomed or needed in the house. Too much is already going on in there, without you dragging your issues in there, on top of everything else. Anne gets sick and the whole lot of them just falls apart. Well, I'll deal with those young'uns, and I'm leaving the sick people upstairs to you and Roy. I didn't offer to come over here and get all that sick breathing all over me.

"Well, that's what happens. You go and get tied up with these people and you just do what needs to be done. They take care of us; we take care of them. Anyway, come on now. We got things to do, whether you want to do them or not."

Ironically, Karen's tangent on the porch made Marilyn feel better. She didn't know why, but it somehow relaxed her. It gave Marilyn a chance to just stand still, be quiet, and listen to someone else bitch. How Karen delivered the situation, though, was amusing. Marilyn was then able to see this for what it was; there was a crazy sick family, and these three were there to watch the kids and put up with the three pitiful sick people. Okay, so the situation itself maybe wasn't the crisis that Marilyn had built it up to be in her own mind. However, it didn't boost her confidence, either. Karen took the overnight bag from Marilyn's hands, and started for the back door. Marilyn just followed her. They went in the back door, where Marilyn was greeted by the pleasant old house smell. Karen set Marilyn's bag on the cherry bench in the back hall. Marilyn could hear Eliza crying in the kitchen. She followed Karen into the kitchen. Roy was putting Eliza into her booster seat.

"Roy, baby, here. Lexi gave me these after church. She said Jamie gave them to her to give James and Liza since they missed church. Here. Liza, child, you need to be quiet, now. I can't be listening to all that. I know you didn't just lose an arm and that's just exactly how you are acting. You ran into a table. You're gonna have a bruise. Now, get over it. It's just an arm and you have two of them anyway," Karen reasoned with the angry little girl. Roy handed Eliza a coffee can of crayons and rubbed his eyes.

"James! Come on in here if you're wanting this cake!" he bellowed. Karen looked at him in shock.

"Cake? You're giving that baby cake at three o'clock in the afternoon? Have you lost your mind? You know Will would stroke out."

"Then, let Will come down here and take care of things. If they want me to take care of things, I'm taking care of things my way. A piece of pound cake at three o'clock isn't going to kill him, and it's not going to ruin his supper. He's got a good three hours to go before supper. Marilyn, go see if James is in the living room, please," Roy directed. Marilyn, a bit overwhelmed, turned and left the kitchen. She walked up the wide hall and turned to go into the living room.

She peered in and saw James, sitting in the middle of the floor, watching television. He had the big family Bible on the floor in front of him, and he was wearing a blue beach bucket on his head. She found herself smiling at him. She walked over to him and kneeled on the floor beside him.

"Hi, there. What are you watching?" she asked.

"*Spongebob.*"

"I see. I've heard of him. You and Caleb like him, don't you?"

"Yep. So does Liza and Daddy."

"Oh." Marilyn sat awkwardly, watching the yellow sponge battle a jellyfish, on the big screen television. She glanced down at the Bible on the floor.

"You're looking at the Bible? What is that? Oh, Noah's Ark. I liked that story."

"Daddy and Papa said this is the best book in the house."

"Well, your daddy and Papa are right. It's a very good book. Your daddy reads it a lot, doesn't he?"

"We read it every night. I like the pictures."

"Well, your Uncle Roy wants to know if you want this cake that he cut for you, in the kitchen?"

"Yes, ma'am," he replied, looking at a picture of Noah directing a pair of giraffes.

"Well, then, come on, before it gets yucky." Marilyn stood and gestured for James to follow her. He left the Bible, open on the floor, and followed her into the kitchen with the bucket still on his head. Once they reached the kitchen, Roy was sitting down, watching Eliza color. Karen was at the sink washing something. Roy looked up, as James came into the room. He raised his eyebrows amused.

"New hat, son?"

"No, sir. It is just a bucket," James informed him.

James took after his father. James was practical, and his vocabulary, at not even three years old, was downright frightening. The child crawled up into his booster seat and began eating his cake carefully. Marilyn sat quietly feeling a bit awkward.

"So, what can I do?" she asked Roy and Karen.

"Why don't you go on up and see if your man needs anything? He's so pitiful, he'd just lay there and die rather than getting up to get help," Karen muttered. Roy shook his head.

"Well, okay. I can go do that." Marilyn stood and took a deep breath as she left the kitchen. She walked up the hall and began the tiresome journey of walking up the massive staircase. She had always thought the stairs at home, in Kentucky, were bad. But no, those were just standard stairs. These had to have a landing, they were so long. She finally made it to the second floor and made her way down the wide hall to Jerry's bedroom, where she knocked.

"Come in," called a pitiful Jerry. She opened the heavy door and stepped inside.

"Hello, baby," she greeted him. She was greeted by a groan and a hacking cough.

"Jerry? You okay?"

"No, I'm not. I'm siiiiiick," he whined, pitifully.

"See? What the Hell is the point of those damn vitamins? Immunity support, my ass. What do you think you have this time?" she asked.

"Will and I both have it, whatever it is."

"Don't forget Anne," she said oddly.

"Anne? Is Anne sick?"

"How could you not know that?"

"I've been asleep. She was in here, earlier. She seemed okay then," he said, worriedly. He didn't realize Anne was sick. He thought about the children.

"What about the babies? Are they still okay?"

"They're fine. Roy and Karen are taking care of them. I offered to come take care of *you*," she said, suggestively. She began to lean over to get a kiss when he began coughing again. She sat back down.

"I guess it's a good thing I didn't stay in town last night, darling," he smiled.

"Yes, I agree. Well, do you need anything?" she asked. She had hoped being suggestive would ... well, she didn't know. She thought maybe it'd make him feel better. Marilyn liked this man. She loved him. She would do *most* anything for him. That's the first difference between her and Anne Granger. Anne would do *anything*.

Marilyn understood this situation, to a degree. She just couldn't understand it completely. She wanted to. She cared about Jerry too much to say, screw it. She and Jerry had a lot of fun together and enjoyed the arrangement that they had. It was a relationship that was exhilarating yet exhausting at times.

"Well, look. I'm here. If there's anything that you need, I came here, just to take care of you. So just let me know," Marilyn smiled but looked somewhat unsure.

"Well, I would like some juice if you don't mind," he admitted feebly.

"Well, okay! I'll go get you some juice. What kind of juice?"

"Oh, orange juice. I only drink orange juice." Jerry said this with a touch of surprise. Marilyn knew he liked orange juice, didn't she? Whenever they went out for breakfast, he always got orange juice. Perhaps he was just so used to Anne, who always knew what juice he wanted. Oh, well. So, Marilyn didn't know what kind of juice he preferred; she does now.

"Okay, well, I'll go get you some orange juice. Is there anything else that you want?"

"Just a kiss," he puckered his lips to kiss her. She hesitated. Whatever it was he had he could keep for himself. She really didn't want to catch it. But she was in an awkward position. He kept his mouth ready for the kiss. She laughed it off.

"Oh ew! I'm not gonna kiss you! Yuck! You're all germy!"

He looked surprised but unpuckered his lips.

"It could have been on the cheek," he muttered, hurt, and offended.

"What's that?" Marilyn asked, as she got his empty glass from his bedside table.

"Nothing." He laid back into his pillows. Jerry watched her move around the room for a moment. As she got ready to leave, she looked at him.

"What's the matter?"

"Nothing. It's all good." He smiled a sickly smile.

"Oh. Well, alright. I'll be back with the juice." She turned and left the room. Jerry grabbed his washcloth off the bedside table. He preferred to use a washcloth for his runny nose, rather than tissue. This was something he had done since he was a child. He thought a washcloth felt better than tissue. Everyone thought he was weird, but he learned that Anne, too, preferred washcloths to tissue. Rather than deciding Jerry wasn't so weird, after all, everyone just decided Anne was weird, too. Wiping his nose with his washcloth, he thought about Anne. He hoped she and Will were feeling better. He picked up his phone, and dialed Anne's cell phone.

"Hello?" she asked, after the fifth ring.

"Did I wake you up?"

"Yes. What's going on? Do you need something, honey?" she asked, waking up a little.

"No, I don't guess so. Marilyn just came in here. She went downstairs to get me some juice. I just wanted to see if you and Will were feeling any better."

"Marilyn?"

"Yeah, you know, Miss Beales?" Jerry said jokingly. Will, Jason, and Lexi still insisted on calling her Miss Beales, out of habit. So, Will told Anne she needed to call her that, too. It was only polite and respectful, he felt.

"I mean … what's she doing here?" Anne asked.

"I think she came to help out, since we're sick. I guess, anyway. She said she was here to take care of me. She said Roy and Karen were watching the kids. I sent her downstairs to get me some orange juice."

"I see. Well, I mean, I'm not like deathly ill or anything. I'm just sick. In fact, I'm probably not really even sick. I took cold and flu medicine right before I drank bourbon. Dad said that'd probably make me feel bad. So, probably, it's not even really being sick. It's probably just the drugs and booze together. I'll go ahead and get up," Anne rambled. Even as she spoke, Jerry knew what was going on.

"Anne ... Anne, honey, listen. Just let her help-out today. I mean, it was nice of her to want to come out here. Just rest today and let Marilyn help-out. If you get up and take over ... I don't know. Just let it go, today, for me," Jerry felt odd asking this. It was the first time he recalled telling Anne to back off and let Marilyn have her way. He was touched that Anne wanted to be the one to take care of him but oddly, he was more touched by Marilyn's gesture. He knew Marilyn well enough to know she didn't really want to be there doing this. He knew she came because she felt she should and that meant a lot to him. Anne was quiet on the other end of the line. She finally responded to his request.

"Alright. If you want Miss Beales to take care of you today, she can. She can take care of you. It's all good."

"You need some rest anyway, Mama. Whether it's the bug or booze and pills, you do need to rest, you know? Besides, if I know Marilyn, she'll probably be ready to throw in the towel by dark. This isn't really her thing, you know? I think she just wanted to ... I don't know. I just think it was nice of her."

"It's fine, Jerry. You don't have to keep trying to convince me. I told you, it's all good. Regardless, I'll probably be getting up before long. But I won't interfere. I'll let her take care of you, dearest, and I will take care of Will. Okiedokie?"

"Anne, are you mad?"

"I promise you I am not mad. Now get some sleep, sugar. I love you."

"I love you too. I'll see you in a bit, Mama." Jerry blew a germy kiss into the phone, and Anne returned it with a slightly hungover one. Jerry smiled and hung the phone up, setting it beside his bed. The door to the bedroom swung open. There was Marilyn, slightly out of breath.

"Hi, Jerry. Here's your juice. I um think I'm going to maybe go back downstairs and get my bags. I think I'd maybe like to change into something more ... practical." The tight jeans and ankle boots and blouse had seemed like a good idea when she got dressed. When she got dressed, however, she'd dressed to impress a sickly Jerry. Now, she saw just how foolish and pointless that was. She was thinking about her yoga pants and T-shirt she had also packed. Yes, those sounded much more practical. No way in Hell was she going to climb up and down these damn stairs all day, in this outfit. The shoes were just the ultimate mistake.

"Oh, well, okay. You look nice, though. You don't look very comfortable, but you do look nice," he said honestly. She smiled, relaxing a touch.

"No, you're right. I'm not very comfortable, at all. I guess I didn't really think when I selected this outfit. I wanted to look nice for you, and I guess I kind of forgot this wasn't a date. It was silly of me, but at least I did bring some clothes for chilling out too."

"It wasn't silly of you; it was sweet. It was thoughtful. But yes, go get something more comfortable on. You'll be much happier."

Marilyn nodded, deciding he was right. She'd be a lot happier once she was out of these clothes. She was just turning to leave the room to go get her bags when she thought of something. Earlier in the day, she had decided that Jerry was important enough to dress up for, and important enough for her to pack her bags to go take care of him. She looked at him and decided that he was important enough to risk getting sick for. She crossed the room back to his bedside and sat down on the edge of his tester bed. She leaned over, and gave him a kiss on his cheek, then on his mouth.

"You're going to get sick, baby," he told her, withdrawing from the kiss.

"Hey, it comes with the territory. If a kiss makes you feel better, and I know it makes me feel better, then it's all worth it. If I get sick, you'd take care of me, wouldn't you?"

"You know I would. I'd try, anyway."

Marilyn lay in Jerry's aching arms, her head on his chest. It was then that Jerry decided he would try just a little harder to do *a lot* of things regarding Marilyn because, he didn't like that she felt the need to even ask that.

CHAPTER 6

It was late Sunday afternoon. Gary had visited with Jason and Lexi and the kids for a while. Then, Caleb started complaining that he didn't feel well. So, they cut their visit in town short. Gary's fiancée, Kylie Johnston, was volunteering at the medical center today. So, he decided to go to the diner and see what everyone was up to, there. Maybe he'd at least be able to find out what was going on with the assistant football coach at the high school. He was supposedly considering quitting, but nobody had been able to get the facts just yet. He was a good coach (better than the head coach actually), and nobody really wanted him to leave. Some said he was just talking, others speculated something more was going on. Gary wasn't really interested in the gossip aspect of it; he just wanted to know if there were any updates.

He walked down Main Street, stopping to pet a couple of dogs and stopping again to visit with a few locals. He finally made his way to the diner and went inside. The smell of coffee and hot roast beef sandwiches greeted him. The usual chorus of hellos greeted him as well. Folks looked up from their papers and pie to nod to him, as he walked by them.

Gary found his way to an empty booth, grabbed the Sunday paper from the nearby counter, and took his seat. He had just settled in when Tammy Hand came to his booth. He had known Tammy forever, literally. Their parents had been friends, and he didn't remember her ever not being around. As kids, even when he didn't want her around, she was around. She and Faye had been friends and that automatically put her in Gary's and Jerry's social circle.

Now, as a waitress at his favorite restaurant, she was still always around. He couldn't help but like Tammy though. They had dated three different times. Every time they broke up, they stayed friends. It was an odd relationship that they had, but it was a comforting one. There had been a lot of inconsistencies in Gary's life and a lot of confusion, but Tammy was always a staple. So, when she came up to his booth and slid in the booth across from him, he smiled. She set her order pad and pen down on the table and smiled.

"Hiya, Chief. How have you been doing? It's been, what? Four hours since we last saw one another?" she teased.

Gary returned the smile and laughed softly. He folded his newspaper back up and nodded.

"Yes, right about four hours, I guess. How'd you enjoy the sermon this morning?"

"Well, in all honesty, I don't think Brother Lawson is looking too well. It seems to be affecting his services, you think so?"

"Yeah, I know what you mean. But he insists he's fine. You can't argue with the man. He'd preach through a stroke, Tammy."

"I guess so. Listen, I was in the co-op yesterday. I had to get cat food. Anyway, when I was in there, I saw the bulletin board. So, um, Jerry and them, are looking for help, huh?" she asked awkwardly. He looked at her for just a moment.

"Yes, yes, they are. Jerry put the flier up just Saturday in fact. It seems that that big old place is just a touch too much for Anne to handle. So, they are trying to find some help for her. Lexi ... well, Lexi helps her out some to an extent. But it's really, as a friend not as an actual housekeeper. So, most of the time Lexi spends there at the house is spent giggling or arguing. And, well, Lexi needs to spend a bit more time at her own house, taking care of business, in my opinion. But nobody has really asked my opinion. So, yeah, they need some help. Do you know anyone who might be interested?" he asked.

"Well, here's the thing. This job, it's not really working out so well anymore. When Owen died, I had to do something. I mean, I needed the money. But that was several years ago, Gary. This job is hard on me now. My legs ache and swell and I've started getting pains in my back. This is a job for a teenager. It's too much standing for me. So, I was thinking; something like working for Jerry and them might work better,"

"So you're wanting the job? That's what you're saying?" he asked her patiently.

"Well, Mamaw worked for them before. That worked out okay. She told us about all the weird stuff that went on in that house years ago, so the weirdness wouldn't bother me. I spent enough time there with Faye to see my own share. And, you know, it'd be easy for me, Gary. I was a homemaker. That's what I've done all these years. It'd be easier for me to work if I was able to do different kinds of stuff around a house. That's different from just standing here, all day, walking from table to counter."

"Well, what's going on with your ... whatsits? Those feel-good-healing-oils and rocks and things you like?"

"Oh, I'm interested in that, still. I do sell it still, but this is Liberty Creek. I mean, what's that Brady calls it? My 'New Age bullshit?' It's just not something that's huge in demand around here, not yet anyway. I'm not making enough from it yet, to live off it, Gary. Leon! What are you doing?" Tammy's attention turned to Leon Addams, their childhood friend and the high school principal. He was cutting himself a piece of chocolate pie, from the old glass cake stand on the counter. Gary and Tammy both waited for Leon's answer.

"Well, Tammy ... I'm getting myself a piece of pie. *You* sure as Hell didn't appear to have any intention of getting it for me. So, I'm getting it myself." He went so far as to go behind the counter, reach in the cooler, and get the canned whipped cream. He covered his pie with whipped cream, returned the can to the cooler, and walked past Tammy and Gary looking irritated.

"You're a jerk, Leon," Tammy retorted. Leon paused and came back to Gary's booth. He dropped a five-dollar bill on the table, in front of Tammy. Leon smiled, leaned over, and planted a kiss on her cheek.

"That'll cover the coffee and pie. And the rest is your tip. But I got another tip for you. Find another job, sweetheart. Waitressing just isn't your thing." Leon walked away.

Tammy looked pointedly at Gary.

Gary sighed.

"Alright. I will talk to Jerry and them for you."

"Yeah? You will?"

"I will. But listen, honey, it's not my house. I can suggest you, but it doesn't mean anything. I mean, I personally can't see why they'd have any objections to you working there. Like you said, Miss Eula worked there, and they got along with her for … how long did she work there?"

"Oh, good grief. Mamaw must have worked there for 15 years or so …" she guessed.

Gary nodded.

"Yeah. I'm thinking it'd be okay. But listen, the weirdness that goes on there is a little different from the weirdness that went on back then. I mean, William and Lena certainly had their own share of weirdness. And, well, Jerry and Faye had a little too. You were Faye's best friend; you know how weird they were. If anyone knows about it, it should be you. But the weirdness that goes on there, now …"

"Hey, I know. It's all good. Remember where we are, man. Everyone in town knows about the weirdness." She laughed.

Gary looked at her disapprovingly.

"It's not nice of y'all to sit around gossiping about your own folks, Tammy. I wasn't gossiping just now. I was just giving you a heads-up before you went over there to try to work. I'm just saying there is always a lot going on up on that road."

"And who in this town doesn't know that? I mean, really? It's not gossip, Gary. Its' just people talking. We don't sit around making fun of them or anything. It's just observations. It wasn't gossip when everyone started talking about you hooking up with the Johnston girl either. It was just observations."

"Okay. Call it what you like. If what you *do* say about someone is something that you don't want them to *know* you said, it's gossip. That's all I'm going to say. Always ask yourself, *how would they feel if they knew I said this*? And don't look at me like that. I know Mamie comes in here and runs her mouth. I know she talks about people. I'm not saying you do but listening to others do it makes you a part of it."

"Oh, come on! You're talking about what happened to Jackson in Lynchburg, aren't you? I knew you'd say something about that eventually. Look, last week, Mamie came in here asking if I'd seen him. I realized I hadn't seen him in a couple of days, so I simply wondered out loud. She jumps on that and starts in about the arrest. That's when you decided to come in here and raise your eyebrows and shake your head at us. She bailed real quick when she saw you and left *me* looking like the asshole. I was going to explain what happened then, but then George started yelling about orders being ready and I forgot about it."

"It's all fine, Tammy. Don't sweat it, sugar. Like I said, I'll talk to them for you. I'll call Roy tonight. Jerry and Will weren't feeling well this morning."

"Alright. Well, thank you. I appreciate it." Tammy smiled and slid out of the booth. She stuffed her pad in her apron pocket and began to walk away.

"Tammy!" Gary said impatiently but amused.

She looked at him, surprised.

"What is it?"

"Oh, I don't know, my order?"

"Oh yeah. What do you want? The Philly and fries again?" she asked, already writing it down.

"Yes, thank you. And tea, coffee, and two aspirin."

"What's the aspirin for? The headaches again?"

"Yeah," he braced himself for what he knew was coming. Tammy shook her head.

"I told you a hundred times, I have stuff that will help your headaches. Peppermint, lavender, eucalyptus and ..." she began.

Gary finished for her,

"Rosemary! I know, I know. I know you got your oils, honey. I can't help it. I just grew up taking good old-fashioned aspirin and ..." he stopped. Her feelings look hurt.

She managed to make him feel like he, single handedly, was the reason her oils and rocks business wasn't going well in Liberty Creek.

He rubbed his eyes and sighed heavily. Oh, why did women in this town have to be so damn difficult?

"Okay, look. Pick one of those oil things. Come over tomorrow and explain this shit to me one more time. I'll listen, and I promise, this time I'll try to pay attention. What are you working tomorrow?"

"Morning. I'll get off at one," she said happily.

"Fine; come over after work, I guess. But today, just be a doll and give me my aspirin. I just want my aspirin today."

As she went to get his drinks and aspirin, his phone rang.

"Hello?"

"Hey honey bunny," Kylie said on the other end. Gary smiled.

"Hello, pretty lady. What number are you calling from? This isn't your phone."

"Oh, phone here at the nurse's station. Listen, bad news. Brother Lawson came in with chest pains. Lois brought him. They're setting him up in a room, now."

"He's being admitted, then?"

"They're getting ready to start running tests on him. Lanie told me he wanted her to call you. Well, we decided it made more sense for *me* to just call you."

"Call me? What for?"

"He wants you to come see him. Apparently, he wants to talk to you. He wouldn't say what about."

"That sounds kind of unsettling," Gary said, worried and paranoid. "What do you mean by that?"

"Oh, I don't know. The town preacher is taken to hospital with a health crisis, and asks to speak privately with the ex-police chief? I don't know. It just sounds sketchy to me."

"Well, I don't think he's going to confess to any murders or anything. I don't get the impression he's in bad enough shape for any deathbed confessions. And he doesn't really seem the sort to have lived a life of crime. I mean, he's 84 years old, Gary. I don't think it's anything too bad. I actually assumed it was maybe church related." Kylie rolled her eyes and shook her head at the nurses sitting nearby, who were overhearing her end of the conversation.

"Oh. I guess that's possible. Well, I'm just now sitting down to eat at the diner. Let me finish that up, and I'll come that way. Do you want me to bring you supper from the diner?"

"Yeah, that'd be good. They got the beef tips, right? It's Sunday,"

"I'll ask Tammy, but yeah. They should since it's Sunday. The green beans and fried squash?"

"Please? You're too sweet. Oh, speaking of sweet …"

"Tea. Yes, I'll bring you some tea. Tell Lawson I'll be there soon."

Gary and Kylie hung up and his headache began to pound. He was hoping for a quiet night, and now, he'd somehow become Tammy's career counselor, and the preacher wanted him at his hospital bedside for some secret reason. He was rubbing his eyes, where the headache seemed to be the worst, when he heard Tammy putting things on the table.

"Here's your drinks and drugs, baby. The sandwich will be right out."

"Add the beef tips with the squash and green beans please, to go. I need to hurry through all this. Kylie just called, and it seems you were right. Brother Lawson was taken to the hospital this afternoon. I'm going to out there when I'm done."

"Is he alright?"

"Doesn't sound too positive, chest pains. They're admitting him to run tests. But anyway, I do need to hurry. So, go ahead and give me my copy of the ticket so I can pay now, if you don't mind."

"What's that you said a few minutes ago? He'd preach through a stroke? Sounds like he may *have*. I hope he's okay."

She stood beside him and wrote the beef tips meal on the ticket and handed it back to him. He saw his own meal was crossed off. He sighed. The restaurants still insisted on feeding him for free if he was alone. They'd started doing this when he was the police chief, and they still did it to this day. Tammy disappeared to get his food while he pulled out his wallet.

The meal wasn't an enjoyable one for him. He had things on his mind. Within 30 minutes, he was finished eating, and on the road with Kylie's to-go box and tea and a touch of indigestion coming on. He parked at the so-called medical center. His car was 1 of 17 cars in the visitor's parking. He carried the food and tea inside and was greeted by the ladies at the nurse's station. Connie Clemmons, one of the nurses, winked at him.

"Hey, there, Chief. You're looking good tonight. How are ya?"

"Hi, Connie. Well, my eyes hurt, my head hurts, and I'm feeling a bit gassy, you know, from eating my Philly too fast. Anyway, thanks for asking. Is my fiancée around?" he smiled. The other nurses giggled at Gary's reply. Connie just shrugged. Some arms wrapped around his waist from behind and squeezed him.

"Ooooh, my stomach is not in any shape for the squeezing, sweetness." Gary turned around and kissed Kylie, as she took her food from him. She put it on the counter and took his hand.

"Come on with me, hot Daddy. The preacher is asking for you."

"Ohhh, why'd you call me that in front of everybody? They all heard you, and they're laughing." It was one of the things about Kylie he still tried to get used to. Kylie was considerably younger than he was, by 19 years. She was still kind of silly, a far cry from the sullen, strung out Charlotte he'd first given his name to. Even the women he dated since divorcing Charlotte had been different; they were part of a generation that acted like their mothers as soon as they hit 30. Kylie was part of that generation that just somehow avoided maturing. Lexi, Jason, Anne, and Will were among that generation. They acted like they were still 17. Sometimes, this was a refreshing trait of Kylie's. Sometimes, it was kind of frustrating.

Kylie began calling him hot Daddy on their second date. She liked the age difference, said it turned her on. So, she called him Daddy often. He was still trying to get used to that. He liked it, when it was just them, and, yes, he really liked it when she called him that while they made out. He didn't know why he liked that, though, and he felt kind of like a pervert for liking it. But then, Jerry told him that Anne often called him that, too. Considering the relationship between Jerry and Anne, Gary didn't really find that entirely appropriate, either. Especially since Anne *also* called Roy Dad and Daddy because she considered him a father figure. When Gary recalled that Jerry also called Anne Mama quite often, he just gave up.

89

There just was no justifying the kinky weird shit that went on in this crowd. So, Gary went along with the Daddy thing, and even found himself referring to himself as *Daddy* when talking to Kylie. *Come sit with Daddy, get Daddy a glass of tea.* Yes, he was embarrassed that he'd begun doing that. It was embarrassing enough that he did this in the privacy of his own home, but knowing that Kylie was calling him this in public? At work? He waited until they were out of earshot of the nurses, before he held her arm and pulled her, easily, to a stop.

"Come on, now. Don't go doing that in public! What's the matter with you?"

"Doing what?" she asked, baffled.

"Nobody needs to know that you call me Daddy. It makes us look like perverts."

Kylie rolled her eyes at him. He was always so paranoid!

"Oh, good grief. Would you get a grip? They know who my dad was, Gary. They know that you're not really my daddy. I mean, come on! You really think they care? Tonya said she calls Adam sir in bed,"

"Kylie! Have you not ever listened to anything that I've ever said? Stop talking about things like that with people! If Tonya elected to tell you that, it doesn't mean that you should be telling me that. I really didn't want to know that about her, thank you."

"Well, they all know I call you Daddy so get over it. And, on that note, Lexi and Anne and Karen and Marilyn all know that I call you that, too. Now, come on." Kylie led Gary to a hospital room.

"Now, here is Brother Lawson's room. He doesn't feel good; I mean, obviously, or else he wouldn't be here. Get that look off your face now. I'll be back in a few minutes." Kylie kissed his cheek, and reached up, rubbing his bald head. She giggled and left him alone in the hall. He went inside.

Gerald Lawson looked bad; much worse than he had this morning at church. He looked like a very old, tired, sick little man. But he saw Gary and managed a feeble smile.

"Gary, I'm so glad that you made it tonight. Have a seat." He gestured towards the chair beside the bed. Gary made his way to the bed.

"I'm sorry you ended up here, Brother."

"Me, too, son. It's been a long time coming, I suppose. I didn't want to say anything, but I haven't felt my best here lately. I wanted to keep services up. But the doctor is already telling me I need to take it easy. Gary, I wanted to talk to you about something.

"I wanted to know if you'd be willing to take over services for a spell? Not for a long time, mind you. Just until the doctors give me the clearance to start preaching again. I pointed out to them that standing up there for two hours a week doesn't take that much out of a man, but they pointed out that this morning it apparently did. I did have a heart attack, Gary. It was mild, thank God above. But it was bad enough to get the doctors barking orders and making mountains out of molehills.

"I know that this wasn't a route that you particularly wanted to take; I respect that. But I must say that you do an excellent job, from what I've heard. The times you've filled in for me, the congregation has praised your services. You seem to have it in you, well enough to keep the attention of the folks here. What do you say? Would you do it, for me? Just until I am back up and getting around?"

Gary was in an awkward position. How do you tell a possibly dying preacher that you won't take his place for, what? A few weeks? Gary thought about it briefly. He was there, at the church, every Sunday anyway. This would just involve him finding something to talk about every Sunday morning. He would have to preach; this was a little different from nagging people for not behaving in church, or for not showing up at all. He had done this before, several times even. It wasn't that he had a problem with preaching in a fix, but he already had so many things on his mind. Brother Lawson didn't know this. Nobody really knew about the things that were on Gary's mind, these days. Gary just looked at the old man, lying in the bed. Gary smiled, although it was a tired smile.

"Of course, I will. I'll take care of services, starting next week. You can count on me. I do hope that you'll be back soon; it won't be the same without you there."

"Thank you. Your father would have been proud of you."

"Yeah, well, get some sleep. I'll come by tomorrow, alright?"

"Alright, Gary. Thanks again. Goodnight, and God bless you!"

Gary wanted to go home now. He didn't really even feel much like visiting with Kylie again before leaving, but he couldn't leave without saying anything. He made his way back to the nurse's station.

"Could one of you find Kylie for me real quick?" he asked irritably.

They noticed a change in his mood, and simply paged Kylie to come to the nurse's station. She showed up quickly and looked at him curiously.

"What's the matter?"

"I'm ... I'll just talk about it all later, okay? My head hurts, and I think I ate my supper too fast, besides. I talked to Brother Lawson. I told him I'd be back tomorrow."

"Well, what'd he want?"

"Kylie, I *said* we'll just talk about it later. Okay? I'm not mad. Don't look at me like that. I've just had a long night. I want to go home now. So, give me a kiss, and remember; call me when you start for home, okay?"

"Well, okay, if you say so. Go on and get some rest. Thanks for bringing me supper. And yeah, I'll call when I leave here. I should be getting out at 10."

Gary just nodded, kissed her, and patted her belly.

"I love you, doll. I'll see you when you get home."

"I love you too," she told him. He smiled and walked away. Something was wrong, but she would wait until later to find out more.

Gary got in the truck and remembered Tammy. He'd told her he'd call Roy today and he would. He didn't feel like it, but he didn't feel like doing a lot of things he was about to do. He decided to try Jerry instead. Originally, he thought he'd call Roy because he knew Jerry was sick. But no, he'd go ahead and try Jerry. He dug his phone out of his shirt pocket and called Jerry's cell phone.

"Hello?" answered a weak sounding Jerry.

"Hey, man. I know you don't feel good. Are you *any* better?"

"Not really. How'd you know I was sick anyway?"

"I saw Marilyn at the store this afternoon. She told me."

"Oh. Oh yeah, she told me you made her go buy me Cokes. Thanks. I was out of them."

"Yeah. Hey, you know the flier you put up for the housekeeper? You have someone interested in taking the job already."

"Already huh? Who is it?"

"Tammy."

"Tammy Hand or Tammy Waites?"

"Well, Tammy Hand is a waitress and Tammy Waites is a pediatrician. Which do you think, Jerry?"

"Hand, I'm guessing."

"Yeah. And we don't even like Tammy Waites. When is the last time I said Tammy in reference to Tammy Waites?"

"Okay we've established that it's Tammy Hand already. Moving past that now. What'd she say exactly? I mean, she's working at the diner. How's she gonna do both?"

"She's not. She wants to quit working there. It's not good for her. It's giving her leg and back problems, all the standing. She said a job like this though would be a lot of different kinds of work, not just going back and forth between the tables and counter."

"You know though she's not a great waitress. I mean, I love her to pieces, but she never really acted like she wanted to be there."

"She *doesn't* want to be there. She took the job because Owen died. But she said she was raised to be homemaker. That's what her mama was and all the women in her family; that's what Tammy was. She stayed home and took care of the house and raised young'uns. And that's why she thinks it'd make sense to hire her. And she's right. She knows how to do the work, and her grandmother took care of that crazy ass house for y'all. Apparently, incidentally, Miss Eula (Tammy's grandmother who worked for the Grangers) even informed Tammy and them that y'all were bat-shit crazy. Well, she said her grandmother told her about all the weirdness that went on there, same thing."

"Oh well, that would be a plus, not having to hide the weirdness. I'm sure she knows about the weirdness anyway, from hanging out here with Faye all the time. Hell, I like Tammy. Will likes Tammy. Roy likes Tammy. We *all* know *you* like Tammy ... three times, was it?" Jerry teased. He started giggling, but then began coughing.

93

"Yeah, it was three times. Will the girls get along with Tammy, you think?"

"Put it this way; your son suggested LeAnne," Jerry pointed out.

Gary couldn't help but laugh.

"Maxwell? Jason really suggested *LeAnne Maxwell*? The middle-aged waitress or LeAnne, the incredibly gorgeous 27-year-old daughter of the trashiest woman in town? I can see where *this* will be a toss-up!" Gary shook his head. Jason never changed at all.

"Now, don't get me wrong; *I'd* be okay with LeAnne making my bed. But I just don't see it going over well with any of these girls, and especially not Faye."

"Nor do I. So, what do you want me to do, friend? Do you want to give her a shot? That'd be Tammy, incidentally, not LeAnne. Are you wanting to go through an actual interview process, or should I just take down the ad and tell Tammy to put in her notice?"

"You know, I'm thinking Tammy would probably be great. Even Anne likes her. They talk at church. She's always talking to Tammy about that natural healing hippie shit that Tammy's into. Anne's talking about making some jewelry that holds oil balls or something for her even."

"Oil balls? What the Hell is an oil ball?"

"Aw, I don't know. I wasn't really listening. Faye was kinda into all that too. Remember, Faye liked all those colored rocks she called crystals. Anne was just talking; she's *always* talking about *something*. Sometimes, well, I just don't always hear everything she's saying."

"That's your nice way of saying sometimes you quit listening."

"Yeah, I guess so. Anyway, yeah. Go ahead and tell Tammy we'll give it a shot. Find out when she'd be able to start for me, if you don't mind."

"I don't mind. I'll go ahead and call her. She's coming over tomorrow, but she'd probably like to go ahead and hear this tonight."

"Why's she coming over?"

"She started in on me about my headaches at the diner tonight. She's been trying to talk me into trying something besides aspirin. So, I told her she can come over tomorrow and talk to me about it. I mean really the aspirin I've been using doesn't do much."

"Um, was I misinformed or isn't your fiancée a pharmacist?"

"She is, but she doesn't take medicine at all. I thought it was an odd profession for her to go into, given the fact she doesn't believe in taking medicine. She doesn't like seeing me take a bunch of over the counter crap anyway. So, if anything she'll be happy, I'm having Tammy bring her stuff over here. Well, let me let you go. I'm going to go ahead and call her."

"Hey, you okay? You don't sound quite right to me," Jerry asked. Gary sighed. Leave it to Jerry to pick up on that. If there was ever a soul Gary could talk to it was Jerry. He had missed Jerry during those four years, following Faye's passing.

"Well, did you know about Brother Lawson?"

"What about him?"

"He had a heart attack, a mild one, this afternoon. He's stable, but he's wanting me to fill in for him at the church."

"Oh! Well, that's fabulous! I mean not that he had a heart attack. I mean about you filling in. You're good at that. You've done it before, though; why do you sound so pissy about it this time? The way you bitch and nag people for not showing up, I'd think filling in for him would be right up your alley. You could do a whole sermon, dedicate a whole service to guilting people into coming every week. Maybe Roy and Karen would make it to that one anyway. You really do need to talk to them; they don't go enough."

"It's just … I've got things going on right now. There's a lot of stuff on my mind, and this is just a bad time. And, you know he makes it sound like it's just a few weeks. But the older you get the harder it is for you come back after things like heart attacks. He's way up there, Jer. I just don't see this being a few-week commitment."

"Well, don't sweat it yet. Just take it as it comes. He might be right; maybe he can come back soon. Old people out here never die. Look at Gap. I mean, he should have died five times by now, like 200 years ago. Besides what's all this on your mind?"

"Oh, babies and weddings and stuff."

"You mean, you're nervous about the baby coming? You've got lots of time to get used to that! It sounds like a big deal, but it's not really. I mean a baby is a big deal, yeah. But not anything to stress over. And the wedding? Well yeah, that's a good bit sooner. But you still got another month to even have to stress over that. When the kids got married here, we didn't worry about too much at all. Just chill, take it easy. Make it a fun thing."

"Well, I don't know. I can't just turn it all off, you know? There's just things I've got on my mind."

"Okay, here. I'm already feeling a bit better. This is Sunday. How about you come up here Tuesday? We'll hang out, talk. It sounds like you need to talk."

"Alright. Sounds doable. Thanks, Jerry."

"Not a problem. Thank you for hooking us up with Tammy. Go give her a call."

Gary and Jerry exchanged goodbyes and Gary dialed the phone again, this time calling Tammy.

"Hello?" she asked.

"Hey, honey. Look I just got off the phone with Jerry. He said he thinks it should work out just fine. So, if you're really interested in going through with this, he wants to know when you'd be able to start."

"Oh, that's great! Really? Oh, thank you, Gary. Well Judy does the schedules on Thursdays. I could let her know tomorrow to just not schedule me for next week. I'm scheduled through Thursday. The work week starts on Fridays. I guess I could arrange to come out to the house on Friday, if that'd be okay."

"That should be just fine. I'll let him know. I'm glad it worked out for you. Hopefully, things will go how you hope they will, working there. But I'm going to go ahead and go to sleep. Been a long day and night. I'll see you tomorrow. What time are you wanting to do this thing?"

"How about two o'clock? Would that be okay?"

"Yeah, it's fine. I'll see you then. Good night, girl."

"Night, Gary. And thanks again."

"Sure thing."

Gary took a shower and got into his pajama pants. He picked up around the kitchen and did his usual nighttime things. They were staying at his trailer for the time being because they were getting some work done on the house Kylie had grown up in, and now owned. Her parents had really let the place go. The lovely old craftsman was in bad need of some attention, so Gary decided to take care of the things that needed to be done for it.

He sat back on the soft leather couch and began to relax. His headache was still there, but now, he could at least rest. He had fallen asleep and was in the middle of a very peculiar dream when the phone rang startling him awake. It was Kylie calling to say she was leaving the hospital and would be home soon. Waking from that dream to hear Kylie's voice bothered Gary. The dream itself had bothered Gary. Gary began to realize that things in his life were still far more complicated than he'd realized.

CHAPTER 7

While Gary dozed on his couch in town, Jerry was still piled up in his bed on Teague Road. He had enough on his mind already; now, he had to worry about Gary. Gary seldom sounded stressed. Nothing much ever really seemed to bother Gary. But obviously there was something bothering him now.

It was getting late and he could hear the faint noises going on downstairs. It had been a long, and relatively boring day. Marilyn only came up there three times all day. Karen came up there twice to see if he was being taken care of. Then, Anne came in.

Anne wore the old, faded Virginia Tech T-shirt that Will had given her on her second day there. She wore this with a pair of frog- printed pajama pants. It wasn't the sexiest of sleepwear she owned, but Jerry couldn't help but think she looked beautiful. She was being very quiet, as if she were sneaking in there. He smiled at her.

"Hey, Mama. Are you feeling better?"

"Not too much, but I'll survive. I think it's mostly a hangover. How are *you*? I've stayed away long as I could stand it. How's it going though? Is Miss Beales taking care of you?"

"Oh, she's been in and out of here. Karen's come up here too."

Anne didn't need to be told. She could tell by the way Jerry said it; Miss Beales had not done much. Why else would Karen feel the need to check on him?

"Well, I'm about to go downstairs and get a drink. Do you want something?"

"Yeah, one of my Cokes, please," he answered, but he seemed let down about something.

"What's the matter?"

"It's nothing. Never mind. Thanks for coming in here, Mama. I appreciate it." He smiled sweetly, and Anne returned the smile.

She went downstairs.

At the foot of the stairs, Anne did a double take. In the hall, she saw what was, clearly Faye Granger. Faye was there plain as day, looking back at Anne. The times before when Anne saw Faye, she looked relatively happy. The Faye that Anne saw this evening looked curious. The two women stood in the hall looking at one another. Anne felt funny in her stomach, as she always did when she saw Faye's spirit. She had seen her several times, but still had trouble thinking of what to say or do when it happened.

"Jerry's sick. He wants a Coke so I'm going to get him one."

Instead of disappearing, which is what Faye usually chose to do when Anne spoke to her, Faye just stayed there looking at Anne like she wanted to ask a question. Her brown hair fell across her face, and she pushed it back, a habit Faye had had in life, and one that apparently had followed her in death. Anne sighed and left Faye in the hall.

In the kitchen, Marilyn was sitting at the table with Karen and Roy. Karen looked relieved.

"Thank you, Lord. Can I *please* assume that you, being up and walking around means that you're feeling better?"

"I'm fine. Just a headache and a little tired. I wanted a drink. Will is still hot." Anne went to the refrigerator to pull out the pitcher of tea for herself. She poured herself a glass, stood around for a moment, listening to the light conversation in the room. When she was finished with her tea, she returned to the refrigerator to get a Coke for Jerry. But she felt a familiar chill; it wasn't from the refrigerator. It was a different kind of chill; one that was felt from the inside. Anne recognized this and looked toward the sink.

Faye stood beside the sink and shook her head at Anne. Anne was not sure how to handle this. Jerry wanted a Coke, but Faye didn't want her to get him one. Anne didn't really understand Faye's reasoning but who was she to argue with the dead? She decided to just sit down at the table for a moment; maybe she'd get the Coke when Faye went to haunt the cat or something.

While Anne sat at the table for a few minutes, she listened and observed. She thought about how Jerry had acted, when she asked if Marilyn had been taking care of him. He seemed let down. Anne thought about this for a few more minutes before she finally decided to go ahead with her idea.

"Miss Beales, you're not usually here Sunday night, so you might not know; Jerry always comes down here about this time and gets himself a Coke. He might like one up there now if you want to take him one." She said this as civilly and nicely as she could. Marilyn looked at her with a touch a surprise. She composed herself quickly.

"Oh. Yeah, okay." Marilyn got up and went to the cabinet and looked vacantly into it. She closed it and looked in another one. She went to the third cabinet and pulled a plastic cup from the shelf. Anne sighed and went to a different cabinet. She reached in there and pulled out Jerry's favorite glass. It was a big glass mug; he used it and only it. Anne set the mug on the counter in front of Marilyn. Then Anne sat back down. Karen suppressed a smile, while Roy looked at Anne suspiciously. Their attention turned back to Marilyn.

Marilyn was about to put ice in the glass when she stopped. She paused awkwardly and looked back at the three at the table. They were watching her.

"He doesn't take ice in his Coke, does he?"

"Not if they're already cold. He says it makes them watery," Anne explained. Marilyn nodded. She seemed to recall him saying that. Or did she really? She honestly didn't know. But she did seem to recall he didn't like ice in his Coke. So, she reached in the refrigerator and pulled out a bottle of Coke. She looked around the kitchen, as if she was wondering what the next step was.

"So, I guess I'll just run this up there to him."

The others just nodded and smiled. Marilyn left the room, looking a bit confused. Karen looked at Anne.

100

"What was all that about?"

"All what?"

"You helping that woman do something for Jerry. What's going on?"

"Nothing. I was up there talking to him earlier. I just got the impression she hadn't done much for him. He seemed let down. I thought it'd make him feel better if she did something nice for him. He called me this afternoon. He told me she was here. He asked me to back off and let her help. He said she wanted to come here and do something nice, so he wanted me to let her. I guess it was important to him, so I let her do something nice. I did it for *him* not her. So, stop looking at me all goony."

In her mind though, Anne was thinking about Faye. Had Anne really done it for Jerry, or had she done it for Faye? When Anne was going to get the drink for Jerry, Faye shook her head as if she didn't want Anne to get that drink for him. So, Anne had waited long enough to observe things and think things through. That's when she decided to let Marilyn get it. Anne was feeling like all of that wasn't a coincidence. Anne was sure, Faye had wanted Marilyn to take that drink to Jerry.

Jerry was lying in bed, but he wanted to get up now. He'd gotten up a few times to go to the bathroom, but that damn staircase had kept him upstairs all day. His body ached, and he really had not wanted to tackle that staircase. But now, he wanted to get up. He had just convinced himself that it wasn't just because he now knew that Anne was up when Marilyn came in the room.

"Hey handsome. I brought you a Coke. I was informed that you are apparently used to getting one about this time. So, I brought you one."

Jerry sat back into his pillows again. He looked surprised but smiled. He knew that Anne must have been the said informer. He was touched that she'd thought of Marilyn. He was happy to see Marilyn come in his room with his Coke, but he still wanted to go ahead and get up.

"Thank you, Mare. I'm thinking about getting up here in a few minutes. My back is starting to hurt after laying here all day."

"You're getting up? Now? Well it's late. It's ten o'clock! What's the point in getting up now? Just go ahead and sleep in," she argued.

"I don't want to. I want to get up. I've been sleeping all day. I'm tired of sleeping. I'm tired of laying here. I'm going to feel like shit tomorrow as it is. Will's going to bitch about how useless I am."

"Well, Will has spent most of the day in the bed too. He's only been downstairs three times."

"So? Will can do that; it's Sunday. Will doesn't let anything affect his work week though. Even if he feels like Hell in the morning, he'll get up and work. And he'll have plenty to say if I'm not out there helping. It's a cold, he'll say. It's not pneumonia, he'll say. Then he'll point out how our frontier settling forefathers worked with tuberculosis and cholera, through grasshopper plagues and blizzards. Knowing him he'll even have a name and date to use as reference. Then, he'll point out again that it's just a cold, it's 77 degrees outside, and we're a five-minute walk to the house. Believe me; it's easier to just get up and work than to listen to all that shit."

"What an asshole ..." Marilyn muttered.

She'd already heard some of this, to an extent, from him today. Will came downstairs, that first time, looking like death warmed over. Karen told him to take his sickness out of the kitchen, and away from the food. He told her that likely they all already had what he had anyway. He pointed out that he'd already been in the kitchen that very morning. Then he told her that he had to get up and move around because he had things to do tomorrow that weren't going to do themselves. He proceeded to list the things that needed to be done. He finished his orange juice, got a glass of water, and went back upstairs.

The next time he came down he hung out for a little longer. He was going to get dressed and go check on things until Roy assured him things in the stable and barn were tended to already. The third time he came down was just about 20 minutes ago; his hair had been combed and he looked like he had just washed his face. But he was still wearing his Superman pajama pants and white T-shirt. He said something about Anne getting up. Sure enough, just a few minutes later, Anne came in the kitchen and made herself a glass of tea.

"That Coke is what I wanted though," Jerry said, reaching for it. Marilyn handed him his drink and sat beside his bed. He guzzled the glass quickly, then stretched.

"Are you staying the night?" he asked, hopefully.

"Yeah, I can. I have the whole week off. I was planning on staying the night. Is that alright with you?"

It had not dawned on her that perhaps he didn't even want her to stay the night. He hadn't exactly invited her. He didn't even invite her over to spend the day. She couldn't see him saying no, but ...

"Is that alright with you? I mean do you want me to stay the night?" she pressed.

"Yeah, actually I do. Will you stay in here? With me?" he asked. Marilyn was uncomfortable in this room, he knew.

"I will, but I want you to promise me something. Get some rest. Screw Will. If I'm going to stay here, I want to take care of you, Jerry. I at least want to try to. That's the whole reason I'm here. If Will wants to get up and work let him. He'll have Roy and Jason and the hands helping him out. But you and Anne both need more rest. She looks like shit. She was trying to tell Roy she isn't really sick; it's just a hangover. But it's obvious she's sick."

"You're worried about Anne? I must be dreaming," he said this teasingly, but he was genuinely surprised.

"I'm not an asshole, Jerry. I know that there's some mixed feelings between us, but I do love her. You know that. I know she does entirely too much around here. Roy said y'all are trying to get her some help around the place?"

"Yeah. Actually, Gary just called. Seems we found someone already. Tammy wants the job. I think she'd be good for it."

"Tammy from the diner? What about the diner? She going to quit there?"

"Yeah, the job's hard on her it seems."

"Well, y'all have known her long enough. It's not as if she's a stranger or anything. Of course, is anyone a stranger in this town?"

"No. Anyway, Gary said he'd call her and find out when she could start. So, don't worry too much about Anne. Between Lexi and Karen and Tammy, things will be taken care of."

"But back to my point; you two need more rest. Please? Just another day or so. You need it. I think Will needs it, but I'm not even about to try to tell him anything."

"I'll take it easy tomorrow. I'll have to listen to Will, but for you, I'll get another day of rest. I can't guarantee Anne will though."

Meanwhile, Roy and Karen sat at the kitchen table, watching Anne fall asleep as she sat there with them. Karen had an amused look on her face; Roy looked almost angry. He stood up finally and went around the table to where Anne sat. The sound of his chair scooting back made Anne's eyes open briefly, but by the time Roy made it to Anne's chair her eyes were closed again. He laid his hands against her face.

"She's burning up. Why in the Hell does she do this? Anne, honey, get up. You have *got* to go back to bed. This isn't a hangover, baby. You're sick. Come on now; get up."

"What? I'm fine. Stop."

"No! You're not fine! Now get up and get in the damn bed! There's enough people to take care of things around here right now. You're sick. Now get upstairs."

"Stop, I'm okay. I'm just …" and she fell asleep, again. Roy shoved her out of the chair and directed her to the hall. He followed her to the staircase, shoving her every few feet. He followed her up the staircase and to the bedroom she shared with Will. Roy told her to go to bed and she did. She didn't want to admit it, but she was tired. She was also rather achy feeling. This made her mad. This crowd stayed sick. Jerry especially was always sick. Anne took off her pajama pants and laid back in the bed beside a feverish Will. She felt the heat from his body before she even laid her hand upon his cheek. Anne sighed and fell asleep.

Will had plans to get up and accomplish things that next day, but it just didn't happen. Jerry, too, had intended to get up and take care of things, but Marilyn insisted he get extra rest. When she pointed out to him that Will had even elected to stay in the bed, Jerry decided he'd take advantage of the extra off day. Anne decided to do as Will did, staying in bed.

Roy and Karen spent the night at the house in Roy's old bedroom. Lexi and Jason showed up Monday morning to find things somewhat off-kilter. Karen and Marilyn were in the kitchen preparing breakfast. Roy was there with the children at the table. Jason looked around.

"Where's everyone else?"

"Still sick," Roy answered.

"Mommy threw up in the bathroom. It was begusting," James shared.

"They're still sick? What is it?" Lexi asked, putting her bags down.

"I don't really know. They all have a fever, body aches. Anne and Will have thrown-up, but Jerry hasn't ... so far. But I don't think it's a flu or anything. I think it's just a bad cold maybe. We will just do the things that need to be done on the farm today. Let the hands take care of most of it. I am willing to bet the rest of us will be sick soon."

So that's what they did. Lexi helped Marilyn and Karen get breakfast to the table. They sat down with Roy and Jason and the kids and lingered longer than usual. Usually, Will was there pushing them to hurry up so they could get started on work. Today, they just enjoyed the slow morning. The kids ate and went to the living room to watch cartoons.

Lexi tried to be friendly to Marilyn this morning; Marilyn seemed to be somewhat uncomfortable. She didn't look incredibly happy, but she was pleasant enough and spoke with everyone. At one point she said good naturedly,

"Jerry needs few things to feel better; booze, attention, and Anne."

This was said with a laugh, but it brought an uncomfortable pause to the table. Nobody knew quite to say to that.

Lexi finally asked,

"He likes having you here; why do you say that? About needing Anne?"

"Well we both make him feel good, I guess, but only one of us really makes him well. I'm no fool. I can see it. Yes, I'm able to admit she can pull off some things I just can't."

"That doesn't bother you to say those things?" Jason asked her, frowning slightly. She looked surprised but then smiled. It wasn't one of those insincere, tragic smiles though. It seemed to be a truly genuine smile.

"No, Jason, it doesn't. I understand what it is. So, no it doesn't bother me. It's just a trial sometimes. It is what it is."

"What is it? You said you understand what it is, and it is what it is. What is it?"

Marilyn looked at Jason with surprise, as if she thought he already understood the whole crazy screwed up circumstances.

"Florence Nightingale Syndrome."

"Who?" Lexi asked.

"Florence Nightingale. Basically, it's where a patient develops abnormally strong feelings for their caregiver. It can be intimate, romantic feelings, and it can result in sexual feelings. It can also be caregiver developing feelings for the patient. It's very common although not advised. I studied it in school. It makes sense. You feel helpless and someone comes and devotes time and attention to you, so you'll get better. Anne saved his life. He sees her as a Godsend. She came along when he was at his absolute lowest and look what all she did for him. And he returned all the things she provided for him. They take care of each other. I understand it. They both, in my opinion have Nightingale syndrome."

They all sat at that table and looked at each other, processing what Marilyn was saying. So, she understood and was fine with it? Jason cleared his throat.

"So, you're saying that you're fine with the way they hang out and … things?"

"Yes, I am. I understood what he was going through. We talk about it a lot. I know I'm not necessarily the best person to take care of him. He's needy and, well, he doesn't deal with things very well. He's incredibly emotional. I'm glad I can help him through some of it, but well, there are some things I just can't fix for him. There are some things I can provide that Anne can't, and there are some things Anne can provide that I can't. And then there's Faye. Can *either* of us compete with *her*?" she laughed.

Jason, Lexi, Karen, and Roy looked at Marilyn with admiration. She wasn't naïve. She wasn't gullible and foolish or blind. She simply understood something that the rest of them never had been able to figure out. Marilyn remembered something.

"Oh, did Jerry tell anyone? He thinks y'all found your new housekeeper. Gary called him. Tammy Hand is wanting the job."

"Tammy, huh? Well, waitressing certainly wasn't her thing. I'm assuming she's leaving the diner?" Jason asked.

"Yeah."

"When's she going to start?" Lexi asked.

Anne wasn't 100 percent well, even with her prescription. Anne was almost always tired and just didn't seem to be okay to her. Lexi knew that even with her helping, she knew it wasn't enough. She knew she didn't really help as much as she could. She more-or-less visited with Anne and simply helped-out from time to time. Lexi knew that Anne was over here in this huge house, dealing with two meals for these men (including Lexi's own husband). Marilyn frowned at this question, thoughtfully.

"Oh, I don't know, actually. I didn't think to ask," she answered.

Roy sighed.

"Well, she's a good choice. I think she should work out just fine. It's a shame what she went through after that fella of hers died. I don't think she ever quite got over all that. I never did quite understand that relationship; there weren't ever two people any more opposite of one another than those two. He was a bitter old fool, and she's always out trying to help somebody with something. Well that's over and done, I guess. I'm glad she's looking for something besides waitressing. She never looks like she wants to be there. I think a soul should do something that makes them feel good about themselves. Maybe helping us out will be right up her alley."

Faye, there but unseen, agreed with Roy. Tammy was a good choice; she had been Faye's best friend since they were just three years old. Faye had been unhappy about them bringing someone else in her house. It had been one thing when she was there, hiring them. But this time, she'd have no say about who was hired (she thought). She didn't realize that she was still very much so calling the shots around there.

Faye left the kitchen and went upstairs to see her husband. Jerry was dozing, now. He looked rather uncomfortable. His head was at an awkward angle, and she knew him well enough to know he'd wake up with a horrible crick in his neck. So, she did as she had always done; she went to him and used her haunting abilities to wake him just enough. He woke, readjusted himself, and began to fall back asleep. Then he felt it, the presence of his beloved wife. His eyes began to open, and he saw her. Faye was near the foot of the bed wearing the blue shirt he always liked seeing her in. Her brown hair fell over that one side of her face. She pushed her hair out of her eyes. Jerry was torn. He loved seeing her; he really did. But Marilyn would likely not be as happy to find Jerry's deceased wife in his bedroom. He knew Marilyn could see Faye now and he knew that Marilyn could walk through that door at any time.

Faye was his wife. She had loved him enough and had remained faithful enough to stay by his side even in her death. Her love for him was never doubted. There was never any question from anyone in Liberty Creek whether-or-not Faye loved Jerry more than life itself. So, he had a hard time finding a way to tell her that regardless of the unmeasurable love he still felt for her she was no longer welcome to just hang out in their bedroom when Marilyn was visiting.

Jerry found himself smiling at Faye.

"You make moving on hard, woman. You make it very hard for me." He sighed.

"I'm not trying to," she replied. She sounded far away, as she always did. Even when she was three feet away, she sounded very far away, but it was her voice.

"No, I don't guess you are. But baby, Marilyn doesn't understand things yet. Not ... not all the way. She understands you're here. But I don't think she really understands what all you can see and do. She's scared you watch us *do things*."

"Why would I want to watch y'all *do things*?"

It was interesting to Jerry that, even in death, Faye was able to get that impatient, disgusted look on her face that she'd always gotten when she found something to be foolish. Her voice even sounded irritated. This was why it was so hard for him to fully accept she was gone. This wasn't how he'd always pictured ghosts. Jerry always assumed ghosts would be spooky floating people, resembling sheets. They'd sound like ghosts, saying things like "Woooo". But no … Faye just looked like Faye and sounded just like Faye. She was sometimes sort of hazy looking; sometimes she was quite clear and well defined. It was like watching her on a television that sometimes, had bad reception. No, she didn't look or act like a ghost. She looked and acted like his wife. This was why Jerry still felt very much so devoted to her and still felt very much so married. He smiled, amused at the situation.

"Well, I don't know. You've come in here turning lights on before when we were *doing things*. So, you *have* done that. I guess now she feels like maybe you are *always* in the room with us. She's also paranoid that you follow me to her house. I guess I'm just saying before you come orbing into here, maybe you can make sure she's not in here too?"

"I don't care to see anything she does to you, or anything you do to her."

"Then, why did you come in here messing with the lights that time?" he whined.

"I was bored."

And with that, Faye was gone. She was there, and then she wasn't. It was nothing gradual. She usually left with a blurry swoosh. But now she just disappeared as if he'd turned a channel. He sighed but laughed.

Faye didn't go far. While Jerry was upstairs mulling over the situation, Faye went into Will and Anne's room. She knew they were both sick, so she wasn't worried about walking in on them doing anything. She was right; they slept soundly with Will snoring while holding Anne in a strange headlock of sorts. It didn't look like an incredibly comfortable position to sleep in, to Faye. She just looked at them curiously and picked up a few things on the floor. She left them to sleep.

Then Faye went back downstairs. Lexi and Karen sat with Marilyn at the kitchen table. Roy and Jason had gone outside to work. The three women sat at the table, laughing, and talking. Faye moved across the room and stood with them. Part of her felt as though she were there, in her kitchen, serving as hostess. This was her kitchen, her table. But then, a part of her felt very removed from everything taking place at that table.

Truthfully, Faye could have made herself quite visible and joined in the conversation easily. All three of these women had seen her ghost before. They had all heard her speak, even. But she didn't know how it'd go over if she pulled out a chair and started talking about how to make good gravy, something Karen was discussing. Jerry had apparently asked her to please show Anne how to make real gravy, instead of the mix from the envelopes. It pained Faye, really because she always made much better gravy than Karen did; Karen's was lumpy. Faye really wanted to take part in this conversation around her own table.

As the three ladies talked, the chair at the head of the table moved back, ever so slightly. It then moved again, away from the table, scraping against the old oak floor, then stopped. All three ladies stopped what they were doing and looked at the chair. They weren't scared or nervous; they were quite used to things moving unassisted around here. They all held their breath somewhat, and suspiciously watched the old chair continue to move on its own. Karen raised her eyebrows.

"It appears the lady of the house has joined us this morning," she said, smiling.

Lexi relaxed at Karen's smile. Marilyn just looked at the chair. She wasn't quite sure how she felt about this. But Lexi decided to just go with it. She stood up and got a coffee cup. She poured a cup of coffee and put it at the head of the table. Even if Faye couldn't drink it, Lexi was going to make the gesture. Karen laughed and shook her head. At this, Marilyn found herself laughing.

Then, the three ladies continued to talk, and even found a way to make Faye a part of the conversation. Karen acted like nothing was strange. She was the first to include Faye in their conversation when she said,

"Faye, I do wish you'd find a way to give me that recipe for those teacakes you used to make. You up and died before you ever shared it with me. You need to work on that, girl. I've gone too long without your teacakes."

Whereas Faye did not respond, Marilyn asked about the teacakes. The ladies began talking about the teacakes that Faye used to make, and they somehow managed to make Faye feel very much so a part of the conversation. She was at her table with her lifelong friend, her husband's girlfriend, and Jason's wife. She was hosting again in her kitchen.

It wasn't just Jerry keeping the spirit of Faye alive in this house. Everyone made sure that Faye felt welcomed, wanted, loved, and needed. Because they all knew how very, very, important it was to feel needed.

CHAPTER 8

Back in town, Liberty Creek was waking up. It was spring break, so there wasn't too much going on in town. The schools were closed, so everything was a bit quiet this morning. Stores were opening their doors, and people were greeting one another on the wide sidewalks.

Gap Peterson was already sitting in front of the co-op before Gary even had a chance to arrive to open the doors. Gap had already ditched the flannel shirt he wore all fall and winter. Everyone *wished* he'd wear it all year. When Gap decided flannel shirt weather was gone, he didn't trade it in for a T-shirt. No, Gap wore nothing at all under his overalls. The denim overalls looked old enough to be in the Smithsonian (along with Gap). But that was Gap Peterson.

Everyone knew Gap and loved Gap (in their own way). It was often disputed exactly how old Gap was. Gap had always been old. Gary's own father said Gap was old when *he* was a kid. Nobody at all could remember Gap being a young man. This was where the notion came about Gap being dead. Many just decided he was dead, had been for some long time, and they were all simply seeing his ghost.

Men had no real problem with Gap. He made legendary moonshine and grew his own marijuana (and was always willing to share both). He had excellent stories, could accurately tell you what the weather was going to do based on his knee and back, knew more bird calls than anyone in the hills (despite only having about 2 teeth left), could whittle absolutely anything out of a simple stick, currently had three pet raccoons, had hand-raised more forms of wildlife than you could list, had been married to a real Indian, and built his own cabin by hand by himself. This cabin looked like something straight out of a history book, which just helped prove the theory that he was hundreds of years old. This cabin was old, ancient.

However, Gap also had a waist-length beard that *would* have been white, had it not constantly been stained with grape soda, tobacco juice, and whatever food had not made it in his mouth during his last meal. He often told children that he kept a litter of kittens in his beard, too. Whenever someone brought a litter of kittens to the co-op to get rid of, Gap told the kids he'd gotten the kittens out of his beard.

Gap also had a very bad habit of harassing and terrorizing any female living in Liberty Creek. He didn't care if they were three years old or 73 years old. He'd whistle and try to coax them to come see him and sit on his lap. Of course, none of them ever did. They all ran screaming in the other direction. At some point in their lives, every single girl in Liberty Creek had been called Pretty Puss, or Tickle Britches by Gap Peterson.

There was, however, one girl in Liberty Creek who was rather fond of weird old Gap. Ironically, that girl was Gary's granddaughter, Laurie. Laurie would stop and visit with Gap regularly. She thought he was interesting. She was 15, in 10th grade. Whenever he would call her Tickle Britches, she just answered with,

"Hi, Gap."

He was surprised, at first, at her willingness to visit with him. He never really meant any harm when harassing the girls in town. He just did it because he thought it was funny, how they acted. But many years ago, while her mother was inside the co-op buying tomato plants, Laurie sat outside playing with the box of kittens that were looking for a new home. And Gap showed up. He said his usual greeting to the then four-year old. He called her Tickle Britches and asked how she was. She told him she was fine and asked how he was.

That began the unlikely friendship between older-than-the-hills Gap Peterson and now 15- year-old Laurie Raymond. He thought she was one of the kindest people in town. There were times her friends were forced to associate with Gap, should they be with Laurie when coming upon him. They were polite enough, but never could understand why in the world Laurie would like this man so much. Oh, he was nice enough; none of them disliked him. Laurie just seemed to be abnormally fond of him.

On this particular morning, Gary sighed and smiled when he saw Gap in the old rocking chair on the porch of the co-op.

"Good morning, Gap," he greeted him.

"You just now getting here? It's going on seven o'clock. What were you doing all night?"

"Spring break, Gap. School is out. Lots of folks sleeping in today. Anybody been by here, yet?"

"Miss Reppie came by. She told me to give you this, paying you back for something you gave her," Gap said, handing Gary the three dollars.

Gary took the money, thanked Gap, and unlocked the doors. A big gray cat came outside immediately. Gary looked only somewhat surprised. It wasn't his cat. It lived on the next street, but often visited the store. Apparently, Saturday night, it had gotten locked inside when they closed. It was okay, he guessed. They kept a bowl of cat food and water in the store for the neighborhood cats who frequently visited.

"Good morning, Rocky. Hope you enjoyed your stay," he said to the cat, as it stalked out, tail held high.

"If Rocky was in since Saturday night, he likely took himself a dump somewhere inside," Gap predicted.

"Thank you, Gap. I'll be sure to be on the lookout. You gonna help me open up?" Gary asked the old man.

Gap sighed, stood up, and helped Gary open doors and windows. He helped Gary put a few things outside (the ferns, a few other plants, some feed he was trying to get rid of before it was out of date, and an assortment of other odds and ends) and turn on the lights. Then, Gary went to the old deep fridge that had been in this store since 1937. He had always loved this cooler, and as soon as he bought the co-op, he made a vow that he'd never let this cooler go. It was an ugly yellowed color now, with Coca Cola in Bottles written on the front. Gary slid open the glass top, pulled out a grape soda and gave it to Gap. He always gave Gap a grape soda on the house when Gap helped him open-up the store.

"Thank you kindly. So, how is old preacher man? Heard he had himself a spell yesterday after church. Don't seem right that a man would have a heart attack after preaching for two hours, does it? You think he'd be shown an ounce of 'preciation from the big man. Well, how is he?" Gap pressed.

"Brother Lawson is fine. They are running tests and keeping an eye on him, is all. He needs to take some time off from work, to rest."

"Well, what's gonna happen to the church? What are y'all gonna do 'bout services? You filling-in next week?"

"Likely, the next *several* weeks. I'll expect to see you there."

"I expect a lot, but it don't mean I get any of it," Gap argued.

"I wish you'd come more often. Showing up for Easter and Christmas services is admired, but it's not near enough. Folks have offered to give you a ride up there."

"I don't need no charity rides. If I wanna go somewhere I can't get to by walkin', I got a horse. I'll think about it. Ain't making you no promises."

"Well, that's something, I guess. By the way, horses are welcome too."

The men worked quietly, not talking for several minutes. Gap finally broke the silence.

"Gary, I was wondering if I might could ask you something? Since you're doing the preaching thing again?"

"What is it?"

"I was wondering if there might be a way to get just something for Bird's grave."

He said this hesitantly. Gary just looked at the very old man, surprised. Gap seldom talked about his deceased wife, who was said to have been a direct descendant of the Catawba Indian tribe. Only the very oldest members of the community had ever seen this woman or had any information on her. Gap had admitted her name wasn't really Bird, but it was a combination of Catawba words translating to Little Brown Bird and Gap said he never could say it quite right. So, he just called her Bird.

Gary had seen where Bird was buried; she had been buried by Gap, himself, after passing away at home. Nobody knew exactly what it was

115

that she died from; Gary always figured it was something that could have likely been treated, had Gap and Bird chosen to live as if they were in this century. It was predicted it was likely flu or something, but nobody knew for sure. For all they knew, Gap murdered her. She lived in the hills in an ancient cabin, eating whatever Gap had managed to kill in the woods or grow in the yard, died at home, and was promptly buried. Nobody found it necessary to investigate this apparently.

Gap spoke fondly of Bird; Gary didn't really believe he murdered her. But he seldom spoke of her at all. Her grave was a simple cleared place among the trees, about 50 feet behind their cabin off Fishpond Road. Wildflowers grew on it in the spring and summer, and there was a rock at the head of the grave. That was all. Gary cleared his throat and sat down at the old card table by the door. Gap slowly sat down at the table, too. He said nothing.

"What kind of something are you talking about?" Gary asked, softly.

"Well, just thought it'd be nice to have a real stone on it is all. I ain't a'aiming to get anything uppity. Just something plain, her name is all. That'd be enough. I ain't got the money to buy nothing like that, you know? But I can help ya' out around here, if need be."

Gary felt sorry for the old man, who looked like he didn't want to be having this conversation. Gap just stared at the checkers board painted on the table's top. Gary smiled at him.

"Look, let us see what we can do. I can get in touch with Middleton and see what he has to offer us. Give me just a little time to see what can be done for Bird, okay?"

Gap looked at Gary with a look of surprise and shame.

"Why you looking like that, Gap?"

"I know I should have been able to do something for her before now. I don't want to leave this world, and nobody know that she's there, is all. I want somethin' tellin' folks that there's a lady there."

"You've done a lot, Gap. Nobody thinks you haven't done right by her. You took care of her without help from a soul it sounds like, from what I've heard. That's more than enough to be proud of right there."

116

"I guess so."

"I know so. Don't sweat it, friend. We'll see what we can do. I promise you that."

"I thank you for trying, anyway. I'm gonna go finish getting stuff ready."

Gap stood up and hobbled out the front door. Gary just sat for a few more minutes. He knew that Gap wasn't going to go to services Sunday morning. Gap never went to services; this would prove to be beneficial this week.

Gary finally got up and started his day. He would work until Wes got out of his doctor's appointment. Gary worried about Wes and wished the old man would just stay home for once. When Wes's health began to decline, he agreed to sell the co-op to Gary, but not without a catch. He wanted to keep working there. He said it's all he's known all his life. Wes's ancestors opened this co-op in 1857 and it had stayed in Wes's family ever since. Wes had grown up within these walls. So, Gary agreed, but worried about the man constantly. He took comfort in knowing that Eric Clemmons, a local high school senior, came over every day after school to help him out.

Gary was standing behind the long counter, looking at the newspaper, when someone came in the door. He looked up to see Tammy.

"Hey, girly. You putting in your big notice today?"

"Yeah. Hey, what's up with Gap? He didn't even talk to me."

"Oh, he's got things on his mind. Hey? Let me ask you something. I'm thinking about bringing something before the church Sunday. You're a good one to ask; Gap's got himself a request he brought to me this morning. It seems the old man is wanting to put a marker on Bird's grave. The problem being, he doesn't have the money of course. Do you think the folks would be willing to chip in at the church, set up a fund to pay for a marker? A simple marker, he wants ... nothing ostentatious. Just her name, I think."

"Well, that's just kinda sad. I always thought the rock was sad, but somehow, what you just told me is even sadder. I don't see *anyone* in Liberty Creek having a problem with chipping in for something like that. I'm sure Jack would be willing to work with us." Jack Middleton owned Middleton's Monuments on Court Street.

"Yeah, I think so too. I told Gap I'd talk to him. So, you agree with me? It'd be alright to talk to them during services? I guess that'll give me *something* to talk about. I still gotta come up with something to preach about. There's just too much going in my old head," he said tiredly.

"Oh! So, you *are* gonna fill in for Brother Lawson? That's great! You always do a good job filling in. I never could understand why you didn't go ahead and study that at Virginia. You'd have made a wonderful preacher."

"Oh, I didn't make a wonderful police chief?" he teased. She smiled.

"You made a great one of those, too. I was just surprised. I mean, considering the fact that every other man ..."

"In my family studied it and preached, you'd have just assumed I would too. You know what? I had my reasons. And truthfully, I'm sick and so tired of being compared to the God-fearing men in my family. I do what I'm supposed to do ... most of the time. If I wanted to be a cop, why is that a problem? My dad and grandfather were both on the force. They preached on Sundays; I don't ... or I *didn't*. Just lay off with that! I have heard it from every single person in this sad-ass town ... even Jerry and them! Can't you be the single one person who doesn't ask me about that?"

Tammy just looked Gary in shock. "Wow. Where did all that come from? Excuse me! I was simply making conversation. I didn't realize it was going to light a fire under your ass. Anyway, I came in here to get a paper and to say hello. So, hello and can I have a paper?"

"Aw, don't go acting like that, now. I'm just going through some shit right now, and I have all kinds of mess I'm stressed out about. You just had to ask the wrong question."

"Maybe you should talk to somebody then. You talk to Kylie about any of this?"

"Ohhhh, no! No, I'm not able to go there! Not right now, not that, not her." Gary suddenly looked very miserable.

"Not her? What in the world is going on?"

"It's just a lot of stuff, Tammy. There's just a lot of things going on right now, and this was just a really bad week to ask me to preach. I don't feel real good about several things right now. And I just need to think."

"Why don't you talk to Jerry? Or Karen? Or, well, you could talk to me, I guess."

"Karen? Oh, I don't think she'd be a good one either. I'm going to go talk to Jerry tomorrow. I don't know that it'll do any good, but I'm going to try, I guess. He told me to come talk to him about things."

"Well, that's good. I'm sure he can help you out at least some. But my shift starts at eight, and the last week of my job isn't the best time to start showing up late … although what are they gonna do? Fire me?" Tammy asked, smiling.

"Here, girl. Take your paper, on me. Listen, thanks for your offer. You're right; you'd be a good one to talk to. It sure wouldn't be the first time I'd bitched and moaned to you. I do appreciate it. And you know, maybe I'll take you up on it. We'll see what I get accomplished, talking to Jerry."

"Good deal. I'll catch you later, Chief. Still on for today? Two o'clock?"

"Two o'clock. Remember, though; we're staying in the trailer." He confirmed.

"Oh, yeah, the remodeling. Glad you reminded me; I'd have gone to the house."

She got her paper. He went to her and took her in his arms. He needed a hug right now, and Tammy always had extra ones when he had needed one in the past. She pulled away after a moment and told him, "Watch the stress, man. We aren't young anymore and freaking out like that just isn't good for us. I don't need you stroking out or having a heart attack. We're still trying to nurse Lawson back to health, remember?"

They told each other goodbye, and Tammy took her paper to the diner.

Gary was not entirely comfortable talking to Jerry about these things on his mind, either. But he did need to talk to someone.

His day was slow, uneventful. The regulars came into the co-op, talked football, weather, local gossip, and gardening. He wasn't in the mood to be there. Wes did show up, but he was so poorly that Gary was not comfortable leaving him alone. It was okay; Eric was coming to the co-op early today since school was out. He'd still have time to meet Tammy. At two o'clock, Eric finally came in to work.

"Hey, Gary," he greeted Gary, as he threw a backpack behind the counter.

"School's not even in this week."

"I know. That's why I'm here early today."

"I mean, what do you carry in that backpack? It's obviously not school stuff."

"Actually, not true. *To Kill a Mockingbird* is on our required reading list, and it's in there. Plus, my phone, a notebook, my wallet, my Chapstick … just junk."

"So, it's your purse."

"Come on; don't go there." Eric looked impatiently at Gary, who laughed.

"I'm sorry, son. I come from a generation that stuffed everything in their back pocket. If it didn't fit in your pockets, you didn't need it anyway."

"Yeah, well … not as many things existed when you were young," Eric said, smiling.

"Good one. Look, I'm tired. My head hurts and I'm supposed to meet be meeting someone at 2 o'clock. Gap's been helping out today; just let him. Grisby is coming by this afternoon to get his feed, and Lois said if she doesn't make it by here before you close-up, to please put her seeds in the box on the porch. She thinks she'll be running late. Is your mama still wanting a fern?"

"Yes, sir."

"Go on and take her one then. It's a thank you for her helping Laurie with history."

"Hey, how'd Laurie do on the test?"

"She got a B on it. It's a far cry from the F she was expected to get. So, yeah. I wanna tell your mama *thank you*. So, take her a fern."

"Thanks. Now, quit lecturing me. You're gonna be late for your date," Eric scolded. At this, Gary looked at him suspiciously.

"Date? Why'd you call it a *date?*"

"Um, you said you had somewhere to be. I didn't mean it, literally, when I said you had a date. Okay, is *appointment* better?" Eric asked, when he saw the accusing look in Gary's eyes.

"Yeah. Much better. I'm out of here."

Gary grabbed his jacket and his coffee cup, and left to meet Tammy at the trailer behind the co-op. He'd hoped to have a few extra minutes to go by the pharmacy and visit Kylie, but he obviously wasn't going to have the time. He was right; as soon as he went behind the co-op and saw his trailer, he saw Tammy's car there. He walked up to her open car window and scared her.

"Hey, girly. Sorry I'm late. Had to wait up for Eric. I thought he was going to be there a little earlier with school being out. He had told me he'd be there around one. So, I'm sorry I'm late. I didn't even get a chance to go by and see Kylie today."

"No problem. I'm ready when you are," she replied, getting a bag out of her backseat.

"What's that?" he asked warily.

"My oils and stuff, dopey."

"All of that is oils?" he was amazed.

His knowledge of oil ended with canola and vegetable oil. He'd always heard canola was better for your heart. That's about it. He shrugged.

"Ummmm, okay, then. Well, I guess let's go inside and look at oil."

"Try to curb your enthusiasm," she told him jokingly.

So, Gary and Tammy went inside the trailer.

"Wow, it's been awhile since I've been in here! Not too much has changed, I see. A woman's touch here and there; am betting you didn't buy the corn husk angel on the mantle."

Tammy looked around the neat, clean double-wide trailer. It was hard to believe this trailer was 15 years old. Gary had taken very good care of it over the years, making it nicer than several of the houses in town, even. She never did like the mounted deer heads on the wall, but there they still were, staring blankly across the living room with glass eyes. She set her bag down on his coffee table. He went to the refrigerator.

"You want something to drink? Tea? Coke? Coffee? Scotch?" he called from the kitchen.

"Ummm, Scotch sounds more fun, but I think I'll go with the Coke today. So, Kylie's at work?" she asked, feeling somewhat awkward suddenly.

"Uh, yep. She's not off again until Wednesday. Why? Did you want to tell her all about your stuff too?"

"Well, if she wants to know about it, I guess. Did you tell her I was coming over here, today?" she asked.

Gary was making noise with the ice. He didn't hear her. He brought the drinks into the living room and set them on the coffee table. He looked perfectly relaxed.

"Say?" she asked.

"Say, what?"

"Did you tell her I was coming over here to talk about the oils?"

"Yeah. Why are you looking like that? What's the matter?" he looked confused. Tammy didn't say anything right away; she was thinking.

Just here recently, word got out that, Karen had slapped Ruth Morris (her ex-sister-in-law) directly across the face right in front of Main Street Florist. That was bad enough (although it made for interesting talk at the lunch counters at Jenson's and Elderod's). Well, word also got out that within 15 minutes of that happening, Karen's car was spotted at Gary's trailer. Given the speculated history between Gary and Karen and the very well-known current relationship between Roy and Karen (as well as the recently announced engagement of Gary to his much younger fiancée, Kylie), this raised quite a few eyebrows in Liberty Creek.

Now, Tammy was a church goer. She knew Gary was a good man; she often wanted to kick herself for ever letting him go! He was indeed perfection, in her Baptist raised mind. Gary was strong, independent, a leader, smart, a good father, very active member of the church and community, and he was simply beautiful to look at. Yes, she had always admired Gary Connelly. They had attempted dating several times.

The first time they tried dating was in 10th grade. That lasted six months. Then they tried this again, in 12th grade. That time only lasted for five weeks. He was always in trouble as a teenager. It was silly stuff; never anything too bad, but her parents saw him as rebellious and a troublemaker. They pitied his poor parents, such good God-fearing people, and having that wicked, wicked son! It was the wickedness that Tammy liked.

The third time they tried dating was just a couple years ago. Her husband had passed-away several years earlier, and she took the advice of friends and decided to try to see someone, just to get out of the house. Ironically, that someone ended up being Gary; she and Gary struck up a conversation at the diner and he asked her out to dinner for the next night. Again, it didn't quite work out. His mind always seemed a million miles away. She felt sorry for him because he never accepted help from anyone. He insisted on taking care of things himself, and she never could understand why.

Now, he had accepted help from her and here she was, getting paranoid. What if people saw *her* car here, and they started talking about *her*? What if people started thinking she and Gary were having an affair behind Kylie's back?

"Earth to Tammy. What is wrong with you?"

Tammy realized he was leaning in, looking at her oddly. She was embarrassed.

"Oh, hey. It's okay. I was just thinking."

"About what?"

"Is Kylie going to be okay with me being here?"

"Kylie? Why wouldn't she be? Is that what you're all weird about? She knows you're coming over here, today. She said she hoped you gave me something for my headaches. Lighten up, girly. It's not like I've got mood lighting on and playing Bob Seger. I mean, I *can* play some Seger if you *want* me to."

"No, no. That's okay. I mean, nothing against Bob Seger or mood lighting, but I think we're good with what we're working with already." She suddenly felt very weird. This was all fine and good just this morning, but now it was just weird. Especially when she remembered what happened last time she was sitting in this very same room with Gary. How could she forget what happened that night? Unfortunately, she began remembering entirely too much from that night, and didn't realize that a faint smile came across her face.

"Tammy, are you okay?"

She looked at Gary; Gary, who she'd known all her life. Gary, who she did some very inappropriate things with, at just 15 years old. He was wearing his staple black T-shirt, jeans, and boots. His head shaved and his eyes very green, he continued to look at her curiously. Well, she decided to just keep going. He was engaged, and they were still friends. That was the status of things now. Nothing to be done about that. She reached over to her bag and began her presentation.

By the time she was done, Gary had some better understanding of what it was exactly that she did with her oil business. He never really understood what she did, but now he did. And, truthfully, it was even rather interesting.

"So, did smoking weed get you into this?" he asked her.

"*What*? Why'd you ask that?"

"Well, you used to smoke it. I just wondered if it's what got you into like, natural healing and stuff like that?"

"No. I mean, weed was okay and all, but not why I do this."

"So, why do you do this?"

"I don't know. I like that you can use natural things to make you feel better, instead of filling yourself with a bunch of unnecessary stuff. It's fun to learn about too. It's something that I guess I'm proud of. I stayed home all those years; Owen didn't want me working or anything; said it made him look like he couldn't provide if I worked. I remembered Faye and Joan and them, were into that kind of stuff; they had shown me some things before. It looked interesting, but he thought it was foolish to get into. He didn't even want me using the stuff, much less selling it.

"After he died, I had to think of *something* to do, to make some money. I did the waitressing thing but thought it'd be a good time to look-into, maybe making money off this, too. I went on my computer and talked to Joan, and … well, here I am."

"Well, I'm proud of you. You did something you were interested in, something that you wanted to do for you. I'm happy for you."

"Well, thanks. I don't have very many customers yet, but I do have some. Not many here in town; do you know Bessie says its witchcraft? I mean, really?"

"Bessie isn't the sharpest knife in the drawer these days, doll. I think you know that. People all over these parts grew up on natural remedies and tinctures and shit, and they mostly all still use them. It doesn't make them all witches. As for not having many customers here in town, well, you just got yourself one more. Add up whatever it was you said I needed and give me the total. I'll probably have to ask you a few more times how to use it because I'm sure to forget exactly what to do. But that'd be okay, wouldn't it? If I had to call for instructions?" he asked smiling.

She returned the smile.

"Yes, that'd be okay. But are you sure that you really want it? I mean, you're not just saying that to make me feel better? Because if you don't really want it, I don't want you wasting your money on something that's just going to sit around in a cabinet somewhere."

"I really want it. By the way, part of a sales pitch doesn't include talking potential buyers *out* of a sale, doll. Just roll with it." He patted her knee and stood up to get more Coke.

Gary and Tammy sat and visited for another 20 minutes. He was somewhat more relaxed by the time Tammy left and Kylie came home.

He was more relaxed, but the things that had been on his mind all week were still on his mind. He considered even talking to Kylie about these things when she got home. But being in the early stages of her pregnancy, she ran in the front door, past him, and made a beeline for the bathroom. She shut the door and spent the next 10 minutes vomiting. She came out of the bathroom, got a glass of water, and kissed Gary. She went to the bedroom, where Gary found her sound asleep ten minutes later.

He went to sleep that night, dreading what was possibly waiting for him in his dreams again. Tomorrow would be okay. Tomorrow, he'd be able to talk to Jerry.

CHAPTER 9

Tuesday morning found Will, Jerry, and Anne all groggy and a bit cranky but otherwise alright. Marilyn was glad. She wasn't enjoying playing nursemaid to Jerry as much as she thought she would. There was nothing sweet or romantic or touching about taking care of Jerry when he was sick. He was pitiful and coughed incessantly. She wasn't even sleeping with him, after all. His cough was so horrible, it kept waking her up. He insisted she sleep in Eliza's room. He looked horrible, and she didn't want whatever it was he had. She had already kissed on him and stuff, to make him feel better. She hoped she didn't get sick.

Then, there was the ritual of hosting Jason, Lexi, their children, Karen and Roy. Of course, Karen and Roy were staying there, but it still meant extra people that needed feeding. It meant a lot of talking and refills and getting up and down during mealtimes. It meant getting one kid a sippy cup and wiping another kid's chin and passing something to somebody throughout the entire meal. Honestly, Marilyn had a whole new respect for Anne; Anne, after all, had managed to do this every day for several years without killing anyone yet. Marilyn was impressed.

This morning, everyone was at the table, including the three invalids. Marilyn was getting a touch of a headache, and she figured it must have been because she was going crazy. She had already seen Faye three times since arriving Sunday. This wasn't particularly a frightening thing for Marilyn; Faye seemed peaceable enough. However, it did make things awkward.

When Marilyn saw Faye, Faye was only smiling one of the three times. The other two times, she looked suspicious. She looked like she was waiting for something or up to something.

Last night, Marilyn had made her way down the dark, creepy staircase to the first floor. It was late; everyone was asleep. Marilyn had been sleeping in the big tester bed in Eliza's bedroom. She woke up, feeling uncomfortable. She couldn't put her finger on it. She sat up and looked around the semi-dark room. The big windows were open, allowing a soft breeze to blow through the screens. The breeze sent the long sheer white curtains stirring in the room. Marilyn pulled back the blankets and got out of bed. She crept quietly across the big bedroom, past the sleeping little girl. She left the room and walked down the dark upstairs hall. She wanted to get something to drink, so she made her way downstairs to the kitchen. As she made it to the first floor and turned to go down the hall to the kitchen, she was greeted, immediately, by a figure standing in the middle of the hall. It was right in her path, only about six feet away.

Marilyn quite nearly had a heart attack right there in the hall. It was the only time in her entire life she'd been *so* scared, she couldn't even scream. She'd *wanted* to scream, but it couldn't quite come out. She was scared not so much because she saw Faye, but because there was a ghost in the hall at two o'clock in the morning, in a very old, very creepy, very haunted house. It also didn't help matters that Marilyn was alone with it.

It was obviously Faye; although when she saw Faye she wasn't ever quite as clear as how others described seeing her. Marilyn could make out what appeared to be pants and a top, but it was difficult to make out details. Everything was blurry except her face. Faye's face was always very clear. Tonight, it looked curiously at Marilyn. Marilyn stopped cold and just looked at the spirit in the hall.

"What do you want?" Marilyn asked quietly.

"What's mine," replied Faye's voice. It sounded far away, and sad. Marilyn's heart was hammering in her chest. She worked hard at steadying her voice.

"It's *still* yours. I assure you, it's *all* still *yours.*"

Faye's spirit turned suddenly and disappeared down the hall with an odd dull light. The swift, sudden movement of the spirit terrified Marilyn. She sat down in the straight back chair a few feet away and tried to collect herself. Her legs were shaking, and the blood was pounding in her ears. She realized her hands were shaking too. She couldn't stop trembling.

The temperature in the hall suddenly dropped. It was as if a winter wind blew past Marilyn. Just as soon as it was there, it was gone, and the temperature was normal again. Marilyn couldn't help it; she broke down in tears. She wasn't scared exactly. She was confused and incredibly overcome, emotionally, by what just happened. She couldn't collect her thoughts. She had trouble convincing herself that she was really, even awake.

She finally calmed down enough to stand up, and she made her way to the kitchen. When she got there, she decided she didn't want water or a Coke or any of Anne's sweet tea. No, Marilyn needed something strong. Marilyn went to the liquor cabinet and pulled out Jerry's beloved bourbon. She took one of his glasses and poured herself some. She returned the bottle to the cabinet and sat down at the very, old kitchen table. She looked around the kitchen. It was dark except for the light over the sink.

Marilyn had suspicions about this house. She didn't think it was simply ghosts who elected to stay here. She had reasons to think this house kept them here. Sure, they seemed to enjoy being here, but this house, she was convinced this house had something about it that simply possessed people. She felt silly, at first, even thinking about the word *possessed*. That wasn't a word she ever thought about much, before. It also wasn't a word she ever took seriously.

But now, she thought about it a lot, and she certainly took it very seriously. These walls seemed to breathe. To Marilyn, these windows seemed like eyes, watching everything that went on inside and outside. The very, old furnishings seemed to hold the very life of everyone who had ever used them. Sitting at this table, seemingly alone, Marilyn felt she was sitting there with nine other people. These chairs didn't feel empty to Marilyn. She felt that this table, and these chairs, had a life of their own. And it creeped her out, terribly. How could she feel inanimate objects had feelings, thoughts of their own? It was ludicrous, but it was true.

Marilyn thought about the curtains hanging on the windows. They were all very light, sheer curtains during the spring and summer. She recalled, a conversation she had with Jerry about these curtains once. She had commented about how pretty something heavier and richer would be in the house. Jerry reminded her that they put heavier drapes up in the fall. Okay, but then he said something that sent chills down her back. He'd told her,

"Whenever the weather is nice enough to keep all the windows open, we do. So, we keep the curtains light. It helps the house breathe. It couldn't breathe as well with big heavy window coverings."

He said this with such seriousness, so calmly. An outsider might have likely taken that to mean, it lets fresh air in the house. Marilyn wasn't an outsider, however. And she truly, believed that Jerry meant what he said. Whether he realized it or not.

The sheer curtains rising and falling with each breeze that blew inside was like the rise and fall of breathing body. And those *settling sounds* as everyone called them, the noises this house made in the night ... well, Marilyn had an opinion about those, too.

Her grandmother had lived in a very old house; and yes, it creaked and groaned from time to time. This house was different. This house creaked and groaned, itself. When this house creaked and groaned, Marilyn felt as it were simply stretching, tired from sitting for almost two centuries. But there were other noises. There were noises she herself had heard, and nobody could convince her that those were standard settling noises of an old house. The noises Marilyn often heard were a collection of murmurs, very low voices of a sort, whispering things that could not be interpreted. They appeared to often be talking over one another. As soon as you thought you heard it, it was gone. There was another sound this house made that Marilyn could only compare to the sounds heard through a stethoscope. It was subtle; only there when you really listened for it. But it really sounded to Marilyn like the sounds of a heart, and blood, working together. It reminded her of the sound of a pounding headache when you can literally feel and hear the blood pounding inside your head. It was faint, but it was there.

There were too many reasons for Marilyn Beales to believe that this house had a mind and life of its own. While she sat at the kitchen table tonight, the rich smell of tobacco wafted through the kitchen. She looked up and saw without any doubt a touch of smoke at the other end of the table. It lingered briefly next to the top of the old Windsor backed chair before disappearing.

When she saw that, her thoughts went in a million different directions. Should she scream and run to the bedroom? Should she pack her shit and leave right then? She ended up not doing either of those things. She looked in the direction where the smoke had been. She licked her lips, which had suddenly become very dry.

"I'm not in here alone, am I?" she asked, to no one in particular.

She watched as the heavy, full Natural Bridge saltshaker knocked itself over, spilling salt across the top of the table. The shaker then proceeded to roll back and forth, emptying more salt onto the tabletop. She watched as something smoothed the spilled salt out evenly. She was breathing heavily but couldn't stop watching what was taking place before her. Something ran through the salt, writing in it. Marilyn could clearly see what it said: *No.*

Marilyn pushed her chair back slowly, as quietly as possible. She looked at her half empty glass of bourbon and quickly finished it off. She took her glass to the sink, not looking back at the table. She closed the door to the liquor cabinet and left the kitchen.

Marilyn made her way back to Eliza's bedroom. She lay down in the big tester bed and decided she didn't really feel comfortable closing her eyes. But her eyes did close. She remembered trying to keep her eyes open. But then, when her eyes tried to close again, Marilyn just let them close. Her eyes closed, and all other senses seemed to take over.

She could feel the breezes that blew through the open windows better; the breezes were warm, but with the chill of springtime nights still in them. She was aware of these breezes earlier, but now, she really felt them. They felt nice, comforting, and refreshing. She could hear soft noises around her; they weren't frightening. These noises were the same noises she'd heard before, but she wasn't suspicious of them, or worried by them tonight. Marilyn fell asleep to the sounds that played around her. Clarissa Buchanan stood at the window, humming Green Grow the Lilacs, while the long curtains made soft whipping noises, and the rocking chair near the crib began to rock on the old hardwood floor.

That had been last night. Now, in the morning, Marilyn was thinking of her comfortable house in town. After the things Marilyn experienced last night, she wasn't exactly afraid or even unsure how to handle the situation anymore. She came to terms with what was going on here, in this house, but that didn't mean she really wanted to spend the night here, again. Not right now, anyway. Yes, Anne walking around was a welcomed sight.

Anne looked around at the crowd gathered in the kitchen. She poured herself a glass of tea, sat at the table, and looked at Caleb.

"Well? Did you go see your classroom yesterday?" she asked him.

"Nope," he said with a broad smile.

"Why not? Did you run away again?"

"The teacher made a mistake. She told us Sunday, at church. She had forgotten that school would be closed this week for spring break. We'll go when its back in session," Lexi explained.

"Oh! So, you got lucky, huh?" Anne yawned.

"I smell coffee," Jerry said as he staggered into the kitchen. He looked terrible. Anne looked pointedly at Marilyn. Marilyn sighed and stood up to go make Jerry a cup of coffee. She was torn. Part of her appreciated Anne giving her the chance to do things for Jerry; the other part of her wished Anne would take pity on her and do it herself. Marilyn wasn't used to waiting on a man. Jerry didn't require much work at her house on the weekends.

Then, Marilyn thought about something. If this was really, how he was raised and if this was simply how he liked being treated, well … that's just Jerry. It wasn't anything he could really help. He wasn't a demanding, arrogant asshole. He never came right out and asked anyone for anything. He was endlessly polite and appreciative.

She started to think about a few things. She had wanted this man for years, and during those years, she knew he was adored by his woman. She knew Faye worshipped the ground he walked on and had since they were five years old. In short, Marilyn knew exactly what she was asking for. She knew exactly what she was getting herself into. She deliberately went after a man who she knew had been waited on and fussed over all his life. She deliberately went after a recovering, depressed, drunken widower. She knew this at the time and did it anyway.

Jerry worked that morning, but he came back inside after about four hours. Shortly before lunch, he came inside looking flushed and his eyes were red. He was sweating. Anne looked up at him, startled. It wasn't hot enough outside yet to cause him to sweat like that.

"Jerry! What's wrong?" She scooted her chair back to go to him. At this, Marilyn looked up and saw Jerry herself. He looked terrible. Marilyn felt bad for him. She stood up and went to him. As Anne was feeling his forehead, Marilyn went to the refrigerator to get him a cold bottle of water. Lexi sat at the table.

"You look like shit, Jerry," she told him.

"Lexi, really?" Marilyn looked at her in disgust.

"He does. I didn't mean anything by it. I told him this morning he didn't need to try working. Him and Anne both still look bad. Will looks good, but they don't."

"Shut up," Anne told Lexi irritably. She was discovering that Jerry was not necessarily hot though. If anything, he was cool. She thought about something.

"Hey, I think your fever's breaking. I think you *did* try getting up too soon. Go back to bed," Anne advised. Marilyn agreed, as much as she hated to, but Jerry shook his sweaty head.

"No, Gary's coming over today."

"Well, we'll tell him to just come back another day," Marilyn suggested. Jerry dismissed this though.

"No. He has something that he wants to talk about. I told him to come over. I'm the one who told him to come over. He'll be here after lunch."

"I'm sure he'd understand," Marilyn started. Anne had already dropped it. She could tell by his tone of voice that he had every intention of seeing his plans through. Jerry looked at Marilyn impatiently. He stood in what Will called his *coaching position*. He put his hands on his hips and set his jaw. When he did this, he was usually about to lecture someone. Anne, knowing she wasn't the one who was going to get lectured, elected to sit back at the table. Jerry sighed.

"Look. He's not coming over here to talk about football or the weather or deer meat. He is having problems. I am not getting into those problems with any of you because it doesn't concern any of you. Gary needs a friend to talk to, and I said he could talk to me. So, he is coming over here to talk. I appreciate your concern, but I am not going to tell him to not come over today. He will be over here about 1:30."

"She's just trying to help. If you insist on having company, fine. But why don't you at least go get some rest first? Take a shower now that your fever broke. You'll feel better and less … sweaty. When Gary gets here, we'll let you know," Anne said, sounding bored. She wasn't talking to Jerry in her usual loving, wheedling tone of voice. She was simply trying to appease him, and Jerry caught on to this. He didn't want to go to bed, but he decided this was a reasonable compromise.

"Fine! I'll go take a shower and lay down. But! I mean it! When Gary comes over, you let me know or send him upstairs. I mean it!" He said this, pointing an angry finger at all three of them, then directed a look at Marilyn. She had to wonder what Gary's crisis was. She wasn't going to ask.

"Fine, go upstairs. You're being an ass, anyway," Marilyn told him. She crossed her arms in front of her. She didn't want to deal with him right now.

Jerry glared at her but kissed her anyway. He walked past Anne's chair, and pulled her hair. Lexi just shook her head.

Shortly after, Will came in for lunch. He was usually the last one to make it inside, so the girls were surprised to see him in there first this time. Lexi, especially, took notice of him. He was in need of a haircut, so his blond hair had started curling. He had just shaved that morning, so his goatee was short and neat looking. He looked tired but otherwise he looked great. Will wore his jeans and work boots, with the usual plain white work T-shirt. Lexi couldn't help but admire him. Will went to the sink, where he washed his hands. Anne handed him the dishtowel for his hands.

"That is the dishtowel. Where is the hand-towel?" he asked patiently. He was perfectly polite, but his question received a heavy sigh from Anne.

"Oh, good grief. What is the difference?"

"The difference is quite obvious. One is a dishtowel; its name indicates that it is a towel designated to dry dishes. The other one is a hand-towel. Its name indicates that it is a towel designated to dry hands. When one washes their hands, and then dries them off, dead skin cells come off in the process. When this happens, the towel used is left with traces of dead skin cells on it. I personally do not feel that a towel covered with the dead skin cells of numerous different people is an appropriate item to use to dry newly washed dishes. Now do you?" Will asked this while holding his still wet hands up in front of him. He said this in all seriousness.

Anne just went to the pantry and pulled out a clean towel. She delivered it to her husband.

"You have issues. Here is a brand new, clean, dead skin cell free towel."

"This has the blue stripes on it. Mom used the blue striped towels for *dishes*. Where are the ones with the red stripes?"

"Who cares? It's clean."

"You will not let anyone else use the pink washcloths you use on your face. What is the difference? I already said ... one is for dishes and one is for hands. The blue striped is for dishes. You know that. We have already had this discussion, like, four years ago."

"I'll go get the damned towel! I swear," Anne muttered as she walked to the pantry.

"If it is something worth saying, say it loud enough for everyone to hear it. If you do not want others to know what you are saying, then it is best to not say it out loud to begin with," Will advised.

Will was always coming out with things like that; Lexi often wondered if he'd stumbled across a book at some point, full of words of wisdom. She liked the things he came out with, but he sure came out with a lot of them.

Will continued to hold his hands up in front of him, like a surgeon getting his gloves ready for a major medical procedure. Anne stomped back and handed him an elderly looking white towel with faded red stripes. He took the towel graciously. He dried his hands on it, carefully and meticulously. Lexi giggled at the attention he paid to drying off his hands. Then, he leaned in, kissed Anne on the mouth, and hung the hand-towel on the hook by the sink.

"Now, we may eat." He smiled at everyone in the kitchen. Marilyn looked oddly at him but couldn't help but smile.

Marilyn had known him for so long, now. She had witnessed his meticulous behavior in school. He was always meticulously groomed, had perfect grades, and his grammar was so perfect it was annoying as Hell. She recalled once he came into her office breathing heavily because his progress report said he'd gotten a 99 average in world history. She told him to stop stressing over it; it was probably a mistake (it was).

Will wanted perfection and Will wanted a system. These things had to work for Will; there wasn't any room for compromise. There wasn't even room in Will's structured life for the wrong towel.

Will sat at the table and smiled warmly at everyone. Roy had come in during the towel incident, washed his hands, shook the excess water off in the sink, wiped his hands on his jeans; that was good enough for Roy. Jason came in right after Will got his towel, took the towel from the hook, and dried off his own hands. He tossed the towel on the counter.

"Hey! Hang that up!" Will shouted at him. Jason hung up the towel and sat down. They were finally all sitting at the table, minus Jerry. Roy looked around.

"Where's brother?"

"Taking a shower. His fever broke. He's taking a shower, then he's going to rest for a while before Gary comes over," Marilyn explained.

"Why is Dad coming over? He usually works at the co-op on Tuesdays," Jason asked.

"He said your dad just wanted to come over and hang out, talk about some things," Anne cut in. Anne knew that if Marilyn told about Gary having a problem, Jason would get all worried and start asking questions. But Jason was already on top of things.

"He's got something going on. I don't know what it is, but he's been all stressed out acting here lately. I called him last night, and he screamed at the remote because he put it on the wrong channel. Then, he bitched about his ice melting in his glass too quick. He's got something going on. Oh well, maybe he'll talk to Jerry about it.

"Anyway, Caleb? You gonna lead us in the blessing, son?" he asked the little boy who was looking at his reflection in his spoon.

Caleb sighed, tried to lay the spoon down, and dropped it on the floor. He reached over to pick it up, banged his forehead on the edge of the table, fell out of his chair and began howling in tears. Lunch had begun.

They began eating as a big blue knot formed on Caleb's forehead. Caleb began worrying he was going to have to go to the hospital and get brain surgery. Karen shook her head at him.

"Child, you are too little to be a hypochondriac. You have a knot. It's not your first. It won't be your last, either. We'll watch it. Always something going on here. I'll give y'all that."

"Of course, it's always something. I didn't expect to have these things happening every single day. I mean, *every single day*! Every single day, something is going on. I didn't expect this. I never expected that *every* day I'd be dealing with a whole new crisis," Jason whined.

Marilyn laughed, but she didn't sound amused.

"Get over it. That's what it is. I guess for some people, things work out how they expected things to, but I don't think it happens often enough to count. I thought the same thing, for a while. I got over it," she told him. Jason looked interested.

"You? Things didn't work out for you how you wanted them to?" He was surprised because she seemed to have things going well for her. She was beautiful, seemed to be in great health, had a good career, a nice house, a new car every couple of years, and a well-to-do boyfriend who lived in a historic mansion. He couldn't imagine what she was referring to. Marilyn looked at him, with a very insincere smile.

"Sure, Jason. My parents laid out thousands and thousands and thousands of dollars for me to study psychology for seven long grueling years at the University of Kentucky, to earn my doctoral of psychology, so that I could be a guidance counselor at *Mayberry High School*! Do you really think when I started that I imagined I'd one day be nagging kids about grades, giving girls pregnancy tests, and talking to a bunch of completely clueless know-it-alls about college applications? You know what I *want* to tell them? Don't spend too much money on college because chances are, you're going to end up right back here, working on Main Street. Chances are they're going to work at the school, co-op, the lumber mill, or running the register in one of the two stores. Maybe they'll luck out and work at that sad-ass medical center, changing the sheets on one of the what? 50 beds?" Marilyn stabbed her potato salad with her fork. Everyone else had stopped eating and listened to her rant. Will, Jason, and Lexi especially took offense to it. Will bristled.

"Oh, really? So, which one was I? Was I one of those who you had to bitch out about their grades? Is this about that straight A record that I had? Or was I one of the clueless know-it-alls? I mean, really? Let me remind you about the time I came to you, suggesting we organize the food drive for Thanksgiving in ninth grade. Or how about when I came to you with the idea for organizing the creek clean up? Or when I offered to help you with the numerous other things, I offered to help you with?"

"Wow, you sure were a suck-up," Anne commented.

Jason cleared his throat.

"So, I guess I was one of the ones who you had to chew out about grades, huh? Yeah, well, you know what? I rather enjoyed spending time in your office with you. You were badass. But I resent us being referred to as clueless know-it-alls.

"And, what's that supposed to mean, anyway? Don't waste money on college because we're all just going to end up here with dead end jobs anyway? I'm sorry, but as a lifelong resident of this town, I take offense to that. We all do okay here. We've managed to keep this town running without the support of chain stores. We have managed to build, open, and operate an impressive list of locally owned businesses. Personally, I think that takes some skill. Will and I do just fine. I did just fine *before* I came to work here. Kylie is a pharmacist. My dad is a retired cop, police chief and an ordained minister. I see no shame in any of that.

"And Jerry and Uncle Roy and Karen all do just fine. You act like anyone that comes out of our schools are just doomed to live out their lives here being *nothings*. What if you had told Will that, what you want to say to kids? He went to VT and studied business management and we're all pretty lucky as shit that he did! Uncle Roy and Jerry studied farming and stuff. They went to school and became something, even if it was something that they chose to practice here in our sad ass little town."

"Oh, come on, Jason. I'm not talking so much about the older generations. You all turned out okay for the most part. You don't have a clue what I have to listen to every day. They don't even want to do anything! They come right out and say they plan to work at the salon or the bread store or the co-op. I mean, come on! Eric has no intention of going to college! He says he doesn't need to! He wants to run the damned co-op! Do you know what Laurie told me? She actually told me that she's going to get a job working at Tess's Tresses. I said okay, doing what? She said *answering the phone and things*. Answering the phone and what? Sweeping up hair? That's really her goal? Working in a salon?"

"Well, I worked in a salon. Faye worked in a salon," Lexi pointed out, a little insulted. She obviously wasn't the only one. The empty chair where Jerry usually sat pulled away from the table by itself. It appeared Faye had joined in the conversation. Marilyn looked at the haunted chair, along with everyone else. Marilyn wasn't even fazed by it anymore. She just sighed.

"Oh, good grief! Lexi … *and Faye* (directing a look at Jerry's haunted chair*)*; you two both went to school! You two studied cosmetology at least! I mean, even a community college is better than nothing! Laurie doesn't even plan on doing that! It's that way with *most* of the girls here."

Karen smiled and tried to reassure Marilyn.

"But Marilyn, it may seem that way, but it's not what it looks like really. Our girls grow up to teach school, work in the stores around here, work as nurses and doctors. We open and run businesses too. Both the salons are owned by women. There are several businesses here owned by women.

"Just because you have a few light-headed girls that come into your office not knowing what they'll be doing five or 10 or even 15 years down the road, it doesn't mean that they'll never amount to anything. It's true that our sights we set are a bit small town, but this *is* a *small town.*

"And, Marilyn, dear, please stop making it sound like what you do isn't important. What you do *is* important, to a good-many kids. There is no shame at all in being a guidance counselor for a bunch of messed up teenagers. They're crazy at this age; they need someone to talk to. You are a very well-liked staff member. It might not be what you expected to do for a living, but if you chose psychology, it's because you wanted to help people. And, honey, that's just exactly what you're doing. They're teenagers, but they're still people."

"Laurie's not one of the one's coming to you for pregnancy tests, is she?" Jason asked Marilyn suspiciously.

"No, not yet anyway. But even if she did, I wouldn't tell you; that confidentiality bullshit, you know? But just keep in mind … I mean, she *is* related to *you,* after all," she said quite seriously.

Karen smiled but said nothing. Nothing much else was said during lunch. They were all thinking about the things that Marilyn had said.

This was Liberty Creek, and it may not have the big city amenities or the big city jobs, but they all felt Marilyn was being a bit harsh and unfair. Honestly, Marilyn even felt bad about it. She liked this town, obviously, or she wouldn't have stayed all these years. It's just, this wasn't the way she had seen things going for her, so many years ago. She looked around the table a couple of times, seeing everyone quietly eating.

"I'm … I'm sorry. I didn't mean for it to come out quite like all that. It may not be what I expected to do with a degree, but y'all must know I like it here or else I wouldn't have stayed here this long. It's just, I was just talking, I guess," she said quietly.

"That's the problem with you women; you all talk too damn much. A man can't hear himself think around here, the way y'all are always talking," Roy muttered. Lexi glared at him and Anne ignored him. Marilyn wondered if he was serious, when Karen slapped him on the back of the head.

"Fool, you need to shut up. We got plenty we *ought* to be saying to you idiot men, but we keep it to ourselves. Trust me, you think we talk too much? We can show you how much we *can* talk if we *want* to."

"See? You gotta talk about it," he joked. Karen poked him in the ribs.

Caleb sighed heavily, "My head bump is hot. Is my brain breaking?" he inquired. They all looked at him.

Karen, the nurse, set her fork down. She scooted her chair back.

"Come on child. We'll go look at it. I'll get you a bag of frozen peas for it."

"But I just ate."

Karen laughed and led Caleb to the mud room to investigate his knot and get a bag of peas from the deep freezer.

Lunch ended, and the girls began clearing the table and cleaning the kitchen. Anne pulled a plate down from the cabinet.

"Is that for Jerry?" Marilyn asked.

"Yeah. Um, I guess the barbeque and potato salad. Loaf bread, not the buns. He's not going to eat the coleslaw. It feels wrong to be eating this on Tuesday instead of Sunday. Roy and Karen trying to get out of cooking, I guess."

"I guess. Well, we'll fix the plate up and I guess run it up there to him. Are you taking it up there? I mean, I didn't know if you were planning on taking it up there, or ..." Marilyn began. Anne smiled tiredly.

"You take it up there. Me and Lexi will finish up down here."

"*Lexi and I* will finish up down here," Will corrected.

"I thought you left. Why are you still inside?" Anne asked him.

"Because I forgot my kiss." He kissed Anne on the mouth and slapped her behind hard. Then, he turned to Marilyn.

"Miss Beales listen to Karen. You are a great counselor. Everyone around town likes you. It might not be what you imagined, but we're glad you're here. I hope that means something. Our family wouldn't be the same if you weren't a part of it." He leaned forward and planted a kiss on her cheek and hugged her tight. As he pulled away, she smiled a *thank you* at him. She wasn't able to say it out loud. Marilyn was too touched; it was the first time any of them had referred to her as *family*.

CHAPTER 10

J erry had to admit, he felt a little better by the time he finished his shower. He still didn't feel like eating anything though. He went up the hall to his bedroom. As he walked past the wall sconces, they flickered. He paid them little mind. He simply muttered,

"Why don't you just say hello, Faye?"

At this the lights all went dark, then turned on very bright, then they all went dark again. Jerry went in his bedroom and closed the door. He pulled the towel off from around his waist and was about to put blue jeans on. Then, he decided he didn't care if he was having company; it was just Gary. Jerry decided the cheeseburger printed pajama pants looked more comfortable. These had been a gift from smart-ass Anne, who constantly lectured him about his obsession with ground beef. So, Jerry slipped on the pajama pants and a gray T-shirt.

Jerry's big bed looked so inviting and comfortable, that he was tired before he ever even laid down. He slipped between the cool sheets and lay beneath the heavy quilt. He yawned, and his eyes dropped until he was sound asleep. He smelled that familiar smell of Charlie cologne and smiled in his sleep. Jerry and Faye took an afternoon nap, waiting for Gary to arrive.

At exactly 1:30pm, Gary's truck pulled up beside the house. He got out and stood in the yard for just a moment looking around. He could hear horses, and distant conversations taking place at the stable. He finally went up the front steps and through the front door without knocking. The screen door slammed behind him, announcing his arrival. He went directly to the heart of the house, the kitchen. He knew that's where he'd find most of the folks in here.

Lexi was pouring Eliza a drink in her sippy cup. Karen was walking through the kitchen with a bag of Cheetos in her hand.

"Well, hey there, good looking. How you doing?" she asked, winking at him.

"I'm ... alright. I'm alright. How are you?" he asked, kissing Karen's cheek, and noticing Anne struggling to reach a bowl on a high shelf.

"I'm doing okay. About to go work some more, on these damn accounts. I'll catch you later sugar." Karen patted his cheek.

Gary nodded and walked over to Anne and pointed to a bowl. "This one, honey?"

"The one under it, please." Anne waited while Gary retrieved the bowl and handed it to her.

"Thank you. Jerry's upstairs. His fever broke today. He took a shower and laid down for a little while. But he wanted us to be sure to let him know when you got here. You can go on upstairs if you want. Would you like a drink or anything?"

"Um, yeah, thanks. Coke."

Anne went to the extra refrigerator in the mud room, where Jerry kept his Cokes. She retrieved Gary a cold one and delivered it to him.

"Thank you, honey. Hello, Lexi. Aren't you going to talk to me?"

"Hi. This stupid lid won't screw on straight. It keeps leaking," she complained. Gary handed his Coke back to Anne and put the sippy cup lid on securely. He kissed Lexi on the top of her head. He took his Coke back from Anne and kissed her on top of her head, too.

"Now, I'm going upstairs to see Jerry for a bit," he informed them.

"Hey! Wait a minute. Take this with you." Anne handed Gary a small plate with four Vienna sausages on it. He looked at her curiously.

"Miss Priss. Caleb thought he wanted them, then decided he didn't. They'll just go bad. Nobody ever wants refrigerated Vienna sausages. So, take them to Miss Priss. Thank you, dear."

"Well, you're welcome, I guess. These things sure do stink, though." Gary never could get into Vienna sausages. They always smelled like, well, cat food to him. They were disgusting. But he obediently carried the blue Fiestaware plate upstairs to the cat.

Gary finally reached the second floor and knocked on Jerry's bedroom door.

"Come in!" Jerry called from the other side.

Gary opened the door with one hand while balancing his drink and the sausages in the other. As he entered the room, he saw Jerry sitting at the occasional table in the middle of the room. Jerry smiled tiredly as Gary made his way to the table. Gary set the Vienna sausage plate down before Jerry. Jerry looked curiously at Gary.

"Awww, you brought lunch. That was thoughtful of you."

"Anne made me bring it up here for your damn cat. Trust me; I've managed to go over 60 years without eating these disgusting things. I can go the rest of my life without having them. So here ya go."

Jerry took the plate and carried it over to Miss Priss's placemat that sat in the corner of his room. She jumped off his bed and ran over to investigate her lunch. She began eating, and Gary looked at her in disgust.

"Ewww, that noise she makes, eating. She's *smacking* Jerry. It sounds so ... wet."

"This is Miss Priss's room. You are merely a guest in it. You leave Miss Priss alone. Keep eating your lunchy sweet kitty girl," Jerry told her lovingly.

"*Lunchy?*"

"Did you come here to talk about my cat or your problems?"

"My problems, I guess."

"Alright then. Would you like a piece of gum first?" Jerry offered the pack of Trident.

"*Trident?* What happened to that cinnamon crap you used to chew all the time?"

"Anne said sugar free is better for me. It really sucks. She also cut back on my tea. She's making me drink water between every glass of tea."

"Oh. Well, she loves you, man. She wants to keep you around for a long time, I guess. It's not the end of the world. I'd think it'd be kinda nice to have some woman fussing over you so much. Quit complaining."

"Doesn't Kylie fuss over you?"

"Eh, not exactly. I mean, she does. I take that back. But not to the extent Anne fusses over you. Does Marilyn fuss over you?"

"She's trying to, I think. It's nice. It's not Faye. Faye really laid it on thick, you know? Anne pretty much does what Faye did. Marilyn, though, she's not into that stuff. She doesn't offer to do stuff for me or anything. And, I don't know, I offer to do stuff for her, and I try to make nice gestures to her. I guess we're still learning about each other. She's trying … I think."

"You know, you were lucky to have had Faye. I mean, she wasn't really typical. These days, a lot of women would say she was crazy for falling all over you like she did and then, to have Anne do the same thing … maybe expecting to be lucky enough to have *three* women treat you like that just isn't practical. Maybe, just maybe, lay off Marilyn some? She's not Faye, and she's not Anne. She grew up differently. And, well …" Gary began, but he didn't know how to finish what he'd started.

"Well, what?" Jerry pressed.

"Um, nothing. Just what I was saying. I don't want to talk about you and your women anymore. I *thought* I came here to talk about *me*."

"Oh, well, okay. Start talking. What's your problem?" Jerry asked. Gary sighed. He thought for a moment before answering. Then, he almost whispered,

"I think I'm going to Hell."

Jerry chewed his gum slowly, his brow furrowed. He looked carefully at Gary for a moment before asking,

"What did you *do*?"

"It's not one thing particular. It's all the things I've done. I mean, come on! You know the things I've done. This thing that Lawson is asking me to do is just a stretch. There's too much going on. How am I supposed to do this right, when I'm going through all of …" Gary rambled before Jerry interrupted him.

"Hey! What are you talking about? What things? What are you going through? Is this still about the wedding and baby? Are you really this worked up over that?"

"No! It's not that! Well, not *just* that. I've been thinking about the things I've done, Jer. You know the things I'm talking about. I don't feel right preaching after I did … *that*. I mean, how am I supposed to preach in a church? I know I've filled in a time or two, but this is different. You know it's going to be different. This is going to be several weeks or longer. And it just feels different. It feels *wrong*."

"Those things you did, you didn't do them alone. And I'd do them again, if I had to. Anyone you ask would say the same thing. Stop beating yourself up over that. All of that. Now, what else is this all about?"

"I'm doing the same thing all over again. I realized that. I got a girl pregnant before marrying her; I did that once and it did not work out well for me! And now, all I can think about is how I did the same thing all over again!"

"No. This is *not* the same thing all over again! Really?"

"Yes! It *is* the same thing!" Gary argued. He buried his face in his hands. His nerves were starting to get the best of him. He then realized there was someone he wanted to be there. It wasn't Kylie or Jason or Karen. He wanted Tammy to be there. He wanted Tammy to hand him something that would chill him out. She had a million bottles of shit in that bag of hers. She had even told him she had great stuff in there for nerves.

"No, it's not the same thing! Charlotte was a loser! She was a strung-out drug addict who never gave a damn about you or Jason! *How* can you compare *Kylie* to that piece of shit?"

"Hey! You shut the fuck up! That was my *wife*! I've never said anything like that about Faye!"

"What the Hell are you talking about? Of course, you never said anything like that about *Faye*! Apples and oranges, man! Faye never did the shit Charlotte did! Why *would* you say things like that about Faye? And *what is your deal*? After 43 years, you're defending her behavior? Are you serious?"

"I'm not defending what she did! I'm just saying that maybe it wasn't always her fault that she did that stuff. I mean, her parents were assholes when she was growing up. They made her life impossible! She had problems. Her parents never did anything to help her. They never tried to be parents to her. All the fuck they were interested in was keeping their precious reputation clean. I knew she had issues, and I thought I could help! But what the fuck did I do? I got her pregnant and then expected her to be the perfect wife, despite all the bullshit I knew she had gone through. What kind of husband is that?" Gary asked. His eyes were very bright. Jerry just sat quietly and listened. When Gary finished his rant, Jerry leaned forward.

"You are seriously blaming *yourself* for what happened? Gary? How can you really believe that any of that was your fault? You knew she was doing that shit before you got her pregnant. You knew she had something going on. Okay, so you didn't know what exactly it was that *was* going on, but you admitted to me that you had suspicions. That with Char, that didn't happen *because* you got her got pregnant and expected her to be a wife and mother!

"You cannot let what happened between you two screw-up what you've got with Kylie. You and Kylie are different! Kylie was successful and happy and clean and sober when you started going out with her. I mean, I guess she *still is*, but you know what I mean. Charlotte was fucked up. Regardless of how or why or whose fault it was, she was fucked up. You tried to see something different in her, and I commend you. But it's just who she was. Kylie was not fucked up. You got married to Charlotte because you got her pregnant and your families treated you both like trash until you married her. That marriage? That wasn't done for the right reasons.

"But Kylie? You fell in love, asked her to marry you, then you got her pregnant. Totally different. That whole thing was out of love, not manipulation and blackmail."

"I *did love* Charlotte. I can't help it; I feel like I failed her terribly. Jerry ... I dream about her. The past several months, I've had a *whole lot* of dreams about her," Gary confessed, reluctantly. He'd kept this inside for so long.

"Well, what kinds of dreams?" Jerry was entirely too familiar of dreams about dead wives.

"Well, there's been a few bad ones, dreams where she's dead. But listen … most of the dreams? Most of the dreams are real nice. I mean, they're really, really nice, Jer. It's like it's Charlotte, but she's better. She's doing good. But she's our age and good. In these dreams, I see her how she *could have* been. Then, I wonder, or is it just maybe how she is *now*?"

"Well, what's she doing in them? What's she saying? Anything?"

"I don't know if you'd understand that part or not; I'm still trying to, myself."

"Try me."

"We make love, Jerry. We spend time together with Jason, and Lexi and the babies. She's pretty, again, but older. It's like, I feel like I'm having an affair with my dead ex-wife. That's not good, Jerry. There's no way that's good. I've started liking those dreams. I wake up, smiling. I wake up missing her."

"Our minds do these things to us, Gary. Do you only see her in your sleep? I mean, she's not coming to you when you're awake?" Jerry asked barely above a whisper. Gary looked oddly at him.

"There's been a couple of times, I thought I was dreaming about her, but then, I'd realize I wasn't even really, asleep. But that doesn't mean she's, I mean, there's a place, you know? Where you aren't really awake, but you haven't quite fallen asleep yet either."

"Yeah, I know that place. But just be honest with me. In your own opinion, do you think you only see her in your dreams? Or do you think you see her other times?" Jerry was uncomfortable about this. Jerry knew that Jason had his mother's ashes in his house. He also knew that, given the conditions they'd found her body in, Charlotte very likely had a torturously painful and lingering death. Charlotte's ashes were currently residing in a proven haunted house, which was located on a piece of property just ten minutes away that was a paranormal investigator's dream come true. If Charlotte was indeed haunting, Jerry wanted to know because he just didn't think her ghost would be a nice one to have around for some reason.

"I don't know really. I honestly don't know anymore. I'm confused, Jerry. I don't think I've ever been so confused about anything. I don't want Kylie to find out about all of this and think I don't want to marry her and have the baby with her. I do. I mean, I'm worried and nervous and all but I do love her, and I do love the baby. I want them. But this Charlotte thing is really messing with me."

"It's gotta be psychological. I mean, you're probably just nervous about this relationship and kinda having flashbacks to the first time you did this whole marriage baby thing. Maybe? Does that sound good?"

"Maybe, but it doesn't change the fact that I've started thinking about Charlotte again. There was a time when all I could do was think about the bad things. I mean, there were just so many bad things, you know? Now, I've started remembering the little things about her that were nice. I mean, there was a reason I hooked up with her. There were things about her that were nice, for a while, anyway. I think after some time, I stopped seeing the nice things and just saw the bad things."

"Look, with all due respect, when your wife overdoses on cocaine in the bathroom, while her cop husband is at work and her sick baby is wearing nothing but a shitty diaper in the freezing living room, well, it's kinda hard to give a shit that she still makes you coffee in the morning, Gary! Oh, well, she forgot your one-year-old in the car at the Buy and Bag but hey! She rubbed your shoulders for you! You found him eating detergent when you came home that time, while she was on the phone with her dealer! But hey! She put pecans in your chicken salad for you! *Of course,* you stopped seeing all the nice things! When all her bullshit took over, that's what happened!"

Gary looked at his lap and broke down in tears. Jerry immediately felt horrible.

"Look, I saw what you went through after we got back here from Blacksburg. I saw her out and running around like a teenager when she should have been taking care of a baby. I saw you busting your ass trying to make things right by that baby. Faye and I both hated her as much as we could without going to Hell for it. Faye loved her at a point too, but when we came home for Christmas that time and she saw Char at the store with Jason? Charlotte was all dolled up, and Jason looked like a refugee. Faye wanted to take that baby away from her so bad she didn't know what to do. We saw the things she did, and we saw the things she *should have* done but never gave enough of a shit to do them.

149

"Of course, I'm not going to have anything nice to say about her. Yes, it was your wife. It was Jason's mama. And, as far as that goes, I'll respect all that. But I'm sorry. I simply can't forgive what she did to y'all. It wasn't fair."

"It wasn't her fault. She had problems. It wasn't like smoking a cigarette, Jerry. That, what she did, was not so easy to just quit."

"She could have gotten help. She chose not to."

"Like you?" Gary asked, suddenly looking Jerry in the eye. Jerry looked at him curiously.

"Like me? What the fuck are you talking about? You're the one who's got a cigar box full of weed in his gun case!"

"Your drinking! That's what I'm talking about. Look at what *your* habit did to *your* family! Let me remind you, I watched how you treated your own family! I saw what drinking has done to you. How can you, of all people, sit in judgement of Charlotte? As for my weed? You tell me one time! You tell me one fucking time that my stash of weed has impaired me! You tell me one fucking time that my weed has kept me from doing my job as a daddy! Tell me just one time that my weed kept me from seeing my own son for three years, Jerry! Or my Scotch!"

"You really want to throw my weed up in my face? I have always done what was expected of me! Always!"

"Maybe that's been your problem. Maybe you've always done what everyone else expected you to do and not enough of what you really wanted to do. Always doing what's expected of you isn't necessarily the best road to take. Where did that get you? Really?

"That aside, I resent what you just said to me. I've always enjoyed drinking, Gary. Since we were 12 years old, I've enjoyed booze. And you know damn well that it *never* affected my home life. What happened to me, when Faye died, wasn't because of my drinking. It was because my best friend in the world, my wife, died. I was depressed, and I was crazy. I dealt with it the only way I knew how. It wasn't a recreational high for me, and it *was* for Charlotte.

"But you're totally right. Who am I to sit in judgment of her or you? If you two screw each other every night in your dreams, well, that's certainly between y'all. Who am I to say anything about what happens in our dreams? I still dream about sleeping with my daughter-in-law. I mean, is it right? Hell no. But you know, it's not like there a switch or a button that we can turn to adjust these things, right? It is what it is.

"What bothers *me* is you're talking like giving Charlotte another chance to prove herself is an option. Do you *hear* yourself? You're talking like she's wanting to work on things! Do you realize that? She is not able to do that, Gary. Even if it was a ghost thing she had going on … *it can't happen*. It is not worth giving up what you've got, to rediscover Charlotte."

"But you and Faye …" Gary started. Then, he stopped. What *was* he thinking? What was it, exactly, that he was getting at anyway? Jerry rubbed his eyes.

"Me and Faye. Let us talk about that. I'm not going to run her off. This is her home. This is her family. I am her husband. I'm letting her stay. However, I am *not* going to let her dictate what I do with my life anymore. There was a time, I think, I let her influence too much. But not anymore. I miss her. I honestly miss her more and more every single day. I don't miss her any less. I have not gotten over this *at all*. I am, however, learning to move forward.

"I've thought about a few things the past couple of days. I've not been fair to Marilyn during all of this. I mean, I really haven't. I'm doing a few things differently from now on. I've not said anything to anyone yet, but I'm taking Marilyn out of town. I'm taking her away from here for a week or so."

"That's big. Where are you taking her?"

"I don't know yet. I'm still having to get used to the idea. You know, I've not gone on a trip since I took Faye to Ocean City. It's been a long time. I'm kinda nervous about it, but I'm going to do this. See, Gary, at *some* point you have *got* to accept things. It might feel like someone is stabbing you in the gut with a rusted ice pick, but it is what it is. You just make up your mind that you have to move on."

"You and Anne, though, you moved on from *that*?" Gary inquired. Jerry frowned slightly, chewing on his bottom lip. He cleared his throat.

"Well, that's different. That whole relationship is different. The point is, you and Kylie have started building something really great and

I know you're happy with her. Everyone knows you are. Everyone in town is happy for y'all. You *are* happy with her, right?"

"Of course, I'm happy with her. She's sweet, funny, nice, and smart. She has a lot of things going for her. She makes me laugh. She takes 30 years off me. Being alone all this time was worth it. I mean, what if I'd settled for someone who didn't do these things for me? She totally turned my life around, gave me a reason to care again," Gary said. Jerry nodded.

"Being in love again is awesome, isn't it? It's pretty fabulous. I mean, every morning is better, waking up to have them there. All of the little things they do, and all of the cute little annoying habits they have; it makes you wonder how you managed to get by without them," Jerry said, smiling with his eyes bright and happy.

Gary smiled back, but it was a sad, understanding smile. He leaned back in his chair.

"You're not talking about Marilyn, are you? Or even Faye. You're talking about Anne. I mean, that's okay. I understand. You said the part about waking up every day, having them there. You said that about the annoying habits and wondering how you ever got along without them. I know you're talking about Anne. And it's true. I can see that. Anne is always here, always taking care of you, and you're around her all day every day, living with her quirks and her weird ways. I'm not judging. She's pretty amazing.

"I'll be honest with you; I think she completes you. I see you two together, and it's like you two just ... well, you make a great couple and I know that that's not right, but it's just true. *Why*, Jerry? If you love her so much and she loves you so much, and everything, why did you back off like you did? I've heard enough over the years to know that you two were involved long before she and Will were. So, why did you give it away?"

"She's young and deserved to experience being married and having children. I couldn't ever give that to her. Well, the children part, yeah. *That* part's easy. *That* part is fun, even. But I made a vow to Faye that I'd marry *her*. Wives aren't something I feel you should trade in. I never divorced Faye. I believe in marrying once. I married once, took a wife, an excellent wife. I won't marry again. Of course, it's nothing for you to take personally. You had every reason and right to get a divorce. But what went on with me and Faye is different. We were happily married, and I guess I can say that we still are.

"Here's the thing, Gary: I wasn't given a choice in the matter. I was forced to get better. I was forced to move on, whether I was ready to or not. Will told Anne once, that what Anne and I have, had to change or else he'd move them out of the house. That was after I slapped her that time. He knew; he knew that something was going on. He told her that things simply had to change, or else they'd leave me. Well, obviously, that wasn't an option! I mean, the thought of him taking her away from me!

"Well, I'd already started seeing Marilyn, by the time that happened. I just decided that was it for me. I mean, I couldn't stop loving Anne, but I could move on. I could accept that this is just the way things are and move on."

"*Have* you really moved on in your opinion? I see you two together, Jerry. I know it's not just me that sees it. Everyone sees it. Obviously even Will sees it."

"What the fuck is there to do about it? Everyone knows that you can't just turn these things off! Marilyn knows I am in love with Anne. Will, Roy, Karen, and even your son and Lexi *all* know that I am in love with Anne. *Anne* knows I am in love with Anne. They understand. I am not going to pretend that I don't love her. There's no shame in loving someone who saves your life and takes care of you. No, I'm not going to apologize to anyone. I'm not sorry I love her, not at all.

"But I could never have asked her to give herself to me. She deserved more. Will can give her all that, and I can still be with her. This arrangement works. He knows his wife and the kids are taken care of even when he's not here. He's come right out and told me that they couldn't be in better hands if they were in his own. I can't have his wife, but I take care of her. And I take care of her as if she were my own. He knows it's a blessing, not a problem."

"And Mare? She's as understanding?"

"Yeah, but like I said, things are going to have to change. She shouldn't have to ever wonder about certain things, and she said something that really bothered me. She asked, if *she* got sick, I'd take care of her, wouldn't I? Wouldn't I? Did she really have to ask that? I don't think it was a rhetorical question. I think she honestly wanted to know, and that really bothered me."

"How do you think this'll all go over with Faye?"

"Faye? Faye wants me to move on, long as I don't forget to bring her along. She doesn't make this easy for me, at all. She's always bitching and lecturing me about Anne, but she doesn't ever really say anything about Marilyn. She doesn't complain about her. In the beginning, she was a pain in the ass about me seeing her. Now? Not so much.

"But I will say this; I have to wonder how this is going to end up working out for you and Kylie and Charlotte? I mean, I thought *my* situation was fucked up, but … well, look at what's going on with *you*. The new preacher is engaged to his pregnant fiancée who made out with his own son 25 years ago, and his dead ex-wife is wanting to date him again. There's a reason we're friends, I guess. So, is our talk helping you out any so far?" Jerry asked, cheerfully.

"Um, I'm going to need a lot of Scotch and a designated driver."

CHAPTER 11

While Jerry was counseling Gary over Scotch and cigars, Jason was working in the breeding stable. He was in the middle of cleaning a stall when his phone rang. He looked at the phone, and saw it was Laurie.

"Hello, dear," he answered tiredly.

"Hi Daddy," Laurie said sweetly, too sweetly. She usually reserved *Daddy* for when she was sucking up to him for something.

He sighed,

"Hi, daughter. How are you?"

"Oh, I'm doing okay. How are you doing today?"

"I'm fine, just working. Is there something you'd like to ask me?" he asked, smiling.

"Oh, well, not really. I was just wondering; did you know it's spring break?"

"Yes, Laurie," he said patiently.

"Oh, well, like, I was wondering if, since we're out of school this week, if it'd be okay if I maybe had a few friends spend the night."

"Do you mean here? You want them to spend the night here?" he asked apprehensively.

"Well, yeah. Why would I ask *you* if they could spend the night at *Mom's*?"

"So, you're talking about having like a slumber party?"

"Ugggh, no Dad. I'm in *high school*. They aren't slumber parties anymore; not since, like, sixth grade. Hello! It's just a sleepover."

"Well, how many are you talking about? What do you call a few? What night are you wanting to do this? And make it quick; I'm working."

"Just two, Stacia and Jennifer. I guess maybe tomorrow night?"

"Ohhhh, a week-night?" Jason whined.

"Well, Dad! That's the point of it being spring break! We can do this because we don't have school the next day."

"But *we* still have *work* the next day," he reminded her.

She sighed heavily.

"We won't bother you! We'll hang out around the house and whatever. It's not like you have to *babysit* us. I believe we can find enough to do around there. Come on!"

"Oh, fine! Let me tell Lex and see if she'd spaz about it. If she doesn't care, it's okay with me. I'll call you back later about it. Like I said, I'm working."

"Thank you, Daddy. I love you," she added.

"I love you, too. I'll talk to you later. Bye-bye, honey."

Oh, Jason was not really looking forward to having three teenaged girls hanging around the house! Laurie was obnoxious enough these days. He was constantly having to referee spats between Laurie and Lexi and Laurie and Caleb.

Laurie and Lexi were always at each other's throats because Laurie felt she was old enough to be treated like an adult. The problem was, she didn't *act* old enough to be treated like an adult. She had won a beauty walk at the high school, made the cheerleading squad, and was now rather impossible to be around. Yes, Laurie was somewhat full of herself these days. This caused numerous arguments between her and Lexi.

Caleb had discovered older sisters and was having a fine time going out of his way to make his own mad. He thoroughly enjoyed doing things to make her chase him and scream at him. He would sneak in her room and go through her things. Jason had no choice but to start punishing the child for these things, but it seemed to have very little effect on him.

Jason thought about Laurie's request on and off for the rest of the afternoon. When the day ended, Jason sat down in the office for a few minutes. Roy came to the doorway.

"Hey, you seen Luke?"

"Nope. I've been in here most of the afternoon. He was with Jonathon trying to fix the truck when I saw him last. That was right after lunch though. Why?"

"Because the workday is fucking over and there are five things left that he was supposed to do, that he *didn't* do! And I don't want to listen to Will bitch about for it three hours! You know tomorrow is Wednesday, and that means in the morning he'll come through here for his damned inspection! And I want everything done!"

"Um, go see if they're in the barn. I'm assuming you looked around here already?"

"Yes, I did. I am getting sick and tired of chasing his ass all over this property looking for him! Every single time I need him for something, I can never find him! I want someone else in here." Roy turned to stomp off. Jason called him back.

"Oh, come on, Uncle Roy! Don't go getting ready to fire him yet. I'll talk to him. Let me talk to him! He's a good guy, just … chill out, okay?"

"No. I won't chill out. I am going to find him and then I am going to kill him." Roy left the doorway. Jason fumbled for his phone and called Luke. Finally, on the fifth ring, Luke answered it.

"Hello?"

"Luke, Uncle Roy is looking for you. What the hell is the deal? He said there's five things on the list that you haven't even done yet!"

"I'll do them. I'll get them done today. It's not like I haven't been working the farm. I've been helping Jonathon with the truck most of the day. He doesn't know the difference in a radiator hose and heater bypass hose. I mean, really, man, he doesn't know shit. If we're going to get the work truck, well, working, then I have to help him out with it."

"Will is going to be coming through here tomorrow morning. It needs to be done before then or else he'll bitch."

"I live spitting distance to the stable, man. I can work on it all night if I have to. Get a grip! It will be taken of! Look, if Will wants things run properly, then he has to understand that sometimes *other* shit comes up that isn't on his list!"

"Oh, fine! I'll find Uncle Roy and tell him. I guess I'll go ahead and tell Will what's going on, then."

"Fine. Whatever. I'll catch you later. Bye." Luke hung up the phone. Jason sighed heavily. He liked Luke; really, he did. They all liked Luke. But Luke wasn't like the others. He didn't give a damn if he pissed Will off. This stressed Jason out because he was always paranoid a big fight was going to break out, and Will would either end up firing Luke or Luke would just end up quitting. Jason didn't want to lose Luke. The phone rang again, immediately. Laurie.

"What is it, Laurie?" Jason answered irritably.

"Well? Did you ask her yet?"

"No! I am working! I told you I would let you know something!"

"Well, when?" Laurie whined.

"Oh, good grief! I'll ask her now! Leave me alone, and I will let you know when I am done talking to her. Do you hear me?"

"Yes, sir."

"Bye!" Jason hung up and called his wife.

"Hello, honey," she greeted him warmly.

"Yeah, hi. Listen, Laurie is bugging the shit out of me. She wants to know if she can have a slumber party ... oh sorry, sleepover ... here tomorrow night."

"Well, I guess so ... if it's okay with you. I don't guess I care. How many is she inviting?"

"Um, two? Stacia, and that Jennifer girl. I don't like her hanging out with her, but not a lot I can do about what she does when she isn't here. Me telling her that Jennifer can't come to the sleepover thing doesn't mean she won't keep hanging out with her."

"Yeah, my mom hated most of my friends in school. I still hung out with them. Jennifer is okay."

"Okay then. I'll call her and tell her. I guess I'll have to get something for them to eat, dammit. Is there enough pizza in the freezer, do you think?"

"Well, I bought seven. So, I'm guessing yeah."

"Okay. I can't believe I'm agreeing to do this."

"Hey? Why out here? All her friends are there in town. Why do they want to have it out here?"

"I don't know. Maybe her mom won't let her have it there, for some reason."

"Okay. I'll head home in a bit. I'll see you when you get there," Lexi told him. They exchanged goodbyes and hung up.

"What's going on?" Anne asked.

"Laurie wants to have a sleepover at the house tomorrow night. I'm not really looking forward to it, but maybe it will at least keep her upstairs," Lexi answered glumly.

"Are you two still at it that bad?"

"Oh yeah. I get told that I'm not her mother, that only Jason can tell her what to do. She even told me that if I don't lay off, she'd quit coming over at all. All that will do is hurt Jason. It isn't worth it."

"Lexi! She's blackmailing you! She's telling you to let her have her own way or else she'll punish Jason and that it'd be all your fault!"

"Yeah, basically."

"You can't let that little twit do that!"

"Do what? Which little twit are we referring to?" Marilyn asked good naturedly as she came into the kitchen. Lexi and Anne exchanged looks. Well, Marilyn *was* Laurie's school guidance counselor after all. Lexi had never had to go see Marilyn much, in school. She never had any pressing issues or anything. However, Lexi realized that Marilyn might be a good one to go to with this.

"Can I tell you something just between us for now?" she asked hesitantly. Marilyn looked at Anne.

"Well, between you and me and Anne, sure. What's the matter?"

So, Lexi told Marilyn what Laurie was doing. Marilyn sat at the table, brow furrowed, with a disgusted look on her face.

"Lexi, let me explain something. She *is* going through things; I know that for a fact. But you cannot let her get away with this. You need to tell Jason what she is threatening. That isn't fair to you or the people who have got to live with y'all. You know what? I'll talk to her," Marilyn decided quickly.

Marilyn seemed to be doing better today. It was as if her mood had lifted and she had gotten a sudden burst of energy. She was smiling instead of looking worried and weary. She moved about the house easily as if she had spent her whole life there, instead of clinging to the crowd in the kitchen, as she had been doing.

Lexi just shrugged. She didn't care. If Marilyn wanted to take over Laurie's issues, that was fine with Lexi.

The girls in the kitchen could hear Jerry and Gary coming down the hall talking. They came into the kitchen, Gary looking chilled out and Jerry looking very sleepy.

"Did y'all have fun, kids?" Anne asked.

"Um, yeah. Yeah, I guess you can say that. But now, I'm tired and wanting to go to bed. I'm headed home." Gary hugged Lexi and Anne. He excused himself to go to the office so he could tell Karen goodbye. As soon as he was out of the room, Jerry whispered to Anne,

"Y'all thought *I* was fucked up? *That* man isn't doing any better."

"Later, Jerry," Anne told him quietly. She wasn't going to talk about him with Lexi in the room and Gary still in the house. Jerry went to get some tea.

"Hey! Did y'all drink booze upstairs?" Anne asked accusingly, after smelling a familiar smell on Jerry.

"Yeah, a little. He wanted some Scotch."

"You are supposed to drink a glass of water between every drink of tea. Maybe you should have some after drinking Scotch."

"Oh, come on! I want some tea dammit!" he yelled.

"Fine! I won't worry about your blood sugar or your arteries or your other stuff. You eat and drink whatever you want and slow down all your essential organs and things. I'll stop trying to take care of you!"

Jerry, who was very tired of Anne monitoring his diet, went to the refrigerator and got a bottle of water. He guzzled it down, staring Anne in the eye the entire time. He drank the 20-ounce bottle of water so fast that it gave him a slight pain in his gut. He took the now empty bottle and put it in the sink for Anne to wash and reuse. He belched.

"Now? Now can I have tea?" he asked. She looked at him with amusement and disgust. She poured him a glass of tea.

While that went on in the kitchen, Gary was sneaking up behind Karen, in the office. He grabbed her arms and said,

"Boo!" She turned around and hit him.

"Fool, you should know better than all that! You don't go creeping up on folks in this house!"

"You didn't have to hit me! You ... what was ... hey! You stabbed me with your pen! I'm bleeding!"

Gary was astounded to see blood running down his arm, and he was beginning to realize that it hurt badly. Karen saw the blood and jumped up and to tend to him. She felt bad now. She inspected the wound and told him to hold on; she'd go get the first aid kit from the half bath. Gary sat down and looked mournfully at his arm. He wondered if he'd get some sort of poisoning from it. Karen returned quickly and put her retired nurse skills to use. She cleaned the wound and put a bandage over it. She kissed his cheek.

"Baby, I am so sorry. You know I wouldn't have stabbed you on purpose. You know that right?" she asked worriedly. He smiled at her pretty face, while he rubbed his arm. He hugged her.

"Yes, Karen. I know you didn't mean to stab me. It hurts like the devil, but I forgive you."

"Let me know if it gets infected or starts to ooze or anything."

"Well, okay, but I'll just hope that doesn't happen."

"Did you come all the way in here just to scare me?" she asked, oddly flattered.

"No. I came in here because I didn't want to leave without telling you goodbye first. It seemed tacky. But then you went and *stabbed* me."

"Hush your mouth. I hear you're filling in for Brother Lawson."

"That I am. Are you going to be making it to morning services?"

"If you're gonna be preaching, I guess I can arrange to come. You do that well enough."

"Well, thank you. It's nice to know I have a fan club," Gary joked.

"You know I've *always* been in your ol' fan club. Everything you do, you do well. Don't go acting all surprised and embarrassed. You know it's true enough."

"I wasn't a good husband. I didn't do *that* well," he said this quietly, with an odd look on his face. Karen stepped back and studied his face.

"What are you talking about? You talking about Kylie or Charlotte?"

"Charlotte. I wasn't really a great husband to her."

"Let me talk to you about Charlotte. You were a good husband. She wasn't a good wife. I knew her during all of that, baby. And I can tell you that being a mama and wife were not big priorities for her. Why are you talking all this nonsense over 40 years later? Why do you look like that? What's happening?" Karen asked. Jerry had been good to talk to, but he kind of lacked the practical advice he was getting from Karen.

"I already talked to Jerry about it," he tried shrugging it off but looked purely miserable.

"It don't look to me like it helped so much."

"I'm not comfortable getting into it with many people, Karen. It's difficult."

"Will it go away if you don't get into it with many people?"

"No," he admitted. Karen raised her eyebrows at him. Gary sighed and briefed Karen. She shook her head at him.

"Listen to yourself. That woman is your dead ex-wife. She is not an option. You are making it sound as if you are wanting to give her a second shot! Do you see how crazy that all sounds? I'm going to tell you this, Jerry might *seem* like the ideal one to talk to about this because of his messed-up relationship with Faye. But it's just the opposite. *He* isn't going to tell you you're crazy, because he's crazy, too! You are both romantically involved with your dead wives, fool. You talk to his ass about it and start listening to him? You'll be double dating over a Ouija board before the week is over! You need to stop listening to him *now*."

"I didn't think about it like that. He knew I was upset and offered to let me come up and talk about my problems. So, I did. I'm glad; I enjoyed our talk."

"But what did y'all decide?"

"Nothing. He said I shouldn't let this screw up my relationship with Kylie. He kinda pointed out how his relationship with Faye has affected his relationship with Marilyn."

"I imagine his relationship with Anne doesn't help his relationship with Marilyn either. But that's just my opinion," Karen pointed out. Gary nodded.

"Yes, that's just your opinion and neither here nor there. We aren't talking about Jerry and Anne, Karen. Do I need to take a strap to you, *too*? I've already had enough of Kylie's incessant gossiping. I can see that breaking her of it is going to be a process. What is the matter with you people? I have said this over and over again. If it is something that you wouldn't want them to know you said, then obviously it's something that should have never been said in the first place."

"Well, that's the thing right there. I have no problem telling that old fool that I imagine his mooning all over Anne probably pisses Marilyn off. I ain't saying nothing I don't want him to know I said. Go get him; I'll tell him right now."

"No, we won't get into all of that. Quit getting all spastic; you get loud when you get worked up. They're gonna hear you all the way in the kitchen. Hush now."

"Anyway, I think you need to go get your head examined. That ain't right and you know it's not right. But you know what I think? Do you even care?" Karen asked.

"Go for it."

"I think it's all just nerves. I think you're spending entirely too much time getting all worked up over this new wife and baby and you're just remembering how shitty it was *before*. That's what I think. And you know what? It may *have* been shitty before, but that don't mean it's gonna be this time too. Kylie isn't all strung out on all that garbage. She isn't gonna be hanging out with friends all the time instead of raising that baby because, well, she doesn't even *have* very many, does she? I mean, she doesn't seem to ever do very much unless it's with you. That's what I think. I think you have just thought so much about this that you've gotten your britches in a bunch. Stop it, now. You're a big boy ... and a right good looking one too. You are getting married and having a baby and that's all there is to it."

"Well, now that you have explained it with absolutely zero compassion, I understand fully. Thank you, dearest," he said with mock gratitude. Karen knew he was being sarcastic but just smiled lovingly at him.

"You're welcome baby. That's what you needed; someone who would tell you like it is, not sugarcoat it and tell you what you want to hear. Now as for that comment you made about taking a strap to me? That might could be arranged." Karen smiled wickedly. Gary laughed, shaking his head.

"Y'all are the horniest, most messed up women I've ever come across. This house does it to y'all, I do believe. Thanks. I'm gone, I guess. Kylie will be getting off soon and I'm tired. I'll catch you later, princess."

Gary hugged Karen and kissed her cheek. She returned both, smiling at him calling her *princess*. He had begun calling her that while they were having their totally inappropriate (but quite fun) affair. Gary went home.

Faye had been active during the day. She eavesdropped on the conversation that went on between Gary and her husband. Faye wondered if Gary's problem was a result of just paranoia or a dead ex-wife who wouldn't let him move on. Faye saw that as completely different from her own relationship with her own widowed husband. Faye wasn't Jerry's ex-wife. She was his deceased wife, and that was just different. She wondered if crazy old Charlotte was actually haunting Gary in his dreams? Charlotte didn't seem the type to haunt to Faye. But there was a time Charlotte also didn't seem the type to get strung out on heroin. So, Faye didn't know. Maybe it was like Jerry and Karen said; maybe Gary was just paranoid after what he'd been through.

Faye then eavesdropped on Gary and Karen. Faye was dead, but she was convinced that even dead, she still had more sense than anyone in this house. Karen was still sweet on Gary. Faye firmly believed this. Oh, Faye didn't think it was necessarily *love*, but there was definitely something still stuck in the cracks there. Faye knew about Gary's crush on Karen forever ago. That comment Karen made about Gary taking a strap to her? Yeah.

When Jerry, Faye, and Gary had been in seventh grade, Karen was in 10th. There had been one afternoon, a big crowd of them were spending the day playing in the creek. Faye, Jerry, Roy, Karen, Leon Addams, Charlotte, Virginia Thomas (a friend of Karen's from school), Gary, Mamie Lowery and a few others were having a fine time that day!

Faye had looked over at Gary, who was only 12 years old, and saw the look of admiration on his face as he checked out Karen in her red swimsuit. Karen was petite but well developed already. Faye giggled at Gary's goony behavior. That was no big deal though; after all, he was only 12 and had a really, bad haircut. However, once Gary entered high school, he flirted with Karen shamelessly. He always sat in her section when she was waitressing at the diner. In 10th grade, Jerry told Faye that Gary had confessed he thought he was in love with Karen. He went so far as to call her house and hang up on her when she answered (this was in the days before caller ID). Yes, Gary had been sweet on Karen for quite a while, and Faye was pretty sure he still was.

Gary got home and saw Kylie's car was already home; this surprised him because she'd been staying at work later the past week or so. They were rearranging the pharmacy (again), and she often stayed late to help. He missed her. He thought with her being pregnant, she'd be home more. He didn't know why he thought that; he just did. He'd spent so much time alone, once Kylie came into his life, he wanted her around all the time. He began to wonder how this was going to work out once the baby came. He suddenly had a horrible thought; what if she intended to put the child in daycare?

Before he got too worked up, he went in the trailer. Kylie was sitting on the couch, talking on the phone. She had her shoes off and was looking quite comfortable. When he shut the door behind him, she turned quickly to see him.

"Hey, Angie? Listen, Gary just ... I know, right? But hey ... I know! She's totally going to get it. He's never going to go for it. She is totally smoking something if she thinks he's going to fall for it. He'll bust her; just wait. Anyway, yeah, I know. Anyway, Gary is here. I need to let you go ... I don't know. I'll think about it. So, let me call you back later. I need to go talk to him. But it's been great. I'll talk to you later ... okay ... okay ... okay ... yeah ... no ... okay. Bye."

Kylie hung up the phone and turned to smile at Gary, who was looking rather irritated. She was surprised. She stood up and went to him to get a hug and kiss. He gave her both but didn't seem happy about it.

"What's the matter with you?" she asked.

"I'm not getting into it again right now."

"Getting into what? What's wrong?" she pressed, as she followed him into the kitchen. He took orange juice from the refrigerator, poured a glass, and sat at the island bar.

"Kylie, I spent over 40 years telling Jason to not talk about people. I have let it be known that I do not approve of gossiping about people. I heard all kinds of shit being said about Charlotte, Jason, and Jerry. I do not like it. When it was my family being talked about, I didn't like it. When it was my dearest friend in the world, I did not like it. Therefore, I'd never do that to anyone else. You are simply *going to have to stop.*"

"We were just talking about Paige; she's totally having an affair with Rod. It's just a matter of time before …" she began. Gary was astounded. He couldn't believe that after what he'd just said, she started gossiping again! He interrupted her.

"I think one of the problems I had in my first marriage was that I didn't have expectations of Charlotte. When nobody has expectations of you, you tend to slack. This time around *is* going to be *different.* If you insist on acting like a child, I'll talk to you like you're a child. Listen carefully; you will not continue to talk about people. If you are going to be my wife, and have my child, then there are a few things that you are going to work on, and that is a big one. I will put up with some things. I will compromise on some things. I will look in the other direction about some things. But I will not compromise on this. Rest assure; if it keeps up, I will resort to finding ways to teach you a lesson. Let's not let it get to that point. Agreed?" he asked a glaring Kylie.

"Agreed," she said but without enthusiasm.

Dating Gary had been a different experience for her. He was the first much older man she'd ever dated. Therefore, his standards and expectations of people were a bit different from what she was used to.

Even her dad had not been this anal. Gary Connelly, she had always known, *was* that anal.

Kylie remembered when he busted her brother for playing his music too loud in his car. He'd also given her brother a ticket for the pipes on his car, saying his car was too loud. He'd banned the use of *lawnmowers and like equipment* on Sundays. He gave out three $150 tickets to guys who were wearing their jeans too low and showing their boxers and underwear. After the third ticket was given, guys started making sure their jeans were pulled up though.

Gary put up with very little. Gary had no problem at all fining you if you didn't follow the rules. And *if* the townsfolk were relieved when he retired, they needn't have been. No, because somehow (everyone knew how), Gary still had just as much say now as he did when he was the chief of police. If Gary had a problem with the way something was being handled, somehow, it was always handled to Gary's satisfaction. Yes, it was one of *those towns*.

Kylie had always thought that Gary was cute, though. He had not known this, but when she was in ninth grade, she developed somewhat of a crush on him. This happened while he was filling in for Brother Lawson for a couple of weeks. His hair was so dark, and his eyes were so green she could see them from the second pew. He wore a dark suit and his muscular frame looked fabulous in it. She felt bad for hoping that Brother Lawson kept his flu for another week, but she did. Her friends thought she was weird when she confessed her crush on the preacher police chief. When she referred to him as *the hot, sexy preacher daddy,* well, they thought she had lost her mind.

Teenagers in Liberty Creek often didn't like Gary because he kept them in line. Parents and adults in general liked Gary very much *because* he kept the teenagers in line. This was amusing to most of them, however, because growing up Gary was notorious for getting into trouble.

His own father had even arrested him one night, making him and Jerry spend the night the jail. That night he and Jerry had broken into the Masonic Lodge.

But Gary was still Gary. He had grown up in an extremely religious household. His own father was a stern, serious man who, in addition to being, the preacher at Liberty Creek Baptist, was an officer for the Liberty Creek Police Department. He had been Gary's inspiration as far as being a cop. Gary, however, had always insisted he'd not grow up to be the overzealous religious type. Growing up, he couldn't stand living in a religious household. His parents picked apart his music, his friends, and his interest in girls. They were purely appalled that he got his girlfriend pregnant, not long out of high school. And, to add insult to injury, it had been that Charlotte Banks girl, who was wicked and tacky in their opinion. Gary spent most of his life being lectured, being punished, and apologizing for things he wasn't the least bit sorry for doing. Then, he became a single father, with a drug addict ex-wife. Suddenly all the things that his parents had lectured about all those years began to make sense to him.

Kylie knew these things about him, and she understood these things. It didn't make it any easier, adjusting to these things, though. He was obviously in a bad mood today, and she didn't feel that what she had to tell him was going to make his mood any better.

"Gary, listen. They think he's going to be okay, but Brother Lawson had another heart attack this afternoon. Dana called me. They're running tests but think he's going to have to have surgery. This one, well, it was bad. That's why I went ahead and came home, to talk to you. He's going to be out for a long time. You need to decide, I guess, what to do about filling in for him. I know we were just thinking it'd be a two or three-week thing. I really think it's going to be a lot longer than that. He's no spring chicken, baby. He's 86. He may never make it back to preaching. So, now you know. I guess you just need to decide what to do. Does the church need to start looking for another preacher, do you think?" Kylie asked quietly. She knew he was already stressed about things. He was stressed about the idea of preaching for just a short period; she didn't know how he'd handle this.

"He's really so bad off?" he asked quietly.

"He really is. I'm sorry. Look, he might be able to come back, but it'd be awhile if they're going to have to do the surgery. If he has to have surgery, it can take six or eight weeks before he starts feeling better. It could take six *months* before he actually feels the full benefits of the procedure. So, what do you want to do?"

"Um, I guess I'll preach for now. I told him I'd help him out. I've done it before. It's no big deal. I mean, I wasn't expecting it to go on for that long, but ... he might be okay enough to come back. I'm tired today though. What is going on with supper? I want to go to bed after supper."

"The pot pie stuff has been in the crock pot since this morning. It should be ready to go ahead and put in the crust."

"Excellent. I'm going to take a shower. How are you feeling? Everything okay?"

"It's fine. Gary?" she asked as he was popping aspirin. He took a swig of water and looked her, tiredly. He looked older now than he had just 10 minutes ago.

"What is it, baby?" he asked.

"I'm sorry."

"For what?"

"Well, I'm sorry that you're having to deal with this right now. I know that you've got your mind on stuff. I don't know what, but you seem distracted and unhappy. But I'm also sorry that I made you mad about the thing with Paige and Rod. I know you hate it when people talk about others. A lot of people just don't see it like you do."

"Regarding Paige and Rod and a lot of people not seeing it like I do. I have no control over what other people do or how they see things. I do, however, have control in my own house. I've made it painfully clear what my expectations are. Gossiping will not be tolerated in my family. There is nothing else to say about that.

"Regarding me having things on my mind, yes. I have things on my mind. I'm dealing, though. It'll be fine."

"Hey, is it about the baby? Or me? You seemed okay until just about a week ago. And that's when I started talking about fixing up a bedroom for the baby. I was just wondering if everything is okay about the baby."

"If you are asking, do I still love and want the baby, the answer is yes. There's just a lot going on in my head; it's not you or the baby. It's just everything altogether and I'm having to sort stuff, prioritize, and all that. Okay?" he asked, taking her hands in his own.

"Okay. So, what about what I asked you about the other day? About the wedding?"

"If that is when you want to have it, we can have it then. Jason wants to have the reception at their place, so I do need to tell them a day. So, first Saturday in May? That's when you want to do this?"

"Yes, I want to do it before I start showing."

"Okay, I'll talk to him about it. I thank you for putting it off until May though. Like I said, April is still a very bad month for Jerry."

"No problem. So, you're going to preach?"

"Yes, Kylie," he answered. He was so tired.

Kylie just nodded, and Gary went to shower. Kylie sat in the living room and thought. She loved Gary; he came into her life when she really did need someone, even just an old friend. He gave her everything that she needed in life to help her move forward during her mother's demise. But he was also an incredibly good-looking, retired police chief in his 60s. That was cool. She was marrying a still very influential ex police chief. He was kinky, crazy, funny, and full of life. He was just a crazy guy who she'd kinda-sorta known forever. Now, she was marrying a *preacher*?

She could hear Gary fumbling around in the kitchen for something. She just stayed there on the couch thinking. She looked across the room at his huge gun case. Kylie thought about Gary's impressive arsenal of guns and his ridiculously huge collection of knives. She thought about his shaved head and usual outfit of black T-shirts, jeans, and boots. She thought about his NRA bumper stickers. She thought about the fact that he smoked weed (often) and that he frequently drank Scotch. She thought about the other night when he spent the entire evening cleaning his guns. That didn't sound like a preacher. She worried that Gary was going to change, now.

But then, Gary came in the living room and stood in front of her. He was completely naked, with a big cigar in his mouth, a glass of Scotch in his hand, and asked her if she wanted to join him in the shower. Kylie smiled at her fiancée. She decided she didn't have anything to worry about; Gary would always be Gary.

CHAPTER 12

Tuesday night, Laurie was on the phone with Stacia, giving her the good news.

"We can do it. Dad had to ask Lex first because I don't know why, but he did, and she doesn't care! So, tomorrow night, we'll all ride up to my dad's, and we might be able to even stay more than one night. I mean, obviously I can, but they might let y'all spend the night more than just tomorrow night," Laurie bubbled over excitedly.

"So, are we going to do what we talked about?"

"Of course! I already talked to Jennifer. It's totally all set."

"This is going to totally kick ass! I can't wait! How are we going to get up there?"

"I'll ask my grandfather to take us. He goes up there all the time anyway."

"Do you think he'd take all of us then?"

"Yeah, he does everything I ask him to do. He'll do it."

"Well, if you say so. I'll let mom know then. I'm going to call Jennifer real quick. I'll call you back later, okay?"

"Okay. I'll call Poppy."

Stacia called Jennifer while Laurie dialed her grandfather. He was helping Kylie with the dishes after dinner when his phone rang. He tossed the towel on the counter and answered his phone.

"Hello?"

"Hey, Poppy. Listen, I was wondering … would you be willing to drive me and a couple of friends up to Dad's tomorrow?"

"Who's going? What for? Does your daddy and Lexi know about it?"

"Yes, sir. I'm having friends spend the night there tomorrow night. Dad and Lexi said it's okay."

"Who are these friends?" Gary asked suspiciously.

Laurie sighed.

"Jennifer and Stacia. Come on ... will you?"

"I don't like Jennifer, but you insist on hanging out with her. Alright. What time do you want me to pick you up?"

"Three o'clock?"

"Fine. Be ready though."

"Thank you, Poppy. How are you doing today?" she decided to add. She didn't want to sound like she'd only called for a favor, even if it was true. Laurie truly, loved Gary. She had liked him even before she and Jason had started talking and spending time together. Gary sank into the kitchen chair.

"Oh, I'm okay. Just tired and a lot going on. How are you, dear?"

"I'm okay, I guess. How's Kylie?"

"She's okay. Hey? When are you wanting me to take you shooting? You keep talking about learning to shoot a gun. I told you to just let me know when."

"Saturday? Or Sunday? Would one of those be okay?"

"Well, either is fine."

"Hey, let's do it Sunday then. Can't we go practice with Uncle Will and Anne?"

"Yeah, don't see why they'd mind. Hey, Brother Lawson had another heart attack today. It looks like I'm going to be filling in for him for a while."

"So, you're going to be, like, preaching?"

"Yeah, it looks like."

"Well, I guess that's cool. I mean, I'm sorry he's sick," Laurie said, awkwardly.

She had never attended church regularly. Once in a blue moon her mom would go, but it was not enough to even remember. Her mother said that her own family had simply never been church-goers. It wasn't that Laurie would have minded going; all her friends went. Honestly, it felt to Laurie like her family was the *only* family in Liberty Creek that *didn't* go.

"Well, I'm sorry he's sick too. I thought it'd just be for a few weeks, but it looks like it may be much longer. Either way, we'll just pray he gets better soon," Gary said.

"Yeah, that sucks. But I'll bet you do a good job. You are good at acting like that."

"Good at acting like what?" Gary asked.

"You know, preachy or preacherish."

"I'm afraid I'm not quite sure how to take that," Gary replied, indignantly.

"Oh, it's not a *bad* thing. You just lecture us about how we act and what we say and all that. You have rules about what you should and shouldn't do on Sunday. You say the blessing and pray and all that. You're, well, preacherish. That's all." She couldn't understand why he was acting all offended. You'd think a preacher would be happy to know he was preacherish.

"Alright, Laurie. Anyway, be ready at three tomorrow."

"Thank you, Poppy. Or do I call you Reverend Poppy? Or Brother Poppy?" she teased. At this, Gary found himself smiling.

"Just Poppy is fine, dearest. I'll see you tomorrow."

"Alright. Night-night. I love you."

"I love you, too. Goodnight."

Laurie went in the kitchen and told her mother that yes, she could have a sleepover at Jason's and yes, Gary would give them all a ride up to the farm. Then, she told her mother about Gary becoming the substitute preacher at Liberty Creek Baptist. Stacy Mitchell listened as her daughter explained the situation. She didn't say anything, really. She said she hoped Brother Lawson recovered. Even though she didn't attend church (she had her reasons) she knew who Brother Lawson was. He was a kind old man, and she truly hated to hear he was bad off.

Laurie went to her bedroom and did what 15-year-old girls do. She turned her music on too loud and read a magazine that her mother didn't know she had. This magazine had all kinds of great things:

fashion, makeup, celebrities, relationships, and sex. The parts Laurie liked the best were the parts about fashion, makeup, and sex though.

Laurie hadn't tried this sex thing out yet; she was only 15. But when she started hanging out with boys, her mother got paranoid. Laurie's father was Jason Connelly after all. Stacy was no fool; she knew girls were doing things they shouldn't be doing at Laurie's age. Everyone in town knew that horrible Jennifer girl was dropping her jeans on dates. So, at Laurie's 15-year checkup, Stacy just went ahead and decided she'd rather be safe than sorry. She got Laurie on birth control, an act that resulted in a very belligerent, loud, angry Jason calling Stacy on the phone while she was at work.

But Laurie often thought, if she was on the pill *anyway*, but she still hadn't gotten up the nerve yet. She hung out with a few different guys from school. The unfortunate part was her grandfather, right there in town, knew who *every single one of them* were. Everyone knew Gary was her grandfather, and so half of the guys at her school were too scared to date her.

She had gone to the diner with Randall Wedgeworth one night, and Gary had come in. Laurie thought Randall would die right there. His eyes darted around the diner as if he were looking for an escape route. Gary came to the table and spoke politely to his granddaughter and her friend. Laurie didn't see what the problem was. Her grandfather was sweet as could be. But what Laurie didn't see was what her grandfather did behind her, as he was leaving. Randall saw what her grandfather did, though. He saw Gary look directly at him. He saw Gary smile, point his finger at Randall, then point at Laurie, then pat the gun on his hip, wink, and leave.

Randall watched the six-foot Gary stroll out of the diner. He wore jeans and a black police department t-shirt with boots. No, Laurie didn't have to worry about using her birth control pills because of Randall! He had heard they weren't 100 percent effective and he had absolutely no intention of being the one to accidentally get *that* man's granddaughter pregnant!

It was frustrating for poor Laurie. She wanted to start dating and experiencing all these things she kept hearing and reading about, but her grandfather had terrified every guy in Liberty Creek out of even holding her hand in public.

Laurie was reading an especially interesting article about women sharing the kinkiest thing they had ever done when her mother knocked on the door. Laurie threw her blanket over the magazine. She called her mother in the room. Her mother came in and gestured for Laurie to turn her music down, so she did. Stacy sat on the edge of the bed.

"Listen, I wanted to talk to you about something. I think that maybe, since your grandfather is going to be preaching there for a while, it'd be nice if you went to his services," she said carefully. Laurie looked at her puzzled.

"You mean, I have to start going to church? I thought you said Dad shouldn't try pressuring me to go just because they go. But because Poppy is preaching now, I should?"

"Why not, Laurie? You love him, and he's doing a good thing. Even if your daddy and I didn't always get along, I've always liked your grandfather. I think it'd just be the respectful thing for his own family to attend his services. And considering all that's been going on around here lately, maybe it'd be a good idea for you to go to church."

"It's not your fault, Jack leaving. You know he's just a jerk. I don't know why you want him to come back. He treats us both like crap. He's a bully redneck."

"Laurie, I'm not getting into all of this right now. I don't expect you to understand. It wasn't your relationship, and it wasn't your problem, so you just can't …"

"Excuse me? Um, yes, it was my problem. When you two fight all the time, and he screams and cusses us, slaps us around, and screws around on you? It is totally my problem. Why do parents think that just because *they* are fighting with *each other*, the *kids* aren't a part of it? That is so stupid! *Of course*, we're a part of it when y'all act like that. And now, knowing that you are wanting him to come *back* here?

"What am I supposed to do? Listen to the fighting and crying again? Go back to wondering what to expect when I come home from school? I hate him. I can't understand what you ever saw in him. Why in the world did you leave Daddy for that asshole? I mean, *what* were you *thinking*?" Laurie was angry now, and what made her so angry was her mother suggesting *Laurie* go to church, when *she* was knowingly trying to convince her abusive husband to come back home to them!

Stacy glared at Laurie.

"That is enough. You need to watch your mouth. Its growing faster than the rest of you. I will not be talked to like that by my own daughter."

"Oh, I'm sorry. You'll only be willing to be talked to like that by your own *husband*. You know what? I hate y'all. I hate the so-called relationship y'all have. You guys have made me *miserable*! I have even talked to Miss Beales about y'all! That is how miserable y'all have made me! I go to her, like every single week, and talk about y'all! She knows about y'all! Yeah! You think the crap that goes on in here is a *secret* and nobody knows? She knows! Don't look at me like that! I had to have *someone* to talk to! I sure as hell couldn't ever talk to my own *mom*! I've been talking to Miss Beales about your screwed-up relationship since sixth grade! Almost four years! She knows *everything*! Whatever! Do what you want, but if Jack comes back here, I'm leaving."

"Excuse me?"

"If you let Jack come back here, I'm leaving. I'll go stay with Daddy. I'll go stay with Poppy and Kylie. I have places to go. In fact, as soon as he left you, I was *glad.* I felt like I could finally move on and quit pretending to think of him as a parent. You tell me, oh, he's the one who's taken care of us all these years. *I don't care.* He didn't think *too* much of me. He never tried to even adopt me. I've lived with him my entire life and he never even talked about the adoption thing. I lived with my mom and the only dad I knew for 14 years, and I didn't even have either of y'all's last name.

"Well, you know what? I don't want your maiden name anymore. *You* don't even want your maiden name anymore. I want my father's last name. You stay Stacy Mitchell. I'm done being Laurie Raymond. I'm going to talk to Daddy tomorrow about changing my name to Connelly. I'm going to be like my friends and have my dad's last name. I'm tired of being your bastard kid." Laurie pulled her magazine out from under her blanket and started looking at it.

"What are you reading? *Cosmopolitan*? Have you lost your mind? You don't need to be reading *Cosmo* yet! I've told you, there are magazines for girls your age, and this is not one of them! Laurie! Are you listening to me?"

"Don't worry about it, Mom. I'm gonna start going to church, remember? I'll be forgiven."

"You are getting way out of line, girl!"

"I don't care. I'm tired of all of this. Jack leaves, and suddenly, you're all interested in my life and asking questions about my friends and guys I like and whether-or-not I go to Hell? You never gave a damn about how I felt or what I was doing or *anything*. You never wanted to be bothered with it. I mean, come on! It was easier for you to just get me on the pill than it was for you to tell me reasons why I shouldn't screw someone? So, you give me the all-clear to fuck around but I'm *not* old enough to read *Cosmo*?" Laurie shouted. Her mother slapped her across the face.

"You went too far!" Stacy shouted back.

"No, *you* did! I heard you on the phone tonight, calling that asshole back! *Begging* him to come back! *You* went too far when *you* did *that!*" Laurie stood up and went to the bathroom. She locked the door and cried. She waited several minutes and cautiously opened the door. She could hear her mother in the kitchen, slamming cabinets.

At 11:47 p.m., Laurie crept to her bedroom and began stuffing a few crucial items into her backpack. Laurie grabbed the backpack, her hoodie, and turned her radio up loud again. She opened her window, crawled through it, and left in the night.

In the meantime, back on Teague Road, everything was very quiet. Marilyn and Jerry were lying in his massive tester bed, watching a movie. There were no blinking lights or doors opening and closing. They were just having a nice, quiet evening alone. Will and Anne had already gone to bed.

Earlier, at 8:30 p.m., Jerry had joined Will, Anne, Roy and Karen in putting the babies to bed. Roy had announced tonight that he felt he and Karen could go back to sleeping at home tomorrow night. They decided to go ahead and stay tonight though.

When the time came for Will and Anne to go to bed, Anne and Will both gave Jerry a hug and kiss goodnight. Marilyn watched with interest. She found it unusual, but incredibly touching that a man Will's age, with Will's obnoxious, dominating personality, would be so openly affectionate and loving towards his dad. Will's kiss on his dad's cheek was too sweet for words.

Will and Anne had been sitting at the table with Marilyn and Jerry, talking about their day. Jerry had his cheese and crackers in front of him. Anne had prepared these for him because he hadn't felt like eating supper that night. After about an hour, Will and Anne decided to call it a night. What Marilyn then saw changed everything she had thought about these people and their relationships.

Will and Anne stood up, and Will went to his father's side, leaned forward and hugged him tight and kissed his scruffy cheek. They exchanged goodnights and love yous. Then it was Anne's turn; she went to Jerry's side, leaned forward, and hugged him tight and kissed his scruffy cheek. They, too, exchanged goodnights and love yous. Marilyn felt as if she were watching two kids telling their dad goodnight.

It was as simple as that. Will then came over to Marilyn, hugged her neck, kissed her cheek, and told her goodnight. Anne hugged Marilyn and told her goodnight.

Marilyn wasn't sure what she had been expecting at bedtime in this house. But what she saw was not perverted or twisted. It was normal and sweet. She knew she had no way of knowing what went on in this house at bedtime, when she wasn't there, but she did know that there was no awkwardness or discomfort between these three people tonight. And the fact that Will and Anne had included her in their bedtime goodnight rounds made her feel very happy. It was also the second time that Will Granger had made her feel as if she had been accepted as one of them. She wasn't his mother, but she felt as though he had at least accepted her as his father's new love. Well, one of them anyway.

But now, it was going on midnight and the house was quiet, except for the television in Jerry's room. Even the spirits were keeping low tonight. There had been so many bad nights in this house, full of nightmares and tears and sickness. Tonight, however, everyone was content, feeling well (for the most part) and happy. Marilyn fell asleep in the crook of Jerry's arm.

Gary was resting peacefully, too, in his bedroom on Court Street. He was having no dreams of his ex-wife tonight; he wasn't dreaming at all. Kylie slept soundly through the night, unusual for her during this stage of her pregnancy. She had been battling nausea. Gary thought he kept hearing something in his sleep, but it was distant and muffled and he thought it wasn't real. But the phone ringing beside his bed was very real; it woke him with a start. He looked at his alarm clock and saw it was almost half past midnight. He looked at the phone in a panic. He just knew something horrible had happened. Otherwise, why would someone be calling him so late? Everyone knew he went to bed reasonably early.

The caller was Laurie. If she was calling him at 12:30 a.m. to ask about a ride to her damn slumber party, he'd personally go find her, right now, and beat her. He answered it.

"Laurie, if you are calling me about dragging your ass to your daddy's tomorrow, I am going to come beat you."

"Poppy? Are y'all awake?" Laurie asked.

"No, we are not awake. Why in the ..." he started.

"Well, I tried knocking and nobody answered, so I thought you might be asleep. That's why I just called," Laurie told him, sounding out of breath. He took just a moment to process this.

"You tried to knock?" he asked confused. What was she talking about? Then, he seemed to recall that odd noise in his sleep.

"I'm outside. I'm on your porch. I tried to knock on the door, but nobody answered," she repeated. He looked back at the clock, waking up more. He sat up in the bed.

"You're on my porch? It's 12:34 in the morning! What are you talking about you're on my porch? Are you serious?" he roared into the phone.

"Please don't yell at me. Can I please just come inside? Please?" she begged. He realized she sounded as if she were crying. He told her to hold on. He hung up the phone, got out of bed, and pulled on a pair of pajama pants.

"What's going on?" Kylie asked from her side of the bed.

"There's no telling. Just go back to sleep, baby. I've got it handled."

Gary walked through the dark double wide and turned the front porch light on before opening the door. Laurie sat on his porch chair with a backpack, crying. He looked at her curiously.

"Get in here. What is going on? Does your mama know where you are?"

"I left! And I am *not* going back there! I will not! And you can't make me! If you try to make me, I'll just go stay with Daddy!"

"Get in here." He took her arm and pulled her inside.

Laurie came in her grandfather's living room and tossed her backpack to the floor.

"Pick that up. Put it on the chair. We don't throw things on the floor here; you know better than that by now," Gary directed. Laurie picked up the bag and set it on the big leather recliner.

"Now, sit down and tell me what this is all about," Gary said tiredly. He sank onto his couch and rubbed his forehead. Laurie sat at the other end of the couch.

She reenacted the whole horrible, terrible situation, the phone call Stacy made to Jack, and the fight Laurie had had with her mother. Gary just listened to her rant until she appeared to be done. He sighed and sat up.

"So, you ran away from home? That's what you're telling me?"

"Yes, sir."

"It's after midnight, and your mother doesn't have a clue where you are?"

"Nope and have you noticed? She hasn't called you. She hasn't even called me! She obviously hasn't called Daddy because he'd have called you or me by now. She probably thinks I'm still home. She pays no attention to anything I do! Guess what? I sneak out all the time. Yeah, she doesn't have a clue! When Jack dumped her, suddenly she tries to act like Mom of the Year, pretending she cares about what's going on with me. It's like, once a week she remembers she has a kid."

"I'm going to ask you a few things, and I'm going to tell you a few things. I expect absolute honesty. If I find out you're lying to me to help your case, that car you were promised next year? Not even going to happen. And, if you're lying about anything, I will find out. I promise you that. I refuse to put up with a girl crying victim, only to find out she's taking advantage of the system. Do you hear me?"

"Yes, sir."

"Has Jack ever laid a hand on you, with exception of popping you on the butt, growing up? I'm not talking about little spanks. You know what I'm talking about. Has he really hit you?"

"He shoves and pushes me. He gets in my face, like inches away, and screams at me and stuff. He's gotten so close, he's like, spit on me while he yells at me. He hits Mom all the time. When he slaps Mom around and I can tell they're in there fighting, I go to my room."

"You know for a fact he has hit your mother?"

"Yes, sir."

"And she's trying to get him to come back home?"

"She's been begging him."

"And you don't want to be there if he's there?"

"No! I'm tired of how things always are when he's there."

"Okay, look, you need to call your mama," Gary began but was quickly interrupted by Laurie.

"No way! I don't want to call her!"

"Yes way. You will call her. It's just a matter of time before she realizes you've left. Then, she'll end up freaking out, calling your daddy, maybe even the cops. Let's not let it escalate to that point.

"Look, babycakes, if you are unhappy at your mama's, you are old enough to decide where you want to go. Jack has a terrible reputation in town; it's your word against his. You don't even have to have a reason at your age to move in with another relative. Long as we can provide you with supervision and a safe place to stay, you are fine. It's up to you if you stay here or at your daddy's. But you simply have got to call your mama. Do you want me to call her?"

"Would you?"

"Yes, I would. Let me get my phone." Gary stood to go get his telephone from the island counter. He sat back down beside Laurie and called Stacy, who was very surprised to get a phone call from him after midnight.

"What's going on, Gary?"

"Well, Laurie apparently had a falling out with you this evening?"

"Did she call you about that? I am going to go in there ..."

"No, she didn't. She came over to the house. She um snuck out. Listen, before you go getting your panties in a wad; she has every right at 15 to decide where she'd rather stay. She's gonna stay with me for the time being. I don't know yet if she'll want to stay in town or go stay with her daddy. But it is up to her at her age. She isn't happy there with Jack, and I can't say I blame her. He's a dick, Stacy. She feels your relationship with him is more important to you than your relationship with her. And, well, your daughter is begging you to not bring him back, and you are trying to anyway. So, I guess she's right."

"She's not staying there. She's being a spoiled brat."

"Stacy, not to be mean or anything, but right now, your husband is in the bed with Joan Ritchie. He's not in the bed with you. And the example y'all are setting isn't one to be admired. We can involve the courts if you want, but I don't think you want to. Things tend to go downhill really quick when kids are subjected to that kinda stuff."

Stacy was quiet for a moment. She agreed with him but didn't tell him so.

"She's staying with you?"

"For the time being, yes. We'll talk about it more, tomorrow. It's after midnight. I'm tired, and I want to go to bed. I still need to get her situated. So, let's pick this up tomorrow. Okay?"

"Yeah, fine. Hey? Would you let her know I love her?"

"Your child should already know such things, Stacy. But sure."

Gary hung up the phone and looked at Laurie, who sat on the couch watching him.

"Come here, love."

He held his hand out to her. She stood and walked over to him. He wrapped his arms around her, resting his chin on top of her head. He heard her start sniffling.

"Your mama said she loves you."

"I'm sorry I woke you up, Poppy."

"Oh, it's just silly ol' sleep. I get it every night. You should have said something to us before, Laurie. You should have never let it get this far. I take that back; you had your reasons for keeping quiet about it. Perhaps we just didn't give you reason to think you could talk to us quite yet about these kinds of things. But please ... in the future, if there is ever anything you need to talk about, talk to us about it. You can talk to me about *absolutely anything*. If you ever get yourself in a situation and you don't know how to get out of it, just tell me. I'll help you through *absolutely anything* you could throw my way. Alright? Do you trust me enough to promise me that you'll do that?"

"Yes, sir."

"I love you, Laurie."

"I love you, too. Can I sleep in here?"

"You wouldn't rather sleep in the guest room?"

"No, sir. I want to sleep in here, with the TV and the lights," she told him, looking somewhat frightened.

"Are you okay?"

"I just don't want to be in a dark, quiet, closed up room right now. So, can I?"

"Yeah. Keep the TV on, and the foyer light will be enough light to make you feel better, I'd think. You think?"

"Yes, sir." Laurie looked around awkwardly.

"Did you grab something to sleep in?"

"No, sir. I didn't grab any clothes at all, I don't guess."

"Let me go grab some of Kylie's pajamas for you. I'll drive you over to your mama's tomorrow, so you can pick up some clothes." Gary brought Laurie some pajamas, kissed her goodnight, and checked the locks. He went to bed. As he started for the hall, he turned and told his granddaughter,

"Hey, holler if you need anything tonight. Really. Goodnight. I love you."

Not quite 15 minutes later, Laurie got a text message on her phone from her mother. It didn't say she loved her, or that she was sorry, or that she wanted her to come home. It said, *I can't believe you told that woman at the school about our private lives all these years. Jack always said you were nothing but a shit starter, always wanting attention. Looks like he's right. What are we going to do with you?*

Laurie hugged the pillow Gary gave her tight and cried herself to sleep.

The next morning, Gary went to the living room and woke Laurie up. She opened her eyes and looked confused.

"Wake up, Laurie. It's time for breakfast. Kylie's setting the table. Go fix your hair and come on in the kitchen."

"Fix my hair?"

"Yes. I like people at my table to look nice. Go wash your face and brush your hair. Washing your face will help you wake up. Come on, now. It's almost nine."

It was spring break, and Laurie had gotten used to sleeping in until ten or so at least. But her grandfather stood over her waiting for her to get up. She dragged herself off the couch and stumbled down the hall. She realized she forgot her hairbrush, as well as her toothbrush and numerous other things. Her grandfather kept his head shaved down to the skin, so he was as bald as he could possibly be. He wasn't likely to have a hairbrush she could borrow. But Kylie probably would. She went ahead and washed her face first. She went to the kitchen and asked Kylie if she could use her brush.

"Yeah, of course. It's on the dresser."

Laurie felt weird going in her grandfather's bedroom, for some reason. She'd spent countless hours in his trailer and house since she and Jason started talking again. But she had never had many reasons to go in his bedroom. It was a neat, clean bedroom. The bed was already made and everything. She looked around the room for a moment and took the brush from the dresser top. She looked in the big mirror over the dresser, brushed her hair, and went to have breakfast with Gary and Kylie.

Kylie was a nice woman; Laurie liked her a lot. Laurie had to admit that she liked Kylie more than she liked Lexi. Kylie had red, shoulder-length, layered hair. She had a very fair complexion and had hazel almond shaped eyes. She was always smiling and just a very pleasant person to be around.

Lexi, on the other hand took everything personally. Lexi seemed to always be suspicious of everything and always overreacted about everything. It never mattered what Laurie said Lexi would want to know what she had meant by it. It was just exhausting being around Lexi for very long. She kept trying to like Lexi, but it wasn't always easy. Laurie felt like she was in the way at her dad's house because Lexi made her feel like she was.

This morning, Kylie, wearing a long, fluffy light green bathrobe, acted like it was nothing at all unusual for Laurie to be there. Kylie talked and visited and chatted away. Gary said very little. He looked stressed out. He finally spoke up.

"Listen, Laurie, we're going to go get you some of your clothes and things after breakfast. You don't have to make any permanent decisions right this minute, but where are you aiming to stay? Here? Your daddy's? Have you thought about this at all?"

"Well, my friends are all here, and school, and, well, I love Dad and all, but I don't think I really want to live there all the time. I mean, they're always busy and between Caleb and Teague ... I don't know. The thing is, me and Lexi don't always get along so great. I can handle her okay on weekends and stuff like that. But I just ..."

She didn't know how to finish this. What if Gary and Kylie didn't even want her to stay here, with them? Kylie was expecting her first baby and was going to be a newlywed. This might be a really bad time to have a 15-year-old move in.

"You don't want to stay with your daddy then? That's what you're saying?"

"Well, is that okay? Is it alright if I don't want to stay up there? I don't want him to be offended or anything."

"Is that what you're worried about?"

"Well, and I mean I don't know if y'all really want ... well, like I know I didn't exactly ask if I even could come here. I just kinda showed up. So, I don't know if it's going to be a problem, you know, me being here."

"Oh, good grief! Don't worry about that!" Kylie exclaimed, smiling.

"No, don't worry about that. If I had a problem with it, I'd have not given you options. As for your daddy, well, we'll just say that you wanna stay in town where your friends are and everything. You've lived in town all your life, have a social life here, school. He'll understand. We don't have to tell him you don't want to stay with Lexi."

He almost told her to try to work on the thing with Lexi but changed his mind. Lexi was not the easiest person to get along with. He loved her dearly; he loved her as if she were his own. He'd known her ever since Jason began dating her in high school. But she was highly emotional, easily offended, easily triggered.

"Okay then. I guess I want to stay here. If that's really okay with y'all."

"It is, but we have some things to talk about."

"Like what?" Laurie asked.

"Oh, I don't know! How about when you told me last night that you sneak out your window all the time? Heads up; things you got away with at your mom's, you won't get away with here. If you even try to test me, you will find yourself locked up tighter than a tick, my dearest. You will not sleep all day, and there is a curfew at night. Homework will be done before doing anything fun and you will be expected to do your part around here. No friends inside if Kylie or I aren't home. I'm sure I'll think of a few more things."

"Goody," Laurie said sarcastically. Gary just smiled.

The rest of that day wasn't a very pleasant one for Laurie. Gary did take her to her mother's and waited in the living room while Laurie got her stuff. She was worried her mother would try to start something, so Gary came inside with her. Laurie put her belongings in bags, and Gary helped her carry the stuff to his truck. Her mother never even left the kitchen to talk to her.

That afternoon, Laurie and Gary picked up Jennifer and Stacia to take them up to Jason's. The girls' constant, incessant yammering and giggling made Gary's headache. From the moment he picked them up, they never shut up. He thought if he heard 'I'm just saying' or 'oh but you know what' or 'I know, right' or 'don't even' or 'no way' many more times, he'd pull over and make these girls walk.

He paid little attention to their conversation until Stacia mentioned Lance calling her. He snapped to attention at this. Lance Braye was 18 years old. Stacia was 15. Gary was not Stacia's father, so he couldn't really say anything about it. But well, he did anyway.

"Lance? Lance Braye? What is Lance Braye doing calling you? Have you lost your mind? You are 15 years old. He is 18. That makes him a legal adult, and you a minor and him a pervert. What can you possibly have in common with someone three years older than you? Do your parents know about this?"

Needless to say, Stacia said nothing. Laurie, however, came to her rescue.

"Oh, wow. Like, really? A three-year age difference bothers you that much and *you're* marrying someone like almost a quarter of a century younger than you? That is totally not fair. See? See? You adults do this *all the time*! Grown-ups are *all the time* doing this. So, like, it's okay when your all old and everything but it's not ok to love someone when you're 15 and 18? You know, maybe had you known Kylie better when she was 15, you'd have decided back then that you loved her, and you wouldn't have had to have waited all this time. Right? Right?

"You know, we are basically like, *women*. Yeah. We're practically *women* and y'all treat us like *children*. We know what love is, Poppy. We are all, practically, like adults. I really think it is time that we start getting the respect we deserve. I think we should be treated liked adults." Laurie said all this very indignantly.

Gary didn't like Kylie being referred to as almost a quarter of a century younger than him. That sounded much worse than 22 years. He resented Laurie scolding him in front of Stacia and Jennifer, too.

"Let me tell you something. When you are an adult you can make all the stupid decisions you want to. As long you live under my roof then you will not go getting involved with someone that is an adult. You are a kid, yes, a *kid*! Any man that is 18 years or older is an *adult*. And that is wrong. When you are 18 and he is 21, then you will both be adults and you can do whatever the hell you want. And Stacia, you had best pay close attention to what I just said. Lance is breaking the law if he so much as touches you. If he were to have sex with you ..."

"Poppy! Stop it! Oh gross! I cannot believe you just said that in front of my friends. I am dying. I am totally dying. Just never mind now. I don't even want friends. I don't want a boyfriend. I cannot believe you. They aren't even talking about doing that!" Which wasn't true at all, but Laurie felt she had to defend her friend somehow. Actually, they had discussed sex several times, according to Stacia.

"Well, you just remember what I said. I'll wear your young ass out if I ever find out you're cavorting with someone 18 or older. You just wait."

"*I'm* not doing anything! Stacia said Lance called *her*! You don't even know what it was about. But still! He wasn't calling *me*!"

"And he won't be," Gary muttered.

"You are so embarrassing," Laurie muttered back.

They drove the rest of the way to Jason's house in silence. When they got to the house, they all got out of the truck. Laurie took Gary by the arm and took him several feet away from the others. She looked up at him pleadingly with bright green eyes.

"Poppy, seriously now. Please, please, please, don't say anything to Daddy about any of what we talked about in the truck. Please? I'm really begging you. He isn't around me enough to understand those kinds of things yet. I mean, if you want to lecture me about it later, just do that. But please don't go getting him all mad about it. Please, Poppy?"

"Fine," Gary said sullenly.

"Oh, don't act like that. Really, look, I'm okay talking to you about it, just not Daddy. Not yet. And not in front of my friends. I cannot believe you said that stuff," she added. Gary glared at her. She looked at him with annoyance.

Of the men who had been in her life, Gary was the one she loved the most and trusted the most. Even during all those years when Laurie and Jason had nothing to do with one another, Laurie and Gary had somewhat of a relationship. Laurie's mother would always stop and visit with Gary for as far back as Laurie could remember. Stacy had been very open and honest with Laurie about who this man was; he was her grandfather. Laurie would often see him around town several times a week. She never really referred to him as Grandpa or Grandfather or anything, though. He was always just *sir*.

Laurie never understood why her mother disliked her father so much yet seemed ridiculously fond of his father. She questioned this several times only to be told repeatedly that she was too young to understand.

Laurie was very fond of Gary Connelly. He was always smiling and such a nice man. Yet, he was just that to her, a nice man. There was never any quality time spent with him because Stacy worried that Gary would let her hang out with Jason. This never seemed quite fair to Laurie. From the time she was born, Jack Mitchell was there. And Laurie was told to call him Daddy. But this man never acted like he liked her or loved her. He never acted like he wanted her around. He made her feel like she was in the way, a problem maker, and once he even told her that they'd have more money if it wasn't for her. But he was Daddy.

Divorce was a rare occurrence in Liberty Creek. It just didn't happen. The times it did, it was justified, and it was always a very last resort. Brother Lawson would go through great pains and endless hours of free therapy in a desperate attempt to keep couples together. But it did happen. Kayla Richards parents were an example.

Kayla was a good friend of Laurie's. They bonded in first grade. The older they got they would talk about the fact that they didn't really know their dads. Kayla's mother said horrible things about Shane Bowers. Kayla grew up believing these things, until one day in seventh grade.

Kayla's grandmother, her mom's mother, took Kayla aside and told her the truth. She told her that Kayla's mother had spent too many years making herself the victim and Shane the villain, and she wasn't going to put up with it anymore. She told Kayla that her father was a wonderful man and she hoped one day Kayla would try to get to know him.

Three weeks later, after school, Kayla went to the hardware store downtown where she knew her father worked. Much to Shane's surprise, they ended up visiting for almost 20 minutes. After that, Kayla told her mother that she felt she had a right to get to spend time with her own dad like all her friends got to do. She told her mom it didn't matter if *she* didn't like Shane; Kayla wanted to get to know him herself.

It was a process, and not a very easy one, but in time, Kayla and Shane began spending more and more time together. It was Kayla that encouraged Laurie to talk to Jason the next time she saw him. So, Laurie did. It just happened to be soon after Laurie had found out that Jason's mother had passed-away.

Now, Laurie and Jason had a much better relationship. He was feeling more and more like a dad to her. But there were 14 years of not speaking at all to make up for. Jason and Laurie spent much of their time together trying to figure the other one out. Jason was over eager, always quick to please her and always defending her rotten behavior. Laurie often felt bad about getting into spats with Lexi though; Laurie knew they were usually her own fault.

At the same time, it was nice to have so much of her dad's attention. She enjoyed the attention she got from the Grangers, and she truly-loved the attention she got from Gary, yes, even his obnoxious, overprotective ways.

She had come from a home where she had always been largely ignored. She didn't want to cause trouble. She just wanted some attention.

If she planned to stay with Gary, she'd have that. Gary would see to it that her every move was monitored and that no boy in Liberty Creek would ever touch her. Kylie would have to chill him out a bit because Gary could be a little bit, well, obsessive about things. Kylie also knew that Gary had never had much use for Jack and Stacy Mitchell.

Laurie's confession to Gary about what it was like growing up in the Mitchell house had not gone over well with Gary. He'd never liked them but had long ago decided it was him simply judging them because of how Stacy had treated Jason. Now, he knew differently. Now, he knew he had other reasons to not like them. This afternoon, Laurie had shown him the text message Stacy had sent her runaway daughter the night before.

Gary had mixed feelings about Marilyn Beales's involvement in all of this. Part of him felt if she had known it was so bad for Laurie at home, why had she not done something about it? On the other hand, Gary wanted to kiss Marilyn on the mouth for being there for Laurie all these years. And Jason still didn't know a thing that had happened.

Laurie stood on her tiptoes and pulled Gary's neck down, so she could give him a kiss on the cheek. She hugged him tight.

"I love you, Poppy."

"I love you, baby girl."

He watched the three giggling teenaged girls go up the front porch steps of the big farmhouse, dragging backpacks and pillows with them. He slowly followed them inside. Once inside, he felt foolish because Jason would be in the stable this time of day, not hanging out in the house. So, he went to the stable, dreading the conversation he was about to have with Jason.

It would be awkward telling Jason that Laurie wanted to live with him, instead of with her own father; even with the very legitimate reasons they had come up with to spare Jason's feelings. He went in the stable and found Jason.

CHAPTER 13

Wednesday afternoon at lunch, it was quiet. Lexi had elected to stay at her own house since she knew Laurie would be arriving with company that afternoon. Marilyn, Jerry, Karen, Roy, Will, and Anne ate lunch with James and Eliza.

Will had come inside and had gone to the living room to retrieve the children. When he came back to the kitchen, everyone else had already gathered around the big old table. Anne looked up at him as she filled glasses with tea.

"What took you so long?" she asked. Will just smiled. He looked bright eyed and kind of sappy. It reminded Anne of his expression when she told him she was pregnant. He wasn't looking at Anne this time, though. He was looking at Jerry this way.

"Daddy, you aren't going to town Friday night," he told Jerry, looking fairly-ready to burst. Jerry just looked at Will. He looked confused. Marilyn looked confused, too.

"Why aren't I?" Jerry asked.

"I just saw on television (Will didn't even say T.V; Will said the whole word) that a certain movie is going to be on Friday night. Can you guess what movie that is?" Will teased.

He looked purely in love. His weird behavior certainly had Anne's attention. Jerry looked thoughtful for just a moment before looking at Will in disbelief.

"You don't mean ... no. You don't mean *that's* coming on?" Jerry asked, his enthusiasm beginning to grow. Will nodded.

"Yep. *That's* coming on! *Arthur*! Can you believe it? It's been, like, forever!"

"Oh, man! *Arthur*? Yeah, it's been *years*! Oh, man! Well, hell, yeah I'm staying home on Friday night!" Jerry was obviously excited. But Will wasn't done.

"But that's not the best part! It's not *just Arthur* that's coming on! After *Arthur*, they are going to have a *Dustin Hoffman marathon*! It's kicking off with *Tootsie* and *Kramer vs Kramer!* There's going to be more! They're just kicking off with those two!" Will was so excited now that he was gesturing with his hands. Jerry looked absolutely ecstatic.

"Ohhh, do you suppose they'll show *The Graduate?*"

"Well, what Hoffman marathon would be complete without *that*? Of course, they'll show *that!*" Will responded, acting as though Jerry should have known better.

Anne had long known about Will and Jerry's abnormal shared obsession with Dustin Hoffman. She liked Dustin Hoffman and all; she didn't have any animosity toward the man or anything. However, she was surprised that any channel would really have a movie marathon in his honor. And it followed an almost 40-year-old Dudley Moore movie? What a weird lineup for a Friday night.

"Dustin Hoffman marathon? Did he die?" Anne asked, surprised.

Jerry and Will both looked at her as if she had said something horrible. Will scolded her like a child who had said a bad word.

"Did he *die*? What is wrong with you? Why would you say something like that?"

"I don't know. I mean, him dying is the only reason I could think of why anyone would have a Dustin Hoffman marathon." Now, she was just trying to think of what she could possibly find to do during the *Dudley Moore and Dustin Hoffman Movie Night*. Marilyn was thinking along the same lines.

"Hey, that won't be a problem. Really. I'll just go back Friday and take care of some stuff around the house and all. I mean, if I don't go back before then," Marilyn added, embarrassed that she had just sort of invited herself to stay the rest of the week. Apparently, Jerry wasn't bothered by her self-invite to stay several more days.

"You're sure you're okay with it? Will and I always watch *Arthur* together," Jerry asked

"*Why*? What is it with *Arthur*?" Anne asked.

"Ummm, have you ever seen *Arthur*?" Will inquired, astounded.

How could she ask that? *Arthur* was fabulous. The soundtrack alone was fabulous. Will was only seven years old when he first saw *Arthur*. He had already been taking piano lessons from Miss Flora Martin for three years by that time. He had loved the movie so much that he sang the songs from it incessantly. So, for Christmas, Jerry and Faye had gotten him a Christopher Cross songbook so he could learn to play the theme song on the piano. He had every single song in the songbook perfected within two years, the first one being *Arthur's Theme*. That's where Will's obsession with Christopher Cross and playing 80's showtunes began.

"Yeah, I've seen it. It was okay and all. I just think y'all are kinda weird. But whatever. Y'all watch *Arthur* and *Tootsie* and things. I'll make earrings or something that night."

Anne and Marilyn may have been making other plans to avoid movie night with Jerry and Will, but Faye was excited. She too had loved *Arthur*. And she loved *anything* with Dustin Hoffman in it. So, Faye had already decided she was going to be sitting in on movie night with her boys. Roy was just looking at Jerry and Will, shaking his head.

"You two and *Arthur*, of all movies to be enamored with!"

"Well, we didn't invite you to watch it with us," Jerry pointed out, insulted. He and Will exchanged an ill look with one another.

"I'll lose sleep over that I'm sure," Roy replied, bored. Karen sort of snorted.

"We don't need your old invites. We're gonna watch us *The Waltons*, and *Gunsmoke* and *Frasier*. So, we don't even care. Besides, we don't want to listen to y'all sing all through it. I used to like Christopher Cross until I had to listen to his songs nonstop every day for 20 something years. *Every* time you'd sit down at that damn piano, you felt compelled to play *Sailing*. No, I didn't like him anymore.

"You played it well enough; don't go looking at me like that. I just got tired as shit of hearing it. Anyway, y'all have fun with your cheesy movies. We're gonna do just fine by ourselves. We'll get us some barbeque and be happy as two dead pigs in the sunshine." Karen put a bite of potato salad in her mouth.

"Do any of you watch movies or shows that were produced in the last oh, 20 years?" Anne asked.

"The classics are the best, Mama," Jerry replied.

"Whatever."

"Anyway, I thought you'd like to hear that. It is weird, Lexi not being here. It seems quieter. Why did she stay home again? I was not paying attention, earlier," Will asked. Nobody noticed that he didn't mention it was weird without Jason, Caleb or Teague there. Except Karen.

"Laurie is having a sleepover tonight at the house. Lex said they'd be up here this afternoon, so she stayed home to stress over it. Well, she said she was staying home to get the house ready for them. I thought that was funny because she seems to actually think that those girls are going to want to hang out in the living room with them or something. They're going to Laurie's room, where they'll stay all night and all day tomorrow until someone runs them off."

"Well, I guess that explains it," Will said simply. The rest of the meal was quiet. They finished up lunch, and the men went outside to work. Karen went to the office to work on the accounts, and Anne sat in the kitchen alone. She finally got up and wandered into the pantry to get a clean dishtowel out of the drawer. She saw one of the drawers was already open. It was a drawer Anne never even used, back among Jerry's junk drawers. She went to it and looked inside. It was full of folded papers. The papers were all the same size. Curious, she picked up one of the papers and unfolded it. It was written in Jerry's handwriting, in pencil.

Faye,

If I could only see one thing for the rest of my life, it'd be you. Every day with you is a blessing. I'll see you after work, and just know that you'll be on my mind until then.

Yours Always, Jerry

Anne didn't know how to react to that, so she just fought back tears. She picked up another one, then another one. This drawer was full of literally, hundreds of notes that Jerry Granger had apparently left his wife every morning before going to work. She had saved them all. She had stacked them neatly, packing them full into this drawer. Anne opened the drawer below it. By the time she was done, Anne had opened four wide, deep drawers absolutely full of love notes Jerry and Faye had written to one another throughout the course of their marriage.

These notes had been left at the coffee pot every single morning. Sometimes the notes would also remind the other of an appointment or of something that needed to be picked up in town. But these notes always, always expressed the undying love these two had for one another. It was the sweetest thing Anne had ever seen. She didn't read them all, of course. She felt bad, reading the ones that she had read. Faye often signed hers, *Your Biggest Fan* and Jerry almost always signed his *Yours Always*.

Anne closed the drawers, quietly. She felt she had invaded their privacy. She hadn't tried to do that; it was innocent enough when she had started looking in the first drawer. But why was that drawer open to begin with?

While Anne was thinking about the love notes in her own kitchen, Jason was in the tack room at the other end of the farm. Jonathon came in.

"Hey, man. I just saw your dad's truck. I thought you'd like to know he's here."

"Yeah, thanks. He brought Laurie and a couple of her friends up to spend the night."

"Oh, a slumber party!" Jonathon laughed.

"Oh no. They don't call it that anymore. Apparently, that is, like, so fifth grade. Now, it's just having some friends sleep over."

"Oh, well. Still, it's a slumber party," Jonathon shrugged. Jason nodded.

"Yeah, I know, right? Hey, would you put these back up on their pegs for me? I'm gonna go find Dad."

"Will do." Jonathon took the bridles from Jason, and Jason left to go find Gary. It didn't take long; as soon as Jason stepped out into the warm March sunshine, Gary was there.

"Hey, Jay."

"Hey. You wanna go to the house and sit for a while?"

"Oh. Oh, uh no. Not yet, not now. Let's just go sit over here for a bit instead. It's nice out," Gary suggested. Jason shrugged and joined his dad. They sat across from one another at the big wooden picnic table. Gary started.

"So, the girls are here. Did, um, Stacy contact you at all this morning?" he asked. Jason recalled that she had.

"Yeah, she did. She sent a text saying that we needed to talk about Laurie. I figured it was her getting all paranoid about the girls all coming up here or something. I just ignored her. She probably sent more when I ignored that one. I wouldn't know though. The phone is in the office. Why? How would you know that?" he frowned.

"Listen, I don't think she was wanting to talk about the girls sleeping up here. She and Laurie had a falling out last night. Apparently, Stacy is trying to convince Jack to come home and Laurie doesn't want to be there when he does. Laurie snuck out last night, after a big ol' fight with Stacy. She came to my house well after midnight. She came over with nothing but a poorly packed backpack and ended up crashing on the couch.

"I took Laurie over there to get her clothes and stuff this morning. And I can lay money that's why Stacy is calling you."

"Well, Laurie is old enough to decide if she doesn't want to live with Stacy and that dick. She can come here, no problem. I'll talk to her."

"Well, see, we talked about it already this morning; she thinks she might want to stay with me and Kylie. You know, she's used to living in town …"

"You mean, she *said* that? She said she wants to live with *y'all?*"

"Before you go getting all pissy, think about it. I'm sure it isn't anything personal. Like I said …"

"You know, she has a mother and a father. If she doesn't want to live with the mother, then doesn't it stand to reason she should stay with her father?" Jason couldn't help it; he was offended. He had been so excited that they had started bonding. He continued.

"Well, what if I want her to try to live with *us*? Do I just not have any say in how this goes? Again? Am I there again? Where I have no say whatsoever in what my daughter does? Not *even* where she *lives*? Really?"

"Look, she has her friends and school, and we've talked about her getting a job in town this summer. It makes sense that she'd stay in town."

"Well, I don't know if I agree with you. I think this summer, with school being out, would be an excellent opportunity for her to stay with me and spend more time with her family up here," Jason pointed out. At this, Gary inadvertently raised his brows doubtfully as he looked away.

"What was that for?" Jason wanted to know.

"What was what for?"

"I saw what you did with your eyebrows, like what I said was stupid?"

"Okay, son, let me put it this way. With all due respect, I really, honestly don't know that this would be an ideal place for Laurie to live right now. The child desperately needs some stability in her life and this place, these people? As much as I love all y'all to pieces, the word *stability* just isn't something that comes to mind when describing y'all. This crowd is many things; stable is not one of them."

"What? Lexi is a stay at home wife and mother," Jason began but was interrupted by a now irritated Gary.

"Bullshit! Stay at *whose* home wife and mother? Whose wife? Whose mother? She's never home in her own damn house. Will has two wives and four kids and a *you*. Lexi needs to keep her ass at home more often. I'll tell you that. She needs to be taking care of her own damn house. That's why I offered to help the fellas find a housekeeper. Maybe when Tammy gets out here and starts helping Anne out more, Lexi will realize she has a house of her own to take care of."

"Where is all of that coming from? Lexi spends more time at home. She likes staying at the Granger's because of Anne."

"Okay, Jason. I'm not going to get into this with you. I was letting you know what was going on, in hopes that you would have an ounce of compassion in your self-centered little world. I was thinking *maybe* you'd support your daughter who has been going through some shit. But I see instead, you are going to find a way to make yourself the victim here. Don't feel bad for the 15-year-old whose mother doesn't give a damn about her. Because, after all, you don't know how *that* feels, do you? No! Instead, let's feel bad for the grown-ass man whose feelings are hurt his daughter wants to stay in town, where she has lived her entire fucking life!

"You are a piece of work! You were just saying, when your mama died, what a great father I was. But you don't think I'm the one for Laurie to live with?"

"It's not like that."

"Well, what's it like?"

"I think I should have been consulted. I think someone should have talked to me about it!"

"What do you think I'm doing?"

"You already made the decision!"

"No! *She* already made the decision! And you agreed that she was old enough to make up her own mind about where she wanted to stay, but apparently you meant to add, long as it's with you. Oh, screw it. I'm gone. I used to be so proud of you. But more and more every day, I'm seeing you turn into a self-centered, whiney, victimized, attention-sucking brat. I see now that I've raised nothing but a good kid who turned out to be a real dick of a man."

Gary got up and walked away. Jason wanted to say something but couldn't think of what it'd be. Gary went back to the house. He could hear Lexi arguing with Caleb in the kitchen as soon as he walked through the back door.

"No, Caleb, you can't."

"But why not?"

"Because school doesn't work that way."

"Well, who makes us go to school?"

"The government."

"Who are they?"

"The people who make people in America do things."

"But I thought we were free in America to do what we want."

"Well, some things, yes."

"Is school one of those things?"

"No. Every kid has to go to school. It is the law!"

"What if a kid had to go to the hospital because his dog chewed his head off? Does *he* have to go to school?"

"Ummm, well, technically sick kids don't have to go to school until they're better."

"I'm sick."

"Stop it, Caleb."

"Can I call those people who make us do things? The dudderdent?"

"Government, and no."

"Why not? I want to tell them something."

"Because you're just not allowed to."

"So, this isn't a free country?" Caleb reasoned. Lexi sighed heavily.

"Caleb, son, go find something to do," Gary joined in.

"See? It's not a free country. People make me do things," he muttered.

"And you're sure he's only five?" Gary asked.

"Hey, Dad."

"Hey, Lex. Did the girls already go upstairs?"

"Yeah, they had to put their things away. Hey? What's the matter? You look stressed." Lexi kissed his cheek.

"Laurie and Stacy had a falling out, primarily about Jack. Laurie ran away in the night, came to my house. She wants to stay with me, in town, which pissed Jay off."

"Why does that make him mad? He knows Stacy and Jack are idiots."

"*He* wants her to live *here* with *y'all*," Gary answered. At this, Lexi stopped breathing for a minute.

"No! no no no no no no! Please, don't listen to him. Me and Laurie? We don't know each other well enough yet. We don't much, well, like each other. We have to give that time before she moves in. Please?"

"She's *not* moving up here. She's staying with *me*, which is where she said she wants to stay. Jason is offended she doesn't want to stay here, is all."

"Well, her friends are there, her school is there, you are there. It's all she's ever known. Of course, a teenaged girl is going to want to stay in town."

"Your husband doesn't see it that way. I want to talk to Laurie before I leave, though. I'll be back down in a minute." Gary went to the top of the stairs and called Laurie's name. She came out of her room giggling. She came to the top of the stairs and stood before him.

"Yes sir?"

"Heads up, girly. I told your dad what we discussed about you staying with me. I told him you wanted to stay for your friends, school, and a summer job and all that. He's taking it personally. Don't let it bother you. If he gives you a hard time, call me. Lexi is on your side, so maybe between Lexi and the fact you've got company, he'll lay low."

Laurie just nodded.

"Are you okay?" he asked her.

"Yeah. I just wish he wouldn't act like that. It's not that I don't love him. I'm just not comfortable enough with him and Lexi to be here with them every day all day. I'm still getting used to the weekends and things." Laurie's mouth began to wobble, and her eyes got very bright. Gary stepped up the last three steps and took her in his arms.

"It's a bunch of people still trying to figure each other out, baby. It takes time. Roy and Karen are still figuring it out. They've known each other all their lives but trying to be a family, living together, is just a whole different ballgame. It'll take a little bit of time, but it'll happen. Like I said, if you need me, just call me. My advice to you would be to be pleasant, act as though nothing is wrong, treat your daddy like you always do. Don't go acting all cold and hateful about this. It won't accomplish a thing."

"Alright."

"Alright. I'll call you sometime tomorrow. Behave yourselves and don't drive Lex crazy."

"Yes sir."

Gary hugged Laurie again, and kissed her cheek. She returned both.

"I love you, Poppy."

"I love you, too. Goodnight, baby."

Laurie watched her grandfather go downstairs. He turned the corner downstairs and disappeared into the living room. She stood alone in the hall for just a moment. She realized she wasn't as excited about her sleepover as she had been.

Gary went home after telling Lexi and the babies goodbye. He told Kylie he had some phone calls to make so she left him alone.

Later that night, at the Granger's, Will was looking through papers in the office. Marilyn was in the shower. Anne was sitting in the living room with Jerry. She was watching television and he was reading something in a magazine. She noticed him, several times, squinting at the magazine.

"Do you want me to turn another lamp on?" Anne asked.

"How's that?" Jerry asked, still frowning at the magazine.

"You look like you can't see the magazine very well. I asked if you wanted me to turn on another lamp?"

"Oh, no. That's okay. This one is fine."

"Then, why are you squinting like that?" she pressed.

"Aw, I think I'm just tired. My eyes are wanting to close on me." He laughed it off, but Anne had her own suspicions. She didn't feel like getting him all worked up right now. She muted the television. She stood up and joined him on the couch. He threw his arm on the back of couch as she sat beside him. She cuddled up against him. It was warm and quiet in the living room. The windows were open, bringing in the sounds of the bugs in the yard.

"What are you reading?" she asked. He kissed the top of her head.

"Um, article in here about people who specialize in historic architecture remodeling. It's pretty interesting."

"Oh, did you get that because of the work you're wanting to get done here?"

"Yeah, it's been awhile since we last had it done. They've become more advanced in all of that since we last had someone out here to do it. Pretty amazing what they can do now."

"So, they what, specialize in remodeling historic places to make sure they don't screw up the historic stuff?"

"Yes. They also make reproduction things to replace the historic accents that can't be saved for whatever reason ... because of rot, being aged, vandalized, whatever."

"That's neat."

"It is. I'm going to be getting in touch with a crowd out of South Carolina this summer. I'm wanting to get some stuff done around here before winter sets in. The columns look rough. The woodwork is starting to look like shit. The plaster on the porch needs touching up."

"The plaster? What about under the geraniums?"

"Oh, no. They never touch that. We've had to get the plaster redone several times over the years. We just tell them to do it around the geraniums," Jerry assured her. Anne nodded. It was a nice, quiet, sleepy conversation they were having.

"Hey?" Anne asked.

"Yeah, Mama?"

"This place is haunted ..."

"You don't say?"

"Well I was just wondering, when you do things like remodel these old places, does it mess up stuff like ghosts? I mean, does replacing real historic stuff with fake historic stuff change things?"

"Oh, baby, they aren't here because of the old floorboards or the glass in the windows or the old doors. It's the house itself, the land it's on. Think about all the old places that have been knocked down and something new built on top on the property. The new structure is often haunted. Well, look at Jason and Lexi's place."

"Why do you think they stay here?"

"Because of the love. Of course, there's been all kinds of theories. There's those who think this place is possessed by something evil."

"You've got to be kidding."

"I know, right? But well, our dear Marilyn just happens to be one of the many who do."

"But why?"

"She thinks there's something here that makes people stay here, not just dead people. She thinks there's something here that makes us feel obligated to stay here, come back here, in life. And then, when we die, we just can't leave it. It's true; everything that's happened here hasn't been lovely. Some horrific things happened on this property. Many people died on this property. Battles took place on this property. This land just has a lot of history. Not just this land, mind you, this whole town.

"There's a reason we won't let chain stores in this town. There's a reason we hang onto every old thing we have here; all our lives we have been told this town belongs to those who founded it. What started the hauntings is still up in the air, although there have been theories there too. It has to do with energies. Some ugly things have happened on this property, and some pretty fucked up things have happened in our town. Middleton's ghost still wanders downtown. The old jail is haunted. The old creek bridge is haunted. The co-op is haunted. Many buildings downtown are haunted. That tree on Main Street is haunted,"

"A tree? Why would a tree be haunted?" Anne interrupted.

"Lynchings, baby," Jerry said sadly.

"Oh."

"Like I said, some pretty fucked up things have happened in our town."

"What does the tree do?"

"Blows when there's no wind, the ground under a certain limb has a hole that won't stay filled. It's the limb where the lynchings took place. They filled it up all the time, and next day, it'd be dug right back out. Someone tried to burn it down several times, but the fire always goes out. It leaves a slight burn spot but nothing more. Fella was going to cut the tree down once, in early 1900s, and a lower branch broke off for no reason at all and fell slap on him. Killed him. Folks left the tree alone after that. They reason, if it's that haunted, even cutting the tree down won't stop the area from being haunted. Anything you put there in its place would be haunted. Some claim to have seen actual ghosts, very unpleasant ghosts from what I've heard. You can often hear an odd creaking sound beneath the tree; it's said it's the sound of swinging rope with something heavy hanging from it. Use your imagination there. What happened at that tree wasn't nice obviously."

"But why wouldn't it be a good thing to get rid of the tree? Even for the ghosts? If something that terrible happened to them, why wouldn't they want it gone?" Anne wondered.

"Because they'd rather us remember what folks done to them. Gary arranged for the historic marker to be put up, to commemorate those who were hanged. He thought maybe it'd make things better. But well, whereas they may have appreciated the gesture, folks guess it just wasn't enough. So, see, different things lead to this kind of stuff. Faye stays here because she loves us. They stay at the tree because they died a horrific death, are unhappy about it, and they just can't get over it," Jerry said with a sigh.

"Well, that sucks."

"Simply put, yes it does."

"Do you think there's any truth to what those people think, about why this place is haunted? Do you think something evil does it?" Anne asked worriedly. Jerry sighed and set his magazine down. He looked across the room, where the old rocking chair had begun rocking on its own. He smiled.

He pulled his arm from the back of the couch to around Anne's shoulders, and hugged her closer. He said, very quietly,

"There may be some truth to it, given the history of the property. But I think the love in this place is far stronger than anything evil that may be here. This house is just full of love. And I'll tell you what I think; I really, truly, think that this house has a spirit all its own. I think this house hears, sees, and feels everything that happens here, good things and bad things. And I think that's where it gets its strength. I think it's gotten its strength from those who have lived here, spent time here, and lost their lives here."

"I think that sounds really nice. So, you think this house has feelings?"

"I do. I've seen and heard and felt too much to think otherwise. Do you think it does?"

Anne looked at the rocking chair and looked around the big old room. She watched as the curtains at the window suddenly blew into the room, even though the dark spring night was still and completely windless. The windchimes outside that very window didn't move at all. Anne smiled at the curtains.

"Yeah, I think it does, too."

CHAPTER 14

Laurie sat on the bed with Jennifer, watching as Stacia unloaded her backpack. It was late now. They had eaten pizza with Jason, Lexi, and the kids. Laurie thought about asking if they could eat up in her room but decided against it. She saw this as an opportunity to try to make things right with her father.

So, the seven of them all gathered around the big table in the dining room and ate several pizzas. Conversation was polite and light with no heavy discussions. Caleb whined about the *dudderdent* dictating his childhood and how he was being expected to relinquish his rights, which he insisted was against the law. Jennifer didn't help the situation when she brought up the option of homeschool. That released a whole new argument from Caleb. Now, was angry at Lexi for withholding this information from him.

The girls helped Lexi clean up the kitchen and wash the dishes before going back up to Laurie's room. They had been up here for several hours. Now, Laurie and Jennifer watched as Stacia pulled a Ouija board from her backpack.

"This is going to be so kickass," Jennifer said excitedly. Laurie wasn't sure.

"Yeah, but these things are just toys, right? I mean, they sell them at toy stores. So, they don't really do anything, right?"

"Well, I've heard differently. This is the perfect place to find out, though. I mean, come on! This is perfect! If these things do work, then we will definitely know before long," Stacia said.

"Well, it's getting awfully late. If we're going to do this, we need to hurry up and go do it. Daddy gets up *really* early during the week. We need to be done and back here and asleep before he gets up," Laurie warned.

"Are they in the bed already?" Jennifer asked Laurie.

"Yeah. Like I said, they get up real early. Like at five. So, they go to bed real early too."

"Well, then, let's go do this." Stacia said, getting up and pulling her shoes back on.

"Yeah ... I guess let's do this." Laurie was getting more and more uncomfortable, though. She had seen enough at the Granger's, especially, to know it was indeed haunted. There had even been numerous incidents in this house, but Laurie had not told her friends that. She didn't know how they would react to that.

The three girls quietly got several things together and put them in Laurie's backpack and Stacia stuffed the Ouija board back in her own. Laurie very carefully opened her bedroom door and looked down the dark hall. She gestured for her friends to follow her. The three girls crept down the hall, down the stairs, out the back door, and across the yard.

The woods were exceptionally creepy tonight. This house was literally, smack in the middle of the woods. A narrow dirt path creeping through the woods served as the driveway. Once you got to the end of that path, there was a clearing in the woods, and the house sat in the clearing. Behind the house, in front of the house, and on either side of the house was woods. You had to walk or drive down a whole other path through the woods behind the house to get to the stable. Beyond the piece of land that the stable sat on a footpath went over a hill in the pasture to the Sewell Family Graveyard. This is where the girls were headed tonight.

They giggled nervously, walking through the thick black woods, lit only by a high full moon and a flashlight with somewhat low batteries. This was the Appalachian Mountains; it was impossible for the girls to not hear numerous different noises coming from these woods. They had gotten almost to the clearing where the stable was, when they heard an animal they couldn't identify.

"What the hell was that?" Stacia asked. Laurie didn't know.

"I don't know. It wasn't a cougar. I've heard the cougars. That's not a cougar."

"Is it a bear? A wolf? Coyote? Deer? Fox?" Jennifer rambled.

"Would you hush? Whatever it is, we don't want it to hear us," Laurie whispered.

"I brought my mom's taser, just in case," Stacia assured them.

"Oh, okay. Sure! *You* get close enough to a *bear* to tase it! My ass will be back home in the bed before you're done doing *that*!" Laurie told her.

"Let's just hurry up. These woods are creepier than I thought they'd be," Jennifer told them. The girls wandered through the rest of the woods until they came to the clearing where the stable stood.

Jonathon and Luke were sitting in folding chairs, near the door to the stable, just talking. They did this often at night. The men enjoyed sitting outside in the dark, talking, smoking, and drinking. But their trailer, within view of the stable, didn't have a porch. So, instead the men would sit near the doorway of the stable. It was a good place to relax they decided. It was close enough to the fridge in the stable, had a fabulous view of the sky and the distant mountains, and they could hear the pleasant sounds coming from within the stable, the soft noise horses tended to make in the night.

On this night, Jonathon caught a glimpse of what appeared to be a flashlight. His first thought was to go in the stable and get the gun. He went so far as to sit forward in his chair. Then he heard the chattering of three girls. He smiled knowingly.

"Hey, man, what's that?" Luke asked, just now taking notice.

"Slumber party, my friend."

"What? That's *Laurie*? What are they doing?" Luke asked quietly. He didn't like that. He happened to like Laurie (a lot!) and he immediately wanted to catch up to them and send them home. Jonathon, who was 28 years old, wasn't as worried as the 19-year-old Luke was.

"I'm willing to bet they're heading for the Sewell graves. What *else* would they be doing out here at night? They're looking for something scary. I say if they want a good scare, we give them one," Jonathon suggested with a grin. His hand brushed back his too-long brown hair as he stood up. Luke looked at Jonathon skeptically.

Most everyone liked Jonathon. He was too tall, standing at six feet four inches. He had strong facial features, warm brown eyes, and shoulder length hair. Sometimes his hair was pulled back in a ponytail or man-bun, which they all used to make fun of but eventually stopped. He had a long, lanky frame and an earring. His outfit usually consisted of jeans, boots, and vintage rock band T-shirts. Jonathon was always laid back, never letting much bother him. He saw the good things in life and enjoyed a good time. So, his plan to follow the slumber party into the field didn't surprise Luke much.

"Man, there's all kinds of shit in these hills. They can get themselves killed," Luke argued. Jonathon nodded.

"I'm grabbing the gun; come on."

Jonathon crept right inside the door where a pistol was kept in the cabinet. He retrieved the gun, and he and Luke quietly followed the three girls into the woods.

The girls walked for what seemed forever before they came to the area of the pasture, at the very edge of the woods. This area was fenced off with an elderly wrought iron fence. The girls stood for what felt like forever before Laurie opened the gate. They went inside the graveyard, Luke and Jonathon watching from the trees.

"Okay. Find Thomas's grave. It's taller than the other ones; I think it's up this way," Laurie told the others.

"Ewwwww look at that. It's a *dead* thing," Jennifer said, grossed out. She was shining her flashlight down on a partially eaten raccoon.

They all stopped to study the carcass.

"Oh, it's just a raccoon. My brother eats those," Stacia said with disinterest.

"That is disgusting," Laurie told her.

"Good grief, it stinks!" Jennifer whined.

"Then, here's a suggestion; let's get away from it. We're *supposed* to be looking for Thomas's grave, not doing a wildlife analysis," Laurie told her sarcastically.

"Well, what do you think killed it? Why did it just leave it, instead of eating it?" Jennifer wondered.

"Well, would *you* eat it if it smelled like that?" Stacia giggled.

"Y'all! Come on! You are totally not taking this seriously. Why are we even out here, then? If you're just going to act like that, let's go back to the house," Laurie scolded. She didn't want to be out here anyway. She was uncomfortable with this whole situation.

"Oh, fine! You are being way too uptight! We were just looking at a dead thing. I mean, it *is* a graveyard. Get a grip already. There, there's a tall one. Is that the grave?" Stacia shone the light up the hill. Under an ancient cedar tree was a tall granite tombstone.

"Yeah, that's it. Uncle Will showed it to me before. He said the guy blew his brains out when his son got murdered by an Indian," Laurie told them.

They stood there, shining the light on the obelisk tombstone.

"That the guy who got shot with an arrow at the well at y'all's place?" Jennifer asked.

"Yeah, the son. Indian shot him in the back while he was getting water. The son's grave is right there, that one," Laurie pointed to another grave, about 10 feet from Thomas's.

"That story is kinda sad," Jennifer remarked.

"I know, right? Like, his daughter, lots of babies, his wife, then his son, then him. They all died here at the house. Well, at the house that used to be where ours is now," Laurie told them.

"Well, let's get this done. Come on," Stacia instructed the other two. They walked up to Thomas's grave and began unloading their backpacks.

"What are they doing?" Luke asked from behind another cedar tree.

"I don't know, yet. Sshhhh," Jonathon shushed him.

"This is just a bad idea."

"Hush."

The girls set up the Ouija board and pulled out candles. Stacia lit the candles. She then began trying to summon the spirit of Thomas Sewell. During all of this, Jonathon and Luke crept closer to the girls, finally crouching behind a monstrous nandina bush and two azaleas. They were now only about 20 feet away from the girls. The sound of their heavy boots walking over the fallen leaves got the attention of the girls. They looked around them in panic.

"What was that?" Jennifer asked loudly.

"Um, maybe just trees?" Laurie suggested.

"Trees? *Trees?* Trees that *walk?* What kind of place *is* this, Laurie?"

"Oh, okay! It's a bear. Maybe that raccoon is a zombie. Is any of *that* better? *Hello*! It is *dark!* I am here with you guys! How in the hell do you expect me to know what it is, when y'all don't? News alert! I have never ever ever done this before!"

"Let's just do this. Maybe it was just a dead limb falling or something," Stacia suggested, even though she didn't believe it.

"Can we please not use the word *dead*?" Jennifer asked.

"Okay. Anyway, let's start. Stacia?" Laurie pressed. Sitting on top of Thomas Sewell's centuries year old grave, the girls faced one another in a circle. They put their hands on the plastic planchette. Then, Stacia started calling the spirit of Thomas.

"We are here to contact the spirit of Thomas Sewell … or, like, any of his family since they're here too. Thomas Sewell, do you hear me? Please talk to us."

At this, Jonathon had a stroke. A séance! These three idiot girls were *trying* to summon the dead on the *most* haunted piece of property in the whole region?

"A séance! Bull*shit*!" Jonathon whispered in a panic to Luke. Luke nodded.

"Come on. Follow me but be quiet. We have to stop this shit quick." They had a quick meeting where they set a plan.

"Did y'all hear that? It sounded like voices. I thought the ghosts were supposed to just talk on the board thingee! I don't want to actually *hear them*!" Jennifer said tearfully.

Almost immediately there was a loud, swift stomping coming toward them through the fallen leaves in the graveyard. They couldn't tell which direction it was coming from, and they had already turned off their flashlights for the séance, so they didn't even have any way to see what it was coming after them. The three tea lights they brought for the séance really didn't do much in the way of lighting. All three girls looked fearfully, all around them but saw nothing but black woods and the ominous, dark, looming tombstones that were among the trees growing in the graveyard. The girls weren't sure whether to stay seated and just get killed there or jump up and run in any direction they could. Suddenly they all screamed.

There, in the moonlight, two tall dark creatures were nearly right on top of them. One of them grabbed Laurie and pulled her away from the séance circle and another one grabbed Stacia and pulled her in the opposite direction. Jennifer, who already hadn't been handling the entire situation well, kept screaming. She didn't know if something was going to grab her next, or if she was expected to try to help the other two. They'd been pulled in two opposite directions, so she decided that'd be hard to do. She was left alone at the Ouija board, while her two friends were screaming in the dark. Well, she was going to die tonight, she'd decided.

Then, among the girls' screams, there was a man's voice.

"Okay! Hey! Shut up! Shut up, already! It's okay! It's just us!" It said. At this, Luke started laughing. Laurie did not.

"Jonathon? *Jonathon?* Luke? Seriously? You, *assholes!*" Laurie said. She started hitting Luke, who had been the one who dragged her away, screaming. She pounded him with her fists. While she did this, Stacia was slapping and shoving Jonathon, who had dragged *her* away. Jennifer just sat on the grave in shock.

"Quit hitting me! Ow! Laurie, chill out!"

"You are a jerk! A big jerk! What's the matter with y'all? Really?"

"What's the matter with *y'all*? Have you any idea how very *stupid* this was? Y'all were trying to summon the *dead*? You don't even have to summon them around here! They're already here! They're everywhere! Why in the hell would you *try* to bring them here?" Jonathon asked.

"It's a Ouija board! That's what they are for! And you just screwed it up! We might could have found out if these things work and you had to go and do that!" Stacia answered.

"You don't need a damn Ouija board to talk to dead people around here! Hell, all you gotta do is sit still long enough and *they'll* come talk to *you!*"

"Whatever. Jennifer, why are you still sitting there, like that?" Stacia asked. Jennifer just sat there, looking odd.

They looked at her for a moment; Jonathon worried she was in some sort of shock.

"Don't be mad, Laurie. Y'all could have gotten hurt, doing this! There's all kinds of shit that lives in these hills," Luke told her.

"Y'all had your fun. Get your stuff together and come on. No way in Hell am I leaving y'all out here. Come on, now," Jonathon told them. Stacia and Laurie gathered their things while Jennifer just looked kind of dazed. They began to walk towards the gate. Jonathon, Stacia, and Jennifer led the way with Laurie and Luke dragging behind several feet.

"Hey, you're not mad, are you? I mean, we saw y'all walking past the stable and just didn't want anything to happen to y'all. That's why we followed y'all," Luke told Laurie. She looked at him knowingly.

"I'm so sure scaring us wasn't on your mind at all."

"Well, maybe a little bit. But anyway, I just wanted to tell you that. I really like you and didn't want you to be all mad and pissy at me. I mean, I don't care if you're mad at *him,* just don't want you mad at *me,*" he laughed. Laurie felt very warm for it to just be March.

"Well, thanks I guess. I mean, it's nice that you really like me and don't want me to be mad at you. It's okay, I guess. I won't be mad at you because, well, I like you too, and all."

They walked out of the graveyard, Luke closing the gate behind them.

Jonathon had been right; the girls didn't need a Ouija board to contact anyone. Had they just sat long enough, listened hard enough, and looked close enough, they would have seen the wife of Thomas Sewell lurking at the edge of the trees. She watched and heard all that went on. She watched the girls go back to the house, *her house.*

The group talked and visited and laughed on the way back to the house. It was still creepy, but somehow the dark woods weren't so bad with Jonathon and Luke there with them. Eventually, they reached the clearing where the house stood. The group lingered for another moment, chatting.

Finally, Jonathon spoke up,

"Look, you girls are lucky Jason hasn't figured out what you've done, yet. You'd better get back before he gets up to take a leak or something and decides to check on y'all."

"Yeah, I guess so. Well, I'm not going to thank y'all for what you did; it was plain mean. But well, I guess it was kinda fun, everything else," Laurie told Jonathon and Luke.

"No problem, wasn't expecting a thanks," Jonathon laughed.

"Well, I didn't say I wouldn't thank y'all for walking us back home. So, thanks. Good night, Luke," Laurie said, smiling lovingly at Luke.

"Good night, Laurie. I guess I'll see you tomorrow."

"Yeah, we'll come out the stable. Anyway, night Jonathon. Come on, y'all."

Jennifer and Stacia told the boys goodnight, and they followed Laurie back to the house, giggling about that night's adventure.

"Oh, my word! Luke was totally into you!" Stacia told Laurie.

"Oh, no, he wasn't. He just works for my dad. He and Jonathon were just keeping an eye on us."

"You are clueless! Yeah! He was definitely keeping an eye on you, more like *both* eyes on you!" Jennifer said, giggling.

"Don't you like him? You were totally acting like it," Stacia asked.

"Well, yeah I like him and all," Laurie admitted. How could she not like Luke? He was exciting. He had hair so dark it was almost black and eyes just as dark. His hair was neat and cut short, but his arms and chest were nearly covered in tattoos. Luke drove a motorcycle and a red 1965 El Camino he had lovingly restored. He was only 19 years old, but he was the only man who worked the farm who was not intimidated *at all* by Will. He didn't give a shit what Will said or expected. Will's lists didn't impress Luke, and his nervous breakdowns didn't impress Luke. Luke liked Will, and Will liked Luke.

Will could tell that he had very little impact on Luke. This frustrated him; Roy was all the time telling Will that Luke wasn't doing things according to plan, but Will did notice that what Luke did, Luke did quite well. So, Will laid off Luke. Luke was the *only* thing that Will made an exception for on the farm. In his own private thoughts, out of all the farmhands they had hired, Luke was the most valuable.

Laurie had always thought Luke was good looking. But she had never imagined he liked her. She was only 15; he was 19. She smiled to herself, thinking about him. Then, she remembered Gary. There was no way on the planet Gary would be okay with this.

The girls snuck in the back door, giggling. They crept up the stairs and reached the second floor. They turned to go to Laurie's room, when Lexi came out of Teague's bedroom. She saw the girls with backpacks and stopped. The girls froze. They couldn't believe they had gotten this far only to be caught now! Ten feet from Laurie's bedroom door! Lexi smiled.

"You'd better hurry up and get in your room. Get to sleep; you'll be expected to join us for breakfast," Lexi winked at the girls, and they smiled cautiously. They went to Laurie's room. Laurie paused at the door.

"Lexi?"

"Yeah?"

"Thanks. For, you know ..."

"I know. It's all good. What's a sleepover without sneaking out?"

"Yeah, I know, right? Night, Lex. I love you." Laurie stepped into the hall and gave Lexi a hug and kiss goodnight.

"Night, Laurie. I hope y'all had fun. Hurry to bed now. I love you too."

Lexi laid in the bed and thought about Laurie. She herself had grown up in a house with a mom who wasn't too involved and no father figure. It had been hard, and it had been lonely. It had been very trying at times. Lexi dated a lot, but her mother never knew anything about the guys she went out with. Her mother had no idea that she had lost her virginity to Jason Connelly when she was just 16 years old.

Her mother had never set boundaries, had never looked twice at a report card. When Lexi brought home bad grades, her mother made the expected threats. Her mother would tell her she couldn't use the phone and that she couldn't go out for a month. That very night, Lexi would be on the phone, and that very next weekend, she was out with friends. Her mother made threats, but never enforced them. That's when Lexi learned that her mother didn't really care; it was just her mom saying things she knew moms were supposed to say.

Lexi had never even met her father. Ronald Pierce went to work one day when Lexi's mother was three months pregnant ... and never came home. At first, her mother worried something had happened to him on the way home. Then, she realized that he had taken all his most important belongings with him. That's when she realized he had left her.

She had the baby, and the baby was raised in daycare until she started kindergarten. Daycare was where Lexi and Jason first met; Lexi wasn't even four months old, and Jason was two years old. It was a very relaxed daycare and all the children played together, regardless of age. For whatever reason, Jason would often play with the funny baby girl with the head full of dark hair. The older Lexi got, the more Lexi and Jason would play. They were friends.

Lexi lay in bed remembering what it was like to be 15 years old in a house with a mother who wasn't interested in anything you did. Her mother never made it to Lexi's events at school. She never made it to anything that was important to Lexi. She'd often thought it was a shame she didn't have a dad; maybe a dad would have done these things for her.

Lexi and Jason bonded over this over the years. He understood what it was like to be raised by a single parent and to wonder where your other one was. He wanted a mom; she wanted a dad. Once, when he was in third grade and she was in first, they tried to get their parents to date. Their parents became friends, but nothing more. There were many reasons Lexi and Jason stayed close over the years. One main reason was they understood each other. Lexi realized tonight that she had not always been 100 percent fair to Laurie. She had been there, herself; she should know better. She should have been able to see what Laurie was going through all this time. She thought about what Gary had told her, and she decided to try her best to understand Laurie and to be a friend to Laurie. She also decided to try to maybe be a little more of a mother to her.

Lexi wondered what it was going to be like for Laurie, living with Gary. Gary was by far the strictest parent she had ever known. He wasn't unfair; he just had expectations and those expectations were met. Lexi worried it was going to be an extreme adjustment for Laurie. She knew that Gary had already done a good bit for Laurie ever since Laurie and Jason began talking. He got her a tutor when she was in danger of failing history. He'd promised her a car when she turned 16. He invited her over often for dinner and made several dates with her, just to spend some quality time with her. So, maybe Gary had this down, after all, Lexi thought.

The next morning, Jason had just left a relatively pleasant breakfast with his family and two extra teenage girls. He was in the stable when his phone rang. He saw it was Stacy. He sighed but answered it.

"Hello."

"Jason?"

"Yep."

"You could have called me back! I called you yesterday! We need to talk! Now!"

"Hey! Don't start yelling at me! I'll hang up! I promise you that!"

"I don't give a shit! I'll just call you back. Do you know that that girl has been telling *all* our personal family problems to that slut of Jerry's? I mean, really? She has been telling God knows what to that woman for years, Jason! Years! Since sixth grade!"

"Hey! You wait a minute! Are you talking about Miss Beales?"

"Yes, I'm talking about her!"

"Okay, first off, watch how you talk about *her*! Her and Karen are the closest thing I've ever had to a mom, so shut the fuck up! Slut? Really? You're calling the woman a slut, based on what? Because she's dating Jerry? Seriously? And I don't know what all Laurie has told her, but hello! Miss Beales is her guidance counselor. What's the matter with her talking to her?"

"Oh, really? Think about it, Jason. She told that woman *everything*. That woman knows everything that has gone on in this house! She has got to learn to stop running her mouth! What happens in my house is no business of that woman's! Now, she knows all kinds of shit about us and it's all because of that damned brat!"

"Excuse me? What in the hell has gone on in that house that you're so damned worried about? You have my curiosity! Obviously, you have been having some pretty serious shit going on in there, or else you wouldn't be so paranoid and angry!

"And who do you think you are, calling that child a *damned brat*? Really? Your own daughter? You know what? My dad came over here yesterday and told me that Laurie was going to stay with him, and I was mad because I wanted her to stay here. But you know, anywhere would be better than her staying with you!

"I don't know what all she told Miss Beales, but if I find out that anything screwed up has gone on in that house, with my daughter living there? I will have your ass in court so fast you won't know what hit you!"

"Your dad thinks he can just take my daughter away from me? He's wrong! I'll get her ass back here. She will *not* treat me this way, after all I do for her. Her and your daddy will be sorry. Just you wait. She'll be back here!"

"No, see, she will *not* be going back *there*! She's old enough to decide that! She can go where she *wants* to! And you just called her a *damned brat*! And you claim you want her? You don't want her! You want the state assistance for having her! You want someone to treat like shit, when Jack isn't around to treat *you* like shit!"

Jason was about to say more when he heard a tiny sneeze. He looked up to see Laurie standing there, holding Caleb's hand. Caleb was wiping his nose with the back of his hand. Laurie stood there, listening to every word between her mother and father. Tears were running down her cheeks. Jason hung up on Stacy.

"Laurie, what are you doing? Why aren't you in the house?"

"Caleb was annoying Lexi with questions about school. She told me to bring him to you."

Jason rubbed his eyes. His phone rang again. He turned it off. He went to the door and called to Luke, who was brushing a horse.

"Luke! Will you come here and get Caleb for me, please?"

Luke wandered over to the doorway to retrieve the child. He saw Laurie.

"Hey, what's wrong? Are you okay?" he asked her worriedly. She just looked at him.

"It's all just a mess. It'll be okay. Just take him, please. We need to talk," Jason directed him. Luke looked at Laurie one more time and took Caleb with him. Jason sighed, looking at Laurie.

"You were not supposed to hear any of that. I would have never, never, never said any of that had I known you were standing there. That was between your mother and me. You didn't need to hear any of that."

"She said that stuff? She called Miss Beales a *slut*? She was saying mean things about Miss Beales and Papa (which is what all the kids called Jerry)? You said something about Karen; is she saying mean things about Karen? She called *me* a *damned brat*?" Laurie asked, still crying.

"Your mom was overreacting,"

"Is she going to try to make me stay with her? I don't want to. I want to stay with Poppy and Kylie. I don't want to go back there. She doesn't like me, I don't think." Laurie started crying harder.

"You are not going back to that house. Don't worry about that. You're going to stay with Poppy. Okay? Don't stress, honey. It's all fine. Ignore her threats. Come on, Laurie. You know your grandfather. He has ways of making things work out."

"Are you mad at me? Are you mad because I want to stay with Poppy and Kylie?"

"No! Why do you think that? I ... well, I mean I was a little bit offended at first, I guess. But I talked to Lex about it, and it makes sense, I guess. I mean, I can see why you'd want to stay there in town. It's okay. Just promise me that this summer you'll spend some extra time up here with us, too, not just weekends. Can you at least do that?"

"I can do that."

"Okay, then. It's all good."

Right then, Jonathon came in the stable with Caleb.

"I took him away from Luke. I'm going to saddle up and take him riding. That okay?"

"Yeah, take him riding. It's fine. Hey, Laurie? Are you going to be okay? We gonna be alright?" he asked Laurie. Laurie nodded and wiped her eyes. She turned to go back to the house. Jonathon looked at her.

"Hey? You okay?"

"Yeah, Jonathon. I'm fine. Thanks. Bye."

She stalked out of the stable and made her way across the thick green grass, covered with dew. She was having a very bad day already, and it wasn't even nine o'clock.

"Hey, Laurie?" someone called behind her. She turned to see Luke. He was walking up to her, looking over his shoulder every few seconds. She brushed her long brown hair behind her shoulder and crossed her arms in front of her. The chilly spring morning made her wish she'd remembered to grab her sweatshirt.

"Yeah? Hi," she greeted him. She looked at him sort of differently this morning. Somehow, their brief encounter last night had changed things.

"I was just wanting to make sure you were okay. You didn't get in trouble for last night, did you?"

"Oh, that? Just now? No. It's a parent thing. Just, well, my mom and I aren't getting along right now. So, I'm going to stay with my grandfather. It's just causing some arguments right now."

"I see. Well, it's a shame you won't be staying up here, instead."

"It is? You think so?" she asked, suddenly very flattered.

"Well, yeah. Maybe it'd be nice to hang out some."

"Well, I promised my dad that I'd spend extra time up here this summer."

"That'd be nice," Luke agreed. Laurie smiled, in spite of the tears still stinging her eyes.

"Well, I need to get back to the house. It was nice talking to you. I guess I'll see you again later on. We're going to come out and go riding this afternoon."

"Good. I'll see you then ... I hope," he smiled.

"You will. Bye, Luke," Laurie said teasingly. She turned and walked away, feeling flushed and nervous. She couldn't believe it! Luke had kinda-sorta flirted with her! He acted worried about her! He acted like he really wanted to see her again! It was too good to be true. Laurie couldn't believe it!

While Laurie and Luke stood there talking, Roy had come out of the barn and saw them. He laughed and shook his head. When he saw Luke about 10 minutes later, Roy smiled at him.

"Hey, Luke, gonna keep this short and sweet. You do know Laurie is 15, right?"

"Yep."

"You do know you are 19, right?"

"Right."

"You remember who her grandfather is, right?"

"Yep. I do."

"You are a brave but *stupid* son of a bitch. Good luck to you, son; you're gonna *need* it."

"You gonna say something to him?" Luke asked, irritably. Roy laughed.

"You know what, Luke? I ain't saying shit, not a word. This *one* time, just for *once*, I'm just gonna sit back and *watch*."

CHAPTER 15

Thursday on the farm went by fairly uneventful. The girls finished helping Lexi in the kitchen. Lexi announced she was going to spend a while at the Granger's. So, the girls decided to go on to the stable.

Back in town, Gary was getting ready to go to the church to meet with Jeremy Clancy. Jason had recently informed Gary that Jeremy was planning on getting baptized this upcoming week at the church. That was all well and good, except for the fact that Jeremy was doing it for the single fact that his probation officer coaxed him into it. So, last night Gary had called Jeremy and told him that he really wanted to talk to him about things. Jeremy agreed, irritably, to meet Gary at the church today.

Gary was standing at the pulpit, looking around the quiet, empty church. It was a small church, with four windows on each side and a stained glass one behind the pulpit. There were six small Sunday school classrooms in the separate building that had been constructed behind the church in 1852. This building also served as a kitchen and dining hall for family reunions and fellowship dinners.

Here in the church, the silver colored offering plate was sitting on top of the piano, next to the *Broadman Hymnal*. The blue felt in the bottom was beginning to peel. This reminded Gary that Jason and Will had both commented on the need for a new offering plate.

Like in the building that served as Sunday School and the dining hall, the narrow boards of the old hardwood floor were slightly warped in places, the white painted wooden walls and ceiling looking a bit weathered. The dreadfully heavy old wooden pews sat where they'd been sitting since 1851, just 10 years after the church had been constructed. Cushions were added to the seats in 1943 to make them just a little more comfortable. They've been replaced every decade or so. During the sweltering summer days, the fabric of the cushions gave the church a heavy velvety smell that always made Gary feel somewhat nauseated. The large wooden cross hung on the wall; the same wooden cross that had originally hung in the original church across the road.

The mouse hole was still near the third row from the front between two boards. It had been there since 1857, but nobody did much about it. In the winter, a brick was laid in front of it during services. For over a century and a half, kids felt sorry for the generations of brown mice that were often spotted near it, so they never blocked it off entirely. Gary looked at this mouse hole, now. He shook his head, remembering catching Jason, six years old, leaving his smuggled Ritz crackers from Sunday School on the floor for the mice.

This church was the heart of the town; Gary had always loved this church, even when he didn't particularly love being a preacher's kid. He remembered the sweaty summer Sunday mornings in this church before they equipped it with the four pitiful ceiling fans, which really did nothing but stir the hot air around. Everyone had a handheld fan, crafted from a cardboard advertisement stapled to a craft stick. These fans usually advertised the co-op, Elderod's Pharmacy, Main Street Diner or the Clip and Curl. The fans did little more than swat flies away. Given the sad excuse for the ceiling-fan cooling system the church had now, these fans were still used regularly.

When Gary was just an infant, radiators were installed to help out the two wood burning stoves. Gary recalled freezing on winter Sunday mornings when the radiators didn't do much unless you were sitting right next to them. He remembered the bats nesting in the eaves. Smiling, he remembered the time, in 1965, when a 37-inch black racer snake came in through the mouse hole for Sunday morning services. He remembered Jason's baptism. This reminded him of why he was here this afternoon.

After another ten minutes, a very bored looking Jeremy Clancy came in the door. He walked up the center aisle toward Gary, who was now sitting on the steps in front of the pulpit. Gary smiled. Jeremy smiled back, but he didn't appear to really mean it. Gary stood to greet him.

"Hey, son. How you doing?" Gary asked, offering his hand to shake. Jeremy shook it.

"Fine, I guess. How are you?"

"Oh, I'm doing pretty fair. I'm keeping myself pretty busy. How's your mama? She doing any better these days?"

"No, she won't leave the house, won't go to a doctor, won't do anything. She just sits and sleeps. She's lost too much weight because she won't even eat right."

"She took your daddy's passing hard. I'm sorry she seems to be giving up," Gary said sadly. He thought about Jerry now.

As if reading his mind, Jeremy asked,

"Hey? Do you think it's like Jerry though? Do you think she'll eventually get better?"

"It takes a lot, Jeremy. Jerry didn't do that on his own. It took several years of depression, friends, and family intervening, and it took Anne. Everyone doesn't have an Anne. But if your mama would just be willing to see someone, get some help, she may see things can be okay again. It's a process."

"Yeah."

"But you're doing okay, right? You're doing better, staying out of trouble. I'm sure that has to be helping her out some."

"Yeah. I guess so."

"I need to talk to you about something. I'm filling in for Brother Lawson, as you might know."

"Yeah, I heard. He doing any better?"

"Well, Kylie says he's looking bad to her, but they're going to do surgery on him next week. Time will tell, I suppose. We'll pray he gets through it fine and recovers quickly. But um, I think you and I need to discuss your plans for this upcoming Sunday."

"What about them?"

"I'm not going to baptize you Sunday," Gary said simply. Jeremy looked at him suspiciously.

"Why not?"

"Because you should not go before the church and claim you have accepted the Lord into your heart as your Savior when in fact, you're merely trying to look good for your probation officer. This is something serious, something very serious, Jeremy. This isn't cheating on a test to get ahead in class. This is *using Jesus*. You just don't do that. If you want to improve your image around town, there's ways to do that, sincere, admirable ways to do that."

"Yeah, sure."

"Yeah. There's a lot of things you can do to volunteer around here. Help clean up the cemeteries, help Wyatt with the Neuters & Spays for Strays Weeks, do the church yardwork, volunteer at the fire station, help the older folks with stuff they need done. Hanson has been trying to paint that fence of his for three months. He's too old and it's not gonna ever get done, not by him. Paint it for him. Help maintain the park. There's things you can do to make yourself look good. Come on, Jeremy. Work with me here."

"Oh, come on. I just want to be left alone. If I'm home and left alone, that's what people around here want to see. They don't want to see me out around town. They follow me around stores and act like they're waiting for me to swipe something, hit someone, or catch something else on fire."

"Then give them a reason to *quit* expecting that of you! Come on, look. It's spring and everything is growing over in the cemeteries again. You're not working, so come out here Friday and clean the place up a little. Get the weed eater and get around the tombstones and the fence and everything. The riding mower is in the outbuilding."

"This isn't a choice, is it? You're making me do it."

"Let me point something out to you without coming across as a conceited jerk. You impress me and get me on your side, and you'll be in good with most everyone in town. Prove your worth, and I can convince anyone here to give you a job. But you have to prove you're worth the time and effort we put into you."

"But no baptism?"

"Not this week, no. I simply refuse to do it, knowing your reasons."

"Whatever, man. I can't believe this. You try to do something good to …"

"No! You tried to do something deceitful, insincere, and manipulative. There's nothing good about what you were trying to do, Jeremy."

"Fine."

"We're gonna work on this. You're only 40 years old. That's not too old to make changes in your life. Look at me! Look at the changes I've made! If I can make changes, you can make changes. Do you really think, 23 years ago, I thought at 63, I'd be getting married with a baby on the way, with a teenaged granddaughter living with me? Do you?"

"Probably not," Jeremy agreed.

"Definitely not. So, do we have a deal? No baptism until it's for the right reasons, and you'll help me out with the churchyard?"

"Alright, Chief."

"Alright! How about you come out here tomorrow morning and cut all the grass first? That'd be a good place to start. The keys to the mower and shed are at the co-op. Just stop by there in the morning and pick them up, okay?"

"Fine." Jeremy stood up but didn't go anywhere. He just turned around and looked at Gary still sitting on his step.

"How long do you think you'll be filling in for Lawson?"

"Oh, I don't know. Several weeks, at least. Why?"

"You're good at that. I mean, he's nice, of course. He's a preacher. But you have a different way of talking to people. You talk to us like you're worried about how things work out for us while we're still here, not just what's going to happen when we're dead. Folks like that."

"I do care about what happens to y'all while you're still here. This is our town, our people. Of course, I'm going to care about those things."

"If Lawson doesn't pull through this, are you going to take over?"

"We're going to hope he pulls through this," Gary answered quietly and pointedly.

"I know that. But if he *doesn't*, are you going to take over?"

"I don't know, Jeremy. I'd prefer to not anticipate something like that. The most important thing is Brother Lawson getting better."

"You won't answer that. Alright then. I'll drop it. I'm going to run now. Don't stress; I'll go pick the key up in the morning and take care of the grass and everything."

"Thank you."

Jeremy left, and Gary remained sitting for half an hour, just thinking. He thought about what he was getting himself into. He remembered his promise to Gap and stood up. He left the church, locked it up tight, and got in his truck. He drove to the creek bridge, where he could finally get cell phone reception, and called Jack Middleton to discuss Bird's headstone.

"Yeah, we can do something for ol' Gap and Bird. Just bring it up at services Sunday. I'll go ahead and come up with an idea for the headstone now, and y'all just spend the next couple weeks getting together whatever donations y'all can. Whatever the folks can come up with will be enough. I'm not going to give y'all a price to come up with. It's for Gap. It'll be taken care of. Like I said, just tell them if they're wanting to donate anything to try to get it turned in within the next couple of weeks."

"Thanks, Jack. We appreciate it."

"Well, I think it's right sweet what you and Tammy are wanting to do."

"Yeah, well, we just thought it'd be nice. Anyway, I'll bring it up Sunday. Thanks again, Jack. I'll holler back to you later."

So, that was two preacher things that Gary had already gotten accomplished. He relaxed a little bit.

Thursday night, he rested comfortably at home, with Kylie asleep in his arms. He had called Laurie to check on her, and she said everything was fine. She said Jason and Lexi had told them they could sleep over again tonight. She admitted she had walked in on a very awkward conversation between her mother and father, but everything was okay. She told Gary about the day they'd spent riding horses, conveniently leaving out the part about Luke volunteering to be the one who would ride with them. Jason insisted someone accompany the girls on the trails, so Luke readily said he'd do it. The afternoon ended with Luke giving Laurie a kiss on the cheek behind the stable. But Gary didn't need to know about that, even if Roy already did.

Meanwhile, Jerry, Will, Anne, and Marilyn were sitting in the kitchen following a game of Scrabble. Will had won again. Will always won Scrabble. They visited for about an hour before Will decided it was bedtime.

"Come on, Anne. Let's go to bed. It is late, and I have to work tomorrow. You going to bed anytime soon, Dad? You gonna feel like working tomorrow? If not, that is fine. I was just wondering if we should get you up or not."

"Yeah, I think so. I may not put in a full day, but I'll get up and do something. I'm starting to get a backache, lying in bed all the time."

"Alright, then. We'll see you in the morning. Good night." Will and Anne, again, hugged and kissed Jerry and Marilyn. They went to bed. Jerry looked at Marilyn.

"I have an idea. I was thinking; the weather is turning pretty finally. I was wondering how you would like to maybe go on a trip? Just the two of us? We could go to Charleston, or Savannah, Maine or DC, or just somewhere like Natural Bridge. What do you think? How would you like that?" he asked, smiling.

"You mean it? Just the two of us?" she asked disbelievingly.

"Well, yeah. I think it's time that we do something like that. I think we've been together long enough now. I mean, that's what I think."

"Do you think you're up to that? You think you're ready and comfortable with it?"

"Well, it was my idea. I love you, and I don't think I've been very fair to you. I've expected you to be in a relationship with me, and Anne and Faye. And, well, whereas that may always be to an extent, I do think there's some things I can do to make it all up to you. I think us doing something, just the two of us, alone, would be good for us."

"Thank you. I think it would be too. I'd love that."

"Well, alright then. We'll talk some more about it and decide where exactly we want to go and when would be a good time. Okay?"

"Okay. I'm going to run to the bathroom. I'll be back in a few."

"Hey, just go ahead and go on upstairs. I'm going to lock up down here and go to bed. I'll be up there in just a few, dear," he assured her. Marilyn, nearly giddy with excitement after Jerry's vacation proposal, smiled at him, nodded, and left the room.

Jerry rubbed his blurry eyes. It had been difficult playing Scrabble tonight. He seemed to be having a slightly hard time reading the letters on the tiles. But he'd never admit this out loud. He hoped it was just from being sick and sleepy the past few days. He stood up and saw Faye at the deep farmhouse sink. She was just looking at him. He sighed.

"Hello, you sexy thing," he greeted her with a sleepy smile.

"You did a good thing, Jerry."

"Did I? When?"

"Taking her away from here. It's good for you. Anne confuses you."

"Anne isn't the *only* one! You don't think it's just a tad confusing knowing my wife's ghost is stalking my girlfriend? Knowing that you're watching every single thing that goes on? I need my privacy, love. I'm getting tired and I'm getting stressed and confused, yes, confused. I don't want you to go anywhere. I want you to stay right here with me, forever and ever. If I could leave this world right now and spend eternity with you, I would. But it'd mean leaving Will and Anne and Roy and Karen and the babies, and that'd just suck.

"If I could go to that place, wherever it is, where I could just hold you and feel you again, whenever I want to ... but if I want to spend forever with you, I'm just going to have to wait my turn. Until then, I'm going to have to pretend like I've moved on. Good night, darling. I love you."

Jerry turned the lights off on his beloved wife, and he went upstairs to their bedroom, where Marilyn waited for him. Their bedroom. Was it still Jerry and Faye's bedroom? Was it just Jerry's? No, it was Jerry and Faye's bedroom. He was sorry about that for Marilyn's sake, but it's just the way things were. He was sorry to Faye, too. It was so obviously wrong to have his girlfriend in his wife's bed. And people wondered why Jerry Granger had issues.

Jerry went in the bedroom where Marilyn was lying in the bed nude. Jerry paused in the doorway and looked across the semi dark

230

room, lit only by the lamp on the bedside table. In the light, Jerry could see her olive complexion, the curves of her bare hips and breasts. He could see the chestnut colored waves of hair tumbling over her bare shoulders, down her bare back and lying across her warm breasts. The blanket was pulled completely back, so Jerry could see all her naked body waiting for him.

He looked at her, without expression for several minutes. He pushed the door to all the way and walked toward her slowly. Jerry took off his shirt and jeans. When he got down to his boxers, he threw those on the floor too. Jerry got in the bed with Marilyn and made long, sweet love to her before they finally fell asleep in each other's arms.

Friday morning, they were startled awake by Will banging on the bedroom door.

"Dad! You have got to get up! Tammy is starting this morning! You are one of the men of the house and you need to be down there when she arrives. Now, come on!" Will bellowed.

"Ohhhh, come on! I'm tired!"

"And I do not give a shit! She will be here in about 20 minutes! Now, come on or I will come in there!"

"I'm naked, Will!" Marilyn warned him.

"I did not need to hear that, nor do I care, Miss Beales! You can stay in here all morning if you like. I am talking to Dad! Dad is a head of the household, and he needs to be down there to greet his new employee. It is only proper! Now, I mean it!"

"Fine! Just shut the Hell up already! I'm so tired of your nagging and bitching all the damn time!"

"It is neither nagging nor bitching! It is enforcing expectations I have of the people who live here! Now, hurry up!"

"I am going to kick your ass if you don't shut up, boy! I mean it! Get away from my door before I come out of here naked and all! I'll do it!"

"No, do not do that," Will told him hastily.

"Then go away, you damn fool! I'll be down there in a few minutes!"

"Fine!"

"Fine!"

Will made his way downstairs. Anne was half asleep and almost put the coffee pot in the refrigerator. Will stopped her and wordlessly took it from her hands. He put it on the coffee maker and turned to see her holding a cup, looking confused. He took the cup from her and set it beside the coffee maker. He put his hands on her shoulders and talked to her quietly and deliberately.

"Anne, go sit down, baby. Let me get you your medicine, okay? You are acting kind of drifty this morning. Do not worry about anything ... no, do not worry about breakfast stuff yet. We are getting help here for you today. Tammy is coming. She will be here even before Lexi gets here. Just go sit down for me and let me take care of things this morning while we wait for Dad and Miss Beales to get down here. Sit down, here you go. Now, just stay right there for a minute." Will directed a very addled Anne to her seat at the kitchen table. He made her a glass of sweet tea and got her medicine for her. Anne just sat and watched Will. She was very tired this morning. Her head hurt, and she just didn't feel great.

Jerry and Marilyn made their way to the kitchen. They saw Will keeping busy in the kitchen. Marilyn, not thinking much of this, went to help him. But for Jerry, seeing Will do this was cause for worry. He went to Anne who sat still in her chair, looking out the window. He sat beside her and put his hand on her arm.

"Mama? What's the matter? You having a bad time this morning? Son? Has she had her pill?"

"Just a few minutes ago. It has to kick in."

"Why are you having a bad morning, baby? Did you get enough sleep?" Jerry scooted his chair near her and put his arm around her shoulder. She leaned into him. Marilyn brought Jerry coffee and continued to help Will out.

At seven o'clock, they all heard a woman's voice calling from the front screen door. Will excused himself rather formally and went to greet Tammy. He would have told his father to join him, but Jerry was talking to Anne in a rather one-sided conversation. As Will approached the door, he smiled warmly.

"Well, good morning to you, Miss Tammy!" he pushed open the screen, and she smiled back at him as she walked through the wide doorway.

"Hey, there, Will. How are you doing, honey?" she asked as she hugged his neck and he kissed her cheek.

"Oh, I am doing pretty well, thank you. Get back, dog! Come on inside. Daddy and Anne are in the kitchen. Well, Miss Beales is in there, too. Come on and get yourself some coffee and breakfast," he coaxed.

Tammy laughed.

"I thought I was here to work!"

"Well, our workday always starts with coffee and breakfast!"

"Part of my job was fixing the breakfast, I thought."

"Yeah, helping fix it, then helping us eat it! Now, come on. The folks are waiting."

Tammy had been in this house numerous times over the years, too many to count really. She and Faye had been best friends. Tammy had only been in this house nine times since Faye had passed-away though. She had come to pay her respects the day after Faye had died, and she had come for Will's wedding and Jason's wedding and the Halloween party they all had several years ago. The other times had been times when she'd prepared some meals for Jerry following the funeral. There had been a time when Tammy was in this house at least once a week. In one way, that time seemed so far away. In another way, it seemed like only last week she and Faye sat in the kitchen drinking Cokes and having one of their several hour visits. Tammy missed Faye. There were so many things that Tammy had been able to talk to Faye about, things she had never been able to discuss with anybody else, things she had not discussed with anyone at all since she lost her best friend. Yes, Tammy missed Faye very much.

This house sort of made Tammy sad these days. As she walked into the kitchen behind Will, this sadness was overwhelming. She smiled at everyone. Jerry, who had been sitting beside Anne, rubbing her back, stood and hugged her.

"Hey there, girl! Welcome to work!"

"Oh, thank you. Hello, Anne. How are you doing?" Tammy replied. Anne smiled a small smile.

"Hey, Tammy." There seemed to be little emotion. Tammy looked curious enough to draw attention from Will, Jerry, and Marilyn. Marilyn tried to make light of everything.

"So, Tammy. How's it feel, to have left the diner? Sit down; let someone else serve you coffee for once!" She brought a cup and spoon on a saucer to Tammy's seat. Tammy looked up to smile at her and for just a spilt second (was it even that long?) she thought she saw Faye in the seat at the chair next to the head of the table across from Anne. Just as soon as she thought she saw her, she was gone. Apparently, her expression gave her away.

"Tammy? What's the matter?" Jerry asked.

"Oh, nothing. It's just a little weird to be sitting here again. It's, well, it's been awhile, is all. Here, Marilyn, let me help you with that."

Marilyn was carrying food to the table as Will prepared it. That was interesting to Tammy. She had never really imagined Will the domestic type. But he stood at the stove, dishing what appeared to be two dozen scrambled eggs into a green Fiestaware serving bowl.

Will was a pleasant man. Tammy had heard he was somewhat neurotic and overbearing, but she just couldn't see that. He was smiling, visiting, and seemed to be perfectly happy to be helping serve breakfast. Anne just sat beside Jerry and watched. She looked sleepy. Will left the room and returned a few minutes later with sweet little Eliza in his arms and James dragging behind him. Will deposited Eliza on the floor. Both children hugged and kissed Jerry and Anne, but neither seemed surprised to see Tammy sitting there. Although both very young, they knew her from church. James looked at her.

"Hi."

"Hi, James. I like those pajamas."

"Thank you, Miss Tammy." He took his sippy cup to Will.

"Daddy, I want some juice."

"You will have to wait a moment. I am busy."

"Daddyyyyy. I want juice now," he whined.

"James," was all Will said. And that was enough. James sighed and went to Jerry.

"Papa, can I have juice?"

"*May* you have juice; not *can* you have juice," Will corrected.

"Didn't Daddy tell you to wait a moment?" Anne finally spoke up.

"He said he was busy. Papa is not."

"That's true. I'm not busy. Give me the cup, son." Jerry stood up and immediately tripped over Eliza who was crawling out from under the table, playing with the cat. Jerry tried to catch his balance, without success. He fell over her, the cup dropped to the floor, and Eliza cried while James laughed at it all. Anne stood up and she and Marilyn helped Jerry back up. He checked himself for breaks or sprains. James picked the cup up off the floor and set it in front of Tammy.

"Are *you* allowed to get me juice?" Tammy laughed and picked the cup up and prepared the child juice. She set the now almost empty jug of orange juice on the counter, and almost immediately, the jug flung itself to the floor. Tammy just looked at it, stunned. Everyone else started laughing.

"I'm sorry, I don't know how I did that. I don't know how I *could* have done that," Tammy tried to figure out how that had happened.

Will explained it for her,

"You didn't do that, Miss Tammy. Mama did that. Don't worry about it. Just set it back it up on the counter, if you don't mind." Will went back to getting breakfast to the table. As Tammy set the haunted orange juice back on the counter, the screen door at the back of the hall opened and slammed shut. Caleb came in the kitchen, announcing his arrival.

"Okay, everybody! We're here!"

Miss Priss fled from the room immediately. Lexi came in, carrying Teague and his diaper bag, while Jason came in carrying a cardboard box.

"What's with the box?" Jerry asked.

"This is some stuff from the breeding stable. I need Karen to go through it. It was crammed in the drawers in the desk. I don't know what the Hell any of it is. Well, I take that back; I know it's all horse related. But that's about it. Hello, Miss Tammy."

"Hello, Jason. Hey, Lexi." She and Lexi hugged. Caleb came up to Tammy. He liked Tammy a lot. She was one of his Sunday school teachers.

"Hey, Miss Tammy," he smiled angelically at her, even batting his eyelashes. She leaned over and kissed his cheek.

"Hello, sweetheart. How are you this morning?"

"Well, the weather is good, so we should be able to get a lot of work done anyway," Caleb remarked. He went to the refrigerator and pulled out the jug of chocolate milk. He set it on the counter and looked at Marilyn.

"I'll have some of that with my breakfast, please," he told her, sounding about 40 years old.

Marilyn just smiled.

"Yes, sir. I'll have that out to your table in just a moment."

"Thank you." Caleb crawled up in his booster seat at the table. Tammy half expected him to throw back a cup of coffee and finish with a cigarette.

Eventually, everyone was seated at the table, and Jerry said the blessing. Breakfast was pleasant and comfortable. Afterward, the men all stood and grabbed an assortment of things from their sunglasses to to-go coffees to water bottles and phones. Jerry gestured for Tammy to follow him out into the hall during the chaos. In just a moment they were standing together by the back staircase.

"What's up?" Tammy asked.

Jerry craned his neck to make sure Anne was still out of earshot.

"Anne's having one of her days, it looks like. She took her pill, so it shouldn't be too long before it kicks in. In the meantime, don't be offended if she doesn't talk too much. She just tends to act kinda slow and drifty during these spells."

"She's okay though?"

"She will be. Don't fret. Lexi and Karen will both be in here with y'all. They know how to deal with her. And Mare is here. Really, it's not a big deal. The only reason I even brought you out here to talk to you about it is because you seemed bothered that she sorta ignored you in there."

"No, I just wondered what was going on with her. I mean, I know about her problems. I just didn't know that's what this was about," Tammy explained.

Jerry smiled.

"It's all good, sweetheart. Just filling you in on things. But I'm about to go on outside. There's work to do. If you have any questions before Anne is acting normal, just ask Lex or Karen. They'll help you out. You have anything you want to ask me?"

"Um, well, we haven't really discussed my job at all. What do you want me to do? Anything specific I should know?"

"Oh! Um, just help pick up around the house, both downstairs and upstairs. Pick which day of the week you want to do the mopping. Other than that, basic housekeeping stuff. Do windows, dusting, polishing, sweeping, vacuuming the area rugs, helping with the meals and clean up. Don't worry about the laundry though. And when you see Faye just tell her hello, great seeing her, ask how she is. She'll be fine. Okay then ... oh! Miss Priss has *got* to have my bedroom door open."

"Gotcha. I think I can handle things okay. And the part about seeing Faye? You're serious, aren't you?" Tammy asked. She had heard too many times that Faye was still very much so the woman of the house here.

"Yep, dead serious. Well, bad choice of words, perhaps. So, have a good time and relax! We're friends, remember! And on that note; this isn't anything formal. If you need to take a personal day, take a personal day. Just try to let us know the day before if you can. If you need to leave early or arrive late, that's okay too. As for sick days, if you don't feel well one day, just go ahead and arrange to stay home and we'll go from there. That way you can get well faster, and you won't be over here breathing all over us." Jerry kissed Tammy's cheek and went to the kitchen to fuss over Anne for another full 15 minutes before joining the others at work, despite having just announced he was going outside now to work.

It was a pleasant day, for the most part. Along ten in the morning, Anne began acting normal again. Lexi and Anne spent much of the day giggling, but both girls helped Tammy out with the housework. Anne could have easily sat in the comfort of her chair all day and had Tammy take care of the house; after all, that is what Tammy had been hired to do. Instead Anne helped with numerous things.

After lunch, Tammy was wiping the furniture in the beautiful living room. The windows were wide open, and the smells of the mountain valley came through them on warm spring breezes. It was a nice job, Tammy decided. She was glad she had taken it.

"Tammy?" a familiar voice from behind her called. She immediately knew that voice, and without really thinking turned to answer it.

"Yes?" As she turned around, she saw her dearest friend in the world, Faye Granger, standing in front of the big window. Tammy's stomach suddenly hurt, then her arms began to ache. Everything on Tammy began to ache. She drew a ragged breath.

"Oh, Faye."

At this, a smiling Faye brushed the hair from her face and turned to leave the room. Faye had been relatively clear while standing there, but as she left, it was like a thick white fog with an odd light to it. Faye's exit was so quick that *it* scared Tammy more than talking to her dead best friend in the living room had.

Tammy said nothing about her experience. It was something she wanted to think about alone for a while. It was a very private moment for Tammy, and it had been a little frightening. But that night at home, Tammy lay in her bed thinking.

She spent the majority of the day surrounded by friends in a beautiful old home, out in the country. And, she had seen her very best friend. Her friend may very well have been dead, but she still spoke to Tammy.

Faye had delivered a big laughing smile at Tammy when Tammy turned around to answer her. Remembering that made Tammy laugh now.

It was true; that Granger crowd never changed. Even when they die, they still stay the same laughing, smiling, very, very weird family that everyone was so fond of. Tammy went to sleep, looking forward to Monday and to whatever weird, dysfunctional things it'd bring at the Granger's.

CHAPTER 16

Walter Loftis, who had just recently arrived in Liberty Creek to establish himself as the next large animal vet (when Dr. Corbin retired the next week) sat at the bar in The Tavern on Friday night. He had had a very long day. He'd spent the day helping Barton on his farm. It had been a relatively miserable experience. The man did not need to own horses. When Will Granger had told him that Barton didn't need to own a cat, much less a horse, he wasn't kidding. It was mind boggling to Walter, how that idiot Barton had become the one who took over the Granger's customers when Jerry had his nervous breakdown many years ago. Walter couldn't imagine what an adjustment that must have been for not just the horses but their owners!

Ray Barton was having problems; that was as plain as the nose on his face. The property was looking rough and in bad need of a makeover. Walter felt that the conditions were so bad that the horses there needed to be taken away. But Walter had just arrived in Liberty Creek. These people were all quite tight, and he worried if he started anything against one of them, he'd wake in the night to an angry mob with torches in his yard.

"Here ya go, Walter. It's a good thing you don't have far to walk," Keith Barkley told him with a tired smile. Walter shook his head.

"I have a feeling I'll be in here often the way things have been going since I got here."

"Well, you won't be alone."

"Really, it's just not going well."

"Oh, come on, man! You just got here! I mean, these folks are friendly for the most part, but they're not going to have you to dinner within three days."

"I've been here longer than three days, but I'm not really expecting dinner invites. Anyway, you're wrong. Mrs. Duncan and Miss Reynolds have both already invited me over for dinner. Oh, yeah, and that Patsy ... McKinney is it? She asked me over."

"Okay, Miss Debbie- you know, Mrs. Duncan- is okay. She's sweet; one of those who wants to make sure everyone feels loved. Miss Reynolds, did you actually go to her house for dinner?"

"Mrs. Duncan *was* sweet. She and her husband were very nice. Miss Reynolds, not yet."

"Well, Miss Reynolds is nice too. Don't get me wrong. She's really nice. She's funny and cute enough. But you do know she owns The Doll House down the street, right? I mean, she's got a serious thing going on with dolls. Honestly, she kind of scares me. Glenn, you know, the mailman, he went in there the other day and said she was sitting at her table with a bunch of doll body parts all spread out in front of her. He said that once he delivered a box to her and she told him it was a box of *hair and eyes*. I mean, *ew*. But you know, all that doesn't mean she wouldn't make a great dinner date." Keith wiped the bar off with a bar towel then ate a handful of corn nuts.

"Well, I didn't know about her doll thing. But I don't think I'll cancel dinner over it just yet. I told her I'd come over Sunday night. What about Patsy?"

"She's nice too, but the town gossip. She knows who's pregnant before the mother does. She talks about folks too much; Gary Connelly is always chewing her out about that shit. Maybe with him filling in for Lawson, he can find a way to chew her out in a sermon. That might help get through to her. Probably not though."

Walter just nodded. He took a swig of his beer. Keith continued talking.

"What you need to do is meet you a gal though. There's still a few loose ones here. Miss Reynolds of course. But there's others. Finding you a gal would do you right good."

Walter thought about the one and only woman who *had* sparked his interest since moving here, and it was unfortunate because she was obviously taken. Honestly, though, he just couldn't get his mind off her. He'd seen her in town and around. She was always so pleasant and refined and well-spoken. She was educated and classy. She spoke with a clipped, articulate tone that made her seem above anyone in this town. Her back was always straight, and her head always held high; her chin was always slightly lifted. She had a way of holding herself that made her seem almost regal. Other women here just didn't come close to her.

The door opened, and an angry woman came to the bar and stood beside him. She looked at Keith, sort of wild-eyed. He looked rather bored. He shoved more corn nuts in his mouth and just looked at her.

"Keith, has Jack been in here tonight?" Stacy Mitchell asked.

She'd had a long week and things were not getting any easier. Her husband was missing, her daughter had left home, and she'd been lectured by both Gary and Jason.

"I don't keep a leash on him, Stacy. Why do you keep going through this, anyway? *I* don't like you, but I'm sure there's some other guy in this town who might still would. I mean, this shit with Jack is just getting really old."

"I didn't ask you. And you don't like me? Screw you. I don't like you either."

"You keep coming in here, bitching and moaning about how miserable you are, how bad he treats you, how nothing is ever going your way. Everyone's tired of it. I know I sure as Hell am."

"Just answer the fucking question. Has he been in here tonight?"

"Nope."

"Today?" Stacy pressed. Keith shook his head slowly, as if trying to remember.

"Nope."

"Would you tell me if he had?"

"Nope. Not my business. I'm not going to get involved. If you want to know where your husband is, then perhaps you should ask him to live with you."

"Look! You don't know what's going on."

"I know he left you. Everyone in town knows he left you. He's not a very private man, Stace. All I can say is, if you want to find your husband, maybe you should try looking at his girlfriend's house?" Keith helpfully suggested; a suggestion that didn't go over well.

Stacy took the beer from in front of Walter and slung it all over Keith. Walter was sure she was going to break the bottle, but no. Actually, she just set it carefully on the bar.

"Stacy, you *bitch*!"

"You shouldn't have said that! That was a real asshole thing to say!"

"It's true! You damn well know it's true! Get out of here! You aren't going to come in my bar and throw beer at me!" Keith yelled, wiping his face with his bar towel. Stacy shot him the bird and left with numerous bar patrons watching the scene with interest.

"I'm not paying for that beer. You pissed her off. You buy me another beer," Walter told Keith. Walter was already getting a little sleepy; he had, after all, already downed five beers. Keith glared at him and threw away the now empty bottle. He handed Walter a new one. Walter thought for a moment.

"So, that one is? I've seen her around, but I'm still trying to learn names around here. I know the first name is obviously Stacy."

"Stacy Mitchell, or should I say *Bitchell?* She's married to Jack Mitchell, but you'd never know it. He treats her like shit and they're fighting every fucking week. But you know? She's an idiot. I haven't had any use for her since she pulled that crap on Jason."

"Jason?"

"Connelly."

"From the Granger's place?"

"Yeah."

"Well, what'd she do to him?"

"Got pregnant by him, got pissed off about it, and she kept the baby that she so obviously didn't want. Jason tried to have a relationship with the child, but she wouldn't let him have anything to do with the delivery, didn't even tell him it was born. He found out from his old man. Then, the old bat wouldn't even let him have a relationship with the kid. She hooked up with Jack before Laurie was even born. Jason

242

has always said the reason he didn't fight it was because he thought it'd make things difficult and stressful for the kid.

"Anyway, everyone likes Jason. So, the whole town kinda lost any respect for her after she treated him that way. Then, her hooking up with up the biggest asshole in town didn't help any." Keith just didn't like this woman.

"Here, Keith. Keep the change," a voice beside Walter said. Walter recognized him but didn't know from where.

"Alright. Thanks, Randy. Hey? I didn't even realize you were still in here. You know where Jack is?"

"Jack? No. Why are you wanting to know?" Randy Meadows asked irritably.

"You must have seen Stacy's fit in here just now,"

"Naw. I must have been in the toilet. Maybe I was at the pool table. I didn't see shit. Anyway, I'm gone. I'll catch you later," Randy said. He gave Walter a look that wasn't exactly warm and inviting and left.

Keith went to collect bottles at a table, but Walter thought for a few minutes. Randy had not told the truth. When Stacy flung the beer at Keith, Walter had turned quickly to shield himself from the airborne beer. When he did this, he had seen Randy watching the whole thing. Yes, Randy had been sitting there, underneath the dartboard, beside the jukebox, and he'd watched what happened between Keith and Stacy. Walter was pretty sure he'd seen the whole thing. So, why did Randy pretend to have seen nothing?

Again, Walter felt he was too new here to start anything. He decided to just keep quiet.

Keith came back to the bar and muttered to himself. He looked up at Walter.

"What's eating you?" he asked Walter.

"Nothing. I'm just thinking about all you crazy-ass people. I'm getting tired. I think I'm gonna head on back to the house. The dog's probably wanting out, anyway. But take this and keep the change, man. I appreciate it."

"You appreciate what?"

"Well, folks have been nice and all here, but there's just not really anyone I feel like I'm actual friends with. I mean, the Grangers and them are really nice. Don't get me wrong. I don't know; I guess I'd call them friends. But you're the only one I ever really talk to around here. So, I'm just saying, thanks. I appreciate it."

"Well, like I said, its gonna take a little time. Nobody here really knows you yet. It'd probably help you out to go to church. It'd certainly get you in good with Gary. And well, you *want* to get in *good* with *Gary*," Keith said this almost apologetically. Walter looked at him.

He suddenly remembered a conversation he'd had with Jonathon Beck, at the Granger's boarding stable. He'd been told there was a group of men, 12 to be exact, who pretty much ran this town, and it really had nothing to do with who did or didn't hold a place in local office. Jonathon had also all but warned Walter about Gary Connelly.

Walter had met Gary for the first time when there had been a search party at the Granger's, when Gary's grandson had gone missing. Walter had liked the man for the most part. He was kind of stressed out and mean that day understandably. But overall, Walter guessed he liked him. But Walter didn't know him. Not really. Now, Keith was telling Walter if he wanted to make friends in this Podunk town, he needed to get tight with Gary. Well, paranoia and an eagerness to be accepted got the best of Walter Loftis.

"Yeah, I guess I might can make services Sunday."

"I think it'd be a good thing for you to do that," Keith agreed.

"Yeah. I'm going home. Take care, Keith."

"You, too. See you tomorrow," Keith added, laughing. Walter had been in there almost every night since arriving in Liberty Creek. Walter waved at him and stepped outside.

Main Street lived up to its name, tonight. It was Friday night during spring break. The streets were surprisingly busy for a town so small. People were out wandering around, window shopping. Gangs of teenagers were scattered here-and-there but seemed to be behaving for the most part. Despite the cooler mountain air of the April evening, the majority of the teenaged girls had stripped down to tank tops and ridiculously short shorts and skirts. Walter saw a few smoking cigarettes and saw a few doing things that their mothers would stroke out about, but it was all good. He just stood there for a moment, watching people.

He liked this town. He liked how the businesses were all locally run, and how they had refused any chain stores inside town. Chains were welcomed on the interstate, but they had no place in Liberty Creek. He liked how everyone knew each other and looked out for each other. But he was seeing firsthand that there were a lot of other things going on in this town that weren't so picture perfect. Stacy Mitchell's freak out was evidence enough of that. Let's not forget about the shady warnings about the mysterious dozen men who were keeping things running to satisfaction around here. He had started to suspect who a few of that dozen were; he'd started to suspect people within days of Jonathon first mentioning it.

Walter turned and headed for Walnut Street. He was approaching a truck parked in front of Plott's bookstore. The man standing at the front of this truck, had his back to Walter. Walter couldn't see his face, but he could hear him well. Upon hearing his first sentence, Walter slowed to a stop.

"Let me tell you something, Stacy. I'm not putting up with you and your shit anymore. You told me you were through with him. So, why are you checking the bars for him? Don't hand me that bullshit. I saw you! I was sitting right there when you showed your trashy ass in there tonight! Done with him? Really? Then why are you looking for him? Why do you give a damn where he is? No, you listen to me. I am done. You think you are so smart. Spending time with your daughter tonight? Really? You taking Laurie out bar-hopping with you now? Did you leave her at The Grill while you went to The Tavern looking for your husband? Hell no. She wasn't with you tonight. If she has any sense, she's at Jason's. I'm not stupid. But I *am* pissed off. And you know what? You just fucked up. You are gonna be sorry because what I'm about to do to you is coming. You wait. Because I promise, it's coming."

In his somewhat intoxicated state, in conjunction with his anger, Randy Meadows didn't stop to look around before calling Stacy Mitchell, and he didn't even think to keep his voice down. It wouldn't have mattered; there wasn't anybody in front of Plott's because Plott's and the next several stores had closed for the night. Except Walter had just happened to come out of The Tavern at the right (or wrong, depending on how you looked at it) time.

Randy hung the phone up and slammed his hands into the hood of the truck. At this, Walter ducked into the old wide storefront of Plott's and hid. He felt somewhat silly hiding at his age. But he hid anyway. He stared at the tiny ceramic hexagon tiles in the doorway under his feet. He was in position to see Randy through the windows though. He watched Randy pull back and punch his own passenger side window. He heard the string of profanity that followed when stupid Randy split his knuckles open in the process. This got the attention of several people. Randy put his bleeding fist against his stomach, got in his truck with its now shattered passenger side window, and left.

Everyone else just shrugged and moved along. They had not heard the ominous conversation between a scorned secret boyfriend and his married girlfriend. They had not seen Randy try to put his own fist through his own truck window, or the bloody fist that he ended up with. All they heard was Randy cuss, and saw him get in his truck, and take off. Walter, however, had heard a lot more and entirely too much for his liking.

As Randy drove off, entirely too fast for these streets, Walter came out of hiding. He proceeded to walk toward Walnut Street. He was no longer tired; he was uncomfortable. He didn't know Randy well enough. Was Randy known for running his mouth with a bunch of empty, threats? Or was Randy crazy?

Walter had no way of knowing. He paused; he considered going back to The Tavern and getting the scoop on Randy, but he changed his mind. He was tired and just desperately wanted to go home.

Walter got to his house and unlocked the door quickly. He felt he had heard things he should not have heard tonight. Maybe Randy just meant he'd dump her? That was possible. Walter fell asleep on his couch.

Saturday morning, Liberty Creek woke up as it did every Saturday morning. By ten that morning, the streets, and sidewalks were busy with kids walking and running, riding bikes and skateboards. Adults were out taking care of weekend errands and gathering in front of the co-op.

At his co-op, Gary Connelly was selling seed to Miss Ivy while Rocky, the neighborhood cat was knocking the display of Bic lighters off the counter. Gary shoved Rocky off the counter and sold a newspaper to Leon Addams.

"What was that that went on last night at The Tavern?" Leon asked quietly, as he picked up the lighters from the floor.

"Thanks. Regarding what? I don't hang out at The Tavern very often. I don't know what you're referring to."

"Clint said Stacy came in there madder than a settin' hen. Raised all kinds of hell, but he couldn't hear what exactly was said. I thought you might know because it was Stacy and all."

"Well, first things first; Stacy doesn't confide in me. Stacy has very little to say to me these days. She's not real pleased about Laurie moving in with me, and on top of that, why would ..."

"Laurie is living with you? When did that happen?" Leon interrupted.

"Um, just this week. Anyway, second, why would I discuss Stace with you? It's my granddaughter's mama. You think I'm going to go running my mouth about her? Really, Leon, I expected more out of you. Go to the lunch counter at Jenson's. You'll probably get the scoop there." Gary said this so smoothly that it irritated Leon.

"I wasn't trying to gossip! I was just making sure everything was okay."

"Of course, you were. Well, I thank you for looking out for my folks. We appreciate that."

"I'm serious."

"Like I said, thank you." Gary smiled a very insincere smile.

"God damn it," Leon said, as he turned to leave.

Gary's head flew up quickly.

"Hey! You want to talk like that, there's other places to buy your paper."

"Oh, come on, Gary! I didn't it mean it like that. I was just ... I wasn't even thinking about what I said."

"Seems to be a common problem around here. I'll see you at my services tomorrow," Gary added, knowing that Leon Addams had gotten real slack about his church attendance here lately.

Leon just waved back at Gary, over his shoulder. Being friends with Gary Connelly was a real pain in the ass sometimes. One weekend, you could trust him to hook you up with some moonshine; the next weekend, he'd lecture you with Bible scriptures.

Leon was walking out the door when he saw Jerry and Marilyn coming up the sidewalk.

"Hey, Leon. My, you look … unhappy," Jerry said, smiling.

Marilyn tossed her hair behind her shoulder and laughed. Leon always looked pissed off. He was the principal at the high school, and she had to admit he wasn't the most pleasant person to work with. He ate alone in his office, and Marilyn knew for a fact that he kept an engraved silver flask in his desk drawer. She stumbled upon this while looking for a bottle of Liquid Paper.

"You can't say *anything* around Gary. You gotta be real careful not to offend ol' *Father Flanagan* in there."

"Hey, now. Be nice. What'd you say that pissed him off this time? You do tend to say the worst things at the worst times."

"I asked what happened at The Tavern last night. Clint said Stacy was in there showing her ass. So, I just wondered what Gary knew about it."

"You gossiped. Gary doesn't like gossip and certainly not gossip about his people, Leon. I mean, come on! You ought to know that by now."

"You're his best friend. Are you honestly going to tell me that Gary never talks to you about anybody? He never *ever* tells you about something he heard in town or anything like that?" Leon asked disbelievingly.

"Nope. He never does. He might talk to us about something concerning us or something concerning him. But if it doesn't directly affect one of us then he doesn't talk about it to us."

"Whatever. I'm gone." Leon took off, and Jerry and Marilyn went inside.

"Hey, big guy! What's going on? Can you get away for a bite to eat?" Jerry asked Gary.

"You feeling better? That was a quick recovery for you."

"Aw, I had good nursing; I'm up and running again. Just got to town, and Mare and I were gonna go eat. I thought I'd see if you wanted to go."

"Just got to town? You didn't spend the night here?"

"Naw. Me and Will had a movie night last night."

"Date night," Marilyn corrected him. He glared at her.

"It wasn't a date night. *Arthur* came on last night and then a Dustin Hoffman marathon. Will and I wanted to watch it together. So, I stayed home last night, but Mare came back to town. She had enough of haunted houses."

"No, I just had enough of all of those crazy people. I needed quiet," Marilyn corrected him again. Jerry smiled, and Gary laughed.

"I can see that. Y'all gonna be up there this afternoon though?"

"Yeah. You coming up?" Jerry asked.

Gary nodded.

"I gotta bring the girls back, so yeah."

"Jason mentioned the sleepover. How'd that go over? They stayed a while, didn't they?"

"Yeah, I think it went fine. It's just been a long week. I'm glad Laurie had that this week. It likely got her mind off things, somewhat anyway."

"What's wrong with Laurie?" Jerry asked.

This wasn't gossip. Jerry loved Laurie as if she were another grandchild, and Gary knew this. Gary knew he was asking out of concern, not because he was nosy.

"Big fight between her and ... Hey, Mamie! I got those hanging baskets finally! They were delivered not even an hour ago. They're in the corner by the Burpee seeds. Anyway, Laurie and Stacy got into it and Laurie ran away in the middle of the night several nights ago and came to my house. She was all upset and next day when I took Laurie over there to Stacy's to get her clothes, Stace was all cold and hateful to her. She's going through a lot."

"Laurie or Stacy?"

"Well, both of them, actually. But I'm referring to Laurie. She has a lot on her plate right now."

"Well, that sucks," Jerry said simply.

"In a nutshell, yes. Then, Leon comes in here asking about Stacy starting shit at The Tavern last night. That irritates me. To begin with, Stacy needs to act like a mother and stop acting like a trashy 20-year-old. To end with, what business is it of his? Of course, when you show your ass in public, I guess you automatically become everyone's business. Yeah, I think it's best for Laurie to stay with me. It's like I told Jay, Laurie needs stability. She's not going to find that at Stacy's." Gary was careful to not add that he didn't think she'd find it up on Teague Road either.

"No, not likely. Well, I hope it all works out," Jerry said.

"Yeah, give it time. It's a terrible age, and she's going through some stuff. I think she'll be really happy with you and Kylie. You two are great," Marilyn added.

"Thank you, dear. Your confidence and compliments are appreciated. Anyway, let me go help Mamie. Cokes and a paper?"

"Cokes and paper. You want the ferns, Mare?" Jerry asked.

"Oh, yeah, thanks."

"And four ferns. But what about something to eat? You coming?" Jerry pressed. Gary looked thoughtful for a minute. Eric, who overheard the conversation, saw his boss pondering the offer.

"Go on, Chief. I'll take care of things around here," Eric offered.

"You sure?"

"Yeah, it's fine. Take off. I mean, it's not like it's the first time I've watched the store," Eric pointed out, somewhat insulted his competence was being questioned. Eric had been working here for years. He was graduating this year and would then be working here full-time. And here, Gary was wondering if he had sense enough to run the place on a Saturday morning for a couple of hours.

"True enough. Okay, Eric. I'll leave things in your capable hands. I'll be right there, Jerry. Let me just grab my phone and help Mamie real quick," Gary agreed. First, he rang Jerry up. Jerry and Marilyn walked out to the porch to pick out her ferns. She selected the ones she liked and put them in the holding corner of the front porch. Gary helped Mamie, grabbed his phone, and walked up to Eric.

"Hey, no need to be ill about what I said. I didn't mean I didn't think you were capable of doing the job. I just meant, I felt bad about running out of here and leaving you to do the work."

"It's alright, man. No big deal."

"You're sure?"

"Yeah. It's alright. I mean, I did think you were implying that, but I understand now. It's fine. Really. Go with Mr. Granger and Miss Beales."

"Well, hey. I'm sorry, okay?"

"Alright. It's *fine*," Eric insisted. Gary nodded, and left with his friends.

Eric had heard the conversation, which meant he'd also heard the part about Laurie. He hated that for her. He knew her well enough and thought she was nice. She tended to act (and look) older than her 15 years, and this got her attention from not only the boys in the ninth-grade class, but the 10th 11th and 12th grade classes as well. Eric now knew that Laurie was living with her very overprotective grandfather.

Eric had known Gary his whole life. Eric had started working at the co-op in eighth grade on weekends and during the summers. In 10th grade, he'd started also working after school. Now, he was getting more hours and was looking forward to school letting out, so he could work full-time. He'd thought about college but decided this made sense. He already knew this store like the back of his hand, knew how everything was done and run, and he truly enjoyed the work.

Gary had always been a part of the co-op, being as how he lived right behind it. He and Wes were friends, and he did a lot for the place. So, Eric had gotten to know Gary. And he knew a lot about Gary. A whole lot.

CHAPTER 17

At the Granger's, it was a very typical Saturday morning. Anne was mixing up her bread dough in the big kitchen and James and Eliza were watching cartoons in pajamas. Anne was alone this morning, waiting for Lexi and Jason to bring the kids over. She knew today would be a full house, because Laurie had her friends over to spend the past several days.

She knew that Gary and Kylie would be over, because Gary had to collect Laurie and her friends. She also knew that Lexi had several chores to attend to before coming over. So, it was going to be a lonely morning until everyone came over.

Roy and Karen had gone to a gun show in the next county and wouldn't be getting to the house until after lunch. She knew Jerry and Marilyn wouldn't be back until after lunch too. It was a lonely, boring morning.

Anne had just finished kneading the dough and put it in the big old wooden dough tray that had been in the Granger's family for well over a hundred years. When Anne had first worried about using something so old and special for bread, they had all looked at her as if she were kind of stupid. They pointed out to her that Faye had been using that same dough tray up until her passing. So, Anne used the dough tray.

She covered it with the tea towel to let it rest and rise. She sighed heavily and sat down at the old kitchen table. She took her notebook and was looking over her list of things to do next week when she heard an odd noise. She looked up to see the plastic straw in her glass of tea moving by itself. The straw stirred the sweet tea and ice slowly. Then, the straw began to stir even faster. Anne just watched it. She wasn't real concerned about ghost germs on her straw, and this kind of thing had become quite a normal occurrence.

Anne set her pencil down and rested her chin in her hand and found herself smiling. After about three full minutes of this, Anne took her finger and rested it on the glass rim, which prevented the straw from stirring so easily. The straw stopped. Anne moved her finger, and the straw resumed stirring. Anne let a giggle escape. She blocked the straw again after a moment. Again, the straw stopped. Anne moved her finger, and the straw stirred the tea again. Anne and Faye spent a full 20 minutes playing with Anne's drinking straw.

Meanwhile, Will was working in the boarding stable. He heard the work truck approaching and went to the doorway to see who it was. Luke pulled up beside the stable and got out.

"Hey, Will. Jason said to bring this feed over. Well, he said to bring it yesterday, but I forgot about it. Anyway, it's here now."

Will stuffed his rag in his back pocket and looked in the truck bed. He just nodded. He wondered though why Jason didn't drop it off on his way to the breeding stable. He had gone to the co-op and gotten the feed. He had to drive past this end of the farm to get to the other end of the farm. Will thought it just stood to reason he'd drop the boarding stable's feed off on the way to the breeding stable. Luke watched Will for just a moment. He suppressed a smile; he knew exactly what Will was thinking.

"I don't know why he didn't just bring it by yesterday when he got it. I mean, he had to drive right past here. But what are you gonna do, right?" Luke told him. Will looked up him, squinting in the bright light. He sighed and laughed easily.

"Yeah, what are you gonna do? I mean, really though … it just does not make sense to me why he always does that."

"Who knows why he does a lot of things? Hey, who's that horse? I don't remember that one around here. It's pretty. It's big, isn't it?" Luke commented noticing the chestnut colored Thoroughbred. It was a striking animal. He walked toward the corral where it was tied to the walker. Will followed him.

"Just showed up yesterday. Retired racehorse. Glenn Raleigh bought him. He is a fine animal; I agree." Will leaned on the fence and watched the bored horse walk in circles. Luke thought about something.

"Raleigh lives a good hour away."

"More like an hour and half."

"He's paying for the deluxe services I guess?"

"Of course."

"Y'all are such snobs," Luke said. Will wasn't sure he'd heard correctly.

"We're what?"

"Snobs."

"Wha ... we are ... why ... snobs? Us? We are most certainly not snobs!"

"Of course, you are. Out of all the horses that board here, how many belong to anyone from town? Think about it."

"Well, a few."

"You have how many horses boarding? And only a few are from around here. Doesn't that tell you anything?" Luke asked.

For one of the very few times in his life, Will was at a loss for words. He just looked at Luke, exasperated and confused. So, Luke explained himself.

"Look, you grew up here. You know what people make around here. Nobody from town can *afford* to keep their horses here. The ones that have horses *have* to keep them at Barton's because that's all they can afford. And the horses are treated like shit there. Don't you think some of the folks from town would like to keep their horses here? They like your family. Everyone knows the reputation this place has. Who *wouldn't* want to keep their horses here? But y'all charge so fucking much that there's no way in Hell they *could*.

"Just because y'all are rich doesn't mean that everyone you know is. I mean, Liberty Creek has had your back for how long? How long have they stood by this family? And what do y'all do? You basically tell them that they're not quality enough to keep their horses here. Loftis told me the other day that he's been spending some time at Barton's. He said it's just a matter of time before he gets shut down. What then, Will? What do they do with their horses when that happens? Sell them off?

"I don't know. It just seems to me that you'd offer some boarding options that don't cost so much. But that's just me."

"Well, it's not that we're snobs. I mean, we do not have a problem with the locals boarding here."

"Haven't you ever wondered why anyone would rather board at Barton's? Have you really never asked yourself why anyone would choose that dump over this place?"

"Not really. I mean, he's been boarding horses for years. I guess I just figured he had people he knew."

"No. It's just that they can't afford services here. Will, you have the room here. And, come on, it's not like you need the extra income. Why don't you take at least ten stalls and make them low income boarding for the people who can't afford $500 a month? Because face it; everyone doesn't own their own Chevy dealership, and everyone doesn't have a daddy who is a member of Congress in D.C. That's just bullshit. Janie Landry loves horses, but her dad drives a forklift, Will. Her mom works at The Buy & Bag. Do you really think they have $500 a month laying around to pay rent for a horse? Think about it."

"Well, you make me sound kind of mean. I'm not mean. And I am not a snob. I just never really looked at it that way, before."

"I never said you were mean. I'm just saying its' kind of like private school, you know? Some parents have money and the right name, and they can poke their kids in some really great private school somewhere, while parents without money have to stick their kids in some crappy public school. I mean, the school *here* isn't crappy, but some places have real crappy public schools. Those kids deserve the great attention and education they'd get in the private school, but they get screwed out of it, just because their folks aren't rich enough. And the same goes for the horses."

"So, you think I should offer lower prices for folks from around here. I see." Will looked at the magnificent Thoroughbred.

Granger Horse Farm had built up its reputation as being elite among horse facilities. People knew the horses coming out of there had extremely impressive bloodlines. They knew the horses boarding there were treated as royalty. They knew the grounds were gorgeous and clean;

the pastures had picturesque rolling hills with quaint wooden fences. They knew that the horses there were happy, healthy, and spoiled.

Then Will realized that Luke was right. Those horses at Barton's weren't happy. Will himself felt sorry for them. But he had just never thought it through a whole lot. There were not many of any one thing in Liberty Creek. But he had always just figured they had a horse facility and Barton had a horse facility. He knew theirs was nicer, but it didn't really mean anything to Will. Theirs was older and historic. Theirs was a different level altogether. It didn't make them snobs; it was just a fact that over time they had built up an impressive reputation and clientele.

"And Barton's really is looking bad, Will," Luke pressed. Will nodded. He'd heard enough horror stories from clients who had been forced to board at Barton's during Jerry's decline; clients who were all too eager to return to the Granger's. Will furrowed his brow.

"Alright, you maybe make a good point. I guess there is truth to what you say. Let me talk to Dad, Uncle Roy and Jason. But I do not see any reason why we could not work something reasonable out," Will said carefully.

As obnoxious as he knew it sounded, he simply wasn't used to admitting someone had a better idea than he'd had. Luke, knowing Will well enough already, was surprised and could tell it absolutely pained Will to give in to this.

"Really? You'll think about it?"

"Yes, I will think about it. It does make sense. Just give me time to talk it over with the others. But you know, you still don't have to call us snobs."

"Maybe that wasn't the best word. Maybe I should have used ignorant, sheltered, or close-minded. I guess those would have worked better," Luke agreed. Will punched him in the arm, and both men laughed.

Will and Luke arranged to talk about it again soon. Will finished his work and went to the house for lunch and to wait for his afternoon guests.

Anne was sitting at the kitchen table writing in a notebook. She looked up as he came in the kitchen.

"Hey, boss. You ready for lunch?" she asked. Will kissed his wife on the top of the head and sat down with her at the table. She giggled.

"Hey, watch this." She put her finger on the edge of the glass of tea sitting before her. Then she removed it. Slowly, the straw began stirring the tea in the glass. The straw started stirring faster and faster. Will watched with interest. He began to smile.

"Are you bonding with Mama today?" he asked.

"A little. You sit down; I'll get your food."

"No, I'll get the kids, then we'll all sit down. Where are they?"

"They're in the living room watching T.V."

"I told you to stop poking them in front of that damn thing. They need to be outside playing. There are all kinds of things they could be doing instead of watching television. Growing up, I was allowed to watch Saturday morning cartoons until noon. I had one hour after school. I was allowed to watch some family sitcoms with my parents at night. There was the occasional movie or special. That's it. These kids watch too much."

"I'm sorry. I'll work on that."

"Do you think I'm joking?"

"No! That's why I said I'd work on it. My parents never gave a shit how much TV I watched when I was a kid."

"And didn't you say you wanted to raise these how I was raised instead of how you were raised?"

"Yes."

"Then, when I tell you to do something, just do it. Feel free to ask me my reasons. I will be more than happy to explain my reasoning. But please cooperate."

"But Will? They *were* watching Saturday morning cartoons."

"But Anne? It is one o'clock now. It is no longer Saturday morning. From now on, the TV gets cut off at noon on Saturdays."

"Fine."

"Thank you. It will be better for them. It will also mean you get to spend more time with them from now on," Will said happily.

"Oh goody," Anne replied sarcastically.

Will paused in the doorway. He glared at his wife for a moment. He remembered what his dad had told him about choosing his battles. Will regained his composure and forced a smile.

"Alright! Then we understand one another. I will return in a moment."

"Alright," Anne sighed. She loved Will and she loved their children. But Will expected her to already have parenting down. He expected her to know exactly how to handle every situation. She didn't think this was fair. He often went to Jerry for advice on how to handle things. He wanted to be just like his dad. Anne understood that.

But he wanted her to be just like his mom, and he didn't understand that she didn't have anyone to go to for advice. Will had Jerry to talk to, but Anne didn't have Faye to talk to.

"I'm not Faye. He wants me to be Faye, but I'm not Faye. I'm doing the best that I can. I didn't even know her, but I'm expected to be like her? How am I supposed to do that?" Anne said aloud in the empty kitchen. Well, the kitchen seemed empty.

The straw began to stir the iced tea again. Anne watched it for a moment. She walked over to the table and set the plates down at their places. She felt her eyes smart with tears. She wiped the tears away as they fell down her cheeks faster. The straw stopped stirring. Anne turned to get glasses for the drinks and was only slightly startled to see Faye standing beside the sink.

Her arms were crossed in front of her; this is the way Faye often stood. Hair was falling over one eye, and she was smiling. Whenever Anne saw her, she saw her wearing what Anne thought might be jeans, and a light solid top.

The two women looked at one another. Anne wiped her eyes again when she heard Will and the children approaching up the hall. Faye brushed the hair out of her eyes.

"Look in the cedar chest in our bedroom," Faye said.

"What? Why?" Anne asked. But Faye just smiled and disappeared in that creepy, swift blur that she always left in. Anne was left in the kitchen looking confused and sad.

"Hey, what's going on?" Will asked as he came in the kitchen with the babies. Anne just looked at him blankly.

"Nothing. Here, sit down. I'll have it all on the table in a second." As Anne busied herself, Will put James in his booster seat and Eliza in her highchair. Will walked over to Anne and stood beside her at the counter. He looked worried.

"What is the matter, baby?"

"Nothing, really. I ... well, I saw your mom. I guess it's just still kinda weird for me, is all. It's alright."

"Are you sure? Everything is alright?"

"I'm sure. I promise. Don't worry about it, boss. I'm okay. Really. Let's eat. We need to hurry up and eat before Lexi and them get here. It's going to be a full house this afternoon."

Will took her face in his hands and kissed her once, twice, and again. He smiled at her and all it took to make everything better was seeing that smile, those blue eyes, and that dark blond hair with those sweet little wayward curls showing up in it.

The four of them sat down and had lunch, then cleaned up the kitchen together. They spent a long time waiting for James and Eliza to help with the work, but it was their weekend ritual. The kids always helped clean up in the kitchen after breakfast and lunch. This sometimes meant waiting 20 minutes while Eliza put one piece of silverware in the drawer, and it sometimes meant waiting for what seemed an eternity for James to dry the dishes before handing them to Will to put away. But it was important to Will that they did things like this together.

Yes, Will actually enjoyed doing housework with his family. He was enthusiastic about it even. Will found it fun and enjoyable to hang out in the kitchen with his wife and kids and his dad. Jerry didn't find this weird; Jerry was the same way. Jerry preferred to hang out in the house and help than work outside, these days. Anne enjoyed their enthusiasm, but she thought it was kind of odd. Her own father had been the exact opposite.

Finally, the kitchen work was done, and Anne had just poured up more tea when Jerry and Marilyn came in the front door. Marilyn came and sat in the kitchen, the kids went out back to play in the yard, and Will called Jerry to the living room. After a few minutes, they heard the piano start playing.

"Will plays that beautifully. Why doesn't he do it more often?" Marilyn asked Anne. Anne shrugged. She thought for a minute.

"He does play it often enough; he just doesn't play for others. He plays at night. He's teaching James to play. He plays a lot from the hymnal, but he does play other stuff too. He likes old 80s stuff. I don't know what that it is he's playing right now, though. What is that?" Anne wondered aloud, turning her ear toward the living room.

The piano would start, then stop, then start again. It was the same song over and over, but only a few seconds were played each time. It was as if Will were warming up to play something. Then, the piano kept playing. Marilyn smiled thoughtfully.

"I know that song, I think. I've heard that before ... what is it?" she asked. Then, as if to answer their question, Will's and Jerry's voices began singing together. Anne rolled her eyes.

"Seriously? The song from *Arthur*? Oh, good grief. I should have known; they were way too into that movie last night," Anne said. Marilyn giggled.

"They sound good though! I'm going to go listen to them better. You coming?"

"I'll be in there in a few minutes. It's okay; you can go on in there."

Marilyn went in the living room to watch Jerry and Will sing Christopher Cross songs, and Anne finished up what she was doing. She then joined the others in the living room. Will was seated at the beautiful cherry Steinway grand piano, with Jerry at his side. Anne couldn't help but smile.

They were having such a good time. Jerry sat there, with his graying goatee and his short, gray-blond hair. His blue eyes were happy, and he looked on top of the world. He was dressed simply enough, in a pair of jeans and a red plaid Western style button-up shirt, with the top few buttons undone. He was gorgeous. For the millionth time, Anne found herself ridiculously attracted to this man. Yes, he was sitting inches from her husband, who she was equally attracted to, but in a different way.

Will wore jeans and a T-shirt that said Virginia Tech Pamplin College of Business. This shirt alone made Anne smile. He was the smartest, sharpest, most brilliant man she had ever known. There was nothing in the world that he could not do; she was convinced of this.

Every time these two men were in the same room, there was no confusion for Anne though. Rather, she was over the moon. She loved nothing more than to be with these two together. When the two of them were together, they seemed to bring something out in each other. Anne remembered what it was like for so long. For so long these two didn't exchange words or even a glance. For so long, Will was full of hate and resentment toward his father. Jerry tried to avoid Will. He was full of guilt and confusion and he was so desperately lonely. Anne remembered all of that. She spent many days and nights wondering when it would all change. There were times she wondered if it would change at all.

Then, it all did change. She couldn't tell you when, exactly, it changed. She thought it was maybe that day in the spring, several years ago, when they were cleaning out the attic. Will had taken his father's beloved football and Jerry had chased him through the house and out the door. Roy joined in and the three men ended up playing a lengthy game of catch in the backyard. Years were lifted from each one of them. She thinks that's when things began to change.

Now, Will had resorted to calling Jerry *Daddy* again, and Jerry had again begun being the father figure that Will had so desperately needed. When the two of them were together, they looked like the two happiest men on Earth, when they weren't fighting, that is.

The two ended up singing three Christopher Cross songs before Anne excused herself to go check on the kids again. She walked down the hall and out the back door. James and Eliza were playing in the wooden playhouse in the fenced-off section of the yard. Anne watched for a moment and went back inside. As she approached the back staircase, she paused. She looked at it for a minute, thinking. When this house was constructed, this staircase was originally built for the housekeepers. It was still referred to as the service stairs. These stairs were much more practical than the giant, wide ones at the front of the house. These were fewer steps. However, this staircase gave Anne the creeps for numerous reasons.

The service stairs were darker; they were narrow and creaked and moaned when you walked on them. This staircase smelled old. The old house smell that this home had, seemed to be especially strong on this one staircase. The service stairs were always cold. Even in the middle of July when the rest of the house was sweating and sweltering, this staircase stayed cold. The walls and ceiling were made of dark, narrow boards. This staircase was also the same staircase that Mary Addie Granger had fallen-down and broken her neck on at the beginning of the Civil War.

She had been assisting in an especially difficult childbirth and in her haste to get downstairs quickly, she took the nearby service stairs. In her hurry, it was presumed she'd stumbled down the stairs. She wasn't used to using the very narrow service stairs, and perhaps her full skirts had gotten in the way as she hurried down them. Perhaps she simply missed one of the narrow steps, and had trouble catching her footing with the several yards of skirt material surrounding her feet. Whatever it was that caused the horrific accident, Miss Mary Addie was dead by the time anyone had been able to reach her. She may have died but she had gone nowhere.

The one ghost incident that Anne hated more than any of the numerous creepy things she had witnessed, was the thumping sound that came down the service stairs sometimes. This could happen in the middle of the afternoon, or the middle of the night. It sounded just exactly like a body falling down the stairs. Thankfully, it was not a common occurrence, but it happened enough to creep Anne out. When she heard it, she was actually hearing someone fall to their death. It was assumed this is what it was anyway. The noise from the service stairs reportedly started the very night of Mary Addie's burial. Story goes if you are unfortunate enough to be standing at the foot of the stairs during these hauntings, you can hear the rustle of silk taffeta and feel the thud of a body at your feet on the hardwood floor.

So yes, Anne detested these stairs. However, today she decided to take them upstairs. She wanted to avoid Will, Jerry, or Marilyn seeing her go upstairs right now. She wanted to be left alone. Taking the back stairs would ensure they wouldn't see her go upstairs.

Anne crept up the creepy stairs and found herself in the upstairs hall. She made her way to Jerry's bedroom and walked inside. Miss Priss was sprawled out across the middle of Jerry's huge tester bed. She opened one eye, looked at Anne, and went back to sleep.

Anne spent plenty of time in Jerry's room; she cleaned it, did his laundry, made his bed, changed his sheets, hid her junk food in here, and there were times she had done a few other things in here that she'd rather not talk about. So, she felt quite comfortable in this room. It was a handsome, regal bedroom full of huge pieces of cherry furniture and decorated in rich shades of deep green, deep blue, and touches of deep red and deep gold. It had maintained its historic appearance all these years; so much so that it was one of the rooms visitors to the house requested to see first. Because Jerry was, she had learned quickly, a slob, she tried to keep this room as clean as possible for these visitors.

Anne made her way to the large cedar chest at the foot of the huge bed. She found herself trembling as she knelt before it. She licked her lips several times, as her mouth had become quite dry during this. She looked over her shoulder once, then opened the cedar chest.

The cedar chest contained many things: clothes, books, assorted boxes. After she removed a few things, she found two stacks of notebooks. She picked up a top one and, feeling a little guilty, opened the notebook. The date at the top of the first page was September 03, 1973. This was where Faye wrote that she had just found out she was expecting a baby, and she couldn't wait to share the news with Jerry. Anne quickly looked over the page and began flipping through the pages. She picked the second notebook up and looked through it. As she picked up the third notebook, Anne realized what she had found.

Faye Granger had documented the life of her son, Will. She had written about every milestone, every trying time, every moment of happiness, every moment of worry, and every feeling she felt throughout it all, for 37 years. Her last entry was regarding her concern for him while he lived in Nashville. Anne thumbed through these quickly.

Anne thought about the situation; she had stood in the kitchen earlier, talking aloud. She'd commented on how she didn't know Faye and didn't know how to raise kids like Faye had, because she didn't know Faye, and had no way to ask her for advice. And Faye had sent her to this cedar chest, where Anne found every moment of Will's upbringing documented.

Anne couldn't help it; she began to cry. The woman she had never met, never known, yet had named both of her children after was here. The woman whose wisdom and parenting techniques Anne so desperately wanted was here. The woman who had disliked her for so long for reasons that Anne never could quite understand had come to her with help.

Anne put the most recent notebooks back and took out the first five. She straightened the cedar chest back up and closed its lid. Anne heard Will and Jerry start playing and singing *Never Be the Same* by Christopher Cross downstairs. She picked up the five notebooks from the floor.

Faye perhaps couldn't understand Anne all the way yet, but she could help Anne understand her. This was Faye's family, her husband and son, and now her grandchildren and daughter-in-law. This was her house. And Faye saw an opportunity to show Anne just how important these things were to her, even in death. Death wouldn't change Faye. She simply learned to accommodate it. She would accept it, but only as it being a minor inconvenience in what she still considered her life.

Faye was loving, a great friend, a great mother and wife. But you simply did not show up in Faye's house and take over without knowing that you were *not* doing any of it *alone*. Anne may have been the lady of the house now, but she was not the only one. If Anne needed help being like Faye, Faye could help her with that.

Faye saw this as an opportunity to regain some control around here. Faye knew that Jerry already saw her in Anne, and she knew that there were many times Will saw Faye in Anne. Now Anne wanted Faye's help. Yes, Faye was going to get her house and family back to how she wanted it. And she was going to do it through her daughter-in-law, Anne.

CHAPTER 18

Jeremy Clancy was sullen. Yesterday, he had done what he promised Gary he'd do. He wasn't happy about it, but at least nobody bothered him out there. He got there Friday morning around ten and went to the outbuilding where the riding mower lived between uses. He unlocked the door and sighed heavily. Then, looking at the mower, the realization of what he'd agreed to do sunk in. He hated yard work. He'd always hated yard work.

Today, he told his mother that he wouldn't be getting baptized tomorrow after all. This baptism had already been put off once, the other week. He listened to her tell him how nothing ever worked out for him and how he should be ashamed to have considered getting baptized for such insincere reasons.

Gary had asked Jeremy to please bring him the key when he was done. Since he forgot to Friday, Jeremy ran the key by the co-op on Saturday. Eric greeted him as he walked in the door.

"Hey, Mr. Clancy. How are you this morning?"

"Hey. I suck. How's it going?"

"Pretty good. I just had to talk Gary into leaving me alone. He acts like he's got to watch over me or something. He's always paranoid about leaving me here to work."

"Aw, I don't think it's that. I think he just doesn't like leaving anyone, period."

"What do you mean?"

"You know Gary; he worries about everyone. It doesn't have anything to do with him thinking you can't do the work. I think he just likes feeling needed. Let it go. I need to give him his key back though."

"Key?"

"He made me mow the grass at the church. I guess he wanted it to look nice for his first Sunday preaching. I was supposed to return the shed key yesterday and forgot."

"Oh. He isn't here. He left with Mr. Granger and Miss Beales. They went to lunch. They've been gone for about an hour now, maybe longer. He might be back soon."

"Oh. Well, I guess I can leave it here with you. He said … Oh, go on ahead and wait on him first," Jeremy told Eric.

Eric stepped aside so the man who had just walked in could be waited on. The man, Luther Wilkens, glared at Jeremy. Jeremy glared right back.

Luther didn't like Jeremy because Jeremy had a history of getting in trouble. That was okay with Jeremy because he didn't like Luther either. Luther was Karen Townsend's ex-husband and he was an idiot.

Everyone in town might have known Jeremy had a shady past, but none of the things he had done were too bad: shoplifting, public intoxication, a fight or two (or seven) at The Tavern, and there was that one time he had exposed himself to Kim Reynolds after she had turned him down for a date. He stood in front of the big window to her doll shop and exposed himself in broad daylight. The act itself had made Miss Reynolds laugh hysterically.

However, Gary, who was the police chief at the time just happened to be walking down the street right then. He didn't laugh at it at all. Jeremy spent that night in one of the three cells in the Liberty Creek Police Department. Ironically, it was Kim who ended up paying his bail.

"You're such an idiot, Jeremy," she told him when he was released. He stood with her in the police department lobby and shrugged.

"So, why did you bail me out?"

"Because you make me laugh. And if I had agreed to go out with you, I don't guess you'd have had a reason to do that; not that *that* could really be considered a good reason for you to do that. I mean, really,

Jeremy? But I guess you'd have probably ended up in here by the end of the week for something else anyway," she reasoned. He agreed, and they told each other bye at the door. Jeremy waited for Gary to give him back his wallet and phone.

So, Jeremy may have gotten in trouble, but it wasn't anything terrible. When he had set that fire by the Buy & Bag, he honestly tried to put it out. He realized, almost immediately after setting it, that he really shouldn't have done that, but by then, the mountain breeze had carried it to the shrubbery at the Buy & Bag and it was out of Jeremy's control. He got in a lot of trouble for that one and had to do community service and was fined and all kinds of shit.

But Luther? Luther wasn't the criminal Jeremy was, necessarily. Luther had his own problems. He had been a fairly-nice man for the most part. At least, Luther thought so. He had gone to school and had gotten a job. He moved to Liberty Creek from Alexandria at 39 years old. He had come to help family out with their lumber business. That's when he met Karen Townsend.

Karen wasn't like women he had dated in the past. She was very well educated, very well-spoken, and seemed to be very classy. He had previously held an interest for somewhat wicked women. When he met Karen at the church that very first Sunday, he had immediately taken a liking to her. She was wearing a light pink suit that morning, and he thought she was beautiful.

After three solid months of asking her out, he finally convinced her to go out with him. She didn't seem very happy about it; he felt she was agreeing to go just to shut him up. This was okay with him. They went out on that date and several more afterwards, but she never seemed to be as interested in him as he was in her. He'd comment to his sister, Ruth, about it. He'd talk to his brother-in-law about it. Ruth and Sylvester would just raise their eyebrows and shrug.

After one year of dating, he decided to just go ahead and take a chance. He asked her to marry him. She took seven weeks to answer him.

He had learned several things about Karen Townsend over the past year. He had learned she was very private, and very refined. She was proud, and she was hard-working. She was a landowner. She had inherited the 20 acres she lived on, from her parents when they passed-away. She was very, very close to the family who lived a 15-minute walk up the road from her.

This closeness was fine with Luther. He had already become familiar with the Granger family. He found out about the Granger family the day after he moved to town. You didn't live in Liberty Creek and not know about them. Within a couple weeks after he started dating Karen, he became even more familiar with them.

Jerry and Faye were a fine couple; Luther never doubted that. He quickly even became friends with Jerry. Jerry was a good man, sincere and friendly. His relationship with his wife was something Luther envied. You could just look at Jerry and Faye and see the respect and admiration they had for one another. Luther wanted that for him and Karen.

Then, there was Roy Granger. Roy was Karen's dearest friend in the world. Karen never ran out of good things to say about him. She praised his horsemanship skills and construction skills. She would often tell Luther to just wait until Roy came back to town and get him to help Luther with a project Luther found difficult. That wasn't how Roy built a fence and that wasn't how Roy made chicken coops.

Roy was younger than Luther, more successful than Luther, and God knows he came from a much more privileged household than Luther had. Roy was among The Twelve in town and Luther knew this. He had figured it out immediately. Had Luther not been told on the fourth day of living there, he'd have figured it out on his own within the week anyway. So, in addition to having a life of luxury, he also had a position in town that pretty much guaranteed he'd get things done to his satisfaction. It didn't take long to figure out who the other 11 were. It wasn't a system Luther was used to, but it was one he either had to accept and adjust to or move.

Luther also figured out that, whereas there were not many black people in this town, the ones who were here tended to be quite happy here. They were respected and everyone in town got along with each other. With exception of the several rows of shotgun houses near the creek, there were not black neighborhoods and white neighborhoods.

These rows were predominantly black, simply because these houses had been in families for several generations. It was a quaint, pleasant area. The roads were dirt and the yards were large, beneath massive pecan and oak trees. But for the most part, everyone lived peacefully among each other. This was something that everyone in town liked very much. For this to be a very small, very old town that was very dead set on refusing progress, it surprised Luther how very integrated it was. They had their own churches, but for the most part, everyone lived and worked and played with one another. It didn't take long at all for Luther to fit in and get used to this town.

But getting used to Roy was something Luther never could do. Roy was pleasant enough to talk to, cordial and endlessly polite. Roy never gave any indication that he had any problems with Luther. But Luther had many with Roy. Luther was able to see through Karen as if she were made of glass. Karen was in love. And it wasn't with Luther. Luther saw it more and more every time Roy Granger breezed through town. He began to suspect the truth; his wife had settled for him.

When this realization hit home, Luther became irritable, moody, and very bitter. He didn't know who to be bitter with though. He was bitter with Karen for settling for him. He was bitter that she had given her heart to another and had given him the leftovers. He was bitter knowing that every time he made love to her, he was convinced she was imagining it was Roy.

Luther was bitter with Roy for his perfect upbringing, position and status in town, self-assured way of carrying himself, and healthy bank account. He was bitter with Roy because he was convinced Roy knew about Karen's infatuation with him, and he was simply leading her on.

This wasn't true, of course. Roy honestly had no idea Karen had ever seen him as anything other than a best friend. There were times, over the years, Roy had thought about her. He'd even wondered what it'd be like to be with her, but it was too awkward to bring up before she got married. What if she thought he was crazy? What if she laughed at him? How could that affect their relationship? There were a few times he suspected she liked him like that, but then, he came home from Nashville to discover she'd taken a shine to Luther Wilkens. He assumed his suspicions were wrong, and he moved on. He dated Patsy Kizzire in Nashville, the sales-clerk from Dillards. They dated off and on. He just never could call himself in love with her though.

Then, Faye died, and Jerry lost his mind and Will became a pissed-off drunk. Roy's mind was on a dozen things, and Patsy took offense that she wasn't at the top of the list. Roy couldn't make her understand. She had even said to him on the phone,

"I mean, I understand that's it a terrible thing that happened. But it was just your sister-in-law. I don't understand why you've fallen to pieces like this over it."

Roy didn't go out with her anymore after that. Faye was so much more than just a sister-in-law. Roy was close to Faye. He had known her most all his life. He'd known Faye since he was just four for God's sake. He had seen her at church and around town, and then when she started school with Jerry, Roy saw even more of her. So, Faye had been a friend all his life. It'd been a terrible two years by then. Patsy watched Roy go through what she thought was a rather excessive grieving period for his sister-in-law. She tried to be sympathetic in the beginning, but it seemed like every single time she turned around, Roy was bitching about Jerry. Jerry wasn't answering his phone, returning calls, or letting Roy and Will come home. He heard from Gary that Jerry had changed. Roy just dismissed it as normal behavior of a grieving widower.

Roy complained that Jerry wasn't there for Will like he needed to be. Then, Will became clingy and relied on Roy more and more. Roy didn't mind this at all, but he was suddenly a father to Will and he just did not know how to help him properly. Roy was worried about Will, angry and frustrated with Jerry, and offended by Patsy's lack of empathy.

Then, not long after he stopped talking to Patsy, Karen called and all but directly blamed him for Jerry's condition for two hours.

So, Luther was wrong about Roy. Nobody cared anymore, though.

The damage had been done. Luther resented every single Granger and he resented Gary Connelly and that arrogant son of his. He resented several people.

The night that Luther had broken into the home he had once shared with Karen, he had been drinking. Perhaps, had he been sober, he'd have thought the plan through longer than 11 minutes. But he didn't, and he ended up paying for it.

Even now, Luther had to admit he knew, not so deep inside, that his skin color had nothing to do with what happened afterward. He knew that this town would have reacted the same way had it been a white man who had broken into Karen's house and forced himself on her, after beating her up. That didn't make it any more pleasant when the group of men, both black and white, showed up at his house in the dark cover of night. Luther knew every one of them, and every one of them knew Luther. He knew that they very easily could have found a way for Luther to disappear that night. It would not have been the first time an undesirable citizen of Liberty Creek vanished.

When Luther saw this crowd at his doorstep, he looked at the faces and realized then how very foolish he had been. Several of these men had every reason to be very willing to kill for Karen Wilkens (soon to be back to Karen Townend). The rest of them were simply there to help those several. Luther sighed and shook his head. He was sick to his stomach.

That was a miserable night. It was the single worst night in his life, and he'd give anything in the world to just forget it. The occasional glares he'd receive in town though made it difficult to forget that night. He didn't have a history of doing stupid things. Everyone did something stupid from time to time. That's why these glares made him so mad. When the hell were people around here going to just get over it and forget about that one night, already? They all acted like he was a serial rapist or something. So, when Jeremy looked at Luther in a perfectly friendly way, Luther immediately took it wrong.

"Why don't you put your eyes back in your head, boy?" he asked Jeremy.

"What's your problem? I'm the one that stepped over and told Eric to wait on you, you asshole."

"Oh, really? The felon does a good deed. What did you come in here for that can wait? Were you gonna hold up the co-op? You'll make out better at The Buy & Bag," Luther sneered. Jeremy was tired of Luther and his bullshit.

"If I did have a gun right now, I sure as hell wouldn't be using it to hold the store up. I'd be using it to shoot your sorry …" Jeremy began.

In a panic, Eric interrupted Jeremy.

"Oh, come on y'all! Don't do this when Gary isn't here to make y'all stop! Y'all are gonna go off on each other and get into a big fight right here, knock crap over, make a big old mess, and then Gary will come in here and think he can't leave me alone to run the co-op!"

"Dumb ass …" Luther muttered.

"Mr. Wilkens!" Eric whined.

"Dumb ass? I've done some sorry shit in my time, but I never beat a woman! Who the hell are you to call me a *dumb ass*?" Jeremy asked, loudly.

"Well, thanks for trying, anyway," Eric said, sarcastically. Luther glared at Jeremy.

"Let me tell you something right quick. I came here to get my chicken wire. I did not come here to talk to your stupid ass. And you had best shut the hell up right now. You don't want to go there, boy. You better believe it; you don't want to go there."

"Screw your chicken wire. And I didn't ask you to talk to me. You started running your damn mouth. I was trying to be nice to you, even though you're a dick. But you know what? Now I'm just going to be as big a dick as you are. Eric, I believe you were waiting on me first," Jeremy said. Eric sighed.

"Yeah, I guess …" Eric agreed, recalling that Jeremy didn't even need any help. He just came to return a key.

"Okay! So, here's what I'm wanting you to do for me; go get me one of each of the Burpee seeds. I want you to tell me about each one of them."

"Mr. Clancy, there's like, a hundred different Burpee seeds," Eric said irritably. He now wished Gary had *not* left him alone to go out to lunch.

"I know, right? I guess it's going to take us awhile."

"You're kidding, right?"

"Nope. Hurry up, now. Let's get started!"

Eric glared at Jeremy and shook his head. He prayed Gary would arrive quickly. He'd been gone long enough by now. Maybe he'd be back soon. Eric spent what seemed like a lifetime picking one of each of the stupid Burpees for Jeremy. He carried them to the counter, where he now had two people in line behind Luther.

"Mr. Clancy, really? I've got a line now."

"So, tell me about this seed."

"It's parsnips."

"And? Tell me more about it," Jeremy pressed. Eric sighed.

"It grows parsnips. There really isn't much else to say about it. And that's okra, mustard greens, rhubarb … they grow okra, mustard greens and rhubarb. It's pretty much all any of them do."

"Now, that's pretty. What's it?"

"Kaleidoscope carrots! They grow *kaleidoscope carrots!* That's what they do!" Luther told Jeremy angrily.

"Hey! I wasn't asking you! It's not your job! What the Hell do you know about seeds? *You* are here for *chicken wire*! Shut your ass up!"

"How about you shut me up?" Luther shouted back.

"How about you both shut up? What is going on in here?" Gary's voice boomed in the co-op.

The other customers, who had been watching the scene unfold with interest, stepped back as Gary came storming in the store. Jerry and Marilyn stayed near the door, observing.

"This is not my fault!" Eric immediately excused himself.

"And it's not mine! I was being nice! I even let him go ahead of me! Then, he had to start running his fucking mouth and …" Jeremy started, but Gary interrupted him.

"Hey! We don't talk like that in here! What's the matter with you? Didn't we just have a talk the other day? Luther, what is the problem?"

"He needs to keep his eyes and his mouth to himself."

"His eyes?" Gary asked. Had Jeremy been looking inappropriately at some woman? Gary looked around and saw that the only woman present was Gladys Pearson, who was just four days shy of turning 93 years old. Gary had a hard time believing Jeremy was winking or making lewd tongue gestures or anything at her. He looked quizzically at Luther.

"He's looking at me ugly," Luther said simply.

"Oh, for the love of God, Luther! Grow up! Don't look at him and you won't see how he's looking at you. There. Problem solved," Gary said irritably.

Jeremy disagreed.

"No! It's *not* solved! He made smart-ass comments about me being in here to rob the co-op! All because I was trying to be nice to him, by letting him go ahead of me. I was talking to Eric about your key, and I decided to be nice and let him go ahead and wait on Luther. Why? Why, Gary? What's the use in trying to be nice to anyone around here? I did what you said, and I tried to be nice to this wife-beating asshole! And where did it get me? It got me accused of holding up the co-op!"

"Why'd you accuse him of holding up the co-op?"

"It was a joke," Luther said quietly. But he wasn't quiet because he felt shame. He was thinking how much he hated Jeremy Clancy. He didn't much care for Gary either. But he really hated Jeremy. Gary shook his head, looking at Luther in wonder.

"A joke. It was obviously a funny joke, being as *how nobody is laughing at it!*" Gary roared.

"He just called me a wife-beater."

"You *are* a wife-beater! But he didn't call you that first! Apparently, you started your crap just because he looked at you? Really?"

"You better watch your ..." Luther began.

Gary looked at him with narrowed eyes.

"Watch my what?"

"You going to chew me out for saying shit to that loser? What are you gonna say to him for what he said to me?" Luther asked, low. Gary saw he was in a spot. Luther raised his graying eyebrows at Gary.

"I wanna hear you say something to him about what he said to me, *preacher man.*" Luther said snidely. Gary didn't like either of these men right then.

"Jeremy, to drag up someone's past, especially in public, is not called for. What you said was about as called for as *Luther* suggesting you're here to hold the co-op up. *Both* of you need to grow up. Shame on *both* of you. We all have something in life that we've done that we're not exactly proud of. It makes moving on and repenting kind of hard when people keep bringing these things up. I don't know what to do with either of you, except tell y'all to grow up.

"Luther, go get your chicken wire. We'll take care of the charges later. Jeremy, did you need anything except to give me the key?"

"No."

"What are all these seeds out here for?"

"I was trying to piss him off by having Eric tell me what each one does," Jeremy muttered.

"What they *do?* They're seeds, you doofus! What do you think they do? They grow the things that are in the picture!"

"Just never mind. I don't want them," Jeremy admitted. At this Gary laughed.

"Well, guess what? You, not me and not Eric, are going to take every single one of these, right back to the rack, and you are going to put every one of them exactly where they go. I mean it. They sure as shooting better be where they belong when you are done. Go on, Luther. Go out back and get your wire. Come on up here, Ms. Gladys. Eric will take care of you. And Jeremy, I do expect to see you in services tomorrow."

Gary told Jerry and Marilyn goodbye. Then, Gary went to the back room and laid his head on the table. Rocky jumped off the shelf with the Moon Pie and honeybun stock and jumped up on the table beside Gary's head. Rocky rubbed his own head against Gary's completely shaved, bald one. He did this several times, trying to get a response. When Rocky heard Gary sniffling into the crook of his arm, Rocky took his nose and poked it into Gary's ear. Finally, Gary lifted his head. He looked at the huge gray cat and broke down in new wave of tears. Rocky stepped over Gary's arm on the table and sat in front of him. Since Rocky was in the way and Gary couldn't lay his head back down now, he petted the cat's back, sobbing the entire time.

He ran his hand over the cat's long gray fur and looked into his icy blue eyes.

"Oh, man, I can't do this. Luther was right. I was chewing him out instead of Jeremy. I mean, I should have been chewing them both out. I kinda did, didn't I? Luther didn't really give me a chance to say much. He just assumed I wasn't going to say anything to Jeremy.

"But how am I going to be a preacher if I'm making people think I'm prejudiced? I don't mean like racist. I'm not racist. But am I prejudiced? Did I chew Luther out first because of the Karen thing? I mean, I try to be nice to him and all because you should just do that. But maybe I did go off on him more because of what he did to Karen. I can't help it. I love her. I've always loved her. Of course, I'm going to be mad about how he treated her. I *think* that's why I went off on him first. Do *you* think so?" Gary asked Rocky. Rocky just meowed and laid down beside Gary's arm.

"Okay, I've witnessed some scary stuff around this place, but if the cat starts talking, I'm out of here."

Gary turned around quickly at the sound of Eric's voice. He wiped his eyes quickly.

"Rocky and I were just … hanging out."

"I see that. Listen, I just wanted to clarify a few things for you. I thought maybe it'd help you out some." Eric sat down on the table. Gary took several deep breaths.

Eric smiled.

"Look here; I know you've got all kinds of stuff going on. I heard you telling Mr. Addams about Laurie. I know Kylie's expecting and the wedding's coming up, and now you are having to fill in at the church. And I know that you and Mr. Wilkens aren't exactly friends and I do know why. I know you and Mr. Addams kinda got into it earlier. And, well, I just wanted to tell you that if it makes you feel any better, everyone is excited about you taking over services.

"Not meaning to be disrespectful or anything, but Brother Lawson's sermons are starting to kind of get watered down. I mean he's been preaching for like 90 years or something. I think, maybe, he's kind of running out of things to preach about. It's like we've heard all his sermons already. You kind of bring something new to the church, you know?

"But also, Mr. Wilkens totally instigated that in there. You were right to chew him out first. Mr. Clancy was being nice. He said nice things about you before Mr. Wilkens even got here. I was kind of complaining about how you acted like you didn't trust me to work alone. He said it's not like that and you just worry about everyone in general. Then, a few minutes later, Mr. Wilkens came in, and all Mr. Clancy did was tell me to go ahead and wait on him, and he went to the end of the counter to wait till I was done with Mr. Wilkens. I guess Mr. Clancy looked at Mr. Wilkens and he just read way too much into it.

"Anyway, I guess Mr. Clancy maybe did overreact a little bit. But Mr. Wilkens kind of deserved it. I can see why Mr. Clancy got so mad. But I just wanted to tell you all that. I know I'm just a dumb high school senior with a C average, but for what it's worth? I think you're a great store owner, and a great preacher. You were a great police chief, and well, you still kind of are because you still *act* like the chief and everyone else *acts* like you're still the chief. You're a great boss, and from what I can tell, I think you're probably a pretty-great grandfather and dad. And you're a great friend, to be so old and all.

"So anyway, I'm glad you feel you can talk to Rocky. But just so you know, there's nothing wrong with how you're dealing with everything. I think you kick ass. So, I wish you wouldn't feel like you had to lock yourself in the back room and ask advice from a cat," Eric finished. Gary smiled.

"Thanks, Eric. You made me feel much better. I appreciate it."

"So, we're good?"

"Yes, son. We're good."

"So, does this *maybe* mean I could *maybe* come by your house sometime and *maybe* hang out with Laurie?"

"You're a senior, Eric."

"But I'm already scared of you. So, you wouldn't have to worry about me doing anything that I shouldn't. You know where to find me if I ever did," Eric reasoned. Gary looked at him for a moment.

"We'll talk about it."

Neither of them knew that Laurie was currently behind the barn at the Granger's end of the farm, far away from the watchful eye of her father and in the arms of Luke. It was just as well anyway. Gary already had enough on his plate to have to deal with that just then. He didn't know it yet, but he was about to be dealing with Laurie far more than he had expected he would.

Soon after, Gary and Kylie went to spend the day up on Teague Road. They spent the afternoon visiting and observing the dysfunction that was always thick there. Gary paid attention to the odd behavior he kept sensing from most of the people present, even Laurie's friends and Jonathon and Luke, who had joined them this afternoon. Gary felt as if every single person there had something that they were thinking about but keeping to themselves. And he was right.

CHAPTER 19

Saturday night Will was helping Anne with the dishes. It was very quiet. Jerry was spending the night at Marilyn's, which he usually did on Saturdays. The kids were asleep. Will dried the last plate and put it in the cabinet.

"How was your day? You've been awfully quiet today. Anything wrong?" he asked.

"No, nothing is wrong. It's just been long day. It's been a kind of long week. I guess there is just a lot going on and all."

"A lot going on? Like what? I felt it was a rather chilled out week. I mean, we slept most of it, and you did zero housework until, what, yesterday?" Will argued.

"Well, for me there was a lot going on."

"Okay. Would you be willing to elaborate?"

"Us being sick, Miss Beales being here all week, Tammy working here now, your mom,"

"What about Mom?"

"She's just being more … active. That's all."

"Is that bothering you? I mean is something happening, something different? Hey? You need to talk to me about things like this. This is a ghost we are talking about. I mean when dead people are bothering you, it needs to be talked about."

"It's not like that. Will? I don't … well, I don't think of her as being dead. Is that weird? I mean, it's hard to think of her that way anymore. In the beginning, I could because I didn't know her."

"And, now you do?" Will asked curiously.

"I think so. I mean, I think I *kind of* do. I think I know her as well as someone who never met her before she, well, you know. I mean, I never knew her until after what happened. I didn't get to know her back when she was … oh! It's messed up, Will.

"How do I even say it? I didn't know her when she was still here? She's still here *now*! I didn't know her when her and your dad were still together? They're still together *now*! I didn't know her when she was alive? I can't bring myself to say that because it *really* doesn't seem like she's *dead*. I don't know. I swear, it's like we live here with your parents."

"What happened?"

"I just saw her today, and she was in the kitchen, but until she left, it wasn't even like it was a ghost. It's gotten to where I just see her and think there's Faye. Lexi said that Faye was obviously at the table with her, Karen, and Miss Beales the other morning. Lexi made her a cup of coffee. They apparently hung out at the kitchen table with her, talking to her," Anne told him. Will just looked at Anne oddly.

"Had they perhaps been drinking something *else* before they got into the *coffee*?" he suggested, his brows raised. He said this rather condescendingly. He knew his mother was being more daring these days, but he did not know the others had gotten so comfortable with it.

"Oh, stop it. I don't want to talk about it right now. I have a lot of things on my mind and this thing with your mom is just really complicated."

"Do you have a problem with the situation? Do we need to do something about it?" Will asked, quietly.

Anne looked at him, confused.

"What are you talking about?"

"I mean, it's Mom. Maybe Daddy can talk to her or do something about it. Maybe something can be done if it's getting to be too much for you. I don't want you to be uncomfortable in your own house, Miss Anne."

"Something can be done? There's nothing to do about it. She's your mom. She's your dad's wife. She's Mimi. I didn't say I wanted her to go away. I like having her here. It's just kind of weird still is all. It used to be a lot weirder though.

"I just talked to your dad about this place. He said things that made a lot of sense. He thinks the people who are here are here because they feel love here. And I like that. There are families out there who are all alive and kicking. They aren't dead but they might as well be. The relationships they have with one another suck. But here? It's totally different. Its creepy sometimes, but it's a nice creepy."

"So, you do *not* want to do anything? Because you know … we can talk about building a place of our own. I would feel kinda weird about leaving Daddy, but if it'd help you any, you know, we would still be on the property." Will said this sincerely. He really would have done that for his beloved Anne if it would have made her happy. But he knew as soon as he finished suggesting it that it was foolish on so many levels.

Will knew he could never leave Jerry. No, not even if it meant across the pasture. He knew he would worry about his father day and night. His father was crazy. Will firmly believed this more every day. Jerry had not gotten better in the things that really mattered, in Will's opinion. Oh, Jerry dated now and had gotten back to his old social self. He had spent three years basically being a weird old reclusive mountain man who existed solely off Ramen noodles and booze. He even went out in the yard shooting guns at people who tried to approach the house. But now he was cleaned back up and out and about the town with a new pretty lady on his arm, and two more in his heart.

Yes, as absurd as it sounded, Will could not bring himself to take Anne away from his dad. That would be like, well, it'd be like taking his second wife away from him. He'd already lost his first wife and had still not recovered. No, taking Anne away from him would do him in. The relationship between Jerry and Anne meant too much to Jerry and Anne. The relationship they had meant too much to everyone, including Will.

The only other option was calling someone for an exorcism. That wouldn't happen at all. So, Will realized that there was nothing to do; Anne was right.

"Anne? Don't you worry about him?"

"Him?"

"My dad."

"Oh, *where* have you *been* for how many years now? When *haven't* I worried about him? I was watching him trying to read in the living room Wednesday night. He was reading a magazine. I sat down beside him and saw it. The type wasn't even very small, but he was obviously having a hard time reading it. He kept squinting at it and moving it closer to his face then further away, over and over. I offered to turn on another lamp; he said that wasn't the problem. Of course, he said he was just tired. Will, Jerry needs glasses. It's as plain as the nose on his face. I've been watching him over the past few days. He's having trouble reading."

Will just looked at Anne, his brow slightly furrowed. His blue eyes suddenly looked anxious. His mouth was fixed in a worried purse. This was not something he was expecting to hear. Will crossed his arms in front of him. He looked angry.

"Oh really?" he asked.

"Yeah, really. Why are you looking like that?"

"And you haven't said anything to me about it?"

"I just did. I just noticed it for first time Wednesday night, Will. This is only Saturday. I wanted to watch and make sure I was right. He needs reading glasses. He's going to fight it and argue with us about it. He's not going to like it at all."

"But he's been sick."

"Yeah, so? I don't think it's like surgery, where you can't eat anything solid for twelve hours before you get the surgery. I don't think there's an incubation period or anything for someone who's getting a pair of reading glasses. I mean, it was a cold. I'm pretty sure he can still get glasses. Elderod's has a bigger selection than Jenson's. I remember that's where Karen gets hers. He'd just need to go see which strength he needs."

Anne didn't notice that Will was looking purely sick to his stomach until she turned to look at him.

"Will? What's the matter?"

"Well, maybe he is just tired. Maybe it is nothing, and you are here already diagnosing him with going *blind*? I mean, you yourself just said you only noticed it three days ago. Do you not think that it is just a little soon to be jumping to conclusions? This is someone's *body* we are talking about. You don't take things like this lightly, Anne!"

"You are crazy, Boss. It's a pair of $10 Foster Grant reading glasses, not a sex change. Really, get a grip."

"Yeah, well, I do not want you to say anything to him about it just yet."

"Why?"

"I just don't. I think it is jumping to conclusions, and I think that it is stupid to worry about something that may not even exist. That is why. Now, we have got to get up early for church. So, let's go to bed, dear."

"I think you're being kind of weird."

"Well, I think you are overreacting. Let's just agree that you're wrong and I'm right," Will responded.

Anne looked irritably at Will, who was at least smiling. They made their rounds, checking on kids and lights, and went to bed.

Sunday morning, Anne was getting dressed for church. She hated wearing dresses, but she did like seeing Will in his suits. Will wore suits quite well. Will was in the kitchen drinking coffee and visiting with the kids. They were all dressed and ready and waiting on Anne. Will clapped his hands together once when he saw Anne walk in the room in the navy-blue dress.

"Alright, then! Now, we are ready to roll! Poppy is preaching today!" Will said with great enthusiasm. Like Anne, the children looked half asleep and lacked the enthusiasm their daddy had. James wore tiny khaki pants and a short-sleeved blue knit shirt while Eliza looked like an angel in her long smocked yellow dress. Her dark curls framed her sweet little face. Will looked his family over for inspection and decided he was right proud of them.

"Anne, darling, perhaps you could try to smile? Maybe the children would pick up on your enthusiasm?"

"I'm *not* enthusiastic though. I want to go back to bed."

"Gary is preaching. I think it would be very bad manners to arrive at his first service looking pissed off."

"Well, when I get to the church, I'll smile. Why do I have to smile now? Gary can't see me yet."

"I really wish you would just try to pretend that you enjoy going to church," Will said under his breath.

"Oh, Boss, it's not that I don't enjoy going to church. Church itself is nice enough. I just don't like wearing dresses, and I don't know, it'd just be nice to have just one day a week to sleep in. I mean, every single day of the week! I even have to get up early on Saturday. I'm not used to that yet. I'm used to sleeping in on weekends. It's like I never get a … never mind. Come on kids. James? You need to go to the bathroom before we get in the truck? Go on then. Hurry so we go see Poppy preach." Anne said all this to James in a perfectly sincere, pleasant tone of voice. But something bugged Will.

"Hey, Baby, come here. It's like you never get a *what*?"

"Oh, come on, Will. It's nothing. Let's just drop this for right now." Anne wasn't being hateful, cold, or ugly. She was honestly trying to just dismiss the whole thing so that they could enjoy the day, especially Will. Sunday was a nice day of the week, and Anne enjoyed it for the most part.

After services, there was the pleasant time of visiting in the churchyard with the rest of the congregation. Then, there was the weekly ritual of Rich's Barbeque, which was almost always picked up by Jerry. After church, the kids would usually ride with Jerry into town, and pick up the barbeque. Then they'd bring it home where Will, Anne, Jerry, and the kids would have lunch together. Sometimes, Roy and Karen would join them. Sometimes, Karen and Roy had gun shows and cat shows to attend on Sundays.

Following lunch, it was time for rest. Will and Jerry sometimes took a nap, or they'd all take the kids to the creek or ride horses. Sometimes, they just had a lazy day of doing absolutely nothing. Supper was always leftover barbeque, so Anne wouldn't have to cook. This was something that Will had decided long ago; Anne would not work on Sunday. Once the kids were put to bed, Jerry *always* helped Anne clean up the kitchen while Will watched his favorite program. This was their Sunday routine and it was a pleasant one.

So, it's not that Anne had a problem with Sunday, or even church.

"Please tell me what you were going to say," Will pressed. Anne sighed.

"Will, its nothing much. I just wish I could chill out. I wish that sometimes, I could stay in bed after you get up. I wish I could sleep in until even just nine sometimes. This house is big, Boss. There are five people living here; six counting your mother. There's six, seven, eight people here on any given day. Sometimes more. Do you know how much I sometimes just want quiet? Every day of the week, I feel like I'm running a hotel. Well, not Sunday so much.

"It's just I want a day to sleep in a little. That's all. But I understand; it's a business. It's a farm and ranch. It isn't like it's a bank or something, where you can just work nine to five, five days a week. Its animals that need to be taken care of and you can't just take a day off from things like that." Anne said this nicely, not raising her voice or stressing out. In fact, it seemed she was going out of her way to make sure she didn't stress *Will* out.

Rather than not stressing Will out though, Anne's words cut like a knife. He took her by the arms.

"No. No, I see I have done something terribly wrong here. Listen, you are wrong. This? This right here? This is not a business. This is our *home*. This is not the farm or the ranch. This is where we live and above everything else, you should always *always* feel as if you are at *home* when you are in this house, not at *work*. So right there, we have a serious problem."

"No, really, we don't."

"Yes! We do! Alright, listen to me. From this day forward, weekends are off for you. Saturdays, I will get up with the kids and make the breakfast. We'll do cereal or something like that. There are enough hands here to do the work until you get up. How does 10 sound?"

"Oh, good grief, Will. I don't need to sleep in that late. Just even eight or nine. I just get so tired of waking up before daybreak every single damn day. Sometimes, I'd just kind of like to see what its' like to wake up to sunshine."

"Okay. How about we meet halfway between eight and ten then? Nine? Would that help you out any? Sleep until nine on Saturdays from now on."

"You're sure that wouldn't be a problem?"

"It will not be any problem at all. I mean, you can still cook supper on Saturday night, you know, if you want to," Will said hopefully. Anne smiled.

"Lunch and dinner will be still be *my* thing on Saturday."

They gathered the children together and let Miss Priss back inside. Jerry always insisted she come in at night. Then, in the morning she would meow mournfully after her breakfast to be allowed to go outside. But they weren't allowed to leave Miss Priss outside unsupervised. She had to come back inside when they went to church, That wasn't ever a problem, really. She was incredibly lazy these days and seldom even left the porch.

Anne found Miss Priss sleeping in the huge tub of geraniums. She put her back inside and the family went to church.

While all of this was going on at the Granger home, Gary was trying to get his own family out the door in town.

"Poppy? Is this okay?" Laurie asked, while Gary was finishing his coffee. He looked at his granddaughter. He was very uncomfortable.

"Oh, honey, don't you have something with a little more material?" he asked hopefully. Laurie looked impatiently at him.

"Oh, come on! This isn't bad! Its knee length ... almost."

"Is that the only thing you have?"

"No. I could wear my black vinyl dress. I could wear my stretchy red one or my stretchy hot pink one or my short lace one with the open back. I have a stretchy black one too. I also ..."

"Oh! Never mind! Wear that then. And when we get home, throw all those other ones in the trash."

"Yeah, right. I don't think so. Remember that this isn't like, 1924. I'm not going to wear a prairie dress to church. I'm wearing a dress. Don't be so difficult and old acting."

Gary was quite close to saying something snide back to Laurie when Kylie walked in the room, giggling.

"Yeah, don't be so old acting. Are we ready? What a cute dress! Oh, Laurie you look great! Come on, honey. You're the preacher today, remember? We need to hurry up and get up there."

"Yeah, yeah. Come on then."

286

Gary wasn't exactly nervous. It's not like he hadn't ever preached before. But today was different. Today could be the beginning of something long term. And Gary just wasn't sure how he felt about that yet. He was kind of sick to his stomach. Yes, he *was* nervous. He knew this now. If this turned into a several weeks-thing then he'd be taking on the responsibilities of the preacher of Liberty Creek Baptist. This wasn't like filling in for Brother Lawson, so he could attend the Annual Session of the Virginia Baptist State Convention in Roanoke every May.

Gary had not said this out loud, but he really felt that Brother Lawson didn't have that much longer left. He really hated that. George Lawson had taken over services when Gary's father passed-away in 1977. Everyone loved the old man to bits and were thrilled to have him take over services. He was a kind man, unlike the strict, stern, shouting Paul Connelly.

Paul Connelly, Gary's father, came from parents even more stern and strict than he was. His own father, Archie Connelly, had been as devoted to the church as any man could have been.

It was a complicated upbringing Gary had had. His father was on the pitiful little police force in Liberty Creek and preached every Sunday.

They had a television but were seldom allowed to watch it. The entertainment in the Connelly home came from the radio in the living room. It played a combination of livestock reports, hymns, and radio shows for the most part. Gary could remember lying in bed at night, listening to the radio from down the hall. When he was nine years old, he had saved up enough money to get his own radio, which he purchased at Main Street 5 & Dime and kept next to his bed.

Paul may have been a cop, and he may have been a preacher, but he was also a miserable drunk most of the time. He wasn't a bad father though, quite the contrary. Paul provided for his family and he loved his children and wife. He would start drinking after dinner and would drink until he went to bed. There were numerous times he went to work with vodka in a thermos.

This is what made being a preacher difficult for Gary. As a child, he never quite understood why it was okay for his father to get drunk on Saturday night and go preach about the Devil's influence the next morning. But as Jerry pointed out to Gary in just sixth grade, if anyone understood the influences of the Devil, it would be Gary's father, the drunken preacher cop.

Gary's father taught Gary everything a little boy growing up in a small mountain town needed to know. He taught him to always be there for your neighbors because one day you'd need them to be there for you. He taught Gary to never talk about people because beside it just being wrong, the smaller the town the quicker someone would find out what you said about them. He taught him to always defend those smaller than you, be kind to animals, open doors for girls and old people, and to always do whatever you had to do to take care of the girl you loved. He taught Gary how to fish and how to hunt. He taught Gary to be honest, to put family first, to work hard, and to step up to your mistakes. Of course, he also taught him how to drink beer, how to smoke, and how to drive his 1957 Chevy truck, all at just 11 years old.

All Gary could ever figure out was for whatever reason his father felt the ripe old age of 11 was when you earned your passage into manhood. Gary remembered an uncomfortable amount of times he and his father would sit together drinking Pabst Blue Ribbon beer and smoking a cigarette after dinner. Gary didn't really have a problem with it even now. When Jason was a kid, Gary let him take the occasional swig from his beer, and he didn't freak out when he found out Jason was sneaking cigarettes with his friends. He, too, taught Jason to drive his truck when Jason turned 11.

The more he thought about it, he had turned out okay, despite his father's odd tactics for raising a son. And he had raised Jason somewhat the same way except Gary seldom ever got drunk. He taught his son the same things his own father had taught him, except how to smoke. But he just felt you were supposed to be a certain kind of person to preach in a church. And Gary felt he simply wasn't the kind of man who had any right preaching to others about their behavior when he, himself, had done some things he felt he shouldn't have done.

But the congregation disagreed. It had been a relief when they got the sweet, quiet, pleading Brother Lawson to take over Paul's services.

Then, as much as they had loved Brother Lawson, after 43 years, they were all kind of tired of getting lectured about the same things repeatedly. As Eric had pointed out, Brother Lawson had pretty much covered every book of the Bible several times by now. The Sundays Gary filled in were always a treat. When word got out around Liberty Creek that Gary would be taking services over for an indefinite amount of time, everyone was elated.

He tried thinking about some of these things, but Laurie talked incessantly on the way to the church. She talked about everything, covering every known subject as if she were a set of *Britannicas*. To make matters worse, Kylie joined in several times. Gary's head began to buzz. The drive to the church wasn't long any other morning. This morning, between his nerves and Laurie and Kylie's endless chatter, it was a very long drive.

As Gary's truck reached the church on Foster-Branton Road, he broke into a smile. There was already one vehicle there to meet him for his first morning service. Jerry's truck was parked in the field to the right of the church. He was sitting on his tailgate, waiting for his best friend, the preacher. Marilyn sat beside him in a blue and yellow dress and strappy sandals. The sight of Jerry immediately relaxed him. The sight of Marilyn touched him. Marilyn very seldom attended church. But she had come for Gary's morning service and he was genuinely flattered by the gesture. He parked the truck.

Jerry and Marilyn hopped off the tailgate as Gary, Kylie, and Laurie got out of Gary's truck.

"Hey there, preacher!" Jerry greeted him. Gary laughed and gave Jerry a man-hug. The little group stood outside the quiet little white church exchanging hugs and greetings. After a moment, Jerry followed Gary to the church steps where Gary unlocked the old church door. The ladies stood outside chatting. The two men stepped inside and just stood there, looking around the little church, as the dust particles danced in the light coming through the windows. The stained-glass window behind the pulpit cast a colorful reflection on the old wooden walls and floor. Jerry sat on the back pew.

"I got here early to talk to you. I thought you could use the slap on the back this morning, you know? You doing okay? You have a lot going on."

Gary looked at Jerry and smiled ruefully.

"I'll be okay. Yes, of course there's a lot going on. I spent days thinking of something to talk about this morning. I'm going to talk about helping thy neighbor. We need to. Gap is wanting to put a marker on Bird's grave, but he can't afford it, of course. I talked to Tammy about it. Then I talked to Middleton about getting a marker for a reasonable price. He said to get as much money as I can from the congregation over the next two weeks, and whatever we're able to get will be enough to get a headstone. He likes Gap, you know? And, well, she is an Indian and all. So, I thought doing a sermon on the subject might be appropriate."

"I agree. Well, count me in."

"I already knew I could, friend."

"What about the dreams, Gary? Are you still having them?"

"Yeah."

Gary sat beside Jerry on the pew in the empty church. People would be arriving shortly for Sunday school. Gary sighed. Jerry elbowed him, smiling.

"Listen, you can do this. You're good at it. You really are. And you know what? You talk about how you aren't the right kind of person for this job. Your dad wasn't perfect. Your dad had his own set of problems. But he was a great dad, a great husband, a hard worker, and a great friend and neighbor. And you are all those same things. And I happen to think it's being *those* things that makes a good preacher. Not being perfect, Gary, being real."

Gary stood in the church yard that morning and visited his congregation as they arrived for Sunday School, and wished him luck. After Sunday School everyone gathered outside for the 15- minute break before morning service. Then Gary stood on the church steps as his congregation made their way back inside to the pews. He did get a generous amount of money collected for Bird's headstone. Gap didn't show up for service, but Jeremy Clancy did. In addition to Jeremy, the

Grangers and Marilyn, all the old familiar faces were there. When Caleb saw his grandfather up at the pulpit he called out,

"Hey, Poppy! Here we are!"

The congregation laughed along with Gary. He looked out over this crowd he had known his entire life. He thought to himself, *just talk to them like you always have. Talk to them like you do when you see them on the street, when they drop by the co-op for a newspaper, when you arrest them for indecent exposure, and when they are nervous about nursing their sick boyfriends. Talk to them like you do when they run away from home in the middle of the night, when their beloved wives die, when their husbands beat them up, and when they want to quit their waitressing job. Talk to them like you do when they like boys who are too old for them, when they get in a fight over chicken wire and Burpee seeds, and when they want you to buy essential oils from them.*

And that's just exactly what he did.

CHAPTER 20

A fter church, while the congregation gathered outside, Jeremy caught sight of Kim. He always thought Kim Reynolds was an interesting woman. She had a kind of creepy hobby but that made her interesting. And she was nice to him for the most part. Other people weren't as nice as she was. She laughed at the idiotic things he did. She had always enjoyed showing him the creepy things she had in her shop. Yes, she was probably the most interesting woman in Liberty Creek. He found his way over to her now to chat.

"Hi, Miss Reynolds," he said teasingly.

"Well, hello, Mr. Clancy. What's with the formalities this morning?"

"Aw, it's church. You're supposed to be nice and polite here. That's what I heard anyway."

"That's pretty accurate, I guess. But hey? I thought you were getting baptized this morning? What happened with that?"

"Gary felt I should wait. He didn't think it was the right time."

"He didn't think getting saved to look good in court was a good idea, you mean?" she asked with a smile. He couldn't help but smile back.

"Yeah, I guess that's what I mean. Listen, I know it's kind of last minute and all, but I was wondering if you maybe wanted to get together for dinner tonight?"

"That's sweet of you, and I'd probably even say yes. The thing is I already invited Mr. Loftis over for dinner. It's nothing romantic or anything. I just think he needs to get out and meet folks. I mean, I see him talking to some folks; I saw him talking to Karen the other day and if you ask me, he was being a little too friendly. I really don't think Roy would have been happy with Mr. Loftis at all. But that's just my opinion. Regardless, I think if I can maybe introduce him to some other people maybe he'll start flirting with someone besides Karen."

"Karen and Walter Loftis? No way. Roy would have him hanging from a tree in ten minutes. I don't think you have to worry about that," Jeremy laughed. Kim smiled at the laughing Jeremy. He laughed and smiled so seldom these days.

"*We* know Roy would have him hanging, but poor Walter hasn't been here long enough yet. He doesn't know how crazy this place is. I'm pretty sure he wouldn't have moved here had he known. We gotta help keep the peace, you know? Anyway, we're gossiping at church and Gary will surely blow a gasket if he hears us and if *he* doesn't hear us, *someone* will and tell him."

"It doesn't even have to be a some*one* around here. I swear, sometimes I think even the trees and houses listen and talk," Jeremy muttered, only half joking.

"Well, I can't do dinner but what about lunch? I mean, if you want to," Kim suggested. At this, Jeremy smiled again.

"Alright. I can do lunch. I guess, just follow me into town in your car and we'll meet … where? Rich's? Jenson's?"

"Jenson's. I wish the diner was open on Sunday. I don't want BBQ on a Sunday. I want real food."

"The lunch counter it is. So, anyway, I guess I'll see you there."

"Alright. Sounds good."

Trish Thurmon came up to Kim then and started asking questions about some doll with human hair and eyelashes. The conversation creeped Jeremy out so he started talking to Will and Ricky. It was just rude to jump in your truck and leave as soon as church was over. You were supposed to stand around and ask everyone how they were all doing, find out who was in the hospital, who got bad news from kin out of town, who had to miss services because their Diverticulitis was acting up, who had produce to share, who was going to clean the church next Saturday (it was going to be Tammy's week), and discuss upcoming community events. Today, Brother Lawson's heart condition and absence was a hot topic.

You at least pretended to care about all of these things, saying the standard replies such as: *Is that right?, You don't say?, How 'bout that?, The poor thing!,* and *Just holler if you need anything.* Tammy was always fond of telling people she'd be sure to put them on the prayer list. Jeremy felt most people who said to *just holler if they needed anything* probably secretly spent the next week screening their phone calls. People in this little town took those offers seriously. If you weren't careful, your *Gunsmoke* hour could be messed up by Mamie Lowery calling you to please go ahead and come check on her radiators (since you offered and all).

It wasn't that Jeremy didn't like church; he just wasn't that into it. He had to admit that he didn't understand most of what was talked about. He'd attended Sunday School growing up, just like every other person in this town had.

The Sunday School classes were held in the old wooden building that had been added when the church was four years old. It sat about 70 feet from the actual church. It, like the church, was white and had that same musty smell that the church had. It wasn't a bad smell; it just smelled like very old closets and books. It often smelled like grape Kool-Aid which is what they drank every Sunday morning with their Ritz crackers. In the winter you bumped into the radiators; every person who attended the church had been burned at least once in their life by those radiators. There was always dust lingering in the light that came through the wavy panes of old glass. The floor was warped with cracks between the boards and the interior walls were white boards running the length of the building.

This building served several purposes. It's where family reunions, Christmas parties, bake sales, vacation Bible Schools, and numerous other things were held.

This church and the Sunday school building were special to Jeremy, he supposed. He'd hate for anything to happen to either one of them. But he didn't really know why. He never felt as if he were really wanted there, at least not once he got older. Jeremy had been a good kid for the most part. When he was in high school, he started hanging out with the crowd every parent couldn't stand. Jeremy started shoplifting on dares and smoking under the bleachers. Then, the cheap cigarettes became drugs. He never did anything too serious. He honestly just wasn't that interested in that kind of stuff. But he'd managed to already get a bad reputation in town, so he figured he'd just roll with it.

He had several friends in school, and he'd stayed friends with some of them despite his reputation. Will Granger and Ricky Stephens were good friends of Jeremy's. Then, of course, there was Kim. He wished Kim would see him the same way he saw her, but he couldn't make that happen. He could only keep trying. Now, he looked up at her just as she saw him. She nodded her head toward the cars and smiled. She was ready to go. He turned his attention back to Will and Ricky. Will was talking about painting the church.

"When are you wanting to do that?" Jeremy asked.

"I do not know. I have not put any thought into it until today. Look up there; the paint is chipped and peeling a lot. It just does not look nice. It needs to be dealt with before it gets any worse. I'll pick some paint up and see if I can find someone to do it. I can't get away from the farm right now," Will said, looking worriedly at the steeple with its peeling white paint.

"Well, I guess I could do it," Jeremy offered somewhat shyly. Will looked at him with a touch of surprise. It was easy to *make* Jeremy do community service when it got him out of jail, but it wasn't like Jeremy to *offer* to do community service. He furrowed his blond brow at Jeremy.

"You would? You would paint the church?"

"You don't have to act so surprised."

"Well, I mean, it's admirable. It would certainly be appreciated. I just know you had your heart set on getting your Church of Steve Perry started," Will added, giggling like a girl. Ricky started laughing while Jeremy smiled at the two. They would always remember when Jeremy tried to get several of them to help him start a church that worshiped the band Journey.

"Yeah, well, I still think it could work. Anyway, so what do you say?"

"Oh yeah, man. Of course. If you're willing to paint the whole church, I'll get you the paint." Then Will remembered Jeremy wasn't working right then. He'd lost another job and was still looking for something else. So, Will decided to do something.

"Just give me a couple days to get the paint. It'll be at least tomorrow before I can get it. And, of course, we'll pay you to do the job."

"Pay me? To paint the church? I mean, thanks, but isn't that kind of a church member thing? I mean, I was just offering to do it to help-out. I didn't think I'd get paid for that. I cut the grass out here Friday for Gary. This was just something else I was going to go ahead and do."

"And that's great. It'll certainly help make you look good. But you're doing me a favor. It would be weeks before I could do this myself. And if nobody from the congregation did offer to do it for me, I would have to hire someone anyway. Don't stress over it. We don't have to tell anyone you did it for pay. Okay?"

"Alright, if you think so. I just feel weird about it."

"Hey, Kim! What do you want? You coming over here to annoy us?" Ricky asked. Kim was making her way through the newly mowed grass.

"Sure. Hey, Will. So, you coming?" Kim asked Jeremy, while Will looked on with raised brows.

"Oh, yeah. I was talking to Will about painting the church. Anyway, I gotta go y'all. We have us a lunch date. Will? Let me know when you know something. I'll catch you later. Bye Ricky." Jeremy and Kim walked to their car and truck, leaving a few curious people watching them from the churchyard. Everyone was already surprised to see Jeremy in church today. They were happy he attended but assumed he came to show his support to Gary.

Nobody found it odd that Stacy Mitchell *wasn't* at church this morning; she never attended. They all noticed that her daughter had shown up, however. Laurie clung close to her grandfather before Sunday school started. Then, she began to see friends from school arriving and felt better. She finally broke away from Gary long enough to go socialize. For Sunday School, she went to the high school class where she sat with friends, but when it was time for morning service, Lexi told her she should really sit with Kylie while Gary preached. It was only proper since she lived with them. So, she found Kylie and sat with her on the front pew. People were a little surprised to see Laurie but attributed it to her coming for her grandfather's sermon. Most of them had not yet learned that she was now living with the man.

Whereas Stacy's absence was not noticed, it *was* noticed that Randy Meadows wasn't there. He was always there, and nobody had heard anything about him not being able to make it. Oh well, at some point within the next day or two, someone would find out why he ditched church. And on Gary's first day preaching! How tacky!

Will and Ricky watched Kim and Jeremy with interest, too. Will looked at Ricky.

"What do you make of that?"

"If any two people in this town can handle either of them, it'd be them," Ricky reasoned.

Will agreed with Ricky. He was just about to ask Ricky how things were going with Janine Thomas, the math teacher at the high school, when Laurie wandered up.

"Hey, honey. How's it going?" Will asked her. He decided her dress wasn't as short as Jason acted like it was. It didn't show too much. Will agreed with his dad. When Jason complained about Laurie's dress that morning after Sunday school, Jerry had told him,

"Oh, for crying out loud! She's 15 years old. She has a great body. She's not going to wear Mennonite dresses with a body like *that*. Get over it. You have a 15-year old daughter who could easily pass for at least 18 or 19. Get used to the dresses and all that now because I can tell you this, she's *going* to wear them. Just get over it already. You're acting like she looks like a *hooker*. She looks *nice*."

Jason didn't want to get over it, and he looked curiously at Jerry for raving how good Jason's 15-year-old daughter looked. It was quickly dismissed though. This crowd seemed to have no problem at all discussing things that should be considered inappropriate.

Will looked at Laurie now, in the short white flowing dress. The dress was long sleeved, but the shoulders and arms were cut out, buttoning at the wrist. It had an impressive V-neck and asymmetrical hemline. She wore a dainty gold chain and earrings with her high heeled gold sandals. Oh yeah; Jason and Gary were going to have all kinds of trouble with her.

"Hi y'all. Have y'all seen Poppy and Kylie?"

"I think they're in the church. They went inside with Mavis a few minutes ago," Will answered.

"Oh. I guess I'll wait. I don't even see Daddy and Lexi."

"Look in the cemetery. James and Caleb like to play there."

"Of course."

"Anything wrong?" Will asked. Laurie was looking around the churchyard anxiously.

"No, I mean, I don't guess so." She didn't sound like she was being totally honest. Will and Ricky had both gotten to know Laurie well enough to know she was acting odd.

"Laurie? If you want to see your grandfather, you can go inside, you know," Ricky said.

"Oh … it's okay."

Will shrugged, and Ricky sighed.

"So, Laurie! Did you have a good spring break?" Will asked.

He might as well talk to her since he obviously couldn't talk to Ricky about Ricky sleeping with Laurie's math teacher.

"It was okay. Does Luke not go to church?"

"Luke? He usually does. He didn't today because he had a bad headache, he said. What makes you ask about Luke?" Ricky asked suspiciously. Laurie gave him an exasperated look.

"I was just asking. Good grief. Chill out. Y'all are so spastic."

"Um, no, we're not. Luke is a good employee, and it would simply be a shame to lose him when your grandfather kills him," Will said pointedly. Laurie looked at Will with a bored expression. Why did all these men have to act like dads? Even the kind of young good-looking ones like Will and Ricky and Jonathan acted like they were like 50 or something.

"For starters, he is not that old. He can't even drink yet. Hello! He's just a teenager! And anyway, you act like we're doing something, and I never said we were doing anything. But you know what? I am 15. Next year, I can drive by myself. In two more years, I will be able to do whatever I want. I really think I am old enough to make these kinds of decisions."

"*What* kind of decisions?" Will asked indignantly, immediately with his guard up.

"Like, who I talk to, hang out with, and whatever. And really, Ricky? You are sleeping with my math teacher. So, don't even go there."

"What? Where did you hear that?" Ricky asked, shocked.

"Well, I'm an office assistant and Miss Thomas has a really bad habit of talking to Miss Beales like they're at home or something. I have heard her tell Miss Beales *all kinds* of things about you and her."

"No, you haven't."

"The night she dripped candle wax on your butt, and it ran down your crack and burned you and you cried? She had to get the aloe vera with lidocaine? Remember?"

Will was trying to decide if he should scold Laurie for what he was quite certain Gary would consider inappropriate conversation in the churchyard or ask for more information regarding Ricky and the candle wax. Ricky glared at Laurie. He also made a mental note to go beat Janine, who was standing, just 20 feet away, talking to Mamie Lowery. Laurie smiled with a touch of triumph.

"So, Ricky, you say anything to my grandfather or my dad, but especially Poppy? I will just make sure *everyone* knows about the candle in your butt. I have a right to like a guy. I have a right to talk to a guy. Stop being so old acting. Uncle Will? Will you please not be a creep and go talk to Poppy or Daddy about Luke?"

"Awww, don't ask *me* to get involved in things like this,"

"I'm *not*! I'm asking you for the exact *opposite*. Please *don't* get involved. I'm not asking you to lie. I'm just asking you to not go talk to him about this stuff."

"Hey, Laurie." The three of them turned to see Eric approach them. "Oh! Hey, Eric."

"I, um, asked your grandfather if it was okay if I maybe gave you a ride back to town, and we could maybe go get some lunch? He said it's okay if I ask you."

Will and Ricky were suddenly very interested in the tangled web Laurie was weaving before their eyes. This was getting complicated for Laurie because she'd kinda-sorta been hanging out with Dereck from school. Then, she kinda-sorta flirted and sort of made out with Luke.

But her grandfather really liked Eric. He gushed about what a great employee he was to have at the co-op. Laurie guessed she liked him okay too. She avoided looking at Will and Ricky just then.

"Well, sure. I mean, since Poppy said its okay." She kind of wished he'd asked her before he asked her grandfather, but she guessed she understood it. Eric was probably wanting to suck up to Gary, so he wouldn't have to worry about Gary shooting him.

As Will stood there for a moment though, he began to get irritated.

"Eric? Would you give us just a minute, please? We were discussing something when you came up. Let us finish up really quick and then y'all can go," Will suggested.

Laurie looked at Will curiously. Eric just excused himself and told Laurie he'd be waiting on the church steps.

"What's going on? I'm done taking about all that. I was just ..." Laurie began. Will held up his hand to silence her. She looked confused. Ricky looked interested. Will took a deep breath and sighed. Ricky and Laurie both knew that was not a good sign. Will frowned at Laurie and spoke quietly, since they *were* at church, after all.

"I'm thinking about what you just said to Ricky. Who in Sam Hill do you think you are? You are 15 years old and threatening to blackmail your father's employee? Let me tell you something right now. I recommend you pay very close attention. You do not have anything on *me,* Laurie. And I have nothing to lose by telling your grandfather and your father what you just threatened to do to Ricky. You are standing in the churchyard of the church your own family built, not 15 minutes after your own grandfather gave a sermon in it! And you are not only talking with absolute disrespect to an adult but threatening to blackmail him if he doesn't do what you say? Do you have any idea how absolutely absurd that is?"

Laurie wished she could orb into town right now. This wasn't the first time Will chewed her out about something. It was one of the cons of hanging out on the farm; she automatically had three more dads. And she already knew that when Will got started on a lecture, it wasn't going to be anything quick. This time wasn't any different.

"Laurie! Pay attention to me! Be ashamed of yourself! What would your father and grandfather say if they knew you were going around talking to us like that?"

"But I didn't say I'd do anything to *you*, Uncle Will."

"You said those horrid things to Ricky in front of me! That's just as bad!" he said in an angry whisper. Laurie thought, in 15 years, Will was the first person she ever heard actually use the word *horrid*. But of course, Will wasn't finished.

"I swear you are another example of a girl that *does* need to be beat! I don't care what society says. Some of y'all just need to be beat regularly. Between you, Anne, Lexi, Karen ... apparently Miss Beales and Miss Thomas ... you all just need to be lined up twice a week and have a strap taken to you. We are not done (of course not, Laurie thought) but you have someone waiting for you. Rest assure, this is not over. Tell Ricky you're sorry."

"Sorry Ricky," Laurie said glaring at the grass.

"Whatever, Laurie. You do need to have something done about you though," Ricky told her. Will smiled but it didn't look like his usual nice smile.

"Oh, something will be done," Will assured them. Laurie sighed.

"Can I go now?"

"Go on."

"Good grief. I'm glad I'm not the one who has to raise her," Ricky muttered. Will looked at him.

"Not here, because that would just be tacky, but I am going to want more information on your relationship with Janine. I mean, that sounds like some pretty weird shit."

"I can't believe she talks about that stuff at school! I mean, really? What else does she tell people there?"

"What else is there to tell? Or do I want to know?"

The men laughed as Jerry made his way to them. He was carrying Eliza, and James and Caleb were dragging behind him.

"Hey, Ricky. Son, Caleb is coming home with us today. He claims he feels broken, and he doesn't want to go see Lexi's mama with them this afternoon. I said he can ride back with me and they can just pick him up when they come home," Jerry explained. Will looked at Caleb.

"Broken? What feels broken?"

"My bones and guts are broke. And my head. My head is broke. And my foot," Caleb said this mournfully.

"Well, it certainly does *sound* as if you *are* falling apart. We need to get you fixed as soon as possible. Are you still going to get the barbeque, Dad?"

"Yeah. I'm dropping Marilyn off at her house anyway."

Will bit his tongue, resisting the urge to talk to his father about the incident that took place a few minutes earlier. It was Sunday, and Will didn't like drama on Sundays. It was a day to relax and appreciate things, not start fights.

"Well, alright then. Where's Anne?"

"Her and Lexi are over there talking to Tammy. Anne! Come on, Mama! We're leaving!" Jerry bellowed across the churchyard, startling the several members of the congregation who were still standing around talking. Anne heard him though.

"Why does he *do* that? It's so embarrassing," she muttered to Lexi and Tammy.

They were sympathetic. Lexi told her she'd see her later, and Tammy said she'd see them both when she came to work the next day. Tammy went home. Lexi went to find Jason. Anne approached Jerry and Will, glaring at them like a child whose mother had just called for them over a store loudspeaker.

"Stop doing that!" she told Jerry.

"What?"

"Yelling my name out like that. Everyone heard you."

"Well, I wasn't aiming for *them* to hear me, just you. It worked. Come on, Mama."

"I'm going home with y'all today because I'm broke. My head is broke. I hope I can be a ghost if I get dead!" Caleb said excitedly.

"Caleb! Don't talk like that! That's messed up. And I know you're going home with us. Your mom told me," Anne scolded him. Will and Anne told the kids and Jerry they'd see them at the house and told Marilyn they'd see her later in the week.

Later in the day, after lunch, Caleb told Jerry he wanted to take a nap in Jerry's big bed. He often took naps in Jerry's bed. So, Jerry took the child to the big bedroom and helped him up on the huge regal cherry tester bed. Caleb grabbed Jerry's arm.

"Papa, lay down with me."

Jerry looked at Caleb worriedly. He sat on the edge of the bed. As Caleb kept tugging his arm, Jerry sighed and laid back into the collection of pillows. He and Caleb looked up at the pleated cream-colored fabric above them, on the underside of the bed's old wood framed canopy. The cream and deep-red bed curtains at the head of the bed were pulled back. The smell of the warm heavy fabric and old wood was comforting as mid-afternoon light fell across the room. They lay on top of the quilt and just listened to the quiet. Then Caleb said quietly,

"Papa, tell me the story about the tar-baby."

Jerry turned his head to look at Caleb lying beside him.

"The tar-baby? Where did *you* hear about the tar-baby?" Jerry asked, laughing easily. Good Lord! Jerry hadn't thought about Br'er Rabbit and the tar-baby in so many years!

"Mimi said you used to tell Uncle Will the story about the tar-baby. She said, *tell Papa to tell you the tar-baby story he told Uncle Will when he was a little boy.*"

Jerry felt his eyes smart. He smiled but it hurt. His mind went back to the nights in Will's room, when he and Faye would go together, to tuck Will in. Faye would sit in the armchair beside Will's bed, while Jerry would sit on the bed telling Will about crazy Br'er Rabbit, Br'er Fox, Br'er Bear and the tar-baby. Jerry took a breath now.

"Okay ... I'm going to tell you a story about some pretty silly animals; Br'er Rabbit, Br'er Fox and Br'er Bear,"

Jerry proceeded to tell Caleb the story about the rabbit who got mad at the tar-baby and how he got stuck, then got away and back into the comforts of his briar patch. As Jerry started to sing the familiar words "I

303

was born and raised in the briar patch!", Will stood outside the bedroom door smiling. Even at his age, Will couldn't help but appreciate and love the comical voices his father used when telling this story. He found himself even laughing quietly as possible. He didn't want to disrupt the storytelling. By the time Jerry had finished the story, the broken Caleb was in gales of laughter.

"Do you know another one?" Caleb asked hopefully.

"I do. I know a lot. I know lots of Uncle Remus stories, especially. But you know what? We'll save them and tell them one at a time. If you're going to take a nap today, you need to do it now. If you nap too late, you'll be up all night. I know you, buddy. Give me kisses and hugs. There ya go. Here, cover up with the throw. Move Miss Priss; I need the blanket. Okay, here ya go."

"I love you, Papa."

"And I love you."

"Thank you."

"For what, buddy?"

"You make *me* your little boy too. I like it when you do that."

"Aw, you know what? You *are* my little boy too. Uncle Will is my little boy, James is my little boy, Teague is my little boy, and you're my little boy. I love all of you just like you're mine. And if I have stories for little boys and girls, I promise you I'll tell them to you. Because I love you. And I think Mimi must love you an awful lot too if she wanted you to hear the tar-baby story. Get some sleep, son. I'll come wake you up in a bit."

But Jerry didn't get up. He laid there too long thinking about things, and fell asleep himself, with the child asleep in his arms. When Will went back upstairs about 20 minutes after the story ended, he found his dad and Caleb sleeping in the bed with Miss Priss. She was on Caleb's pillow, right beside his head. Will stood there for just a moment before leaving the room.

Later that night, after Caleb had gone home and the kids were in the bed, Anne went ahead and went to bed herself. She had another headache. So, Jerry and Will sat in the living room and watched television and drank together. When the program they were watching was over, Will took the remote and turned the television off. Jerry looked surprised. Will just smiled kind of goony.

"What'd you turn it off for?" Jerry asked.

"I'm going to bed in a few minutes. But first, I want a story."

"A story? What are you talking about?"

"Tar-baby. I know you still got it in you; I heard you telling the end of the story to Caleb today upstairs."

"*You* want *me* to tell *you* the tar-baby story?" Jerry asked this disbelievingly but with a smile. Will was an odd one; he'd go from acting like he had a stick up his ass all week to wanting a bedtime story from his dad. Will just grinned. He looked rather excited at the thought of it. Jerry shook his head and laughed at his son.

"Okay, well. This is a story about some pretty silly animals, Br'er Rabbit, Br'er Fox and Br'er Bear,"

Both men had a touch too much of bourbon in them by now and both were laughing at Jerry's intoxicated retelling of the story. Will laughed at Jerry's animated voices to the point he was in tears.

And there, in the old rocking chair beside Jerry's recliner, sat Faye. Anyone else would have blamed the chair's rocking on the nonexistent breezes blowing through the big open windows. But Will and Jerry knew it was Faye as soon as the chair began to rock methodically, creaking against the huge area rug. And then, there she was. They were both able to see her, sitting beside her husband in death just as she always had in life. They were both able to see her, smiling at her two most prized possessions, looking just as happy and alive as she always had. She was enjoying the drunken Uncle Remus stories as much as Will was.

They all three loved the children, and they all three loved Anne. But tonight, it was just the three of them together, alone. Their little family was spending some much needed, overdue time together.

Faye was getting better at this; she was figuring out how to get her family back. She was figuring out how to regain control of her house. She was figuring out how to befriend Anne and Marilyn because she knew they were going to have to learn to trust her. Because Faye had every intention of staying the lady of her house. And Anne and Marilyn (although welcome to stay) were going to have to learn to do things her way.

This old house understood this. Jerry was right, and Jeremy was right; this house heard, saw, felt, and told everything. It heard everything. It knew everything.

In the late hours of the night, while Jerry, Will, and Faye gathered in the front parlor, the house sighed. The settling sounds were heard and felt by those in the house, dead and alive. The warm night mountain air outside was damp. The lights inside flickered for just a second, just as the old grandfather clock struck 10 p.m. Soft humming wafted through Eliza's bedroom as a lady stood in front of the window, the soft sound of her taffeta skirts whispering in the dark room. Cigar smoke was heavy in the seemingly empty kitchen. While the deceased made their evening rounds in the house, the family of three sat downstairs laughing at the story of the tar-baby and Br'er Rabbit.

And, the whole time, Faye was finding a new kind of strength within these old walls, and this old house was giving her the courage and power to take back what was hers.

CHAPTER 21

Sunday afternoon and evening had gone well for everyone, really. Caleb wasn't in the best of moods because tomorrow he'd be going to see his kindergarten class he'd be attending in the fall. He was still very angry about this and said he was going to do something about the government making him go to school. Everyone just apologized to him and said they understood.

So, because he was very, very angry at his parents, he wasn't keen on hanging out with them Sunday afternoon. He went with the Grangers which Jason took a little personally but wouldn't say so out loud. Caleb then had a very nice and relaxing day at the big house with the Grangers. Caleb liked it here; it was always a quiet house for the most part. At home, the television was always on, radios were always on, there was always someone arguing about something. He would try to go to his room to get away from all of that, especially when Laurie was there.

The Granger's house was a sleepy house. It was large enough that even if people were talking in the kitchen you couldn't hear it in the living room. Caleb liked the way this house felt and smelled and sounded. He loved Jerry's room the best, and he didn't know why. It was his favorite room in the whole house. Jerry's huge cherry tester bed was so grand and fine Caleb felt like he was sleeping in a castle. The giant furniture and fireplace and rich red, gold, and deep green and dark blue in the room were comforting. His own house had some old furniture that they had purchased; Poppy had given them a big dining table and chairs. That was nice; Caleb liked the furniture. But the furniture in this house, especially Jerry's room was different. It belonged here. It was simply a part of this wonderous house.

Over the past few years, Caleb had explored the attic, the cellar, and the room under the stairs. He found so many amazing things in this house and had become so comfortable with it he feared nothing in it. He would see people who he didn't know, and he knew these were not ordinary people. He knew they were like Mimi. But they never did anything to him, never frightened him. They would see him, he suspected. He had heard some of them speak. Instead of frightening him, all they did was make him feel safer. He knew, in time, that no matter where you were in this house someone was watching out for you. He liked that.

Outside, he had been allowed to explore the numerous other buildings on the property. There was the old smokehouse, the old icehouse, the old tobacco barn, the numerous buildings that had housed slaves, and a small building that had served as a church for the slaves. He enjoyed going in these places; some of them, he could only go in with a grown-up because they were too far from the house. The complex of this plantation had been very well preserved, which made it one of the finest examples of Greek revival architecture in this part of the country. There had been numerous requests made to allow daily tours of the Granger-Teague Plantation. They always had to explain this was not a museum; it was their home. They didn't want their daily lives disrupted by tours.

Yes, Caleb had it made here. He could play for hours among these buildings. He knew the rule; if you can't see the house, you've gone too far. And on this particular Sunday, Caleb kept himself busy outside. Then, he wanted his nap.

While the Sunday was pleasant on Teague Road, it was going fairly-well in town as well. After Jeremy and Kim had their lunch, they hung out for an extra couple of hours. They parted ways in front of the library.

"I had fun, Jeremy. Thanks for inviting me to lunch."

"I didn't. I invited you to supper, but you already had a hot date lined up with Loftis," he reminded Kim. She rolled her eyes.

"It's not a hot date. It's a neighborly gesture. Really, I'm not interested in Walter Loftis. He's not my type."

Jeremy smiled, stepped closer, and put his hand on Kim's arm.

"So, what is your type?" he asked with a wicked grin.

"What if I told you I liked guys with clean records and no prior arson charges?"

"I'd say that leaves me out, but I'd also say you're full of shit."

"Yeah, you're right. I like them bad. I like guys who don't walk around all uptight and stuff. Will, you know? He'd great looking and smart and rich; he's even nice. But he is way too interested in law and order. And that's boring."

"Well, but he has to, you know? I mean, I know you know that he ..."

"Yeah, yeah. I know all that. Still, I like guys who like to start shit from time to time."

"Well, not to brag or anything, but I'm *always* starting shit. You want to join me one day this week, so we can maybe start some together?"

"That's like, the most romantic pickup line I've ever gotten."

"Is that a yes?"

"Yes. You know where to find me during the day. Come find me. Bye, Jeremy. Thank you for this afternoon." Kim stood on tiptoe to kiss Jeremy's cheek. Even then, she had to pull his head down a little. She was only five feet and three inches tall, and he was six feet four inches tall. So, getting a hold of his cheek was no small task.

He went home feeling a little goony, and she went home to get a nap in before she had to get ready for Walter.

Walter had attended church services but felt a little weird when Gary spent entirely too much time talking to him after the service. He felt kind of like he was being interrogated. He'd run into Gary on a few different occasions by now, but they hadn't really talked very much. Gary seemed interested in making up for that now. He had a way of squinting his eyes when listening to Walter answer his questions. Somehow, the narrowed eyes made Walter feel Gary was suspicious of him. Yes, it did feel like an interrogation.

Walter was right, to a degree. Gary wanted to know this man. He was obviously spending time at the Granger's. This mattered because Gary loved the people who lived on Teague Road. And if this man was going to be spending a substantial amount of time with them, then Gary wanted to know more about him.

Also, he had heard that it appeared this man had taken a shine to Karen. Gary put his foot in there for multiple reasons. To begin with, there was the very obvious reason; she was Roy's girlfriend. Roy was one of Gary's dearest friends in the world; he had done too much for Jason and Lexi and Gary's grandchildren. You didn't mess with Roy. Gary wouldn't watch that happen.

The other reason was, of course, that it was Karen. Gary had been incredibly protective of Karen since not very long after she married Luther. Gary saw all the way from Portsmouth that Luther was going to end up being bad news. After Luther beat her up the night that she left home, he became even more protective of her. He'd suspected Luther had been abusing her but never had the hard evidence he needed until that night. Still, Karen begged him to not do anything just yet.

Soon, Luther was forced to leave Karen's house for good. But he still broke in her house one night and forced himself on her before beating her up. Gary didn't care if Luther was drunk and not thinking clearly that night. Luther learned that very night, that you didn't mess with Karen Townsend. Gary made sure of it.

So, yes, if this man was getting tight with Karen, Gary was going to keep his eye on this man. Gary liked him; don't get him wrong! Walter Loftis seemed to be a nice guy, but he was new here and nobody really knew him yet. That was reason enough to find out more about him and watch him. So, Gary would.

The interrogation went okay for the most part, but then Gary asked Walter if he enjoyed hunting. Walter did, and this was met with a smile of approval from Gary.

"Turkey season is coming back up in couple weeks. You should join me when I go hunting one day," Gary said pleasantly.

Walter felt apprehensive.

"Well, I usually just go in the fall …"

"Well, the *spring* gobblers are good shootin' *too*! I *insist*. It'll be great, just us and the woods!"

There was nothing Walter wanted less than to go in the woods alone with Gary Connelly, especially with guns. Suddenly Gary slapped him hard on the back with such force that Walter stumbled forward a few steps. He looked at Gary after he caught his footing. Gary was smiling broadly.

"Don't forget now!"

Oh, Walter would love to forget this was going to happen, but he wouldn't be able to. Gary need not worry about that.

"Fine. Anyway, it was a good service."

"Thank you! I am so glad that you were able to make it. I will be looking for you *next* week. I'm gonna go find my son. You take care now, Walter!" Gary slapped him on the back again and strolled across the churchyard. Walter watched the pretty redheaded woman join him. Walter had met her during the search for Gary's grandson. She was considerably younger than he was, Walter could tell. Well, Gary obviously had a lot going for him. Walter didn't know that she was pregnant, but he did know that Gary was already engaged to marry her. Yes, Gary certainly had it good these days.

Later that day, Walter got ready to go to Kim's for her dinner invite. When he arrived at her house, he was comfortable enough. It was a nice, neat house. It was one of the older, larger homes in town, sitting across the street from the courthouse square. It was on one of the larger properties located in town. The huge home was a historic somewhat Victorian styled home with three outbuildings and a very large dog within the elderly wrought iron fence. Unfortunately, Walter didn't notice the dog until he lifted the gate latch and had already walked halfway down the cobblestone sidewalk to her large front porch.

The rottweiler came out from under a mammoth oak tree. The bottom limbs literally crawled eerily across the ground. So, Walter didn't see the dog until the dog came out from under the tree. He held his hands up at the 104-pound snotting and snarling dog.

"Hey there, little puppy. It's all okay. I'm here to see Kim. Do you know where Kim is? Can you go find Kim? Go find her now. Go on now."

When the dog simply continued to make congested sounding growls at Walter, he decided to just call Kim on the phone. So as not to startle the dog with any sudden moves, Walter slowly took the phone from his shirt pocket. He dialed the phone while the dog cocked its head at Walter. Kim answered on second ring.

"Hey! Where ya at?" she asked when he introduced himself.

"On your sidewalk."

"Okay, why don't you keep going until you get to the front door?"

"You have a dog. It's a real big dog. And I don't like the way it's looking at me or the noise it's making."

"Oh, good grief. Hold on a minute." A moment later, Kim came out the front door. She started down the steps.

"Gacy! Go lay down! Go on! Go to your tree!" The dog let out a huge wet, runny sneeze and growled one last time. He turned and went to the giant tree that apparently belonged solely to him.

"Gacy? Its name is Gacy?" Walter asked.

"Yeah, after John Wayne Gacy," Kim answered, as if it made perfect sense.

"You named your dog after a serial killer?"

"I thought Gacy flowed better than Dahmer."

"Of course. That dog sounds like it might have a cold."

"Oh, upper respiratory infection. He gets them all the time. Its gross. Imagine what it's like having him sleep with you."

"I'd rather not."

"So! Let's go inside!"

The house was charming with its porches, towers, gables, and turrets. The front door featured the old, original stained glass. There was an antique twist doorbell beneath the window, like the one the Granger's and Karen both had at their own front doors. Walter found these doorbells to be most charming. They stepped inside, and Walter drew his breath. The rich old paneling and hardwood floors were stunning. The huge staircase made this house appear completely out of place.

"My God! This place is beautiful! I never imagined it'd look like this inside!"

"Thank you. It's been in my family forever. It was built in 1889. My umpteen greats-back grandfather built it. He was the judge here. Well, judge, among other things. I love it. Since I'm the only kid my parents had, it was left to me. You want a little tour? It's a really cool house."

Walter quickly accepted the tour invite. It was completely different from the Granger's house but equally stunning. Kim showed him numerous interesting and beautiful things in this house. However, one room both terrified him and fascinated him at the same time. She showed him the parlor, which now served as the Doll Room.

In this room, surrounded by huge windows, were more dolls than Walter had even seen together in one place. But there were also the dollhouses. These things were no toys. These were actual houses, with carpet, dishes, flowers, tiny books that really opened, tiny beds with real bedding, and of course the dolls that resided in them. What floored Walter was the fact that each of these seven dollhouses were wired with electricity. Walter had never in his entire life seen anything so amazing as these dollhouses. He couldn't help it; he desperately wanted to play with them.

"Where did these come from? They're beautiful. Oh, wait a minute! No way! Is that a dollhouse of …?" He had not seen this one in front of the mammoth-sized bay window. Then he saw the one beside it. He was sure he had died at the sight of the eighth and ninth dollhouses.

There, before the windows were two dollhouses. They were obviously the main attraction, judging by their location in the room. The first one he saw there was an exact replica of this house. Beside it, was a breathtaking replica of the Granger home. It was like he was looking in the windows of the actual houses! There was even a silver tub on the porch for the geraniums. Kim sat in the big rocking chair and smiled while hundreds of glass-eyed dolls watched from the shelves, tables, and chairs from which they rested.

"Those were built a very long time ago. Most of *these* were. My great-great grandmother was obsessed with dolls. She collected them from all over the world. She had the architect who built this house, build the dollhouse. That was in 1893. She was so excited by it that she had another built of the Granger house. All of these except those three are houses from here in town. That's a replica of a house at Appomattox. That's a copy of the house my four greats grandmother had grown up in. It burned to the ground after being hit by lightning in 1902." Kim proceeded to tell Walter about the dollhouses.

"And I'm building a replica of the co-op now. Look." She removed a small sheet looking thing from something on a table. And he couldn't help himself; he laughed out loud. It was the co-op! It was still under construction, but it really was the co-op!

"But I don't understand. I mean, why in the world wouldn't the Grangers want this in *their* house? It's beautiful."

"My house is on the historic tour. It's open to tours every day from nine to four, except Sunday. And this room is one of the biggest attractions. I have one of the largest collections of antique dolls in the entire state. Well, not just dolls, as you can see. Dolls, doll furniture, doll houses, and stuff. The Grangers know its' part of the tour. Besides, it's ours. Just because it's a model of their house doesn't mean it's theirs. But anyway, the Grangers have come right out and said the dollhouses should stay here. Everyone who has a replica of their house in here agrees this is the best place for them."

Walter stood back and looked around the eerily beautiful room. Kim smiled.

"And its haunted."

"What's haunted?"

"Watch." Kim walked over to the Granger house and began to hum a song. The tiny rocking chairs in the dollhouse began to rock on their own. She opened the front door to the dollhouse, and they watched as it closed by itself immediately.

"It does other things, too. If you play old Civil War songs, the furniture in the ballroom moves against the walls. And look." Kim proceeded to show him other creepy things the other dollhouses did. Then when the haunted dollhouse tour was over, Kim showed Walter the actual dolls that sat around watching them. She had a truly magnificent doll collection, but she first went to one doll in-particular. It was a ghastly, ugly thing with teeth and a cracked face. Kim was excited as she lifted it from its small cradle. She prepared to lay the doll on the floor.

"Watch. It just takes a minute." She lay the doll on its stomach on the old wooden floor. Right before Walter's eyes, the doll flipped itself open and blinked its eyes several times. One hand slowly began to raise. Walter thought he was going to be sick, but Kim just giggled and picked the doll back up. It proceeded to blink its' disgusting glass eyes even as she carried it to the cradle. Then she picked up another doll. This was a rag doll. It had been sitting in a small, child-sized rocking chair. She put the rag doll on an antique armchair nearby. The doll immediately began to pull itself off the armchair, and Walter watched as it dragged itself across the floor like a paraplegic back to its little rocking chair. As the doll lay exhausted on the floor by the rocking chair, Kim picked it up straightened its dress and set it lovingly back in the rocking chair.

"The chair and doll used to both belong to an ancestor of some sort. Some cousin from way back. She used to sit in this chair and hold her doll. Well, when she was four years old, she died from some fever, and they tossed the doll in her chair in her bedroom before they buried the little girl. Now, whenever you try to take the doll out of its chair, it goes back to it."

Kim seemed excited by this story. Walter looked at her oddly.

"And you sleep here? I mean, seriously? You sleep in the same house with dolls that move around the house?"

"Well, I think it's fascinating. I go online and look for haunted dolls. These aren't all haunted, of course. Just those are the ones I know about. Besides I lock these doors every night." She pointed to a section of dolls. He got the creeps. There were at least 20 dolls in this section.

"People like to know which ones are haunted. And it's cool, because I can pull them out at tours and people can actually see them and hear them."

"Hear them?"

"Sure. Some of these, cry, some talk, some laugh, sing, and a couple sort of growl and one kind of chants. At least, that's what it sounds like to me."

Walter sort of wanted to hear them but decided he'd not get any sleep at all if he did. So, he and Kim went ahead and ate. After dinner and a pleasant visit, he looked for his cell phone as he prepared to leave.

They recalled he had set it down in the room with the dolls while he looked at the dollhouses. They went back in there, and he retrieved his phone. He thanked Kim for an interesting evening and a wonderful dinner. They exited the doll room, as they exchanged goodbyes. Then, Walter heard it plain as day; a voice from the shelves told him goodbye.

Walter didn't know what he had gotten himself into, moving here. He walked down the sidewalk to his house and suddenly it felt as if he was being watched. He paused, looked around him, and saw nothing. He wanted to go to The Tavern, but it was Sunday and The Tavern was closed. So, he went home.

Walter had trouble sleeping. He couldn't stop thinking about those glass eyes and cracked faces with teeth. He couldn't stop thinking about the faceless muslin doll that dragged itself a full five feet across the floor right before his eyes. And then there was the doll that had told him goodbye. It was a nice gesture, he supposed but he didn't like it. Well, maybe he did.

Walter did eventually fall asleep, but he dreamed that he was small and in the Granger dollhouse. The Grangers were in there too. And all the other dollhouses had small people living in them too. When Walter would look out the door and windows of the dollhouse, he'd see the dolls from the shelves walking around the room and peering in the windows of the dollhouses. One, with black curls, in a faded yellow dress looked in the window at Walter and told him goodbye. Her eyes clicked as they blinked at him and he saw her tiny teeth as she spoke.

When he woke, he recalled actually seeing that doll. He remembered her. And he worried she remembered him, too.

CHAPTER 22

———⟨∞⟩———

Sunday night, Laurie was back home at Gary's. Yes, she decided she'd just call that home now. When this started, she said she was staying with her grandfather. But right before Sunday evening services, Laurie got a text message from her mother telling her to come get the rest of her stuff if she didn't want to live there, anymore. Stacy was taking this hard. Between Laurie leaving, Jack screwing around with the neighbor, and Randy calling her with threats ... well, she was just having a bad week. So, when she saw Laurie's forgotten cowboy boots in the foyer, she kind of snapped.

Of course, the text sent Laurie into a new fit of tears, which of course made Gary angry at Stacy all over again. He'd tried to be sympathetic. He'd tried to be understanding about all the things Stacy was going through. But now? Now, he was just plain mad. And he was having to go preach to a congregation while he *wanted* to take a big stick and beat his granddaughter's mother. This is why Gary had trouble with the whole preaching thing. He felt like such a hypocrite.

So, Laurie and Gary made the arrangements to go get her things after evening services. After services, they took Kylie home first. She didn't feel well. When they got to the trailer, however, they were surprised to see a sheriff's department car outside. Gary was only slightly uncomfortable by this; he was close to most everyone who worked with the sheriff's department. It wasn't unheard of for them to come see him about an assortment of things; sometimes it was business related, but sometimes it was just to shoot the shit. Gary parked the truck, and they all got out.

The sheriff was sitting on Gary's porch swing. He smiled at them as they came up the steps to the big deck.

"How y'all doing this evening? Kylie … Laurie."

"Fine, thank you. I'm going to go throw up," Kylie replied. Kylie went inside, but Laurie lingered. She was curious what was going on. She assumed something was going on because the only time the law ever showed up at her mother's house was to break up a fight between her mom and Jack. Gary loosened his tie.

"What's going on, Brady?"

Brady Nolan looked at Laurie.

"Laurie, maybe you should go on in the house with Kylie for a minute, honey. I need to talk to your granddaddy. It's business," he suggested. Gary patted Laurie on the back.

"Go on inside. Let me talk to Sheriff Nolan. I'll be in in a few, then we'll go to your mama's," Gary told her. At this, Brady raised his brows. Laurie went inside.

"What's going on, Brady? Couldn't this have waited until tomorrow?"

"No, Gary. It couldn't have. Why were you going to Stacy's?"

"Laurie needs to pick her stuff up. Is that any of your business?" Gary asked a little testily. He was friends with Brady, but Gary wasn't in the mood for this tonight.

"I think it might be. That's why I'm here really. Stacy is getting to be a bit of a problem, Gary. I'm real sorry she's been dumped, but this behavior she's been exhibiting is getting a bit out of hand. Folks are talking and it's nothing nice that they're saying."

"Well, last time I checked, being an idiot isn't against the law. She's going through some shit, Brady. Lay off. If she gets out of hand, let the boys from the department here handle it. This is a woman whose husband is fucking the town librarian. Doesn't make her a criminal. It makes her pissed off and rightfully so."

"What are you going to do about Jack? I can't see you letting this go."

"This all just happened this week. There's a lot going on this week. And I will admit that I have not really given a rat's ass about Jack this week. I have more pressing things going on. I'm sure you heard about

Brother Lawson. My wife is pregnant. My granddaughter is being kicked out by her own mother. Don't come out here and start going on about Jack and Stacy's marital problems."

"Jack has also taken a shine to Janie. She's grown, of course. She thinks she knows everything; nothing I can tell her. But I'm letting you know that I am not taking too well to him talking to her and ... such. I don't think they have anything really going on yet, but I don't intend to wait until they do. It's my little girl! I would like for you to look into things. This is still your town, Gary. And I expect you're still out to keep it clean?"

"Yeah."

"Yeah, especially since you're the new preacher in town. You got a responsibility here, friend. That's all I'm saying. So, you're taking the girl over to get her stuff? She's staying with you and Kylie, now?"

"Yeah. We think it's best for her."

"I think I agree. Well, school starts back tomorrow, so I guess y'all probably want to go ahead and go get her stuff so you can get back home. You know, since it is a school night and all. I'll go on and leave you be, Chief. Hey? We're good. Don't go looking all stressed. It's alright. I just thought we needed to have us *a talk*. You know?"

"Yeah, whatever. By the way, I *do* think this could have waited until tomorrow."

Brady stood up and adjusted his pants' waist around his slight beer gut. He spit tobacco juice off the edge of the deck and patted Gary's arm.

"Take care. I'll holler back at you later."

"Can't wait."

Brady laughed at this and went down the deck steps. He got in his patrol car and left. Gary watched as the taillights disappeared down Elm Street. He went inside.

Laurie was sitting on the couch, waiting for her grandfather. He stopped short when he saw her, Brady's words coming back to him. The child didn't deserve a mother like that.

"Is everything okay, Poppy?"

"Yes, dear. Let's go ahead and run get your stuff."

319

They went and got her things. Stacy stayed in her own bedroom the entire time.

Back at Gary's that night, although the room that had always been the spare room had become Laurie's, she again elected to sleep on the couch in the living room. Gary had helped her carry her things to the bedroom, and Kylie helped her get settled in. So, Gary was surprised when Laurie came in the living room with a pillow and blanket.

"Honey, what are you doing? It's a school night; you need to go to bed."

"I want to sleep in here."

"Why? The bedroom is yours."

"I just do. I want to. I can't?" she asked pitifully. Gary sighed. He felt something was going on there but agreed to let her.

"Okay, look. You can sleep in here long as you need to. But you and I have got to have a talk, baby. We're going to talk tomorrow. Alright?"

"Alright," she agreed. Laurie and Gary hugged and kissed each other goodnight. She told Kylie goodnight, and they all went to bed.

Caleb, however, was up half the night crying about having to go see his new classroom the next day.

Other than all that, Sunday went fairly-well for everyone.

Monday morning, Tammy showed up for work at the Granger home. She felt odd just walking in, even though she had done that often since 1978. The front door was open, so she just knocked on the wood screen door frame and hollered through the screen.

"Y'all! I'm here!"

Jerry came peering around the kitchen doorway. He stepped out in the hall and yelled back at her.

"Then get in here and get to work, woman!"

So, Tammy had returned to *just let yourself in* status around here. She did just that.

"Were you waiting for an engraved invitation?" Jerry teased.

"No, just for a gentleman to open the door for me," she teased back.

At this, Jerry scoffed,

"Well, you'd be waiting a while! Aren't any gentleman around here!" Jerry laughed joyously and threw his arm around her neck when she reached him. As he hugged her, she couldn't help smiling.

Oh, this Jerry was such a far cry from the Jerry they had seen for several years after Faye's passing. It was so nice to see Jerry back to his old self; as often as she saw him now, it just never got old seeing him happy again. Well, at least he acted and looked happy. *Happy* and *happier* are two entirely different things, he was learning. Before they reached the kitchen, Jerry pulled her to a stop and dropped his voice.

"Hey, listen, I have a request, before we go in the kitchen. Can you teach Anne to make real biscuits? I mean, the frozen ones from the store are okay, I guess. But she uses them all the time and they're just not as good. Maybe y'all could even make homemade ones, like a lot? And then freeze *those* so she won't have to mix them up every time?"

"Yeah, but how do I do that without offending her?"

"Oh, easy. When y'all do biscuits this morning, just immediately start mixing homemade ones. If she says anything, just act surprised and tell her you knew homemade biscuits were my favorite, so you just assumed that's what she makes. You know how Faye makes them. Just tell her you know Faye's recipe for homemade biscuits if she's interested."

"And if she's not?" Tammy asked. Jerry looked at her as if that was a silly thing to say.

"She will be. She likes to make me happy. She always does things to make me happy. All you have to do is tell her this makes me happy. She'll do it."

"Well, okay then. I'll do what I can. If she likes to … *make you happy*, maybe you can suggest she take it easy while I'm here? She worked as much as I did Friday. It's not necessary and I feel bad taking pay for a job she's helping me do."

"Well, that'll be tricky. She loves taking care of us. I think, maybe we can pick a few things we can leave for her to be in charge of? You know, like the laundry? If we find a few things for her to keep doing for us, maybe we'll be able to convince her to let you do the rest of it. We'll see."

Tammy watched Jerry go back to the kitchen and she thought about what he'd just said; *You know how Faye makes them.* No, Jerry didn't talk about Faye in the past tense. It would be the first odd behavior of Jerry's that Tammy would really witness while working for the Grangers.

Tammy followed Jerry into the kitchen. She had always liked this room the best. It always smelled so good. Tammy supposed it was a mix of the elderly wooden floors, and the mix of wooden and handmade brick walls. Yes, even the bricks in the wall and massive eight-foot-wide fireplace smelled good. So much old wood just smelled so nice, the old furniture, and the old cabinetry. In the summer it was a pleasant room full of sunshine with country breezes or the drowsy warm smell of rain coming through the screens of the always open windows. In the fall and winter, it was warm and cozy with the fire going in the fireplace, which took up almost half the wall.

It was always a pleasant place for Tammy and Faye to sit and visit. Now, this morning, it was very quiet except for Will, who was standing at the sink singing quietly. He appeared to be washing his hands. Anne was nowhere to be seen.

"Where's Anne?" Tammy asked. Immediately, Anne came out of the pantry. She looked sleepy. Miss Priss followed close at her heels, walking in front of her, around her, behind her, between her feet. The cat meowed mournfully. Jerry smiled lovingly at the cat.

"Does Miss Priss want her num-num? Is she hungry? Does she want her breakfast? Come on, sweet baby kitty. Let daddy get you something to eat." Jerry went in the large walk-in pantry and came out with a can of flaked turkey and cheese cat food. Will shook his head in disgust at his father. He shook the excess water from his hands and wiped them on the hand towel. He kissed Anne on top of her head and took the iron skillet from her hands.

"How are you, Miss Tammy?" Anne asked politely but sleepily.

"I'm fine, dear. Have a seat! Enjoy your coffee ... oh, tea. Let me get stuff started for you," Tammy insisted. Anne shrugged and obliged. She hated mornings. She hated getting up at daybreak and feeding what felt (and sounded) like 40 people every morning. She hated Miss Priss winding around her feet while she tried to cook breakfast. Everyone loved getting together for breakfast at the Granger house. And, well, it's not that Anne disliked the lively breakfast and lunch conversations. She just disliked it happening five days a week in her kitchen.

Tammy knew where everything in this kitchen was kept when Faye had run things. So, she knew where to look for things. When she realized that absolutely nothing had changed since Faye's passing, she was elated! This would certainly make housekeeping in here easier. While Anne sat at the table, Jerry and Will went upstairs to wake up the children. Tammy quietly started making the requested homemade biscuits. She was in the process of mixing the batter when Anne suddenly asked,

"What is that you're making?" She didn't sound angry, just surprised and a little suspicious. Tammy put on her best surprised look.

"What? This? Well, I thought you'd want biscuits with breakfast. I know Faye always made them. Do you not make biscuits? As much as Jerry loves her biscuits, I just assumed y'all still made them."

Tammy worried she sounded fake and stupid, but Anne looked curious. Her guard dropped a little.

"Well, I get the frozen ones. I didn't know they always did homemade ones. But I don't know; I've never made biscuits anyway. I doubt they'd have been very good even if I had tried. My mom never made them. She used the refrigerated ones."

"Oh. Well, Faye is the one who showed me how to make these, years and years ago. I used to use the refrigerated ones, too. I can show you how to make these, easy enough. Let me just finish these up, since they're almost ready to roll out and cut anyway. Do you want to come help cut them?"

Anne looked at Tammy awkwardly for a moment. She felt betrayed somehow that this woman told her something she didn't know about her own men. Then, she worried that her biscuits hadn't been good all these years she'd been making them biscuits. Oh well, they ate them anyway and didn't complain, she reminded herself. As long as they didn't complain, she was fine. Sometimes even if they *did*, she was fine. Anne finally stood and walked over to Tammy, who showed her how to take the elderly metal silver biscuit cutter with the little red handle and stamp out biscuits.

"Tomorrow, I'll show you how to mix them up, that is, if you want me to," Tammy offered. Anne nodded.

"Yeah, thanks. They ... well, they want me to do things like Faye did them, but they don't always remember that I never even knew her. I mean, I know her like she is now, but I've never watched her cook breakfast or raise kids or anything. They forget that, I think," Anne said this almost apologetically.

"I know; I got that impression a while back. I'm sorry. Give it more time and see if anything happens."

They continued to prepare breakfast, and Jerry and Will came downstairs with the kids. In no time at all, Jason and Lexi showed up with Teague and a sullen Caleb. Jason put the baby down in the bouncing exercise seat they kept out for him.

"Well, what's the matter with y'all this morning? You all look like you belong in a funeral procession," Tammy commented.

"Teague is snotty, Caleb is mad he has to go see his classroom today, and I'm mad that Jason won't be able to go with me, so I'll have to deal with these two on my own. It'd be fine if Caleb wasn't being such a creep today," Lexi answered.

"Why can't Jason go?" Anne asked.

"Because I have someone coming to talk to me about a horse today, and it's when Lexi needs to have Caleb at the school," Jason answered.

"Uncle Roy ..." Anne started. Jason interrupted her.

"Uncle Roy has a physical today. He's going to be at the medical center then."

"Aw, don't worry about it, Lexi. I'll go with you. Did you try to get in touch with Gary? He's there in town. He could probably meet you," Jerry offered.

"No. Because I didn't know about this until about ten minutes ago. I thought Jason was going to go with us. I guess I can call him," Lexi said without much interest. Gary had turned into the dad she didn't want. Roy was the dad she wanted. Gary used every opportunity he had alone with Lexi to lecture her about how she wasn't doing her job as a wife and mother. He told her she needed to take care of her own house, not the Granger's house. He told her she needed to take care of Jason's dinner, not Will's dinner. She needed to take care of raising her own children in her own house, not Will's/ Jerry's children in their house. Yes, he said that because he honestly didn't know who the father was of either child and he had a feeling he never would. Maybe they didn't know. Gary felt bad for feeling that way, but he did.

Anyway, Gary had very strong feelings regarding Lexi's relationship with the Grangers. He simply felt she preferred them to her own family and their house to her own. He suspected it had a lot to do with the attention she got while hanging out at the Granger home. It was busier and more active. They tended to have visitors during the day, and the horse boarding stable kept things constantly moving at this end of the farm, especially now that the weather was turning warm. Gary thought to himself that Lexi maybe liked pretending it was *her* big fine house.

It's not that she didn't love the home Jason had built, but it was by itself in the woods, set apart from all the activity that took place on the farm. But the Granger home? Lexi *did* enjoy answering the wide door that opened out to the big, plaster wrap-around porch when visitors came calling on the Grangers. And she did enjoy welcoming these visitors into the wide grand entry hall at the foot of the stairs.

Okay, so maybe she kind of did like thinking of it as her own. Anyway, she didn't want to listen to Gary chew her out today. Jerry was cute and would be much more fun. It'd probably result in some curious stares and become the topic of the week in the teachers' lounge if Jerry Granger accompanied Lexi Connelly and her kids to the school, but who cared? Not Lexi.

"You'll go with me?" Lexi asked, turning on her charm, twirling her hair. Jerry wondered why she dismissed the idea of asking Gary but didn't really care enough to press the matter. Will had all kinds of work he would make Jerry do outside today if he stayed. So, Jerry used Lexi's dilemma to his full advantage.

"Sure, honey. What time?"

"11:30 is when the morning kindergarten leaves. So, we need to leave about 11:00"

"Okay," Jerry agreed happily.

Lexi was suddenly pleasant again, and Jerry was happy until he looked across the kitchen and saw Anne. He sighed when he recognized the look on her face. She often got disgusted with Lexi's pity parties, as Anne called them. And, well, Jerry sort of had to agree with Anne. Lexi was definitely one to pull out the sympathy card. She really worked it. But Jerry wasn't going for Lexi. He genuinely loved Caleb and felt bad for the child. He was already miserable about the thought of going to school in the fall. To make him deal with a cranky Lexi today of all days wouldn't help any. So, Jerry thought if he went it'd maybe help-out just a bit. Jerry shook his head ever so slightly at Anne. He gestured with his hand for her to follow him into the hall. She did.

"First things first; get that look off your face. You know as well as I do that Lexi can make everyone around her miserable as Hell when she's in one of her moods. Caleb already doesn't want to go do this today. I'm not going for her. I just thought that my going might make the experience a touch easier for the child."

"She makes me so sick with her pitiful self. Oh, I have everything so bad! My husband doesn't love on me enough! My kids are mean! My ..." Anne started but Jerry popped her arm.

"Shut up. She's in the next room. Anyway, you do your own share of bitching and moaning. Now, give me some sugar and go in there and be a good girl."

"You just told me to shut up. Get your own sugar," Anne retorted, as she began to walk past him. He stepped in front of her and quickly kissed her smack on the mouth. When she got ready to scold him, he reminded her,

"You told me to get my own sugar. So, I did." He went back to the kitchen. Anne followed him. They visited until Roy and Karen showed up. Then, they all sat down and had breakfast together.

Tammy felt just a touch odd. For the most part, she enjoyed herself. She had known these people all her life. She had missed them all miserably when Faye had passed-away. It was a little odd to eat breakfast with them. She kept wanting to get up and take care of the housekeeping, but they insisted she sit and eat.

Finally, breakfast ended, and all the men left, with Caleb at their heels and James in Will's arms. Eliza went to the living room to play. Anne began cleaning the kitchen. Lexi made faces at Teague, who sat in the highchair.

"Anne, dear, you must let me take care of these things. You are sweet to help, but I'm here to give you a break! You are the lady of the most gorgeous house in this part of the state! Enjoy it!" Tammy gushed. Lexi glared at Tammy for the comment about Anne being the lady of the most gorgeous house in this part of the state. Apparently, Lexi wasn't the only one disgusted by this statement.

Suddenly, the pantry door slammed shut. All three women shouted at the sudden loud noise. Anne stared at the door for a moment before shaking her head.

"No, I'm not the lady of the house. I might be one of them, but I'm surely not the only one. It's all good. Too much goes on here for me to be responsible for all of it. If Faye, Lexi, Karen, Miss Beales, even you? Yeah, if all y'all want to be women of this house with me, have at it. You all do what you want. I'm going to go play with the baby."

Anne left Tammy to the kitchen work. Lexi got up and began helping. Lexi was scraping plates for the dogs when she noticed Tammy looked odd.

"Hey, Miss Tammy? What's wrong?"

"I don't feel like I'm wanted here."

"Of course, you are!"

"I don't know. Do you really think Anne wants me here? I mean, I'm guessing the fellas feel like I'm *needed* here. But does Anne want me here?"

"Anne takes this house and these men very seriously. And, well, she's going through a lot. I mean, Marilyn came here and took care of things when they were all sick. I think that kind of was a blow to her ego or something. Now, they go and get a housekeeper on top of that. She went from being the one running everything to being kinda replaced. At least, that's what I think it is. And well, this Faye thing isn't easy for her. You don't have a clue."

"A clue about what?"

"Faye is, well, a pain in the ass sometimes. Like, just now. You said that, and she slammed the door. You *do* know that she did that, right? And that was so obviously about you saying Anne is the lady of the house. Anne has a lot going on. Don't stress over her, though. You are needed here. Anne isn't physically up to running this place every day. She doesn't get much rest at all. I know I don't help much."

"My grandmother worked for them, years ago. She said it was a big job. A lot of older houses, they close off some of the house and only live in part of it. But not them. She said every room in the house was pretty much still in use, except for the staff rooms. I saw that, of course, spending time here with Faye. It's a lot of house to keep up," Tammy agreed. Lexi shrugged.

"Well, nothing much to be done about that. I mean, they have to sleep, and the bedrooms are upstairs. The only full bathroom is upstairs. So, it's not like they can just close off the upstairs.

"Down here, the only room that isn't really used every day is the back parlor, but even that gets used when Jerry has company. That's where they go talk. Well, and the staff rooms. So, what is there to do about it? It's a big house, but it's a big family. It's not that there's too many rooms; it's just that each room is ginormous."

"You don't mean that Anne has been trying to clean this entire house all this time? By herself? With all of this going on around her?" Tammy asked, dismayed. She was also disgusted with these men. Had they really expected her to maintain a 11,500-square foot house with children underfoot, in addition to the other things she was expected to do and deal with?

"Well, yeah. I mean, in the beginning, that was her job. She was, well, what you are. They said they never thought about getting her help because she *was* the help. It was Uncle Roy who yelled at them about it. Anne kept falling asleep at the table and things. I mean, she really did need more rest and a lot more help. I've got my own house to keep; Jason and Gary, especially Gary, are always bitching about me staying here all the time. But I felt Anne needed someone here. Karen stays in the office, for the most part. Will pays her to work. So, she has an actual job to do here. But anyway, she does need help."

"Seems everyone just took their time getting it."

"I'm not getting into all that, now. Not my circus, not my monkeys."

"Of course, it's your circus and monkeys. You are over here six days a week. You see as much as any of them do. Will needs to be beat, having her do all that this long."

"Will did nothing wrong. Jerry and Will have both expressed concern but you know what? Everyone doesn't have all the answers immediately. Jerry sees more and understands more than Will does. It doesn't make Will a bad husband. It just means he and Jerry have different relationships with her. Will just, well, he needs things brought to his attention more. It's not because he's a bad husband, just the opposite. Will spends so much time trying to make everything perfect for everyone that that's all he sees. He concentrates on the happy things, the nice things. He doesn't see the bad stuff. Anyway, that's what Uncle Roy is for."

"It's all on Roy? That's interesting. Anyway, I think someone should have gotten help in here after the cougar incident. But that's just my opinion. Now that I know she's trying to keep this whole house on her own, I'd stay regardless. Jerry would have never done that to Faye, I know."

"Nobody did anything to Anne though. They hired her *as a housekeeper*. She loved her job. She apparently turned this house and family completely around. This whole crowd was likely just so deliriously happy, they didn't see any problems. Anyway, they see the problems now, and they fixed it. You're here now."

Lexi went to change Teague's diaper. Tammy finished straightening up the kitchen. Yes, she certainly was here, now. She thought about the past many years. She thought about Faye's passing and Jerry's decline. She thought about Roy's and Will's absence throughout it, and Karen's odd part in the situation. She thought about Anne and wondered if Anne had ever wanted to just hit all these people? And looking up, she saw Faye.

Tammy just looked at Faye. Faye looked back at Tammy. Tammy was torn between smiling at her deceased best friend and scolding her. Tammy was beginning to suspect Anne had a few issues. And after the comment Anne made after the door slammed shut, Tammy was beginning to suspect that Faye was maybe one of those issues.

"You being difficult, Faye?" Tammy asked, only half expecting a reply. But Faye did reply, right before exiting the room in the swift creepy blur she always left with. Faye's voice was uncomfortably clear.

"It's my house."

CHAPTER 23

A nne kept to herself for the rest of the day, for the most part. She spent time in the living room playing with Eliza. She fell asleep with Miss Priss for an hour on the couch. On this day, Anne didn't turn her hands really. She said *screw it* and let Tammy take care of things. She wasn't mad at Tammy. She was mad, but it wasn't at Tammy. She didn't know *who* she was mad at. She didn't even really know *why* she was mad.

It was a nice day; the first truly lazy weekday she had experienced since moving here. Even when she had been sick, pregnant, or mauled by a wildcat, she didn't experience what she'd really call any *lazy days*. Those days were stressful and exhausting; nothing relaxing and lazy about them. Even when she'd been attacked by the cougar and had been banned to the couch and bed, waited on hand and foot, it was still an exhausting experience. Just sitting up wore her out. Everything was a chore during that recovery.

The same thing when she had the flu over her first Thanksgiving here; her men had taken very good care of her. But it was another exhausting experience, nonetheless.

Now, she felt fine (physically). So, she was able to just lie back, chill out, and take her time with everything. If she wanted to play with the baby instead of cleaning the gigantic windows in this house, she could. If she wanted to take a nap with the cat, she could. As she sat at the kitchen table with Lexi, she suddenly knew what she wanted to do.

Will was leaning forward on the top rail of the corral; his chin resting on his folded arms. The thin, new grass was green, and the

331

outside smelled of clean, damp dirt and livestock. He was happy. He loved working outside, and he loved it the most in the spring and fall. Nothing in Liberty Creek ever changed, except the seasons.

Will was watching Luke ride a new horse around the corral. It was a somewhat ornery animal and they were trying to teach it to lope. As Luke pointed out, the Appaloosa had other plans for this glorious spring weekday.

"Will, this thing is an asshole," Luke called out, as he rode past Will.

"No, he is high-strung and misunderstood," Will replied.

"Like you?" asked a voice from behind him. Will lifted his chin and turned around in surprise. He smiled and even laughed at the smartass comment.

"Hey, Miss Anne. You escape?" He kissed her.

"Yeah. I got a housekeeper now, you know."

Anne joined Will at the corral, climbing up the first two rails. He directed his attention back to the horse, while he continued to talk to her.

"Yes, I do. I also kind of recall you were a real creep about it. So, are you maybe changing your mind about having a housekeeper? Luke! Why does he keep acting like that when he gets over there by that back corner? Watch what he does. Anyway, are you?" Will directed this last question to his wife.

"Changing my mind? I don't know. Maybe I am. Don't be pushy."

"Pushy? I am not being *pushy*. I am asking a question. I simply hope that you are. I think it will be good for you. I do apologize for having not taken care of this earlier. I love you to bits, and pieces and I do not want to see you tired and sickly. I do not want to see you working so hard and being all hateful and cranky all the time. I want to see you being like ... well, all the women in my family. They all were able to enjoy themselves and have company come calling and things. You worked hard for us for a long time. We appreciate it. But now it's time to take it easy."

"I don't want Tammy doing the laundry."

"Alright."

"I also don't want her to clean our room or your dad's room. I mean, I guess vacuuming and whatever is okay. But as far as stuff like keeping it picked up and the bed made? I want to do that in those two rooms."

"Ummm, alright. Why?"

"Just because. We're grown-ups and our stuff should be left alone. I don't like the idea of someone poking around our stuff. Especially your daddy's room. It's almost always a disaster. I spend more time cleaning up his room than I do the kid's rooms. He really is kind of a slob. Anyway, I don't want her finding his dirty underwear lying around or his booze bottles and stuff. That's not nice."

"Alright. I guess that makes sense. Is there any other weirdness I need to know about? We need to tell Tammy your rules, I suppose. I do not know for sure what Dad told her already. Hey? Watch the horse. Watch what it does when it gets to that place at the back of the corral ... now! Watch it."

Anne and Will watched as the horse shied away from the back corner of the corral. It was obvious the horse was acting odd when it approached that one corner. They both watched as it made its way around the corral again. Sure enough, when it got to that same spot, it sidestepped.

"Hey, Will? That what you're talking about?" Luke called out.

"Yeah."

"I think there's something over there it doesn't like," Anne suggested. She'd worked with horses enough in the past, even before arriving here, to know stuff like that. Will nodded.

"That's what I'm thinking. Come on." Will put his arm around her waist and pulled her off the corral rail. He set her on the ground and started walking around the corral to the area the horse didn't seem to like. Anne dutifully followed him around. They reached the area and Will and Anne looked around for a moment before Will shouted, scaring Anne.

"Oh shit! Go! Go away, Anne! Get back! Luke! Don't ride back around here again!"

"What is it, Will?" Anne asked, craning her neck to see what he saw.

"That!" Will pointed at the thing, but it took Anne a moment to see it. The thing was well disguised in the leaves and still partly dead grass. Then she saw it. There, lying in the leaves, was an Eastern Timber Rattlesnake. The snake was at least four feet long.

"Already? It's kinda early for snakes, isn't it? Uncle Roy always starts bitching about the snakes later I thought, like around May."

"It's early, alright. But not unheard of. Hey, Luke, check it out." Will pointed out the snake to Luke, who had dismounted the horse and tied him to the gate for a moment. He walked over to Will and Anne to see what they'd found. Luke looked at it for a minute.

"Well, we have to kill it," he pointed out. Will nodded. Anne didn't like that, because she felt it was outside minding its own business. Will noticed the sad look on Anne's face and sighed.

"Anne, we can't have rattlesnakes hanging around the place. There are people, children and animals. There are dogs, cats, horses, cows, and soon to be goats. There are ducks. There is also the pack of rabbits, and the 'coons. We cannot have rattlesnakes on the place. Rattlesnakes are assholes, and girl snakes have baby snakes who *also* grow up to be asshole snakes. Stop looking like that. Garter snakes, king snakes, all those are fine. Venomous snakes are not. Go put the horse up, Anne. Luke, get the rifle. I'll keep an eye on it," Will directed.

Anne very seldom argued with Will; she never felt a need to because she usually agreed with him. So, she went to put the horse up. She knew he was having her do that so she wouldn't be out there when he shot the poor snake. It was all well and good; Anne didn't want to see that anyway and Will knew this.

A few minutes later, she was wiping the horse down when they heard the gunshot. The horse was cross tied in the stable, so he couldn't do much when the noise startled him, but he did throw his head back.

"It's alright. Chill out, horsie. They have to kill the snakes. I don't think it's fair to the snakes, but I guess I understand it. They don't want the snake to bite you or us." Anne visited with the horse until Will came back in to put the rifle up. He helped her finish up with the horse, then he put it back in its stall with some feed. Will looked at his wife.

Anne's hair was pulled up in a messy bun, and she wore a Pink Floyd T-shirt with a pair of jeans and boots. He thought she was beautiful.

"You got plans, Miss Anne?"

"Nope. I'm not doing anything today."

"You wanna go riding?"

"We can do that, Boss."

"You want to take Wyatt or ride with me?" he asked, hoping she'd elect to go ride with him. He liked when she sat behind him.

"I want to ride with you, but I haven't ridden Wyatt much lately. I haven't had the time to really."

"Well, how about this? If you really want to ride with me today, we can make the arrangements to go again tomorrow. Tomorrow you can ride Wyatt." Will stepped close to Anne and wrapped his arms around her. He kissed the top of her head.

"Alright, but you think you'll have time to do that today *and* tomorrow?" Anne was surprised.

Will usually spent from seven in the morning until five in the afternoon working, with exception of lunch hour. It was quite unusual for her husband to just stop in the middle of the workday for what he still referred to as *playing*. Now, here he was suggesting playing two days in a row? During the workweek?

"Yes, I think I can arrange it. So? You want to go ride until lunch? It'll give us a good hour and half."

"What about lunch? What will we eat? I honestly haven't even thought about it," Anne realized out loud. She was surprised by this. Will laughed at her shocked expression.

"You don't have to look so worried! There's stuff for sandwiches. We're good. Lexi, Dad, and Uncle Roy and two of the kids won't even be here for lunch. Oh wait. They're leaving at eleven. Okay. Look. I'll call Karen. I'll ask her to watch Eliza and James until we get back at lunch since Lexi and them are going to leave before we get back. James is with Jonathon. We'll just tell Karen and Jonathon that we're going riding and we'll be back for lunch. No big deal."

And that's just what Will did. Karen and Jonathon were both surprised that Will was taking off during the workday to play, but they agreed to watch the kids until Will and Anne returned. Jerry came in the stable as they were putting the bridle on Will's black horse. Jerry looked interested. Out of habit, he threw his arm around Anne's shoulders.

"What's going on? You enjoying your off day?" He directed this question to Anne, but he watched Will. Will answered for both of them, as he was inclined to do.

"Anne is having a lovely day; she's seeing we were right, and she was wrong. She's got time to play now. And we are about to take full advantage of that."

"Going riding?" Jerry asked.

"Yes, sir, we are. I say, why not? She's got help. I've got help. So, we are going to take us a break today. We'll be back here by lunch though. I have some work this afternoon I really do need to take care of," Will admitted. He adjusted the bridle on the horse's head. Jerry just watched quietly for a moment before he took his arm from Anne's shoulder and helped Will. Anne watched. Jerry finished and cleared his throat.

"You're ummm, talking about us having help and how we can take breaks," he started. Will nodded and worked on double-checking the bridle. Jerry continued,

"Well, I was talking to Mare. I'm thinking maybe it's time I took her somewhere. Like, out of town or something for a few days or so. I know it's a busy time of the year though. But I don't know, son; do we really have enough help for us to take breaks? I mean, I know a ride for a couple *hours* is different from a road trip for a few *days*. Anyway, I'm thinking about it. I just wanted to let y'all know."

By now, Will had stopped paying attention to his horse and had given his full attention to his father. Jerry seemed uncomfortable with the conversation, although Will didn't see any reason for him to be uncomfortable at all. Anne didn't even seem particularly bothered by Jerry's announcement. She looked surprised and interested but not bothered.

"Well, Daddy if you want to take Miss Beales out of town, you hardly have to get my permission. I can see why you'd want to do that.

I, well, actually, I was just talking to Uncle Roy about this the other day. I've been thinking about taking Anne and the kids somewhere. I don't know where yet. But I mean its normal. He kind of acted like it was wrong for us to take separate vacations. Don't get me wrong! I think we should arrange another trip, where you go with us. I was thinking about maybe a camping trip to Natural Bridge. Just tell me when you're planning to go, which I'm pretty sure you'd do anyway. I don't know why you act like you're confessing something though."

"Because you tend to lecture. And, well, it's the first time I'd have left this place since … it'd be the first trip I took since I took your mama anywhere. I don't know how *I* feel about it yet. I don't have a date set, but I have already talked to her about it. So, I just thought I'd let y'all know. That's all."

Will just nodded. Jerry looked at Anne. She appeared to be deep in thought but still not angry. He took that as a good sign, at least for now. Suddenly, he was shy and uncomfortable with the situation.

"Well, y'all have a good ride. I'm going to go find James. I wanted to show him something before I leave with Lex." Jerry kissed Anne's cheek and slapped Will's shoulder before leaving.

Will mounted the horse and rode it to the mounting block. Anne stepped up on the block and Will helped lift her onto the horses back. Since they were riding double, they were riding bareback. Anne's five-foot three-inch stature made mounting the large horse difficult without the help of stirrups and a saddle horn. She mounted the horse behind her husband, put her arms around his waist, and they rode out of the stable.

It was a fabulous morning ride; Will had missed this. They used to go riding on weekends often. Here lately, it seemed like something was always in the way of them spending their weekend time together. He couldn't help busy work weeks, but he often felt he was failing miserably at family time.

They came out of the woods and into a clearing in the pasture. Will had the horse break into a run. Laughing, Anne pulled her arms tighter around Will. She too had missed these days. Riding Wyatt was always fun, but honestly, she preferred to ride behind Will on his own horse.

This is why Will had asked. She had been so excited to get Wyatt that first Christmas with them. Yet, seven times out of ten, she preferred to ride behind Will. If she was riding with Roy or Jerry, she took her own horse. But if she was riding with Will, she almost always preferred to ride double on his. This was one of the few things that she reserved just for him. She had no idea how much this one little thing meant to him. In a world where he had to share his wife with his dad, this was something just his.

Jerry was outside the old tobacco barn, showing James and Caleb the birds nest he found. In a few minutes, he'd deliver James back to Jonathon and take Caleb inside to meet with Lexi and Teague. Then, they would all go to town together. Jerry was secretly glad to be leaving the farm today. He was feeling odd and didn't want to be around here all day. He couldn't put his finger on it, but he just wanted an excuse to leave.

At 11, he took Caleb into the house. They went to the kitchen where they met Lexi. She already had her purse and Teague on her hip. She flashed a bright smile at Jerry.

"Hey! I was waiting on y'all! Ready to go?"

"Yeah, let me get the keys. Y'all can go ahead and get in the truck."

"Are we taking your truck?" Lexi looked confused. Jerry looked at her like she was strange.

"Why wouldn't we?"

"Well, I don't know. I mean if I took them alone, I'd have taken mine. I just assumed we were taking it."

"Oh, no. Let's just take mine." For some reason, the concept of Lexi driving him into town was just too weird.

Lexi and Jason always drove the big truck to the Granger's in the morning. From there, Jason got in one of the work trucks and took it back to the other end of the farm. Sometimes, he just stayed at his end of the farm, and at the end of the day, Lexi would drive herself home. The next morning, Jason would just drive the work truck to the Granger's, meet his family for breakfast, get back in the work truck, and go back to the other end of the farm. It was all very complicated. Because there was often a work truck or two at the other end of the farm, Lexi and

Jason seldom rode together. He didn't like leaving her at the Granger's with no transportation should she want to go home or something.

So, Lexi took the kids out to Jerry's truck where she put them in the car seats he already had for James and Eliza. As he got his keys from the desk in the back parlor, Eliza toddled in the room. She held her arms up to him. He sighed but couldn't help but smile. He stuffed the keys in his back pocket and lifted the little girl. She immediately took his face in her tiny hands and kissed his scruffy cheek. His heart melted.

"Baby girl, we have to fetch Miss Karen. Karen! Come on now. I gotta go."

"Go? I wanna go." Eliza smiled at Jerry. He sighed again.

"Oh, my little princess, you just can't go this time. Karen!" He shouted as he made his way down the hall. Karen came out of the office.

"Don't go shouting at me. Come here, baby," Karen said lovingly, trying to take the child from Jerry's arms. Eliza fixed her mouth in what Caleb called her *mad face*. It resembled the mask representing a Greek tragedy. Jerry immediately started apologizing to her, much to Karen's dismay.

"Oh, don't go doing that face! That's not your pretty face! Come on, baby doll! Don't be mad at Papa! I love you, baby-baby! Please be sweet. Papa loves you! I'll do something fun with you as soon as I come home."

"Stop that! That child is getting impossible. Come here and stop acting like that!" Karen tried to pull the child from Jerry's arms, but she dug her little fingers into his shirt collar and wouldn't let go.

"Going with Papa," Eliza informed Karen as she patted Jerry's cheek lovingly.

Karen wanted to throw up. This child acted just like Anne. They both made Karen purely nauseated the way they loved all over Jerry. Jerry looked as if he were torn; part of him loved Eliza wanting to go with him, while part of him was embarrassed by the attention.

"Okay, sweet baby, I have got to go take Miss Lexi and Caleb somewhere. I will be back. Okay? Okay, little sweetheart? Gimme kisses."

"Nooooo take me, Papa," she lay her head on his shoulder. He heard the horn blowing outside.

"Miss Lexi is waiting on me. You have got to stay here with Miss Karen. I'm sorry. It can't be helped right now," Jerry finally scolded the little girl. Karen raised her eyebrows at this.

"Excuse me? She has *got* to stay with me? You're sorry but it can't be helped? I take offense to all that right there."

Jerry set Eliza on the floor and tried to make a quick getaway. The last thing he heard as he walked out the back door was Eliza crying. He got in the truck, now mad that he had to leave a weeping Eliza. He didn't doubt that Eliza had him purely wrapped around her every finger. But that didn't change how he felt. He knew she was spoiled and that he had been the one who had single-handedly done the spoiling.

"What took you? We're going to be late if we don't hurry," Lexi whined.

Jerry cranked the truck up and backed up. He pulled out and started driving up the dirt drive. Lexi could tell he didn't look particularly happy now. He seemed fine a few minutes ago.

"What's the matter, Jerry?"

"Nothing. Nothing is wrong."

"Well, you look mad."

"Lexi, you asked a question which I have already answered. Please, let's not get into this right now. Let's just get to the school and do what we need to do, okay?"

"Okay, but Jerry? Would you just tell me, you're not mad now that you're taking us, are you?"

Jerry almost snapped at her but felt bad. He just shook his head.

"No, Lexi. It's not you. I'm just upset because Eliza wanted to go and made a big fuss when I left her with Karen. Nothing you did."

"Well, Eliza loves you. She's always wanting to go where you go and do what you do. You know that. I guess you're probably her favorite person in the whole family. I think its sweet."

"Well, it wasn't so sweet just now when I made her mad at me."

"Oh, I know you. You'll find something in town to buy for her to suck back up to her. She can't stay mad at you any more than Anne can. And you know you love it," Lexi laughed. Jerry found himself relaxing somewhat. Yes, Lexi was right, he supposed. Jerry did love it honestly.

How could he not? And of course, he'd find something to take home to her as some sort of peace offering.

They pulled up to Liberty Creek Elementary School. Jerry parked the truck and helped Lexi unload Caleb and Teague. Lexi grabbed Caleb's hand, and Jerry held Teague in his arms while he pulled the umbrella stroller out of the truck bed. He expertly opened the stroller with one hand, then put the baby in it. He pushed the stroller while Lexi dragged a very unwilling Caleb up the front steps.

Jerry was amazed at how it seemed just the other day he was walking up these steps with Will.

Liberty Creek Elementary School had been built in 1873. It started out as a very simple structure with wooden walls, four windows, and two rooms. This part of the school still existed, even today. It now served as the main office and nurse's office. Over the years, the school got bigger and was gradually added onto until it turned into the modest one-story brick building it was now. It was last added onto in 1947. That's when they built the multi-purpose room that served as the gym and auditorium. Before they built that, they had no gym and the lunchroom served as the auditorium. Many felt the multi-purpose room was an unnecessary expense, but the construction was proposed after two years of unseasonably cold winters. They simply felt the children would benefit from an indoor gym. It wasn't particularly big or fancy, but it more than served its purpose all these years.

As things in Liberty Creek tended to do, this school had not changed any over the years. They never felt the need to upgrade it and build some fine modern school. This school had done its job just fine, all this time.

Jerry and Lexi went inside and went to the office. It was something Jerry would regret for weeks. As soon as he walked through that old wooden door with the big glass window in it, he felt sick to his stomach. His senses were overwhelmed with memories of the six years he had spent attending this school with Faye. He remembered the six years Will had attended this school, and the countless hours Faye had spent helping out in here while Will attended it. Jerry remembered the numerous times he'd come by here, in this very office, to visit his wife while she volunteered to help with something. Jerry felt the corners of his mouth threatening to turn down.

"Well, hey there, Jerry! How you doin', hon? Been awhile since you come in here! We haven't seen you in here since, well, since Will went here," Brenda Marshall said awkwardly. She had almost said *since Faye helped out here* but caught herself just in time. Still, he didn't look well to her right then.

"Oh, I needed an extra hand today and Jason couldn't make it. He has horse related things going on. Jerry offered to accompany me. Caleb is here to see his classroom!" Lexi told them in the office. Brenda smiled at Caleb, glad to have the conversation off Jerry.

"Hey there, Caleb! Are you excited to see your classroom?" Brenda asked the sullen child enthusiastically.

Caleb glared.

"No, ma'am, I am not. I don't want to come here. The dudderdent is making me, and I'm not really free. The dudderdent *lies*."

"Oh! I see! Well, I am sorry to hear that." Brenda responded. Lexi sighed.

"He means the government, not *dudderdent*. And he wants to stay home and keep working the farm; he thinks he shouldn't have to go to school since he already has a job. He's blaming the government."

"Well! He's certainly a bright little one, isn't he? Already interested in how our government works and already has a job! My, my!" Brenda tried gushing over Caleb, but he managed to make her feel like he knew she was just humoring him. Between Caleb and Jerry, Brenda was more than happy to direct them to Caleb's classroom.

"Y'all know where the kindergarten classes are. He's in room two. Miss Lana is waiting for him. Bye Caleb!" Brenda began pretending to be busy with an empty folder. Jerry managed to feel even worse when she told them the class Caleb would be in. There were two kindergarten classrooms, and Caleb would be in the same one Jerry, Faye, Will, and Gary had all been in.

The four of them made their way down the school hall. This school had not changed a bit except for the slightly newer desks and chairs. The same dark wooden floors, and ugly sickly mint green paint on the walls.

Couldn't they have at least changed the paint color? He knew they had repainted these walls since the good ol' days when the lead-based paint had covered them. He was just surprised they elected to stick with the same ugly green color.

They passed several doors, the washroom, the janitor's closet, and a few bulletin boards and some wall art courtesy of the first graders.

They talked quietly among themselves as they made their way to room *two*. Then, there it was. Lexi went in, announcing their arrival.

"Hey, Lana!"

"Lexi! How you doing? Well, hi Mr. Granger! I wasn't expecting to see you!"

"Well, Jason couldn't make it and I was going to need help with these two. So, Jerry offered to accompany me," Lexi explained again.

Lana Mosely just accepted this explanation and excused herself to get Caleb's file out of the desk. While she fumbled around in her desk, Jerry talked quietly to Lexi.

"Oh, man. This is just weird. This room has not changed *at all*. I mean, *not at all*."

"Was Will in here?" Lexi asked. Lexi was two years behind Will and Jason.

"Not just Will. Me, Faye, and Gary were all in this classroom. And I swear, it looks *exactly the same*. I mean, there's a few more presidents up there since Carter was in office. Still, other than that? I mean, I really swear that's the same desk Miss Barkley had when I was in here. I *know* that's the same pencil sharpener."

Lana overheard this conversation, although Jerry thought she didn't. She laughed at his last observation. As she walked toward them, she smiled at Jerry.

"You're right about the sharpener. They have bragged that they have only had to replace one pencil sharpener since something like 1940. They swear by Boston Pencil Sharpeners. And the desk? You may be right about that, too. Because I *know* it's the same desk Mrs. Rowland had when I was in here."

"Good grief," Jerry replied.

"So, Caleb! You excited? This is where you'll come when school starts! Isn't it a nice classroom?"

"What's that?" Caleb asked eyeing a door suspiciously.

"That's the cloakroom. We keep our coats and things in there. You would put your bookbag in there, your rubber boots, things like that."

Jerry left the stroller by Lana's desk and went to go look in the cloakroom. He opened the door and peered inside. He felt incredibly corny as he felt his eyes smart and a smile begin. Oh, the cloakroom!

He went inside and walked over to the corner where he'd always hung his ugly gray wool coat. The iron hook was still there. And so was the hook that had been right beside it. It was on this hook that little Faye Collins had always hung her own coat. It was right here, where Jerry stood, where he had received his very first kiss from Faye, the little girl who would become his wife 13 years later. He put his hand on her hook and felt his chest swell. He couldn't help it; he cried. A few minutes later, Lexi came to the door alone. Jerry was sitting on the old bench that sat beneath the cloakroom hooks. His face was buried in his hands. Lexi cautiously walked over to him. She sat beside him.

"Jerry? I'm sorry. Is it Faye? Will?"

Jerry wiped his face with his hands and ran his hand through his hair. He looked embarrassed. Lexi put her hand on his knee.

"Lana took Caleb to see the library. He wants to see books about the government. I think he's going to cause us a lot of trouble in the future," she sighed wearily. At this, Jerry couldn't help but laugh.

"He's going to be a handful. She took him ... how long have I been in here?" he was confused.

"About ten minutes, I guess. It's okay; don't look like that. I think Lana understands. Jerry? I am sorry. If I'd known ..."

"No, no, no. Don't worry about that. I offered to come. I just didn't think about it at the time. Going in the office a minute ago, or 15 or 20 now I guess, I felt kinda sick. It felt just like I was going in there to see her again. She used to help out in the office all the time. But then, oh, Lord. Coming in this room made me think about being five again. It made me think about Will and Faye." Jerry stood up and touched a hook with his finger.

"That was mine. That one ... that was Faye's. Her hook started out over there, but she moved it over here after she proclaimed her love for me in front of the entire classroom. The teacher asked us each to stand up and tell the class what we wanted to be when we grew up. It was only like, the second week of school! And Faye stands up and tells the entire class that when *she* grew up, she was going to be my wife. I was so embarrassed. And it was the next day she gave Leon a dime to switch hooks with her.

"It was here, right here where I'm standing, where she kissed me for the first time. It was Halloween. We were about to go to the auditorium for the Halloween party, and I forgot my hat in here; I was Roy Rogers. So, while everyone else was lining up to go to the party, I came in here. And Faye followed me. She was dressed like a witch. I pulled my hat off the shelf, this shelf right here. I looked up and there was Faye. Her face was painted green. She just went for it, leaned over and planted a kiss right on my mouth. She didn't even shoot for the cheek. Then, she told me she was my girlfriend now." While he told this story, he rubbed her hook with his thumb. Lexi wiped her eyes.

"What did *you* want to be when *you* grew up?" she asked. He smiled.

"A cowboy. Gary wanted to be a policeman or work at the Frost Stop," he laughed at the memory. Lexi couldn't help but laugh.

"It sounds like you all did exactly what you wanted to, when you grew up."

"Yeah, yeah, I guess we did. What about you?"

"Oh, I wanted to be a singer. It was the 80s. I really loved music. I used to stand on the hearth with a hairbrush and sing with music videos. I guess we don't all end up being what we want to be when we grow up. But I *am* glad that Faye got what she wanted. That was a pretty awesome thing to reach for."

"Yeah, thank you. I'm glad she got it too."

"You know what? I think about all the fairy tales I read as a kid, all the sappy movies I've watched and all the love songs I've loved listening to, and I swear, the story of you and Faye has to be the sweetest, most beautiful love story of all. I'm glad that y'all have that relationship. It must be fabulous to feel that loved."

345

"I want Caleb to have my hook. I want Lana to save my hook for Caleb," Jerry decided.

Lexi stood up, and Jerry threw his arm around her. They left the cloakroom. Jerry looked around the classroom for just a moment. He took a pencil from Lana's desk and sharpened it, just to do it. He looked out the windows. He looked at the presidents' faces across the top of the chalkboard. Then, he took a piece of chalk, and at the very top left-hand corner of the chalkboard, he wrote *Jerry + Faye = 4ever.*

They went to find Caleb and Lana and found them coming down the hall, Lana pushing the stroller. Jerry felt bad when he realized he'd completely forgotten they'd brought Teague. Caleb had an armful of books.

"Caleb! What do you have?" Lexi asked.

"Books about the dudderdent. Miss Lana said I can go ahead and read them if I take care of them and bring them back. I'm going to learn how to change the dudderdent."

"Aw, look Lexi. *He's* going to be a seditionist when *he* grows up," Jerry told a concerned looking Lexi.

Lexi, recalling her conversation with Jerry in the cloak room, couldn't help but laugh out loud.

Lexi and Jerry thanked Lana Mosely for the lovely visit. Caleb thanked her for the books. They took the stroller and went to get lunch at Jenson's.

Lana returned to her classroom to eat her own lunch that she'd brought from home. She approached her desk and found a newly sharpened pencil set in the middle of the desktop. She glanced up to see *Jerry + Faye = 4ever* written relatively small, at the top of her chalkboard. She bit her lip hard but found herself crying anyway. She sat down to eat her lunch.

Lana Mosely left that written across the top of her chalkboard until her retirement 27 years later. She even took thin quarter round and made a little frame around it to ensure it was never erased. And when she retired, she told the school to tell the next teacher to leave that on the chalkboard. And they did.

CHAPTER 24

Gary was home. He had just come back from his other home, the Craftsman he shared with Kylie. They were remodeling the kitchen and refinishing the floors of the Craftsman, which is why it was just easier to stay in the trailer for now. He kicked back in his recliner, after trying Tammy's headache remedy. He thought a nap would help it.

Laurie would be home in a few hours; he intended to take advantage of the quiet he had until then.

When Laurie got home, she would surely talk. She talked a whole lot. He knew she'd get out of school and go hang out at Jenson's lunch counter for a while anyway. He didn't care. It just meant more quiet time. He was stressed this week. As he began to doze, he found himself wondering if Tammy had anything for stress. If not, well, he had Scotch. And if he were to run out of Scotch, well, he had the liquor store and Jerry.

While Gary napped in his living room, Jerry and Lexi took the kids to lunch at Jenson's. This brought a few curious looks, but after about twelve seconds of wondering, everyone just dismissed it. That crowd on Teague Road was so weird, there really was no telling *why* Jerry was taking his best friend's daughter-in-law and grandchildren out to lunch in middle of a workday, while his best friend slept not two blocks away.

While they waited on the food, Caleb discussed his experience at school.

"They have a place to eat, and I saw kids eating. It smelled funny in there though. It smelled like Miss Mamie's house. They have a place to play basketball inside. There's a playground. But I knew about that because I've already played there before. I like the library. It's got lots of books. You take the book to this lady; I don't remember who she is. Miss Lana told me her name. She looks old and she has a mustache. But she was nice anyway. You write your name on a piece of paper in a pocket in the book and she takes a stamp and bangs it on the book. She said if I spill juice on it or lose it, I have to *pay for it*. I'm a *kid*. I can't *pay for things*. I told her that. Miss Lana told me you and Daddy would pay for it, Mommy. So, it's okay."

"What do you mean, you're just a kid and can't pay for anything? You get at least five dollars a week. You got a job, remember? You have money to pay for things. You spill juice on a book, you should have to pay for it. Not your mama or daddy," Jerry protested. Caleb was not impressed.

"No, Papa. That money is for a truck."

"A truck?" Jerry looked curiously at Lexi. She smiled and nodded.

"Caleb gives all his money to Jason to set back for a truck. He's saved up about $120 I think Jason said the other day," Lexi said proudly. Jerry was floored.

"He's taking his work money and saving up for a *truck*? At *five years old*? What happened to toys?"

"Well, since we're so proud of what he's doing, when there's something we know he really wants, we just get it for him. However, I do agree with Papa. Getting treats is different from destroying things that don't belong to you. If you take a book home and you let something happen to it or lose it, then that money comes out of your truck fund, dear."

Caleb shook his head at this information. This wasn't fair.

"See? I work and make money and have to give it to the lady with the mustache."

"No, son. You take care of the books that you borrow, and you won't have to give money to anyone. Incidentally, that lady with the mustache is named Mrs. Jenson. Her husband's cousins run this restaurant. So, let us stop talking about her mustache, okay? I don't think your granddaddy would like you doing that anyway," Jerry said this, leaned forward and dropping his voice.

Caleb dropped his own voice.

"She's nice. I wasn't being mean. I just said she has a mustache."

Caleb was a curious child. They were all beginning to realize that he was exceptionally bright. This both worked for him and worked against him. People were beginning to have too high of expectations of him, Roy was learning. Roy felt that Caleb was being given entirely too much to handle. It wasn't just the work situation; Roy didn't really feel that Caleb worked too hard. Caleb did just what Roy, Jerry, and Will had done at his age.

No, Roy was more concerned about the emotional things this child was being expected to adjust to. In just a few short years, Caleb Michael Connelly had gone from living alone with his mother, to living with his mother, father, baby brother, and sometimes a hormonal teenaged sister. In addition to this, the child spent every day of the week with three other men, two other women, a ghost, and two other children. There were also the numerous stable hands and clients that Caleb spent several hours around every day.

Caleb had gone from living in a two-bedroom third-floor apartment in town to living in a five-bedroom two-story farmhouse on a sprawling 536-acre horse farm. He went from having a cat named Buck to having horses, cows, ducks, dogs, more cats, and soon he'd be acquiring goats and several chickens. He went from spending his days in Little Friends Daycare at Liberty Creek Methodist Church to spending his days working in the stables, barns, and rolling fields.

He had acquired a ghost grandmother in addition to a 45-year-old grandmother who was soon going to be giving birth to his new uncle or aunt.

In all honesty, Caleb was putting in approximately six hours a day at the stables. He did this by choice, not because they forced the child to. Granted, he was expected to help with little things in the beginning. He was taken out to the stables with the men in the morning just so he could spend time with them. They thought it'd be good for him. The Granger boys were all doing farm work by his age. What they thought would be an interesting activity for Caleb turned into Caleb's full-time job. They had realized, not very long ago, that the little boy was working roughly 36 hours a week. Whenever someone (usually Will) tried to talk him into playing or taking a nap, Caleb would grow very indignant. He saw the other fellas working without stopping to play or nap. So, he wanted to do that too.

They humored Caleb. Whenever he did get sleepy or whiny, they were simply quick to suggest that he take a break.

Jerry looked at Caleb now with concern. Lexi and Jason were obviously quite proud of the fact that their five-year-old was setting back money for a truck. Jerry, however, worried the kid would make arrangements to talk with John Webb at the Valley Bank about setting up his 401k by the time he was in third grade. He realized that Caleb *did* need to get away from them and go to school, even if it was just for four hours five mornings a week.

"Papa? How much?" Caleb asked. Jerry snapped back to attention.

"I'm sorry, son. What did you ask?"

"How much was your truck?"

"Oh, well, that's not a nice question to ask people. You never ask how much someone spent on something."

"You ask how much lots of stuff is. You ask how much people spend on horses, animal food, and stuff. You asked Luke how much he got his saddle for," Caleb pointed out.

Jerry sighed. He drummed his hands on the table and looked at Caleb.

"Okay. My truck costs roughly $31,000."

"Do you think it was worth it?" Caleb asked.

Jerry frowned slightly at Caleb.

"Yes. Yes, as a matter of fact, I do. I like my truck. I like my truck a lot. It's a good truck. And I'm happy I bought it."

Caleb pondered this information for a few minutes. Jerry looked at Lexi, who smiled lovingly at Caleb. Teague sat in stroller, chewing on Lexi's purse strap.

Finally, the food came. Jerry prepared to eat his club sandwich. Lexi was digging into her turkey cobb salad, but Caleb eyed the spaghetti plate suspiciously.

"What's the matter, son?" Jerry asked him.

Caleb ignored him but flagged down the waitress. Lexi and Jerry both looked confused.

"Are there onions in this spaghetti?" he asked the waitress.

"No sir. Did you want onions?"

"You're sure there's not?"

"I'm sure. Will that be all?" she asked as another customer waved her down.

"I guess so. You can go. Thanks," Caleb picked methodically through the spaghetti as if expecting to catch the waitress in a lie.

"So, Caleb. Do you feel any better about going to school now?" Lexi asked.

"Not really. Can I have your bread?"

"You have bread. This is my bread. Why not? You seemed happy enough today."

"I was just being nice. I think we should do what Jennifer said."

"What did Jennifer say?" Jerry asked.

"Well, Mommy said I have to go to school. Mommy said the dudderdant makes every single kid in the world go to school every day. But Mommy didn't know about homeschool. I guess she didn't, *right, Mommy*?" Caleb asked emphatically. "Because if she *knew* about homeschool, she wouldn't have told me I had to go to school. That would be a lie, and Poppy says you should not ever ever ever lie ever for nothing. Jennifer said you can do school stuff at home and the dudderdant said its okay. You don't go to jail if your kid has school at home like Mommy and Daddy said. They said if I didn't go to school they would go to jail. So, I think I want to do that. But I do want to go to the library at the other school. Please can I have your bread?"

"Homeschool isn't necessary. There's no reason why you can't go to school in town. If you don't go to school, you'll miss out on birthday parties and holiday parties and playing with other kids and just all kinds of stuff," Jerry pointed out. Caleb reached for Lexi's bread, which she quickly moved out of his reach.

"And besides, sometimes mommies need a break. I like having you at home, baby. But getting big and going to school is good for a lot of reasons. It gives mommies a chance to take care of things like doctor appointments and naps when she desperately needs a very long one. And it teaches kids how to grow up. It teaches you to listen to other grown-ups and it teaches you that the whole world isn't going to be like it is at home, and it teaches you to deal with it. Things you get away with at home, you might not get away with at school. Things you sometimes say to us, you will get in trouble for saying at …" Lexi started.

Jerry interrupted her.

"Lexi dear, perhaps you should maybe not put so much emphasis on the things that he might not like so much at school. Maybe we can talk about the things he will like."

"I don't want to talk about school. I want more bread. And I want to talk about Uncle Will."

"What about Uncle Will?" Jerry asked.

"Can we go see Poppy at the store?"

"Yeah, I guess. I mean if he's even there. He might not be there. I'll find out, but what about Uncle Will?"

"I want to work with him on the new pen."

"Well, okay. I guess that can be arranged."

"Isn't he about to start on that?" Lexi asked.

Jerry nodded.

"Yeah, he's starting on it this afternoon."

"But Caleb? I thought you were going to help Daddy with the coop for the new chickens. You know we're getting them this week," Lexi argued.

"No, ma'am. I want to help Uncle Will with the new pen. Miss Anne is getting new goats, and Uncle Will is going to make a pen for them. Hey? Ma'am?" Caleb flagged down the waitress.

She sighed and walked over to him.

"Yes, Caleb?" she asked tiredly.

"Yes, would you please bring me seven more pieces of bread?" he asked angelically. Claire Reeves, the waitress, raised her brows at him.

Jerry groaned.

"Aw, Hell. Bring him another piece of bread please. Just one, not seven."

"Papa, please let me have two."

"Okay, two. Bring him two pieces of the bread."

"Can I have three?" Caleb asked.

Jerry glared at him.

"No, you cannot. You had one already, and you may have two more pieces. That is all."

"Fine."

Caleb sat back in the booth, defeated. Claire looked at Jerry.

"Two, not seven?" she asked.

"Yes, two. Thank you, dear."

"Y'all gonna want pie or anything?"

"No, thank you. He isn't eating his spaghetti. We'll forego dessert this time."

"I want pie," Caleb announced quickly.

"No. You didn't eat your spaghetti. That was $3.78, and you didn't eat it. And the extra bread will be $1.25. And your drink was another $.85. Don't ask me to do the math right now because I hate doing math, but I spent enough on you and you didn't eat the most important and most expensive thing. So, no pie."

"Caleb, greedy isn't nice," Lexi reminded him.

Claire brought Caleb his two extra pieces of garlic bread and left the ticket with Jerry. Caleb ate bread. It wasn't until they were getting ready to leave that Lexi realized Teague, in his stroller, had pulled out a pack of cigarettes and was gnawing on them. Jerry looked astounded. He looked at her with disappointment as he placed a few folded bills on the table with the ticket. He called out the waitress.

"Claire, honey? The money's on the table. Tell your mama I said *hey*. Lexi? Cigarettes?" he asked, turning his attention back to Lexi. Caleb watched the scene unfold with interest.

"Oh, Jerry, don't tell Jason. Please, please, please, please, don't tell Jason."

"Can I tell him?" Caleb asked.

"No! Don't tell him anything! Here. Take a quarter. Take two quarters. Go get some gum or something in the machine." She handed Caleb his fifty-cent bribe and turned back to Jerry as Caleb trotted off for the candy machine.

"Okay, look. Here's the thing …" she started.

Before she could finish, Jerry put his hand up. Frowning, he shook his head at her.

"Shame on you! Telling the child to keep a secret from his daddy for you? Smoking, Lexi? What in the world? You've never smoked."

"Well, I did years ago. I quit when I got pregnant with Caleb. I mean, I smoked before I had Savannah. Then, when I thought I had killed her by smoking, I quit. But well, after I had Caleb I kinda started smoking again. But not very much. Then, Caleb said his clothes stunk. Then, Gary picked him up one afternoon from daycare, and then, *he* told me that Caleb's clothes smelled like cigarettes. Then, Gary being Gary lectured me for a full hour about how I was poisoning Caleb and that Caleb was smoking if I was smoking anywhere near him or in the house whether he was there or not. So, I stopped because I thought I was going to kill another kid."

"So, why in the Hell are you doing it again?"

"It's different now! I don't do it in the house, and I don't do it in the car, and I don't do it anywhere around him. I go outside, far away from anyone and do it."

"Why are you doing it at all?" Jerry pressed.

"Oh, not here, Jerry. It's just a bunch of stuff that's … Caleb? Where are you? Caleb?" Lexi began looking around the diner.

Karen's ex-sister-in-law, Ruth Morris, was sitting near the candy machines. She answered Lexi, while pointing under a nearby booth.

"He's under the table, Lexi."

"Under the table? Caleb? *What* are you *doing*? Get out from under there! I'm sorry, y'all. He knows better than this," Lexi apologized to the couple sitting at this booth. Lexi finally took her foot and gently kicked Caleb in the behind. He fell forward.

"*Get out from under there!*" she yelled at him. Jerry sighed and looked at Ruth who was trying her best not to laugh. She shared an understanding look with Jerry and sipped her coffee.

"Lexi, move over and please keep it down. Caleb, son? What in the Sam Hill are you doing? Get out from under there. I'm sorry, Tom.

I don't know what he's doing." Jerry apologized to Tom and Donna Marshall.

Tom just shrugged. Finally, Caleb crawled out from under the table.

"What were you doing?" Jerry asked again. Caleb held up a small bright red rubber ball.

"I got this in the machine, and I dropped it and it rolled under the table. So, I had to get it."

"Well, put it in your pocket, and let's go home now." Jerry's head was starting to hurt, and he had spent enough time in town for the day. So, Jerry opened the door for Caleb and watched as Lexi took Caleb's hand and started to walk out the door with him. Jerry sighed and took a hold of Lexi's arm. She stopped and looked at him curiously. He looked tired.

"Lex, sweetheart, you forgot to get the baby." He nodded his head in the direction of the stroller, still parked next to their booth. Lexi looked baffled then mad. She dropped Caleb's hand and marched back into the diner, where she retrieved Teague who was sitting in his stroller, patiently waiting for someone to come get him. Jerry held the door open for her as she pushed the stroller through it. She looked back at him. "*That's* why I smoke!"

"Why don't you just drink? You don't have to deal with that second-hand smoke bullshit. Wait until they go to bed, get plastered. They never have to know," Jerry suggested.

"I do drink. I mean, not as much as you, but I do drink some. I usually save it for really really bad days. The smoking is just a quick little stress reliever. The drinking is for when I want to completely forget about whatever it was that made me want to drink to begin with. Usually its Jason."

"Don't talk about this is front of Caleb. The child doesn't need to hear all that. Don't ever talk like that about his father in front of him, Lex."

"His father doesn't mind saying crap about me …" Lexi began.

Jerry was getting irritated with Lexi in general now.

"Lexi stop it right now. I mean it. If you have a problem with Jason, then you take it up with Jason. Stop talking about it in front of the kids.

That's just white trash. Now, quit it or I'll leave your ass here and take the kids home without you. You can get Gary to drag you home later."

"Caleb, what's that in your pocket? What's under your shirt?" Lexi asked suddenly. Caleb looked sweetly at his mother.

"My bread."

"Your bread? Your *bread*, Caleb?" Lexi asked in a shrill voice.

"Yesssss," he answered rather condescendingly, lifting his little shirt up enough for her to see the thick slice of garlic bread protruding out of his jean's front pocket. A grease stain was already coming through his pocket. Jerry wished he'd stayed home now.

"Son, why did you put it in your pocket?" he asked.

"Because I wanted to save some for later."

"Then, you should have just carried it out in a napkin, buddy. Not in your pocket. It's not going to be in any shape to eat it now."

"Yes, it is." Caleb began trying to get the pull the bread from his pocket, ripping the bread in several pieces while doing so. He finally dug the last piece out the pocket and inspected it.

"See? It's okay. It's just got some fuzz on it." Caleb popped the bread in his mouth.

"Oh, Caleb! Yuck!" Lexi scolded.

"What? It was just mooshed. It tastes the same." He pushed the rest of the bread back in his pocket. Lexi threw her hands in the air and stomped off with the stroller.

"Oh, Caleb, Caleb, Caleb. You are something else." Jerry took the child's hand and they walked to the truck.

"Papa?"

"Yep?"

"Mommy is mad all the time now. She's always yelling."

"Your mommy is tired. She needs a break, a rest. We all need those. I think your mommy is just maybe busy and needs to chill out."

"Her and Daddy get loud a whole lot," Caleb said quietly, his voice breaking.

Jerry stopped and squatted so that he was eye level with Caleb. He held Caleb's hands in his own and pulled him close. Caleb's eyes were bright, and his little mouth was turning down at the corners. He looked steadily into Jerry's kind blue eyes. The little smile lines around Jerry's eyes were comforting.

"Everybody is too busy right now. It's springtime and folks are all tired and impatient and running 'round doing a dozen things. Sometimes, we maybe say things out loud when we get so busy and tired. Sometimes, maybe we just forget that there are fabulous little boys who are watching us and listening to us. I'll talk to your mama and daddy, okay? Don't worry about it, son. It's gonna be okay. I promise to talk to them."

Caleb sniffled and nodded. Jerry hugged the child tight and kissed his cheek. They walked the last six feet to the truck, where Lexi was glaring suspiciously at them. Jerry unlocked the doors and put Caleb in the backseat behind the passenger seat. Lexi stood at the passenger side door watching. Jerry didn't look at her. He buckled Caleb into the seat.

"Put the baby in the truck Lexi. I want to go home." He shut the door and got in the truck. Lexi silently put Teague in Eliza's car seat and shut the door. She collapsed the stroller and put it in the back of the truck. She got in the truck and sat without saying a word. She could tell that Jerry was not happy. They got back to the Granger's house, and Jerry pulled the truck to his spot near the back porch. He and Lexi got out and began unloading the children. Caleb ran in the house. Lexi had Teague on her hip and approached Jerry.

"Hey, Jerry?"

"What do you want, Lex?"

"What did Caleb say to you? What were y'all talking about?"

"He was telling me how you are always mad and yelling now and how loud you and your husband are these days. You know, Faye and I did have our share of spats. But we never once subjected Will to them. You and Jason have become whiny, self-centered, self-serving, pitiful, put-upon assholes. These kids are going to grow up angry, stressed out, argumentative, distrusting, and verbally abusive adults. They are going to be shitty husbands and fathers because they are going to have Jason as an example. They are going to put up with bossy, pushy, aggressive, and inappropriate women because you are showing them that is what they should expect in a wife. As of right now, if they have any sense, they'll go stay with their grandfather."

Jerry went in the house with a slam of the screen door. Lexi sat on the back step and cried with Teague in her lap. Jerry stomped through his kitchen to find Anne peeling potatoes. He began to walk right past her, thought twice about it, came back and kissed her.

"What's wrong with you?" she asked.

"Lexi and Jason are what's wrong. They won't stop the fighting and bitching and shit in front of those kids. Caleb got yelled at today for a bunch of *nothing*, and as Lexi stomped off to the truck with a stick up her ass, Caleb told me she's always mad and yelling and that her and Jason are always loud; he was about to cry, Anne."

"Where's Lexi now?" she asked quietly.

"I don't know. I guess she's outside. I don't give a damn right now. I'm in a bad mood. I told her exactly what I thought about her and Jason and told her those kids would be better off with Gary. And I mean it. Come tell me when dinner is ready please, Mama."

He kissed her on the mouth, popped her behind, and went to bed.

Anne sighed. She very slowly set her potato peeler on the spoon rest. She washed her hands carefully and then meticulously folded the plaid hand towel and set it on the counter. She stepped out into the hall and started for the back door when she saw Lexi crying on the back step. She went to her.

CHAPTER 25

The screen door slammed shut behind Lexi. She didn't know who it was; she didn't care anymore. Anne sat down on the step beside her. Anne just sighed while Lexi cried.

"Oh, Lexi. What's the matter now? What's going on with you?" Anne asked this tiredly but tried to sound as compassionate as possible, which was hard.

With Lexi, something was always going on. She seemed to have one issue after another. It seemed there was no pleasing her, but at the same time, Anne felt that Jerry had maybe been a little out of line telling Lexi her kids should go live with Gary.

"Nobody cares. You don't even care. You act like you care but you don't really. You just want me to be nice when I'm over here," Lexi spat.

"Well, duh. Of course, I want you to be nice when you're over here. If you're going to be a big butt, of course I'd prefer you act that way at home instead of doing it over here. But well, I don't really want you acting like that at home either. I mean, I feel sorry for the kids having to put up with it and whenever you and Jason are doing this, it makes it uncomfortable for everyone here. Y'all have been through too much to act this way *all the time*. And I honestly just don't understand what in the world he can possibly be doing every single day to make you stay mad *all the time*."

"Oh yeah! Because Jason is sooooooo perfect and sooooooo great and he never does anything wrong, does he?"

"Okay. For starters, he belches, eats entirely too much food at my house, never hangs the dishtowel up, never puts the toilet seat down, never puts his drink on a napkin, talks really loudly, thinks like a 14-year-old half the time, and he chews with his mouth open. So, no, he is far from perfect. He is pretty great, but a long way from perfect."

"Wow really? You're going to sit there and talk shit about my husband like that? Oh! I forgot you're married to Will. He does nothing wrong." When Lexi said this, Anne assumed she was being sarcastic. But she wasn't. Lexi simply remembered that Anne was used to perfect men. She honestly *truly* felt that Will never did anything wrong. Will Granger was amazing. Lexi often wished that as much time as Jason spent around him, he'd be a little more like him.

"You are an idiot," Anne said bluntly.

"Screw you."

"Screw *you*! And Will is not perfect. I mean, he *is* but that doesn't mean he doesn't do some real annoying, obnoxious, stupid things. He is picky and bossy and overbearing and obsessive and neurotic, and he has to make a fucking list for everything he does. He is constantly horny, and he is entirely too smart for his own good. He does nothing wrong? What the hell is up with you, anyway?"

"You wouldn't have a clue. It must be so hard to understand how the rest of the world lives when you're you. You showed up out of nowhere and suddenly have the perfect house and *two* perfect husbands," Lexi muttered through her tears. Anne didn't care if Lexi was crying. Anne stood up.

"I felt sorry for you. I thought maybe you needed to talk about things. But no. Instead you want to insult me for not being as screwed up as you are. I was going to tell Jerry he shouldn't have said the kids would be better off with Gary. But you know what? Maybe they would be. I will tell you this; until you get over yourself and let people know what the hell is wrong with you, stay away from my house. I'm sick and tired of you coming over here and acting like you've got it so bad. You've got two beautiful children, and a step-daughter, who chooses to spend the night with you; I know *I* sure as hell wouldn't. You have a gorgeous, hardworking, church-going husband who hasn't killed you. He has done so much for you! He could have stayed in that trailer with Gary and let you stay in the apartment. But no, he tried to something good for you. But it's never enough, is it? You expect too much out of him!"

"No, I don't!"

"Yes, you do! You always expect him to …" Anne began.

But Lexi cut her off,

"He's having an affair, Anne!"

Anne just stood there, looking at Lexi, trying to make sure she heard what she thought she heard. Anne's face showed confusion, shock, and doubt. She sat down next Lexi again. Anne shook her head decisively.

"No. No, he isn't. Not Jason. I don't know what you heard or saw, but he is *not* having an *affair*. I mean, think about it! He is here every day for 12 hours! From six in the morning until six at night, he's working. Then, he's home, every night. Nobody here has *time* for an affair. And this conversation is completely disrespectful to him. I can't believe you're even considering it."

"Her name is Claudia. He met her in town yesterday," Lexi spat. She had dropped her voice but was obviously getting madder.

"*What*? How do you know?"

"He has been going into town a lot during the week. He always says he has a few things to take care of. Well, now I know who one of those things are!" Lexi broke down in tears again. Anne was stunned. She felt she shouldn't be discussing something so horrific with Lexi. She was uncomfortable with this subject.

"Oh, Lexi, I don't know. I just really don't know. How do you know though? I mean, how did you get her name and how do you know he met her?"

"Um, well, he called her *Claudia* and he told her he'd meet her at 10, and he said he looked forward to seeing her. But he told *me*, he had to run into town to take care of a few things. Apparently one of those things was his erection."

"I just can't see Jason cheating on you."

"Why do you think we broke up to begin with? Michelle Shaner is why we broke up. He has always thought with his dick and she was always interested in his thoughts, if you know what I mean.

"I was four months pregnant when I found out he was groping her ass behind the Frost Stop. He said he was trying to help her get some change out of her pocket because she'd just had her nails done. I mean, really?"

"Well, it *could* have been the truth."

"He was not getting change out of her pocket. I mean, oh yeah. *Jason, I need 37 cents, but my nails are wet. Can you step behind the Frost Stop with me and dig in my pockets to get my change out?* Bullshit."

"I don't know. It's just hard for me to believe. I mean, I know he was kind of promiscuous years ago. But I just don't see him throwing all of this away, as hard as he'd been working for it. And who is Claudia? I don't remember ever hearing of a Claudia in town."

Yes, Anne had lived here long enough already to be wary of any names she didn't know. The townsfolk would be very happy to learn this about her. She had been trained to trust the locals and be suspicious of those who did not belong here. And she did not know who this Claudia person was. Lexi answered her.

"I don't know who she is. Yesterday, he was on his phone on the back porch. I came around the corner of the porch, but he didn't see me; his back was to me. He told her *I'll be in town tomorrow. We should get together then; it's hard for me to get away.* Then he said *Oh me too. I look forward to seeing you. I'll call you when I get to town. Okay, take care Claudia. Bye.* I mean, really, Anne? You're gonna try to tell me that's not sketchy?"

"Okay, it's a little weird. But we don't know who she is or what the call was about, Lexi. I mean, maybe it was work related. Or maybe it's about the co-op or something."

"Do you really believe that? Because I sure as hell don't," Lexi said through tears.

Anne had to admit to herself that she didn't really believe it either. But she just had a hard time believing Jason would cheat on Lexi. She also still felt very wrong talking about him as if he were screwing around when they didn't have any proof that he was. She did understand that Lexi needed someone to talk to. She decided what she needed to do before this went any further though.

She sighed. "Okay, Lex ... here's what I suggest. Let's go inside. You take a nap upstairs; go to 'Liza's room. Just go chill out. Do you want some tea or something?" Anne asked.

Lexi began to calm down a smidge. A nap sounded so nice. A nap in that beautiful massive tester bed especially sounded so nice. Lexi enjoyed the occasional nap here; she could easily pretend it was her gorgeous bed in her gorgeous plantation home. Yes, a nap was just what she needed.

"Okay, you're right. I guess a nap would be nice. It's been a long morning. Yeah, I'll grab some tea and go on upstairs. You're okay with the kids for a little bit?"

"Oh, I'll just throw them outside. That's no big deal."

Lexi went in the kitchen and got a tea refill. Anne lingered in the kitchen until Lexi disappeared up the stairs. Then, Anne went out the back-screen door, waved to the children playing in the yard, and went to the barn to find her husband.

Will was outside surrounded by lumber and chicken wire. He didn't look incredibly busy though. Anne approached him. He looked up and smiled at the sight of her.

"Hi baby. What's going on?"

"Have you got a minute? I kinda need to talk to you about something, I think."

"Yeah, I can take a minute. Is something wrong?" Will sat on the tailgate of his truck.

Anne stood in front of him and chose her words carefully.

"Do you know someone named Claudia?"

"Claudia?" Will asked with a furrowed brow. He narrowed his eyes and chewed his bottom lip for a moment. He finally shook his head slowly.

"No. I can't say I do. I don't think I've ever heard that name. Well, I mean I have heard it, just not familiar with anyone with that name that I know personally. How old is she?" he asked.

Because this was Will, Anne had no doubt in her mind that he was being completely honest with her. One thing Will had never done was lie to her.

"I don't know. I guess she'd be about your age, maybe a little younger. I mean, technically, I guess she could be a year or so older that you even." Anne had to take into consideration Jason was involved in an older woman. Again, Will shook his head,

"No, baby, I'm sorry but I do not know her. Why? Who is she? How do you know her?"

"I don't exactly. Will, Lexi thinks Jason is having an affair. I kind of chewed her out for being so needy and demanding, and I guess I sort of accused her of expecting too much of him. Then, she told me he's having an affair with someone named Claudia. She told me several things, but I don't know. I didn't feel she really had enough on him to be talking like that about him to me. But I guess she did need someone to talk to."

Will was already getting angry with Jason over something he had no proof that Jason even did. He reminded himself he'd not gotten much information about this yet and this *was* Lexi they were talking about. She tended to blow things out of proportion. Will rubbed his eyes. Anne took this to mean he was getting irritated. She defended herself quickly.

"Look, I told you because, whether it's true or not, Lexi doesn't need to tell people about it. She hasn't told him she knows but she's told me. I guess I was wondering if maybe you could talk to him?"

"Well, before we go getting into this, why does Lexi think he's having an affair with someone named Claudia?" he asked her. Anne retold the story Lexi had given her about the overheard phone call. Will looked saddened and very tired suddenly.

"Anne, I'll ask Jason about it. I'm not going to accuse him of anything. I'm simply going to tell him that Lex apparently overheard a phone conversation that she didn't understand, and it made her worry, understandably."

He hopped off his tailgate and brushed the dirt off the seat of his jeans. He looked at his project lying in the yard and looked back and Anne. If this was his wife with these concerns, he'd certainly want it addressed as soon as possible. So, he decided Lexi's concerns needed to be addressed as soon as possible too.

"Go on and don't worry about it. I'm going to run go talk to him now." Will kissed Anne and got in his truck as Anne walked back to the house.

Will drove through the pasture to the other end of the farm.

He pulled up to the breeding stable and got out of his truck. He went inside and called Jason's name.

"In here!" Jason called back from the office.

Will found him sitting at his desk. Jason looked up and smiled.

"What's up?" he asked. Will sat down in the leather chair in front of the desk.

"Hey, what's been going on with you lately?"

"More of the same. Horses, kids, and women."

"How many women?"

He asked only half joking. Jason looked up from his paperwork with a raised brow.

"Um, let's see. Lexi, Anne, Karen, Laurie … yeah, we gotta consider her one now, I guess. And hell, let's throw Miss Beales and your mom in there for good measure."

"That's all?"

"Isn't that enough? I honestly don't think I could handle us dragging anyone else into this. I have to admit, I'm even wondering how Miss Tammy is gonna work out here. Why? Why are you acting weird?"

"Who's Claudia?" Will asked bluntly. Jason looked only mildly surprised.

"Did she call the stable? She shouldn't have called the *boarding* stable; she has this number." Jason's eyes went briefly back to the paperwork. He looked back up, waiting for Will's reply.

"You didn't answer my question," Will said, with a touch of an attitude.

Jason returned the attitude. He set his pen down and leaned back in his desk chair. He smiled a little smile at Will.

"And you didn't answer mine."

"Your wife thinks you're screwing around behind her back … again."

"Why would she think that?" Jason asked clearly confused.

So, Will told him about the phone conversation Anne said Lexi had overheard. Jason closed his eyes and rested his forehead in his hand.

"Oh, good grief. *No.* No, no, no, no, no, no, *not at all.* No, Will. Let me explain what this is about. Laurie is wanting to change her name to Connelly. Dad told me. We are going to have to go to court about all this. Stacy is not going to make this easy on Laurie or Dad or me. We decided to get a lawyer to represent Laurie but one from out of town. We didn't want anyone who had any connections in this town to avoid ... well, you know the kind of shit that goes on. We just wanted someone that was going to be able to be completely impartial to everything. No lawyer in this town is going to be willing to go up against Dad and Stacy knows that. She'll get a lawyer from one of the neighboring counties. So, we decided to do that too to keep it fair.

"Well, I got in touch with an attorney who represents kids in this kind of thing. Her name is Claudia Wilkes. She had gotten some papers put together for us to look over with Laurie. She wanted to talk to me about some things we needed to discuss. She's from Bastian though. We have to get together when we can. I was going to be in town anyway, to get more lumber for your goat pens and the chicken coop. So, I told her yeah, we could meet about the paperwork since I'd be in town anyway. Really? You think I'd screw around on Lexi?"

Will sighed. Jason's explanation was plausible. But his question bugged Will. Will leaned forward and closed his eyes tight for a minute. He felt a headache coming on. He noticed here lately that he and his dad seemed to have contagious headaches. Their headaches tended to come in pairs these days. If one of them had one, it seemed a matter of hours before the other one got one too. He opened his eyes and spoke slowly to Jason.

"You should ask why *Lexi* would think you'd screw around on her? What are you doing, man? You are doing something very wrong. She should not ever have to wonder that. For starters, why didn't you tell Lexi you were meeting an attorney for Laurie?

"When I go to town, I tell everyone where I'm going and what I'm going for and when to expect me back. *Of course,* that's going to look shady to your wife, hearing you on the phone with a woman she's never heard of, making arrangements to meet, after telling this woman what a hard time you have getting away from here! I mean, Jesus, fool! What did you expect her to think? Y'all are always arguing and bitching these days. She probably thinks you don't like her anymore."

"Well, I *don't* like her anymore! I love her more than anything! But my God! She nags and whines and complains nonstop! Nothing is good enough! Nothing is right! *Nobody* wants to be around her anymore. She didn't *used* to be like this.

"I think she's *bored*. I don't think she wants to go back to work necessarily but I have thought about this for weeks. All I can come up with is maybe she spent so many years working that she's getting stressed, bored, frustrated, I don't know. She used to go *do* stuff. When she lived in town, she went to work, was involved in the church daycare parties and things, and she spent time with her friends and going out to lunch and doing playdates and all that shit. Now? She wakes up, hangs out in our house, or hangs out in your house. She goes to church once a week. That is pretty much it.

"I can't wait for Caleb to go to school! Maybe, *just maybe,* she'll get a life again! Maybe she'll do the PTA thing, chaperone field trips, and help with school picture day or birthdays or class Valentines parties or something! Just something! Something to get her the Hell out of here for a little while! She has nothing to do so she looks for things to fight about!" Jason exploded. He had kept this to himself for too long; he saw that now.

He'd known they were having problems, but it'd been easier to sweep it under the porch at the time than deal with it right then. He'd had so much to deal with already, and Lexi acting worse than the hormonal 15-year-old that visited every weekend was just too much. Jason started to rub his eyes. Will had been angry when he came in here, but now he felt sorry for Jason.

"Listen, there might be truth to what you said. Maybe it's true; maybe she is just getting restless. Maybe she does just have too much time on her hands. If that's true, then help her out with it. Suggest she do something."

"Anne doesn't act like that."

"Anne was never in Lexi's position. Anne had a severely screwed up life before she got here. And well, it's still kinda screwed up in some aspects, but she wasn't living on her own, with her own rules, and her own kid, in her own apartment, with her own career, paying her own bills and shit. Lexi was used to being busy and independent. Anne is not. Anne lived under her parents until she moved in with her boyfriend for a few months, then she ran away from home and came here. And well, this is her entire life and she likes it this way. I think, though, that maybe Lexi isn't as happy with the arrangement as you think she is. You have got to see that Lexi and Anne are apples and oranges, man. How can you not see that? Just because they're friends, doesn't mean they're anything alike."

"What am I supposed to do?"

"You're not stupid! Sit down with her and ask her if she's maybe bored out here! If she says yes, then suggest she get away from here two or three times a week. Remind her that she'll be busier when Caleb starts school, that she'll be going to town more for his school stuff. Suggest she do things away from here. And if she says she's *not* bored, ask her what her problem is. Don't yell at her, just ask her like you actually do give a damn what's wrong." Will suggested. He was floored though that Jason would even have to ask this. Jerry was always telling Will how out of touch he was with what Anne needed and wanted; Will agreed with this 100 percent. But even Will could easily see the solution to Jason's problem!

Jason spun around in the office chair a few times, He stopped, looked out the window, and looked back at Will.

"Fine. I'll talk to her tonight. I'm not doing anything behind her back. When do I have *time* for an affair?"

"Well, that's what Anne asked her. Lexi pointed out your trips to town."

"What would you do if Anne suspected you were having an affair?" Jason asked. Will looked at him for just a moment as if amused by the question.

"Every woman in my life is right here on this road. Anne knows that. Do not give them a reason to ask that, Jason. If they have reason to suspect that you have someone in town on the side, then it is not their fault. That is something *you* are doing wrong." Will stood up to walk out. He felt the problem had been fixed for the most part. But Jason stopped him.

"Wait a minute. You're saying all this is my fault?"

"I'm saying ask yourself what you are doing that would make your wife think you were done with her."

Back in the house, Anne went upstairs later and came across Jerry in the hall. He looked grumpy, but he put his arms around her waist and pulled her close to him. She looked up into his eyes.

"You were an asshole," she told him bluntly.

He pulled his head back to look at her better.

"Excuse me?"

"To Lexi. You were an asshole."

"I am never ever *ever* an asshole. I am a very nice guy. I offered to go to the school with her just to be nice to her."

"Well, no, you said you went to be nice to Caleb but anyway ..."

"Why are you saying I'm an asshole, Mama?" Jerry managed to look wounded and on the verge of tears. Anne couldn't help but smile at his sweet face.

"You yelled at her and told her she was an unfit parent, for one."

"I'm sorry, but I'm honestly starting to think that may be the case."

"She's under the impression Jason is having an affair. I think she's suspected it for a while because she said he's always going into town and becoming distant to her. Well, now she's heard him on his phone making plans to meet another woman in town."

At this news, Jerry was mortified. A local was having an affair with Jason?

"She must be mighty stupid to have an affair with Gary's son. Breaking up Gary's little family? Who is it?"

"Don't think she's from around here; Will said he's never heard of anyone named Claudia."

"Claudia?"

"That was this girls name."

"I don't know any Claudia either."

"Well, Will said he was going to go talk to Jason about it. I sent Lexi up here to take a nap," Anne told him. Jerry shook his head.

"Well, I'm sorry she is going through that but none of that excuses the way the two of them have been acting in front of those boys. She talked to Caleb like he was dirt today when we were getting ready to leave lunch. She was all fine at the school and while we ate, but she turned into a monster when I saw her cigarettes."

"Cigarettes?"

"See? All kinds of shit going on that you don't know about either. Lexi needs to grow up. If she is having marital problems, then take it up with who you're married to. She walks around here having one crisis after another. I tried to be nice today. But how she talked to Caleb was completely uncalled for, and I will not apologize for saying I think those kids don't need to be around her and Jason right now. Now, of course, they *are* going to stay with them because they can't live here, and Gary sure as shootin' doesn't need to take on two more kids right now. Yes, they'll stay with Lex and Jason, but it doesn't mean I think it's good for them."

"Well, some say our living conditions aren't ideal *here* either," Anne argued.

"Oh, they're ideal; they're just a bit unorthodox," Jerry smiled and pulled Anne closer to him and kissed her on the mouth.

"I love you so much," Jerry said, making his way near her ear.

He put his hand on her backside and pulled her even closer. It was torment for him; he wanted nothing more than the freedom to do anything he wanted to her. He felt that familiar, painful pull in his heart. He felt that sick feeling he'd get in his stomach when his heart would ache for her. He held her tight against him, his hand on the back of her head, rubbing her long dark curls. He kissed her cheek, then he kissed her mouth easily. Letting out his breath, he laid his cheek against hers. She smiled and did something she knew he liked a lot. She kissed his cheek several times, making her way to his sweet little ear. She nibbled on his earlobe and felt him tense up in her arms. She did it for a moment, enjoying his reaction. He finally started giggling, so she started giggling too. She looked at him.

"You know I love you, too. And everyone *knows* I love you. It's so easy to be in love with you. You are just perfect. You know you are, don't you?"

"I don't know that I'm *perfect*, but I know that I'm happier than I've been in a long time."

"I'm glad, I'm so happy to see you doing so much better."

"You do it to me. You do a lot to me. Every time I see you (he kissed her), every time I touch you (he kissed her again), every time I dream of doing terribly inappropriate things to you in the night (he kissed her again), and every time I see you across the room during the day and fantasize about doing even *more* inappropriate things to you (he kissed her again)."

"Spoken like a true father-in-law," Anne giggled.

"Does anyone here even consider me your father-in-law? I've heard us referred to as many things; *in-laws* hasn't ever been one of them. Most of the things haven't been very nice, of course. Aw well. It's almost two and that means *Jeopardy* is coming on. You know the drill, Mama. Meet me in the living room with some tea and Doritos, daughter-in-law." Jerry gave her a quick kiss on her cheek and went downstairs to find his remote.

Will had finished his chat with Jason and was back in his own yard, next to his barn, eyeing the building supplies at his feet. With his eyes, he surveyed the land he planned to build the goat pen on. While Anne was making Jerry his snack in the kitchen, Lexi stood at the upstairs bedroom window and watched Anne's husband in the yard. And as Jerry got comfortable on the couch, his deceased-but-very-active wife was watching him. While she watched him, Tammy remained upstairs in the bathroom, where she had been cleaning, when she overheard the entire conversation between Jerry and Anne.

CHAPTER 26

The house sat quietly all day, listening, and watching. From every splinter in the wood, every brick in the fireplace, to every grain of dirt in the dark, earthen cellar, this old house was certainly aware of everything that took place within its walls. If there had ever been any question about whether or not this house was alive, this house could have answered that question quickly and confidently. Oh, it was alive! And it was interested in everything going on.

This house kept things in order. It knew the things that were taking place within the family, and it didn't particularly like it. It knew there were new people spending time here, people it had to familiarize itself with. It didn't like these people spending too much time here. And this house had ways to let that be known.

It had not cared for Marilyn Beales at all in the beginning. The things she thought she had felt, she *had* felt. The things she thought she had seen, she *had* seen. And those noises, the soft whispering she had sworn she had heard, she *had* heard. This had been the house telling Marilyn things. It had not been the numerous resident ghosts whispering fervently in the dark halls. It had been the house. The house had been telling Marilyn things; things she didn't understand yet, but things she would in time. It was becoming interested in Marilyn now. She was no longer seen as a threat, but she was watched. It didn't matter what room she was in, she was never alone, and she was always watched. Yes, these walls were quite interested in Marilyn.

Lexi was a curious one for the house. She was considered family, but she was causing problems for the family too. Faye was concerned about

Lexi; something a little different for Faye. She usually found herself worrying over Anne and Jerry; Will, not so much these days. He seemed to have a handle on things. He didn't necessarily do things like Faye wished he would; he very seldom put thought into *anything*. This was a trait his wife and co-workers admired in him. Nobody ever had to wait days or even hours for Will to make up his mind about something. His attitude was the most obvious answer is usually the one that comes to you first. That's the one you should just go with. Many would argue with him on this if asked, but his method of problem solving had yet to fail him. It had always worked out perfectly for him. He realized that the longer you thought about something, the more things you ended up thinking about and considering and then the more confused you got. So, he just didn't bother with all that extra thinking. Between his approach to common sense and his impressive book smarts, Will honestly seemed to know everything.

Everyone else might have liked having his brilliance on hand, but Faye felt he had gotten entirely too self-assured and full of himself. She wished he'd stop every now and then, and at least pay attention to what was going on around him before jumping on decisions. He was so quick to fix problems, yet seldom saw the entire problem. Lexi was one of these problems.

Lexi was lonely. Lexi was bored, frustrated, angry, and Faye genuinely understood why. Jason was becoming an ass. And, well, Faye even kind of understood that. Will gave him entirely too much to handle at once. Jason was killing himself to keep up with the Granger's expectations of him. Faye had even yelled at Jerry about this; Jason had not been raised around this! Jason was still learning! They needed to lay off! Jerry just shrugged to his nagging dead wife, took a bite of his tomato sandwich, and told Faye to take it up with Will.

So, when Jason became the negligent husband, Lexi's eyes wandered to the next best thing, Will. In truth, she was like another wife to him really. She never went home. Faye liked her okay and all, but she agreed with Anne on this one. Lexi needed to go home and take care of her own house every now and then. Lexi would go through phases where she'd spend several days throwing herself into taking care of her own house and being the perfect wife. Then, somewhere along day four, she'd get bored with that and go spend all her time at the Granger's. This would go on for several weeks, then she'd get that wild hair up her ass again and take care of her own for four days.

Lexi used to have a quite active life and now her days were spent pretending she was the lady of the grand Granger Plantation. She enjoyed spending her days here; home wasn't any fun. She liked her house, but she loved this one. Was it her fault though? Or had she merely become one of the many people who became unwillingly attached to this house? Had she become one of the many people who had come through its doors and simply become a part of this house?

Lexi didn't have a choice. The more time she began spending here several years ago, the more this house became interested in her. She and Jason started spending holidays here. The house really took notice. Jason proposed to Lexi in this house, just as many other young suitors had done within these walls for almost 200 years. Then, Jason and Lexi exchanged wedding vows in its front yard. And that, unbeknownst to her, was when Lexi became a true part of this house.

Something as meaningful as wedding vows was just what was needed to make the relationship between Lexi and the house significant. From that very day, Lexi felt a devotion to this house. She was proud of it and wanted to be there. When she and Jason went on their brief honeymoon, she missed the Granger home desperately. While they were living in the trailer on the property, of course Lexi preferred the big, beautiful home to her own.

When their own big new house was completed, Lexi was surprised that she still preferred the Granger home. The farmhouse was nice; it was beautiful. But Lexi felt disconnected from it. Jason, on the other hand, was very fond of their new house. He was quite carried away by it. In all honesty, he'd rather spend his breakfast and lunch there than at the Granger's. Well, sometimes he felt that way. Then, he'd realize that he'd miss the crazy crowd at the Granger's kitchen table. It simply wasn't possible for them to all gather at the Connelly's for these meals. And he knew it just wouldn't feel right anyway. Yes, their weekday breakfasts and lunches would continue to take place at the Granger table. But other than that, Jason enjoyed his time at his own home. He had begun to prefer the breeding stable at his end of the farm over the boarding stable at the Granger's end. He wished Lexi felt the same way; he could tell she didn't.

Jason wondered if she preferred the Granger house because it was more beautiful than her own. He wondered if she liked the company of Anne and Karen. He wondered, sometimes, if she liked the company of Will. He'd always dismiss that quickly though; he dismissed it because he noticed she also liked the company of Jerry. Well, that's why he told himself he dismissed it. He knew, not so deep inside, that he also dismissed it because he simply didn't like to think about it. He may think of them as family, but Jason knew that the fact of the matter was he was not family. He was not a Granger and he couldn't help but wonder if that made a difference to Lexi.

Jason was proud of what he had accomplished though. He had made so many changes to his life and whereas these changes weren't always easy, they were changes he was quite happy with. He wished Lexi would act happier with these changes. Especially after his meeting with Will today, Jason just felt Lexi would have preferred living back in town than with him, on Teague Road. This bothered him. He liked what they had built for themselves. He wanted this to work out for them all. He now had no intention of leaving this property to move back to town. Where Lexi had begun a relationship with the Granger home, Jason had begun a relationship with their own home. He loved his house, despite all the weird things that had begun happening there. Oh, there were many things that had begun happening there.

Doors opened and closed by themselves. Three dishes fell to the floor, shattering, by themselves. Lights were constantly turning on and off. Laurie came out of the kitchen saying something kept petting her hair, but she couldn't see it. Jason ended up having to finish washing the dishes that night. Buck, Caleb's cat, had become a nervous wreck. He was a rather high-strung animal anyway, so he was especially annoying now. Gary had been sitting in the living room last week when all a sudden, all of Caleb's toys dumped themselves out of the box next to the fireplace. There was nobody else in the room at the time. Well, nobody that Gary could see.

Jason and Will had several discussions about these disturbing events. They were happening more and more. Nothing particularly dangerous had happened, they'd decided. Just annoying. The vast majority of the actions seemed to involve the kitchen and the children's toys. Will had told Jerry about this, and Jerry had a suggestion. There had been numerous children in the Sewell family, nine to be exact. Two had been stillborn, one died at just three months. One of the sons had died when he was just three. Two daughters died at four years old and six years old. This may have explained the toys doing strange things by themselves. The sad row of six tiny tombstones in the Sewell family graveyard was a reminder these children had been there. The goings on in the Connelly home suggested they may be there still.

The Connelly-Sewell home had been painstakingly built to look like the one that had stood there before it. They had done an excellent job; it appeared they had done such a good job that even the Sewells couldn't tell the difference. Jason admitted the Sewells appearing to come home was taking some getting used to but really it was no big, huge deal, he guessed. He had enough experience with ghosts at the Granger house; he wasn't afraid of them. He just didn't always understand them.

Jason had often felt there was something more to the Granger house though. He had often wondered if it was just ghosts, in that house watching everything that happened. Sometimes it seemed it was the windows; he felt something very odd about the windows. Jason had never said anything out loud about this because he didn't know if he really believed what he was thought he was thinking. It was preposterous. They were windows. They were just windows, right?

The old wavy panes of glass in the huge windows seemed to play tricks on Jason's eyes. He'd swear he saw things in these windows, especially during cloudy days and at night, when reflections were easier to see. He'd think he saw his reflection, look carefully, and what should be his reflection seemed often to be the reflection of someone else entirely. Jason would look around, only to discover he was there alone. Or so it seemed. Yes, these windows appeared to show Jason another side to something. No, these windows were not just windows to Jason. He didn't like sitting or standing near the windows. He felt they were watching him, and he felt there were others watching him through them.

Lexi, on the other hand, loved the big windows of old glass panes. She had said one of her favorite things about this house was the windows. It was sort of weird to Jason; he noticed that the few things about the Granger's house that gave him the creeps happened to be the very things that Lexi loved about it. Lexi loved the idea that they were surrounded by spirits. She loved the ghost stories and she loved the way that the house itself felt truly alive. She had told Jason that when she walks in the Granger home, she swears she can feel a compression of some sort, as if the house were embracing her. She smiled as she told him this, but he wanted to throw up. He too had felt that, too many times to count. It was followed by an involuntarily holding of the breath. It was a breath you let out, without ever realizing you were holding it to begin with. It was as if the old house was hugging you as you came through its doors, into its arms.

One didn't simply walk into this house and feel its presence. You had to get acquainted with the house; you had to get to really get to know it and give it a chance to get to know you. It was rather like the little rabbits in the yard; for a long time, they'd watch you from the edge of the trees. Over time, they'd creep closer to you. Before long, they would be nothing more than pets that roamed free. They would help themselves to whatever livestock feed they could find, spend exceptionally cold days and nights in the barn and stable, and play with the cats. If you spotted them and tossed them food, they eventually just said *why not?* and loped toward you to retrieve your offer. And that's the way it was with the house.

Your first visit would be rather ordinary. You would likely smile at the beautiful exterior of the home and imagine something grand and spectacular inside; you'd expect to step back in time upon coming through its door. But once inside, you would find yourself surprised by the warm, inviting, homey, and comforting interior. This wasn't a house made to feel like a museum. This wasn't a house filled with hard, uncomfortable horsehair chairs roped off with *Do Not Sit* signs. This wasn't a house filled with pieces all dating back to the 1840s.

This house, whereas it certainly had numerous original pieces in every room, was full of comfortable, overstuffed pieces made for a family who appreciated their time at home. The brown soft leather sofa that Jerry had ordered in 1981 had been used until it simply had to be retired 22 years later. It was then sold to some guy across the county line (which literally brought tears to Jerry's eyes) and immediately replaced with another couch, exactly like the old couch, purchased at the same exact store. The matching recliner and wide armchair and other newer pieces were accompanied by several antiques. It was this way in every room of the house.

Once you got past the shock of finding just a family home within a historic masterpiece, you really took very little time adjusting. You found yourself quite comfortable, quite quickly. Then, that's when the house started adjusting to you. Once you let your guard down was when the house's guard went up. If you returned to the house, the house remembered you, but it wouldn't say anything just yet. It would just stand back and watch you.

The more time you spent there, you would start to notice little things about this house. Just as the more time you spend with someone, you become familiar with their eye color, their voice, the odd little quirks, in the same way, you became familiar with this house. But it wasn't the architecture you find yourself noticing. You found yourself familiar with its smell; it was a smell that you would eventually find yourself smelling even when you weren't there. You'd begin noticing which boards in the old floor creaked under your feet and you eventually learned where the warps were in that floor. After stepping on the warps and slightly losing your balance so many times, you would just find yourself automatically adjusting your step. It was those little things at first.

Then, you found yourself hearing little things. You would wonder if it was a voice, or just perhaps the house settling, or maybe even you hadn't really heard anything at all? You'd look around one last time before shrugging it off and going about your business. These voices and sounds would become more and more frequent the more time you found yourself spending there. Then, you would see something out of the corner of your eye. You would look up to see who had come into the room, only to find nobody standing there. Perhaps you'd see someone behind you, just enough to your left to get a glimpse of them, but again there was nobody there. Eventually, there would be times you'd sense someone standing behind you; you could actually feel them there, even hear them there, breathing behind you and watching you. You would feel the ever so slight breeze of them coming up behind you and would turn to greet them; that's when you would start to get just a little uncomfortable. That's when you realize that not only are you hearing things and seeing things, but you have now been invited to actually *feel* these things.

For the house, this is where the relationship really begins. You have been accepted as safe, not a threat. You have become one of the lucky ones to be invited to get acquainted with all the people who had lived and died there. You were invited to get better acquainted with the house itself. And once that happened, you were unwillingly, unknowingly bound to the house.

You took care of the house and the people who lived there, and you took care of the spirits that crept the wide halls and wandered the fields. And the people, the spirits, and the house all took care of you. And soon, you were fond of, attached to even, the members of the household who appeared to you surrounded by an odd fog or a strange light. They would sometimes simply watch you and sometimes they would smile. Sometimes they would hum a favorite song of theirs from long ago, and sometimes they would carry on lengthy conversations with you. Sometimes they were merely a smell of rich tobacco with a thread of white smoke appearing in the air of a seemingly empty room. Sometimes they were an empty chair rocking or a curtain blowing from a windless window. They were there in many different forms, but they were always there.

At one point you would have been frightened by the very idea of a haunted house. But in time, in this house, you would see these apparitions as nothing more than extended family. They were there, and they had no intention of leaving. You had become part of this house too and leaving didn't appear to be an option anymore. So, y'all just did what you had to do and made the best of the situation. You learned to accept each other, to respect each other, and you learned to love each other and look out for each other. In life and in death you were friends and family.

And in life and in death, this house would always be home. It made sure everyone who belonged here would stay here together. Forever.

CHAPTER 27

M onday proved entirely too eventful for everyone on Teague Road. Jason called it a day early and came by the Granger's house. He found Lexi alone, lying on the couch in the living room like she lived there. He looked around and chuckled.

"Making yourself comfortable? You know, we have a couch at home too."

"Yeah, well, I was here."

"When *aren't* you? I left the stable early to tell you to bring the kids home early today, now would be nice. I want to talk to you about a few things."

"Well, why can't we talk about it here? We're alone," Lexi reasoned. Jason looked around the room again.

"We're never alone in this house. Not the point. It's not our house, and I want to talk about us, and I want to do it in my own damn house. Is this a problem for you?" He raised his voice without meaning to. He was trying to make things better, but he felt like he was having to get permission to talk to his own wife in his own house.

"No, it's not a problem. Let me gather up the kids," Lexi said mildly, with a touch of boredom. She stood up and walked out of the room. Jason followed her. She went to the kitchen where Caleb, James, and Eliza were sitting in the floor rolling a yellow ball back and forth to each other. Teague was in the highchair chewing on a toy. Lexi picked up Teague's bag.

"Come on, Caleb. Daddy wants to go ahead and go home."

"Why? I want to stay here and play with Liza and James."

"Because Daddy wants us to go home now. Get up now; come on. Get your shoes,"

"Do I have to put them on?" Caleb whined.

Jason sighed. He was mad now, because even the kids wanted to stay here.

"Caleb! Just get your shoes. I don't care if you put them on. We're just getting in the truck. Now hurry up. I need to get home and talk to your mama about something," he snapped.

Lexi looked at him.

"Good grief; chill out. It's a four-minute drive we're talking about. And it's not like we're on a schedule or anything."

"No! We *are* on a schedule! We're on *my* schedule! I took off work early to come back here early, to take you home early, so we could go to our house early! So yes, we *are* on a schedule!" Jason yelled. Anne, who was sitting at the table said nothing. Caleb, however, raised his eyebrows. He shook his head at his father's meltdown.

"Okay, okay, okay. I'm getting my shoes," he muttered. Caleb's response only irritated Jason more. Anne stood up and went to the counter to investigate the contents cooking in the crockpot. She didn't want to be in the room right then but worried it'd look obvious if she left right now. It was almost four o'clock; Will wouldn't be in here to stop Jason from killing Lexi for at least another hour, maybe two. Jerry had gone outside to work after he had his snack and watched Jeopardy, so he couldn't help Lexi either. Tammy was still here though; Anne thought Tammy might could help if she needed it.

Caleb found his little shoes, and Lexi flung Teague on her hip. "Get the diaper bag, Jason. Then let's run run run out to the truck! Hurry everyone! Only four minutes to get to the house!" Lexi said anxiously. Jason snatched the bag up angrily. Anne thought Lexi was not helping the situation at all but then she remembered, as far as Lexi knew, Jason was having an affair with Claudia in town. So, for once, Anne kinda-sorta sided with Lexi. Jason stomped out of the kitchen and down the hall. The back-screen door opened and slammed shut. Caleb looked at Lexi. She took her hand and pushed him toward the door.

"Tell Miss Anne and the kids bye-bye."

"Bye, y'all. I wish I was staying here." Caleb left. Lexi looked at Anne briefly before leaving. She looked angry; no, she looked sad and she looked very anxious. Anne then remembered what Jason had said when he came in and yelled at Caleb. Then Anne understood; Lexi was scared Jason was going to tell her about Claudia. Neither Lexi nor Anne had any way of knowing what Jason had told Will in the stable earlier. They didn't know Claudia was just a lawyer and not Jason's mistress.

Lexi didn't want to go home with Jason. She was certain he was going to confess to his affair to her. She lingered in the doorway for a moment, as if she wanted to say something to Anne. Anne just smiled encouragingly at her.

"Lex, if you want to talk later, you can call me if you want to," Anne assured her. Lexi smiled gratefully and left to find Jason outside. They got in the truck and went home. Once inside, Jason directed Caleb to go to the living room where they put Teague in his baby swing.

Jason and Lexi sat at the kitchen table. Jason sighed and just got down to the point.

"Okay, sugarbear, here's the deal. Laurie wants to change her last name to Connelly. It's going to likely go to court because Stacy is a jackass. So, I hired a lawyer from out of town; she's from Bastian. I had my reasons for getting one from out of town. *Because* she's from out of town, meetings are not easy. She came through town on her way to a funeral and brought some paperwork with her for me to look over with Laurie. The lawyer's name is Claudia, Lex. Here." Jason began digging in his wallet, which sat on the table. He pulled out a business card and handed it to Lexi. She took it slowly and looked at it. Jason continued.

"That card is hers. It has her full name, her office address, her phone number, and her email address. Oh, and her fax number and website. Feel free to call her. Or visit her or email her or fax her. I've nothing to hide, nor does she. My feelings are a little hurt by the suspicion, but anyway, I love you and I've always loved you. I'm not seeing anyone else and I have no interest in seeing anyone else. In fact, I'd *like* to see a little more of *you*. I guess we'll just have to schedule something at some point because I don't see any other real way for us to spend time together. I can't just drop by my own damn house during the day and visit with my wife. My wife is in someone else's house during the day. Let me know what day is good for you."

Jason sounded tired but he smiled when he said this. He wasn't mad, honestly, he wasn't. He was tired. He was tired from working, tired from worrying. He was just very tired of everything that was going on. It seemed it was one crisis after another, every day waiting to see what that day's crisis would be.

Right after Jason and Lexi left the Granger house, Tammy came down the hall. Her eyes caught sight of something on the floor beside the foot of the service stairs. She recognized it immediately. There sat the pair of blue canvas slip-on tennis shoes that belonged to Faye. Tammy had been with Faye when she bought these at Brighton's Department Store. Faye had fallen in love with them when she saw them; they were boring to Tammy. They looked like denim and weren't anything outstanding. But Faye had snatched them up immediately. They quickly became her favorite shoes. And there they sat, in the back of the hall, where Faye always kicked them off. In a moment, Tammy realized that those shoes had probably been right there, in that same spot, since Faye last kicked them off several years ago. It made her feel very touched, very happy, and very sad at the same time. It made her think of the several very sad things she had seen since arriving here to work on Friday.

In the bathroom, Faye's long yellow eyelet nightgown still hung on the back of the door. Faye's night cream and jar of Ponds Cold Cream still rested on the shelf above the toilet. In Jerry's bedroom, all of Faye's things, her jewelry box, her Charlie perfume, her many little odds and ends, still rested on the dresser top. A pair of small wide gold hoop earrings still lay in the middle of a gold bangle bracelet, where she had set them after taking them off. Her Aqua Net hairspray still sat beside her earring rack. Faye's purse sat in the straight back chair next to the closet, where her purse always sat. Tammy assumed that when Faye passed-away, Jerry brought her purse home and put it where Faye would have put it. Faye's clothes still hung in the closet. The novel she had been reading still sat on the bedside table. The bookmarker Will had made for her in Sunday School when he was seven years old rested between the pages 128-129. It's as if Jerry made sure everything was ready for Faye when she came home.

Downstairs, there were the shoes by the staircase. There was also her basket of sewing stuff, which still sat beside her big rocking chair. The little antique round table that sat between her rocking chair and Jerry's recliner still had Faye's little dish she kept an odd assortment of things in; thimbles, loose change, tweezers, a small magnifying glass, a few batteries ... things like that. Faye's little dish had not been messed with since she last touched it herself. It was lifted to wipe the table, but its contents had not been touched. It was this way all over the house, right down to the pile of junk mail addressed to Faye that remained on the washstand in the foyer. It appeared also that Anne had gone out of her way to keep every room, especially the kitchen, exactly as it was when she had arrived. Anne had added her own little touches here-and-there but had gone to great lengths to ensure nothing of Faye's would be disturbed. And nothing of Faye's was. Everything was left exactly where Faye had left it. It seemed only fitting, since Faye had gone nowhere. But Tammy wondered; was Faye here because she didn't want to leave or was it simply because Jerry wouldn't let her die?

Tammy dismissed this almost as quickly as it came to mind; this was the Granger house. It seemed nobody really died here.

Tammy made her way into the kitchen to tell Anne she was leaving for the day. She was impressed that supper seemed to be almost ready at only four o'clock in the afternoon. Anne appeared to have everything very well under control. She had spent the day taking things relatively easy and Tammy was happy about that. She had appreciated Lexi and Anne helping out like they did, but she didn't want them to think it was necessary, especially Anne. Tammy felt Anne had already done more than her share over the years. She shook her head just as Anne looked up.

"What's the matter Tammy?" Anne asked.

"Huh? Oh, nothing, dear. I was just, um, amazed you look like you've already got supper done. Even I never had it ready by four!" Tammy walked over to the stove and looked in the boiler on its top.

"Oh, it's not quite ready. I get all the things that take a long time to cook ready first; then I just keep them warm. Then I make the things that cook quick last. I actually start supper as soon as I get lunch cleaned up usually. It kinda depends on what we're having really. So, thanks but don't be too impressed. Supper isn't technically ready by four. We do six o'clock here. At six, everyone is at the table and ready to eat. Dad always griped if we ate after seven, so I try to keep it at six every night. That gives everyone time to work, and Will time to get his shower before he eats." Anne stirred something in a pot.

Tammy was confused.

"Dad? Your dad?" she asked, surprised. Anne had never talked about her biological family. Anne looked at her blankly. Then, it was as if a light came on in her head.

"Oh! I'm talking about Uncle Roy. He's more of a dad to me than anything else. I really do truly love him like a father. He considers me to be a daughter. So, well, I call him Dad a lot. I say it without thinking anymore."

"Well, that's sweet. I mean, I knew you and Roy were close; everyone can see that. I just didn't know it had escalated to you calling him Dad. Relationships on this road are something else. Always have been."

"What do you mean, *always have been*?"

"Just what I said. I mean, I guess it started back when the house was first built. From the time they bought this land from Sewell, this family has somehow managed to make family out of everyone they get close enough to. They took care of Sewell after they bought his place. His health was said to be bad, in his advancing age. His son was never very well to help him out with much, before getting shot by the Indian, of course. Well, the Grangers and Teagues took care of them.

"They actually did the family a favor, buying the property from him. He wasn't able to keep the farm up, they say. He was having a hard time with the crops and the animals and even the house. So, when they bought it all from him, they said they'd take care of his crops and help him out with his livestock and such. Well, they became family. They took such good care of the old fool that they buried him and his son when they found them dead. They offered to lease the house to anyone interested in helping work the land but never had any takers because everyone was scared to death of that house."

Tammy paused and smiled as she looked around this house; there were many who would be scared to death of *this* one had they known what others knew.

Anne nodded.

"I knew they were close to the Sewells. The Sewell graveyard says that just by looking at it. They keep it looking very nice. You'd think it *was* family."

"Well, that's my point. On this road, that's what you become. It's not even optional, I don't think. But really, who would mind? Over the years, so many people have come to visit and have ended up staying weeks, months, and in a few instances, anyway, they stayed years. They show up and don't want to leave.

"I remember back in ... 66? 67? Jane Reynolds came to spend the night here. She was a cousin of theirs of sorts, second cousin twice removed or something. Her grandfather, Archie, was somehow related to one of my cousins, John. In fact, John married Archie's wife's first cousin, Mary Addy. She had a terrible temper, Mary Addy, that is. She used to go outside on her porch and shoot her rifle at the house across the road! In town! She was such an embarrassment to all our folks. They acted like she just didn't exist after a while. And it was such a shame because everyone just loved John so much! And he just couldn't take her anywhere!" Tammy took a breath.

Anne was curious.

"Was she that bad?" she asked.

Tammy got a second wind.

"Oh, she drank and drank like a fish ... and she belched! Yes, she'd just belch right there in the middle of services, in the middle of meals at the table; she even belched during Abraham Wilkes visitation! Everyone just wanted to die, right there with poor old Abraham. It was just terrible. She also wore a red bra with absolutely everything. And the only place that sold such things back then was Gray's over there on Third. They were always the first to get things like that in. Martha Gray, you know her, the older woman who walks around town in those velour running suits year-round? Well, back in the late 60s and especially in the 70s, she was all over the place yelling about women's rights. Hell, even the women got tired of her. Well, she hasn't worn a bra at all since 1973. It's horrible and disgusting but at least after she got older and they were sagging so bad, she started wearing those running suits, so you don't really notice it so much anymore.

"But anyway, she told her husband she wanted to get red and black bras in the shop, and he was so mortified! He was a deacon at the church at the time, and he just couldn't imagine what Gary's daddy would say. He told Roy he wanted to at least wait until Gary's daddy had died but no! She ordered those red and black bras! And stockings too! Red and black lace stockings! Oh, the women all wanted to go in there and look at them so badly, but they just knew it'd look terrible if anyone found out about them doing it. They went and looked but left the store feeling as though they'd just left a whorehouse. The older ladies called her such terrible names for carrying such things in this town. They told her she should just go ahead and open a brothel. She's always been something else. Anyway, Mary Addy went in there and bought those red bras, and she wore them with absolutely everything. It was so terribly awkward seeing her coming toward you during the spring and summer because your eyes automatically went to those enormous breasts in the red bra. And in the spring and summer, of course, she'd be wearing light-colored clothes. You couldn't help but see everything. Oh, poor John." Tammy paused again. Anne was trying hard to follow the story.

"But anyway, back to Jane? She had come here for a wedding. She was supposed to spend Friday night here, attend the wedding on Saturday, and go home Sunday morning. Do you know she ended up staying here *three years?* Yes! Here, at this house! She slept in one of the service rooms. But she came here, and she stayed here, and she died here. Just died. Well, she was 74 years old, so I guess she was about due anyway, but still."

Anne had not heard about this woman. She thought it was kind of weird, but she did know about the guests who came and stayed extended periods of time, never going home. She was starting to think Lexi was one of them. But the way Tammy had worded this had given Anne a strange feeling in her gut. It made her think of something; there was something vaguely familiar about what Tammy was saying. Where had she heard this? Well, she knew she hadn't heard this exact story; she'd never heard of Jane Reynolds. But what was it that made this familiar?

"And then, of course, there's Karen's people, and look at Jason and them. And you! It's been going on for next to 200 years. It's not likely to stop anytime soon or ever of course. I mean, you can look at it two different ways; is it weird? Well, yes, it is. But at the same time, it's nice too, you know? Well, of course, you know. You, I guess, would know that better than anyone right now. Oh, good grief! Look at the time. Well, look. You tell the fellas I said I'd see them, oh! Well, hey, Jerry. I'm on my way out of here. I was just telling Anne to tell y'all goodbye. I'm out of here. I'll see y'all tomorrow." Tammy took her purse from the back of the kitchen chair and hugged Jerry as he kissed her cheek. He looked uncomfortable for some reason. Tammy didn't notice this, but Anne did. Tammy left.

"Jerry? What's the matter?"

"Nothing really. Well, that's not true."

"Well? So, are you going to tell me?" Anne pressed. Jerry covered his mouth with his hand with a look of worry in his eyes. He moved his hand and sighed deeply.

"Luke was at the boarding stable today."

"So? We like Luke. Even Will likes Luke. He said Luke had an idea to offer lower prices to people who want to board a horse but can't afford y'all's yuppie prices. And Will actually agreed to give it a shot?"

"Aw, yeah. He mentioned it. It's not got anything to do with Luke's work. It's got to do with the fact that I heard Luke on the phone in the tack room. He was talking to Laurie."

"Laurie? Jason's Laurie?"

"Yeah. That'd be the Laurie," Jerry said with a frown. Anne shrugged.

"So? What's the big deal?"

"Um, she's 15. He is 19."

"Um, shall we discuss *our* age difference? He has four years on her. You have *20* on me. And I think you are beautiful, gorgeous, sweet, sexy, delectable, wonderful, and perfect. And we have a lot in common. Why is it so absurd to think he and Laurie would have things in common?"

"Gary will kill him."

"Why? That is so stupid. *He's* marrying a woman almost 20 years younger than *him*. You two are such perverts. Anyway, not only did he hook up with the same girl his own son made out with, but he also told Eric he could ask Laurie out. Hello? Eric is a senior, about to graduate. So, he's okay with Eric asking Laurie out. He's okay with banging Kylie, but he'd kill Luke for talking to Laurie on the phone? How stupid. *I* like older guys; I always have. They're sexy. My friend down the street had an uncle I was totally hot for; I was six. There was a kid in our neighborhood who had this incredibly fine daddy. He'd mow the yard in his shorts and no shirt. He had kinda long dark hair, and a great smile. His last name was Sexton. I called him *Sexy Sexton*. I was 10 or 11 years old when that started.

"It's no big deal. Younger girls often like older guys. And older guys like younger girls. Again, you and Gary are proof enough of that. There's nothing wrong with it. And since you are Gary's BFF I think you should chill him out a bit."

"His BFF?"

"Best friend forever," Anne explained.

Jerry rolled his eyes. "I think I might agree with Gary on this one, unfortunately."

"What? Why?" Anne demanded.

Jerry leaned against the counter and took a swig of Anne's tea. He looked deep in thought for a moment.

"Okay, see here, Luke is a good worker. He is a nice guy. But I think he might be a bit out of Laurie's league."

"I think that's between Luke and Laurie. And you know what? If something is meant to be it's going to be. And if they want to see each other bad enough, they'll find a way to see each other. He lives out here! He lives walking distance to Jason's. If he wanted to bad enough, he could sneak into Laurie's room every night. She could sneak down to the stable and make out with him every night. He could offer to take her riding, and they could make out in the woods. Look at us! Look at all the incredibly creative ways we've found to spend time together without anyone finding out."

"Oh, I think more people found out than we gave credit to," Jerry said dryly. Anne looked at him for a second, then dismissed it.

"I'm telling you to leave them alone and don't be an asshole snitch. Nobody likes snitches, Jerry. Don't be that person. If Gary finds out, let Gary deal with it. You butt out."

"Excuse me? Butt out?"

"Yes, butt out. Think about it. Roy knew all kinds of shit was going on between you and me. Okay, you're right. But did he run up to Will? No. He ran his mouth to Karen, yeah. But he didn't try to stop us, did he? Laurie loves you. Tell Gary and that's over. Luke isn't stupid. He knows Gary. He may not be from this sad ass little sleepy town, but he knows enough about it. And he knows enough to know Gary. So, lay off."

"I think it's a mistake." Jerry said this worriedly. Anne walked up to him.

"I think it's not our business. And the more you tell a girl she can't have a guy she wants, the harder she'll fight to get him. I promise you that. Let's look at Jason's track record in high school. Hell, Karen told me girls' parents hated him when he was *12*."

"Oh, fine! I won't tell him. But I just don't feel good about this."

"You don't have to. It's not your problem." Anne smiled. She stood on tiptoe and kissed Jerry on the mouth, a swift little kiss, and it was lucky for them it was not a more involved one because the back screen opened and slammed shut. Anne giggled, and before she even had time to move away from Jerry, Gary was in the kitchen doorway. He held a large paper bag. He looked suspiciously at the two of them. He walked in and set the bag on the table.

"Here ya go, doll. Put this in the freezer," he told Anne. Anne looked skeptically at the bag. She had a feeling she knew what it was. She sighed.

"What is it?"

"Deer meat! Deer steaks, deer sausages, deer chuck, deer jerky," Gary told her as Jerry looked through the bag.

"Aw, man! Thanks! We were about out." Jerry proceeded to unload the bag.

Anne asked something she'd wondered about before.

"What's the deal with you, anyway, Jerry? You have nine guns, a smokehouse, and you live out here in the middle of nowhere. Why don't you hunt? I mean, I don't wish you did, but I am kinda curious. That's weird to me. You eat his deer and turkey and things that *he* kills but you don't hunt?"

"I *used* to hunt. We grew up hunting. When I moved to Blacksburg I didn't so much, unless I was here on a break. But well, that first fall we lived back here, Roy went hunting and brought home a deer. And Will was four. He saw the deer and broke down in tears and told Roy he was mean for killing it. Then another time, Roy brought home three rabbits, and Will saw them and thought they were alive, and that Roy brought them home to be nice. When Will saw they were dead, he cried and cried. He didn't talk to Roy for days. After that, Roy and I just didn't want to hunt anymore. We felt terrible after what it did to Will. Now, we see animals and just don't even think about killing them. Gary kills them for us. And we thank you for that, friend," Jerry tossed to Gary. Gary shook his head.

"That was all very sweet and shit 40 years ago, but don't you think Will could handle it by now?" Gary asked with a smirk.

"Oh, I don't think *I* could though. And no, actually, I don't think Will could either. You don't see how he acts when he sees animals out here. He gets all goony. I mean he acts kinda like a girl. It's embarrassing really. But like I said, we all kinda got that way. We like to see the animals out here, wandering around like they feel safe here. Well, not so much the cougars. Other than the cougars, yeah," Jerry pointed out. He started loading the white paper wrapped meat up in his arms.

"Help me put this in freezer, Mama."

Anne helped Jerry put his beloved deer meat in the deep freezer, on the service porch.

"Oh, did anyone come up here and talk to you today about your ghosts?" Gary asked them. They both looked at him oddly. Jerry shook his head.

"No. Not that I know of. Anne?"

"Don't you think I'd have told you something like that?"

"Simple *yes* or *no* would be sufficient, darling."

"No. What kind of people?" Anne asked Gary. Gary shrugged.

"Oh, some dried-up looking fella from Clifton Forge. He was looking for y'all. Wanted to talk to you about your ghosts, he said,"

"Clifton Forge? He came all the way down here from Clifton Forge? You'd have thought he'd have called first before making a jaunt like that. He just wasted a couple hours." Jerry took another swig of Anne's tea. Anne made him a glass before he drank all hers.

"Well, maybe it wasn't such a waste. You haven't even talked to him yet. How do you know what he even wants to talk about?" Gary argued.

"You just said so yourself, our ghosts."

"So? Maybe he just wants to talk. Maybe he doesn't want to come in here and do any of those silly investigations. Maybe he just wants to come to talk to you about the history. Maybe he just hopes to see if he can see actual evidence that ghosts are here," Gary tried reasoning.

Immediately after Gary said that, the chair at the table pulled back, then the faucet turned itself on. The radio turned itself on, blasting the Eagles, then the empty paper bag that had held the deer meat flung itself to the floor. The kitchen light turned itself off. Then the chair moved back to the table. Jerry, Gary, and Anne looked around the room. Jerry started laughing.

"What ghosts?"

CHAPTER 28

A nne left the kitchen to leave Gary and Jerry alone. She also wanted to go upstairs and get another one of Faye's notebooks out of the cedar chest. Tammy had taken her time leaving today. Then, Anne had to talk to Jerry about Laurie's love life, and then Gary had to show up with more damn deer meat. Then, Faye (or someone) decided on a late afternoon haunting in the kitchen. So, even though Anne was a little late getting up to Jerry's room, she still had until at least 5:15. Will never came in until 5:15 or 5:30.

Anne had been reading Faye's notebooks on the quiet and was surprised how quickly she went through them. She found it fascinating reading. She learned that Will had always been obnoxious. He had been obnoxious since he came into the world apparently. Anne was only in Will's second year and already Anne was admiring Faye's parenting methods. She truly was everything she'd been made out to be.

And Jerry! Good grief! Faye had the patience of a saint. Jerry was outstanding at parenting now, but Anne learned that those first couple of years, Jerry was apparently terrified of Will. He took him to the doctor 11 times before Will was three weeks old. He called from the school every day to check on him. He was a nervous wreck. And poor Faye felt she had two children to tend to.

Faye had very little trouble out of Will. He was a good baby, and Faye was constantly stopped on the street by his admirers.

He was exceptionally alert and would watch things for long periods of time. He would watch Faye intently as she did things around the apartment. Whenever adults around him were talking, he'd stare at them as if trying his best to follow the conversation. This was first noticed at just two weeks old. He slept a regular schedule, seldom waking in the night. He rarely cried. He smiled his first real smile at just five weeks, when Jerry had a sneezing fit in front of him. He was sensitive to loud noises and had no health problems (contrary to what his father thought). He ate cream of wheat at one week old, in addition to his breastmilk diet. He was a happy, healthy, beautiful baby.

Anne saw what happened; Will had set such a high standard at such an early age that Faye was worried the next one wouldn't even compare. In her journal, Faye even said *Why do people make such a fuss about how hard being a mother is? Especially a new mother? This child is an angel, a Godsend, perfection in every way. He's perfect, and he's happy, and I just can't imagine any other child in the world comparing to this one. They keep telling me he's not like most babies. Well, then I think I'll just stick with this one! I don't need another one! Why would I? I have the perfect child and the perfect husband. I have everything in the world I could ever need.*

Well, that alone made Anne want to vomit. Faye obviously made the mistake of telling Will these things at some point. That'd explain his obnoxious OCD. Faye had pinned him as *perfect* since he came into the world, so Will obviously felt a need to live up to this. Anne liked her kids and all, but she didn't feel compelled to build them an alter or anything.

Then, as Will started walking and talking, he became even more obnoxious. He started talking at just seven months. Faye pointed out this was considered profoundly advanced by Will's pediatrician. Will's first word wasn't even normal. He didn't say mama or dada. No, nothing normal for Will. Will's first word had been germ. Whenever he would drop his pacifier, he'd hold it up to Faye and say *"germ"*. He took his first steps at seven months and three days old. He didn't even take a step and fall. He walked nine whole steps from the chair to the table. He was feeding himself four days after he took those steps.

By the time Will was two, Jerry and Faye were certain they had a child genius on their hands (something that would be confirmed at 17 years old, when an IQ test showed him scoring 184, just 16 points shy of being considered an unmeasurable genius). Yes, he was a very bright child. Nobody ever doubted that. His personality just made him shine brighter.

Faye was a mother though, and like any mother, she did have some trials and errors along the way. Anne learned that Faye didn't know what she was doing, wasn't getting much help from the paranoid Jerry, and desperately wanted to go home to get her mother's help. She was surrounded by students in Blacksburg. She didn't really know very many women with children. Her only time to really meet people was when she took night cosmetology classes. Faye just did what she could, as any new mother does. Every time she'd think she was failing miserably at something Will would do something outstanding that would reassure her. And any time she would begin to worry she was not being a great enough wife to Jerry Granger, Jerry would let her know right quick that she was wrong.

Those first two years had been very difficult for Faye, Anne learned. Anne had been given the impression that Faye was perfect, that Faye had it all figured out, that Faye was outstanding at what she did, the perfect mom, wife, and member of the church and community. And Anne realized that it was true. Faye *had* been perfect. Faye had perfectly pulled off being a new mom at just 19 years old. She had perfectly managed to keep her husband and child happy and well cared for. And perhaps by the time she got back home to those who knew her, she *had* perfected this whole mom thing. Anne would find out in future notebooks.

But it boiled down to the fact that like Anne, Faye had her own set of obstacles. She wasn't given an instruction manual telling her how to make everything work out. She just figured it out. And she had done it so wonderfully, so effortlessly, that her own son and husband thought it had just come naturally for her, that she just had it in her the whole time. In truth, it was quietly acquired and learned through mistakes, questions, praying, and a few mild nervous breakdowns in the kitchen of the one-bedroom Apartment Heights apartment in Blacksburg. The breakdowns were done alone, when Jerry was in class or at practice and Will was asleep. They never saw her act like she couldn't handle things. They never even saw her act like things were difficult.

Was it a blessing? Or was it a mistake? In those first two years, Faye apparently listened to a lot of the Eagles (preferring their sadder drinking songs) and drinking vodka on the quiet. She never got drunk; she couldn't. She had a child to take care of. Faye made sure she put her child and husband first, even when she really wanted to get plastered. It was a rewarding two years though. Faye grew up quicker than she ever thought she'd have to, and she learned things on her own. She managed the best she could, and she smiled when people saw her. She would wipe tears of frustration from her cheeks, wash her face, and reapply her powder before Jerry made it home. As Faye saw it, as long as the tears were gone before he got home, she was succeeding.

Faye knew Jerry had worries, and things on his own mind. She knew he wasn't planning on being a father at 20 years old. She was proud of Jerry for sticking it out, and she was proud of him for never really faltering. He worried about the baby, but he never showed her he was worried about them as a family. He never showed her how nervous he really was, but Faye knew. Faye knew because she had known this man since he was five years old.

She knew what was really on Jerry's mind, and he knew that despite the smiles and the clean apartment and meals on the table like clockwork, Faye was struggling a little herself. The disappearing vodka was evidence of that. But Jerry being Jerry knew Faye well enough to know she would die if he found out she was not on top of things. She wanted him to be so proud of her, just like she was of him.

So, Faye pretended to have no worries so Jerry would be proud of how well she handled things. Jerry pretended to believe her so she would be proud of how well she was managing. He made sure he was always readily available though, should she ever decide to come clean. Yes, he did feel much of it had come naturally for her, but he also knew that it was also only natural that there'd be a few bumps along the way.

In turn, Jerry pretended to have no worries either, so Faye would think everything was taken care of and he had this whole thing under control. And Faye pretended to believe him, so he'd feel like he was succeeding at being the head of the household. And over the years, this desire to make the other one feel important and successful and perfect was exactly what made their marriage work so well.

As time would pass, they'd talk about those difficult times. But by then, they were able to talk about them with smiles. During these conversations, they were simply reminded how much they loved one another. They learned that from the very beginning they'd both been willing to do whatever in the world it took to reassure the other one. They spent 37 years reassuring Will that he was the most wonderful thing in their world. This was something Faye would do even in death. From the day she said "I do" to Jerry Granger, she went to all lengths at all costs to prove her love to him and to support him. She did whatever she possibly could to show the same love and support to Will. Faye had no intention of letting something like dying stop her from doing that now.

Yes, Anne learned a lot about Faye by reading about Will's first two years. She learned a lot about Will, and she even learned more about Jerry. All it did was confirm what Anne had suspected all along. This was an extraordinary family. Jerry *had* always been an excellent husband and father and provider. Faye had always been a fabulous wife and mother. And Will had always been a wonderful son and overachiever. Faye had noted that she knew they weren't perfect, but they tried. Anne smiled at this. Faye was wrong; they *were* perfect. They may not have been perfect people, but they were a perfect family. They were perfect for each other.

Anne was able now to look back at the things she herself had been trying so hard to prove. She had started as a homeless housekeeper who wanted to prove she deserved a job and a place to stay. Then, she saw the magnitude of this position and felt the need to prove she could handle it, all of it, the house, the horses, the nightmares, the drinking binges, the meals, and the ghosts. Then, she felt the need to prove she could be the lady of this house, a wife and mother who would live up to the very high standards and expectations set by her deceased mother-in-law.

There had been many times Anne had found herself alone, with the spiral notebook of Faye's laughing with her mother-in-law, laughing with her, worrying about her, and understanding her, and getting to know her. Anne learned that those high standards and high expectations weren't there really. If Anne wanted to be like Faye, she was finding out that she already was.

Anne went into Jerry's bedroom now and shut his heavy door behind her. Jerry and Gary were laughing very loud about something downstairs. She kneeled before Jerry's cedar chest and opened it and reached for the next two notebooks. She thought better of it and grabbed another one. She put everything else back how it was in the chest, closed the top, and stood. She paused as she saw something on the bed. She walked around the massive tester bed and picked up a note. It was like one of the notes that Anne had found in the drawer in the pantry. It was one of the notes that Faye had left Jerry so many years ago. Anne looked at it. She looked at it and felt a smile and a tear at the same time.

Just another love note because I'll never be able to tell you enough how much you are loved. But I'll never stop trying to show you. Your wonderful wife- Me

Anne set the note down very carefully, exactly where she found it. Had Jerry put this here, or had Faye? Anne remembered the drawer of notes she found open, in the pantry. She didn't know the story here; had Faye accessed the notes or had Jerry? It wasn't Anne's concern. She left it alone. She made her way back downstairs and put the notebook on the shelf in the back hall. She went back to the kitchen, where Jerry was alone now. She was baffled.

"Where'd Gary go already?"

"He went to Jason's to drop off more deer meat. I'm going to go shower before Will gets in though; I got nasty today. Gimme kiss, Mama." Jerry puckered his lips and put his hands on Anne's back. He kissed her sweetly on the cheek, and she returned it on his mouth. It was a very brief kiss. He smiled at her for this and took her face in his hands. He didn't kiss her though. He pressed his forehead to hers and just closed his eyes. He then wrapped her in his arms and just held her for several minutes.

"I love you," he whispered in her ear.

"I love you too."

"I love you very much. Especially since I smell beef tips cooking," he murmured. They both laughed softly. They held one another for a few more minutes. He kissed her forehead and patted her back. She went back to work in the kitchen, and he went to shower. Anne began to pull down the plates to set the table.

"Mommy?" James asked from behind her. Anne turned to answer him.

"Yes, James?" She set the plates on the table.

"You said tell you if we see a snake." Anne immediately freaked out.

"Oh no! Did you see a snake?"

"No, but we saw a bear."

"A ... *bear?*"

"It's a big black bear. He's by Papa's truck," James said calmly.

Jerry's truck was parked only about 20 feet from the fenced-in yard the kids played in. Anne had to remember to breathe before she ran out the kitchen, screaming for Jerry. She went out the back door to retrieve Eliza who was in the yard still. Anne stepped out onto the porch and ran down the steps. She opened the gate and searched the yard for Eliza in panic. While scanning the yard, her eyes fell on an enormous black bear. It had to have been around 300 pounds. It was in the process of investigating the little fence surrounding the yard. Anne called Eliza's name, and Eliza's smiling face appeared in the window of the playhouse.

Anne had flashbacks of the cougar but really had no choice. She couldn't decide whether to move slowly and carefully or run like hell. She decided on a cross of both. As she was making her way across the yard, Luke and Will came running from the stable, toward the play yard. Will yelled to get the bear's attention. The bear looked from Will to Anne. Luke started walking toward the bear trying to distract it. Will realized what he was doing and made his way to the fenced-in yard quickly, where he jumped over the fence and met Anne near the playhouse. He opened the door and went in and snatched Eliza up. As he grabbed Anne's arm and made his way to the gate, Jerry appeared on the back porch with a rifle. He shot at the bear, deliberately missing it. The shot was enough to send the bear in the opposite direction, though. Jerry shot the gun two more times. Luke watched as it ran right past him, not 10 feet away from him. Luke was awestruck. He had never seen a bear besides in a zoo. And here, a tremendous black bear was just 10 feet away!

Anne and Will made their way to the porch where Jerry stood with his gun, and James stood behind him watching the excitement. Anne collapsed in relief in the porch chair. Jerry frowned at the retreating bear. He shook his head.

"We're getting another dog," he said to Will, who was still trying to catch his breath.

"Another dog?"

"A big dog. I want a dog that stays with these kids, stays in the yard. I want a dog that stays with Anne and the kids. We have dogs that protect the livestock. I want a dog that protects my family." Jerry patted James on the back and went back inside.

Will had lived out here his entire life. This kind of thing didn't happen often enough to live in fear. There was the occasional wildlife on the property, but they weren't ever a problem. This was a problem. If the bear had reason to think there was a reason to return, he would return. Will had gotten a good look at the bear. It was a male, 300 to 350 pounds. Bears used to keep to themselves a lot more than they have here lately, which was a problem where Will's family was concerned. Will agreed they needed a dog who would stay with the kids and at least alert people if it saw something.

Luke made his way to the porch.

"Okay, I know that was not a good thing that just happened, but that was really something else! That thing was huge! A bear! A real live bear!"

"It's lucky it's not a real *dead* one. Dad could have killed it had he wanted to," Will responded. Anne went inside. She saw Jerry standing next to sink drinking tea. She walked up to him and put her hand on his arm. "My God. You were so so so awesome and so absolutely gorgeous when you came out there on the porch and shot that big ass gun at the bear. You were just flat out *hot*."

Jerry looked at her oddly. He tried not to smile but he blushed as he shook his head. "You are crazy," he told her.

"No. I've just never seen you act all mountain man and shit. And baby, I *like* it." She winked at him.

Will and Luke came inside then with the kids. Jerry was grinning, his face turning pink. Will noticed this, but Luke started talking.

"You need a Rottweiler. We had two when I was growing up. They're great protectors. They're great with kids. They're really good dogs. Some people think they're aggressive killers but they're not. Well, I mean, unless they're trained to be. Boxers are good too. We had one of those," Luke informed them all.

"Rottweilers? They're pretty. Kim has had them for years. I agree, they'd be a good breed to look at." Will sat at the table. The house phone rang. Jerry answered it. It was Roy.

"Hello?" Jerry greeted him.

"What the fuck is going on over there? Who was shooting guns? What were y'all shooting? I tried calling the cell phones, but you and Will didn't answer! What happened?"

"My phone is in the bedroom. I was about to take a shower when I heard Anne hollering. Will? Well, I don't know where his phone is. We kinda had a situation, and phones were the last thing on our minds. It was a bear, brother. A big son of a bitch. I'm figuring about 300 at least, maybe more. He was making his way over the play yard fence! James and Liza had been out there playing. I came running down the stairs, and James is there in the hall and tells me a bear is in the yard! So, I grabbed my rifle and went outside and started shooting. He ran toward Jason's place incidentally. I mean, I know there's a good bit of ground between here and there, but I'm just letting y'all know to look out around there."

"You didn't shoot it?"

"No, I didn't shoot it. I shot at it. It's not a common problem here. I don't want to kill the wildlife unless I feel it's absolute necessary. We're getting another dog though. I want a dog to stay with these kids outside. Caleb already wanders around here, going between the house and barn and stable and shit."

"You should've shot the damn thing, Jerry. It'll probably come back. Kids okay, I guess?"

"Yeah. Anne went running out there to get Eliza, and Will and Luke saw the whole thing and came running. Luke distracted the bear so Will could get to Eliza. As soon as Will dragged Anne and 'Liza away, I shot the gun. It took off."

"Yeah, get a dog. Get a Rottweiler. Kim knows where to find them. Keep Patton with the kids in the meantime. He can stay with the livestock at night but stay with kids during the day. And hey, tell Luke *thank you* for me. Sounds like he was quite handy this evening."

"He was, and I will. I'll go into town tomorrow and talk to Kim," Jerry assured Roy.

Jerry hung up, and Will excused himself to take his shower.

Luke remained standing. Jerry gestured for him to sit down. Luke sat down.

Jerry sat at the head of the table.

"Roy said to tell you thanks for helping us out today with that. I want to tell you that, too."

"Oh, thanks but you know I'd do it. I'd have done it even if Will wasn't there. I'd never let anything happen to these kids or Anne, or Jason's kids or any of these women out here. Y'all know that." Luke fumbled with a napkin. Jerry nodded.

"Yeah, son. I guess I did know that."

"Well, since you saved lives and all, would you like to join us for dinner? Beef tips and rice with homemade bread," Anne coaxed. Luke looked at Jerry, who nodded.

"You're welcome to, if you like,"

So, Anne retreated upstairs to let Will know they'd be having company for dinner. He enjoyed hosting company, so he was fine with this. Anne brushed her hair and got the kids washed up. They were all waiting for Will when he came back downstairs.

They said the blessing, ate their supper, and finished with dessert. Then, the men went to the library to visit and talk horses and dogs. Anne and the kids watched television in the living room. By the time Luke left an hour later, Anne and the kids had completely fallen asleep on the couch. Will and Jerry just looked at them for a moment. Will sighed.

"Anne, baby, get up. Let's get the kids to bed."

Jerry went to the couch and gathered Eliza in his arms. Will picked up the sleeping James and looked back at Anne, who didn't respond. He and Jerry took the two kids upstairs and put them to bed. After the kids were tucked in, Will said he'd just let Anne sleep in the living room. She was obviously exhausted. Jerry nodded.

"Well, I'll grab her a blanket. I'm going back downstairs anyway."

"Dad? Do you think Jason and Lexi are okay? I mean, do you think all this is just temporary, or do you think it's something bad?"

"I think Jason and Lexi need to pay more attention to Jason and Lexi and less attention to us and what happens in our house. I think there are some things that need to be addressed. But I think these things are minor and could be an easy fix. Why? What brought that up?"

"Lexi thought Jason was screwing around with someone named Claudia," Will began.

"Oh, yeah. I heard about that," Jerry remembered.

"How'd you hear about it?"

"Aw, me and Lexi got into it today; she was an absolute bitch at the diner. She was just a creep to poor ol' Caleb. We came home and didn't talk on the way, and then she and I got into it once we got home. I told Anne what happened. Anne went outside to talk to her, and she was apparently crying. She and Anne ended up kinda arguing I think and that's when Lexi told her Jason was messing around with that Claudia chick. I hadn't ever heard of anyone named that though, not around here. You know who it is?"

"I do now. She isn't from around here, that's why you don't know her. She isn't Jason's side dish either; she's the lawyer who's representing Laurie."

"Representing Laurie? For what?"

"She wants to change her name to Connelly. Jason expects a problem out of Stacy. So, he hired a lawyer for Laurie. She's from all the way over in Bastian."

"Why the hell did he get someone from all the way in Bastian?" Jerry asked.

"Someone referred him to her. He wanted someone from out of town who would be impartial to be fair to Stacy. Any local lawyer will side with Gary."

"Whatever. So, he's not sleeping with her?"

"Well, he says he's not. He seemed a bit surprised by the accusation, so I guess I believe him. Like Anne said, when the hell would he have time to have an affair?"

"Well, he makes numerous trips to town throughout the week. A trip to the therapist here, a trip to the co-op there, I guess he could make it work if he wanted to. But I don't see him wanting to. I don't think he'd have gone through all the trouble he's gone through for Lex and those kids if he wasn't in love. I think he's changed. He's had a lot on his back here the past couple years. He could've left anytime he wanted to. You're not the easiest person to work for. He elected to stay, to stick it out. He wouldn't have done that unless he wanted to. And I don't think he did it for him. I think he did it for his woman and children."

"I am not difficult to work for."

"Oh, fuck, Will. You're the biggest pain in the ass in the world to work for. I didn't say you weren't a good boss. I just said you're a pain in the ass. And don't act all surprised. As much time as you spent in gifted classes, you should have sense enough to know you can be a creep. Your uncle says that's what makes you good at what you do though. You're not all soft and shit. You don't put up with mediocre. You expect the best, and that's exactly what you get. All I'm saying is, Jason elected to stick around and work for you. He could have left."

"Jason works *with* me."

"No, son. He works *for* you. He knows it. We all know it. He may be a partner, but he works for you. He knows fully well that he'd never in a thousand years be able to pull his job off without you breathing down his back every day. He does his job as well as he does because you make him. Again, not saying that's a bad thing.

"My point is, he has a lot on his plate right now and his hormonal insecure wife isn't helping any. They'll figure it out though. He's figuring it out. In some cases, I think he's getting a little big headed, to be honest.

He's proud of what he's done and he's proud of what he's got. I don't see him screwing any of that up. I'm going downstairs. Good night, son."

"You'll get her a blanket? You'll take care of Anne?" Will asked Jerry as Jerry started down the stairs. With his back to Will, Jerry smiled.

"Yes, Will. I'll take care of Anne."

Jerry found humor in the way Will had worded that; Jerry's mind went to impure thoughts, which is what had made him smile. But now in the living room, Jerry did just as a father-in-law would do. He grabbed a blanket from the cedar chest that served as a coffee table. He laid it over his darling Anne. She stretched, mumbled in her sleep, and was quiet and still again. He smiled at her and leaned over, kissing her cheek.

He was headed for his recliner and looked around for the remote. When he couldn't find it, he realized it must have been on the couch with Anne. He sighed and went back to the couch. He felt around the cushions behind Anne and then under Anne. He pushed her back a little and found the remote right under her breast. He sighed again and thought for a moment. *It's a boob. Its Anne's boob, and God knows I've already touched that enough for it to not even matter anymore.* So, he took the remote. Immediately, Jerry heard his wife behind him.

"Oh, Jerry. *Really?*"

"I was getting the remote! I was not fondling her! And I *could* have had I wanted to! Go away. You read way too much into everything. You didn't nag this much when you were *alive*. What happened to you anyway? You cross over and turn into an informant for the secret service? Just stop it. Sit down and watch Mary Tyler Moore and behave or go haunt someone else. I've had a long day with women and kids and bears and all kinds of shit. I want some quiet." He directed the remote at Faye, pretending to turn her off.

Jerry got to his recliner and saw a piece of folded paper in the seat. He felt a tug in his gut. He picked it up and set the remote on the table. He read the note. It was one of the ones she'd left him years ago, one of the notes from the drawer.

I love you I love you I love you I love you I love you I love you. A lot. More than you'll ever know~ You Know Who

Jerry folded the note back and held it to his lips for a moment. Tears welled up in his blue eyes. The corners of his mouth turned down, threatening to cry. He looked across the room, at the hazy spirit of his wife, in front of the fireplace.

"I love you too, baby. A lot and trust me, I love you more and more every day. But you've really truly gotten so annoying. But have a seat. Watch some TV with me."

Jerry sat in his recliner and pulled the footrest up. H turned Mary Tyler Moore up just a little, but not too much so he wouldn't wake Anne up. And on the other side of the little table beside Jerry's recliner, Faye's rocking chair began rocking.

CHAPTER 29

⁌

Gary had delivered the excess deer meat, making room in his deep freezer for the spring turkey he'd be acquiring soon. He made several phone calls that day regarding the spring festival that'd happen this Saturday. Sunday was Easter, and he was glad; he could expect a good turnout and that'd help him get more money for Bird's tombstone.

He went to Main Street Diner since Kylie would be late again. If he cooked supper, he'd have dirty dishes to deal with, and he didn't want to deal with that. He went inside and sat down at his favorite table. Almost immediately he felt someone standing beside him. He looked up and broke into a grin at the smiling waitress.

"Jahnese! What are you doing here? You're in the wrong diner, doll."

Jahnese Hobson started laughing and shoved him playfully on the shoulder. She was always such a happy person; it was difficult to not like her. Her mother was Nellie, who Karen had been lifelong friends with. She had the same laughing brown eyes as her mother and her hair was a riot of curls. Just seeing Jahnese always lightened Gary's mood. She pulled out her order pad.

"When Tammy up and ran off to work for the Grangers, they had an opening here. The hours are better than at Jenson's, and well, they pay a little more. So here I am. This is my second day," she said proudly.

"And they hadn't fired you yet, huh? Well, you're doing good then, I guess. If they give you a hard time here, you let me know." He winked. She laughed.

"I'll do that. Hey, I know what y'all are doing for Gap and Bird. Here, take this from me. I don't go to y'all's church, so I'll give it to you now. It's for Bird." Jahnese dug tips out of her pocket and handed some folded bills and a handful of change to Gary.

"If you tell Reverend Carter about what y'all are doing, I'll bet he'd get our congregation to chip in too. Have you thought about doing that?" she asked.

Gary was touched by her donation and a little surprised by her suggestion. Albert Carter was the preacher at Fishpond Church, which was where majority of the black residents of Liberty Creek attended church. It was the church Karen had attended all her life.

"Well, no, I can't say that I have. Middleton said he'd cover whatever we couldn't raise, but I'm sure he'd appreciate not having to cover *as much*. I'll get in touch with Carter. That's a wonderful idea, thank you. And thank you very, very much for the donation."

"It should be about $15. I hope it helps. I like Gap, even if he does still try to get me to sit on his old lap." She shook her head. Gary laughed.

"Well, he's been trying for 35 years, Jahnese. You have to admire his persistence."

"What do you want to eat?" she asked smiling. Gary decided on the club sandwich and fries with a Coke. She wrote it down and disappeared behind the counter. Gary looked around and found a newspaper on the counter. He took it.

"Why don't you read the ones at the co-op?" someone asked.

He saw Walter Loftis sitting at the counter. Walter was smiling. He was making attempt to befriend Gary and worried now that he'd gone about it wrong. Gary smirked.

"Aren't you sitting at the wrong bar? The Tavern is across the street. How are you, Loftis?"

"Oh, I'm okay. I'm just getting supper."

"Do you want to join me?" Gary asked politely.

It was a question technically. But somehow, even given his short time here, Walter knew it was really more of a suggestion. Walter looked around for a moment and gathered his drink and silverware. He joined Gary. Gary folded his paper up and set it on the table. He looked at Walter.

"So, when are you going to tell me about yourself?"

"What do you want to know?"

"Why are you here?"

"To eat supper; I told you that."

"Why are you *here*, in Liberty Creek?"

"Corbin is retiring. There's gonna be a need for a new large animal vet. I was looking for somewhere new to go. This sounded like a good idea. Faulkner and I went to school together in Charlottesville. We kept in touch. He suggested I give this a shot; I needed a change."

"A change from what? Charlottesville is nice enough," Gary argued.

"I wasn't in Charlottesville anymore."

"You know, no matter where you come from, we do things a little different here."

"Yeah, I get that impression."

"Do you, now? Why's that? Oh, thank you Jahnese."

"Well, I may be a foreigner to you screwed up people, but even a foreigner can see that this town is fairly unorthodox. Even a blind, deaf, *dead* foreigner can see that. It doesn't take being in this place a week to see it, Gary."

"Well, I'm a bit interested in what you've observed, Walter. I don't know everything, but I like to think our little town is fairly well behaved. So, what is it that has you concerned?"

Walter looked at Gary and sighed. He realized a little too late he'd likely already said too much. He should have remembered what Jonathan had told him. He should have had that shit memorized. Twelve people in this town who ran things? Of course, Gary was one of them. Why else would Keith have advised him to go to church to get in good with Gary? Of course, there were reasons why it was a good idea to get in good with Gary.

"Oh, Gary. Come on, friend. It's just the stuff that goes on every day. You hear things, you see things, you just learn things," Walter said this with a trace of boredom, in Gary's opinion.

Honestly, it was a trace of discomfort that Gary had simply misinterpreted. Gary leaned forward his folded arms rested on the table. He smiled but it was nothing close to being friendly.

410

"First things first; I'm not your friend. That will come in time. Maybe. I don't know you and you don't know me. And I don't trust or even particularly like anyone I don't know. You shouldn't either, especially in this town. In this town, you need to make it a top priority to get to know everyone. I do mean *everyone*. Because you will be living among everyone. There is no right or wrong side of the tracks here, Walter. We don't *have* any tracks. The doctor sits next to the farmer and the plumber sits next to the lawyer. And you get over it. We don't do uppity. If you live in this town, you learn to live with everybody. And if you can't do that, we can help you leave real quick. That's first.

"Second, I don't know what you're hearing or seeing or learning but you have peaked my interest. Tell me more."

"You need a refill, chief?" Jahnese asked with raised brows. She had overheard that one last thing Gary had said to Walter and that was all she needed to hear. She wanted to get away right quick. The less she heard of this conversation, the happier she'd be.

"Yes, dearest. And add Mr. Loftis's ticket to mine."

Jahnese took Gary's glass and returned with Gary's refill plus his and Walter's orders. She put them on the table and left the two men staring at each other. Walter rubbed his eyes.

"So, I'm supposed to tell you everything I see and hear? Why? So, I can get my ass beat on a dark street corner one night for talking? Fuck that."

"Ah, you're already familiar enough with us to know you'll get your ass beat on a dark corner. Come on, now, Walter. You can see it one of two ways. Let me know what you know and keep shit tight between us or keep shit to yourself and remain a threat as far as I'm concerned. I told you, I don't trust anyone I don't know. And here you go, trying to call me *friend* while admitting you'll withhold shit from me? I tell you what, Walter. That's kinda ass backwards if you ask me."

"Why do you care so much what's going on anyway? Every single thing that happens in this town has to be brought to your attention?" Walter asked. Gary just smiled. Walter sighed.

"I've been advised by a local, Gary. He seems like a fairly good one to listen to. And I'm just covering my ass, man. I don't know everyone yet. I don't know which ones of you are psychopaths, which ones of you are okay, which ones of you aren't. I don't know who will stab me in the back or who will take me to the ER when it happens. I don't know any of you yet. I am so sorry I'm a bit hesitant to write a damn tell-all about people who truly frighten me! Yes! I'm scared of you people! You're all fucking nuts. You are all weird, weird, weird people and you have *got* to know it!" Walter took a swig of his 7-Up and ate a bite of his hot roast beef sandwich. He thought if he chewed for a while, Gary wouldn't ask him any questions until he was done. Gary took a few bites of his own sandwich, then smiled again. Walter rolled his eyes.

"Oh, stop with the smiling, Gary! You're not happy. There's nothing to smile about."

"This reliable source of yours, what'd they tell you? I'm just wanting to make sure nothing was left out, you see."

"There's 12 people who run things around here. I was also told to get in good with you. Why is that Gary? If you don't mind my asking."

"Cause I'm just a really nice guy and therefore a really great friend to have."

"Yeah, I'm sure that's it," Walter muttered. He looked around the diner. Nobody sat anywhere near them, despite the fact numerous empty tables were available. Jahnese brought Gary the ticket. He gestured for her to wait a moment while he took money from his wallet and handed her cash. Then, he smoothly slipped an additional bill in her hand.

"Keep the change, Jahnese. You didn't hear anything that Mr. Loftis and I said here today, did you?" Gary asked with a grin and a wink. Jahnese looked down at the handful of cash. She understood and returned the smile. As far as she was concerned for a $20 tip (which Walter watched her pocket) she didn't hear shit. As Walter watched this exchange, he understood many, many, things immediately. He was suddenly very nervous.

It wasn't an exaggeration. It wasn't a local joke. Gary had this town wrapped around his finger and even the waitresses here had his back. Walter had just literally watched Gary pass Jahnese *hush money* and she wasn't the least bit surprised or confused. This wasn't the first time Jahnese Hobson had witnessed an interesting conversation between

Gary Connelly and someone else. And it wasn't the first time she'd been bribed to keep whatever she heard to herself. This was painfully evident to Walter. She smiled almost apologetically to Walter and left the table. Gary looked back at Walter. He balled up a napkin and set it carefully in the ashtray. Walter watched this, waiting.

"Walter, whether or not you get your ass kicked in this town is up to you. You know that? I want to like you; I mean, think about it! You're in my town! Of course, I want to like you. I don't want anyone here that I don't like. So, just work with me."

"And you're the preacher?" Walter asked in amazement.

"Not *the* preacher. I'm doing a favor for a friend. And ask anyone; I'm a pretty good preacher. They like having me up there. I look out for people around here, Walter. If you're part of my town, I'm going to look out for you. Lots of us will. But if you're an ass, you won't be here for long. If you're good, and care about our little town, well, we'll have your back. You can count on anyone to help you out. But it's a simple *deal.* You help us keep peace and order and you'll be appreciated by the whole town. You become part of the problem, and you'll be dealt with accordingly."

Walter looked at Gary very hard for what seemed an eternity. His gut was starting to hurt. He wanted to go home, now. He looked around and lowered his voice. His voice was unsteady.

"Fine. You have a deal." Walter rubbed his forehead. He didn't know if this was putting him in the clear or setting himself up to be killed. He felt like he'd just sold his soul in the middle of the diner. He looked back at Gary.

"Stacy ... Mitchell? She used to date Jason?" Walter asked quietly.

"Yes. She's my granddaughter's mother. Why?"

"She's in trouble. Well, maybe, I don't really know. Some guy, I don't remember his name, he was in The Tavern when she came in the other night looking for ... I think his name is Jack. When I left, I heard him outside talking to her on the phone. They're having an affair. He was mad she was looking for Jack and threatened to do something to her. He didn't really appear to be drunk. He was mad as fuck though, Gary. When he hung up, he busted his truck window out with his fist.

I didn't know him, so I didn't know if he was full of shit or if he's really going to do something to her. But he sounded serious. I thought about going back in The Tavern and telling Keith, but I didn't want word to get out that I was starting trouble around here already," Walter finished. Gary looked intrigued.

"You don't know who it was?"

"I *really* don't remember the name."

"So, find out. And Wednesday? I'll pick you up at 4 a.m."

"Four? What for?" Walter asked indignantly.

Gary stood up and feigned a look of surprise.

"We're going hunting, remember? Get a name for me. I'll be in touch." Gary stood up and dropped a business card on the table. It was from the Liberty Creek Police Dept. Walter thought he'd been retired from the PD for a while now.

"The bottom number is where to reach me. Have a good one, Walter."

Gary walked past Jahnese, who was wiping a table, patted her on the back, and left. Walter rubbed his forehead some more before he stood to leave. He just wanted to go home. But he remembered what Gary had said. Walter looked around as he slipped into The Tavern. It was early so hopefully not many people would be in there. He was right.

The low lighting made Walter feel better, safer. George Strait was singing on the jukebox, and three men were gathered at the pool table. That was it. Keith smiled as Walter made his way to the bar.

"Always nice to see my regulars!" Keith said, as he put a bottle of Walter's favorite beer on the bar. Walter thanked him and sat down.

"So, ummm, what's going on in here tonight?"

"Early yet, not much yet. Give it a few more hours," Keith told him. Walter nodded.

"The other night? Friday was it? That Stacy gal was in here. Did she ever find Jack?" Walter said this with a little laugh, as if just making idle conversation.

"Oh, hell. I don't know. She hasn't been back."

"I guess you gotta be careful around here, huh? Everyone knowing everyone else, you never know who's watching. I mean, even that other

414

fella that was in here, the one you talked to after Stacy left? What was his name again? Even he knew Stacy?" Walter asked, trying to sound nonchalant.

Keith looked at him oddly, though.

"I don't know," Keith replied, trying to remember.

"Oh, yeah you do. Some guy came up to the counter, and you said you didn't realize he was still here. You asked him if he saw Stacy in here looking for Jack?" Walter was suddenly worried that Keith wouldn't remember, and Walter desperately wanted a name to give Gary. Keith looked thoughtful for a minute.

"Ohhhh, Randy Meadows. He's who you're talking about."

"Randy! That's right. Yeah, that's right."

"Why do you care?"

"Oh, didn't say I cared. I was just talking. Trying to get all these crazy ass people around here straight. I don't know anyone; I told you that."

"Well, Stacy, Randy and Jack are the last three people I'd suggest you try to familiarize yourself with. Stay far away from them, Walter. Far away."

"Well, the way I see it, if I avoid *all* the fucking nutcases in this town, I won't have *any* friends."

"There's nutcases and then there's troublemakers. The shit starters. The assholes. Jack is a thug. Jack treats everyone like shit and he started treating Stacy like shit. My youngest sister goes to school with Laurie. He treats Laurie like shit too. I heard Laurie is staying with Gary now though. So, maybe Laurie is at least happy."

"Yeah."

"Stacy is just a spoiled bitch. And well, Randy? He just has a habit of getting right in the middle of everything wrong that is going on. He hangs out with Jeremy a lot; they both get into trouble all the time. Those two aren't particularly mean; they just have a habit of getting into trouble. We keep drama down here, but if there's drama, Randy will somehow find himself right smack ass in the middle of it. You know?"

"Uh, yeah, I think I understand."

"So, those three, I'd avoid," Keith added. He went to clean the bathroom.

Walter finished his beer. When Keith came back, Walter handed him money, said he had a headache, and he went home.

While Walter was getting himself settled in his house, Laurie was at her grandfather's, on the phone with Luke. She and Luke had been having marathon phone conversations since the sleepover. He told her about the bear and about dinner with the Grangers. She liked the Grangers so she enjoyed hearing about his day. She told him how very brave he was for distracting the big bad bear and he blushed on his end of the phone.

"I'll be back out there this weekend, you know?" she purred into the phone.

"I'm very glad to hear that. I was hoping you would be."

"Oh really?"

"Yeah. You um, you said anything to your dad? Or your grandfather?"

"About what?" she asked alarmed. She hoped he hadn't said anything!

"About us. I mean, I know we aren't like a couple or anything. I was just wondering if they knew we'd been talking."

"Oh no. Definitely no. I mean, it's not because I don't want them to know. I just don't want them to kill you."

"I don't think they would," Luke said hesitantly.

"Just wait. It's not been long enough. Let's just wait," Laurie pleaded.

"Okay. Alright. You know, Will and I get along real good. Maybe Will can talk to your dad."

"Luke! Just ... wait. Okay? We'll figure this out and all. But if I tell them we started talking last week, they'll say it's too soon for me to know I like you like that." Laurie was getting panicked. But Luke smiled.

"Like that? You like me like how?"

"Oh, you know what I mean."

"I hope I do. You're not bringing your friends back up this weekend, are you?"

"No. It's Easter. They'll be staying home this weekend to be with their families. But I'll be going to church with Daddy and Lexi."

"Well, are you going to the festival?"

"Yeah."

"Okay then. So, we'll see each other Friday, and then we'll just happen to run into each other Saturday at the festival. Right? Sound good?"

"Sounds good."

"Okay, well, I guess I'll go to bed. I have to get up early, you know?"

"Yeah, I know. Goodnight, Luke."

"Night, Laurie." The two hung up and Laurie giggled for ten full minutes afterward. Gary knocked on her door.

"Yes, sir?"

"You decent?" he asked.

She rolled her eyes.

"Yes, sir." Gary came in and looked around the room.

"Well, you're making progress. Does it feel like your room yet?" he asked as he looked at her posters.

"Sort of, I guess."

"Who were you in here yammering with all night?"

"Oh, a couple people."

"A boy?" he asked with a smile.

She looked at him. His smile was a sincere smile.

"Um no. Not a boy."

"How did that lunch with Eric go? We haven't talked much since Sunday." Gary sat on the edge of her bed.

"It was fine. He's okay, I guess."

"Well, he's a bit older and all, but I know he's a good kid," Gary said. She just shrugged.

"Everything okay at school?" he asked.

"No, actually. Deanna Moore told everyone in PE that my mom was a drunken whore. I told her to shut up because she didn't know what she was talking about, and she said her dad told her that Mom was in The Tavern Friday night looking for Jack."

"Well, Deanna Moore is right; your mom did go in there looking for Jack. But I hardly see where it was Steven's place to discuss such things with his daughter. Hey? You know Poppy has your back, baby girl. Don't stress. Other than that? Everything okay?"

"I guess so. Can I spend the night at Daddy's Friday though? He wants me to spend more time up there, and I'm here all week. I could just ride with him to the festival and to church Sunday. Then go home with you and Kylie. And I'd see you at the festival."

"That'd be fine."

"And at the festival, I mean I am 15 years old."

"Yes, I know how old you are."

"So, you could maybe talk Daddy into letting me hang out with my friends and whoever instead of having to hang out with him and Lexi *all* day?" Laurie asked. Gary pretended to be hurt. She suppressed a smile while he looked wounded. He poked out his bottom lip.

"Well, maybe I was wanting you to hang out with *me* all day Saturday?"

Laurie looked at him impatiently. He shook his head. "Yes, yes. I'll try to help you out with that. Laurie? Is there anything you wanna talk about? Your mama? Boys? School?"

"No, sir."

"Will you tell me if there ever *is* anything going on? I mean, I know you won't tell me everything. But tell me what you think I *need* to know, even if you don't want me to know. And if nothing else, talk to Kylie or Lex. Talk to Miss Beales or Karen. Just find a grownup you can talk to about things. If you wanna talk to one grownup about some things and a different grown up about other things, that's okay too. Okay?"

"Okay. Everything's okay though. It's just normal stuff going on," Laurie insisted. Gary nodded.

"Alright. Well, I'm going to bed. Get to sleep, yourself. Remember; it's supposed to be bed by ten on school nights. Gimme sugar, baby," Gary pointed at his cheek. Laurie smiled affectionately at her grandfather and kissed his cheek. She hugged him tight. He tried so hard to be there for her and she honestly appreciated it.

"I love you, Poppy."

"I love you, too, sweetheart. Goodnight." Gary made his way to his bedroom where Kylie lay in the bed with a book about being pregnant. She smiled at him.

"Guess what? Right now, the baby is the size of a raspberry. It's got eyelids and lips and even a little nose! And its little tail is almost gone."

"What?"

"Its tail is almost gone. Isn't that so great?"

"Well, I'm sure *it'll* appreciate its tail being gone before it gets here."

"I can't believe we have to wait eight more weeks to find out if it's a boy or girl though. What do you want, Gary?"

"I want a healthy baby. I want a baby that will be taken care of and loved. I want a baby that doesn't have to be raised by daycare workers, which brings up a subject I feel we need to discuss. What're you planning to do when this baby is born? You going to keep working or what?"

"Well, I don't know. I mean, I guess I'd stay home for a while anyway. Maybe later, I might go back to work. I haven't thought about it too much yet. I'd just gotten here and started this job when I started seeing you. Then, we got engaged and then I got pregnant. I just haven't had much time to think this through, what I'm going to do in nine months."

"Seven months now, doll. And I understand things happened quickly, but they happened, and they need to be dealt with. I personally don't want to wait until it gets here to start talking about things. I mean, I'm not an asshole. I did everything I possibly could do when parenting Jason. Hell, I feel like I'm *still* parenting him. My biggest regret though, was that he wasn't raised by family. He had to be raised by daycare workers, and I had a problem with that. *I* didn't have a choice though. *You* do."

"Do I? I don't think I do. You've made it painfully clear what you want me to do."

"Is it such a bad thing? You don't want to be a stay at home mom and wife? You want to keep working at the pharmacy and keeping these obnoxious hours? You work at the pharmacy during the day and you volunteer at the hospital at night. I never fucking see you unless I'm dropping your meals off at the nurse's station. I'm here every damn night by myself unless I hang out at the diner. Pardon me for having expectations in a relationship. I was hoping for something a little different this time around."

"What's that supposed to mean?" Kylie asked suspiciously. Gary sighed heavily.

"Nothing. Just never mind. It's been a long day. It's been a long week. My head hurts and I'm tired, and I'm, well, I'm pissed off in general. Just never mind anything I said tonight. We'll talk about it later." Gary leaned over to turn the lamp beside the bed off.

"No, I want to talk about it now. You were hoping for something different this time around? Are you seriously comparing what we have got to what you had with Charlotte? A hard-working non-addict who is trying to build a life with you … and your granddaughter … is a far cry from what that woman did."

"Oh, Kylie. I just, have things going on in my head. I have shit going on, and I spent the greater part of my adult life *alone*, dealing with everything *alone*. I thought I'd finally have someone home, waiting for me when I got here with things on my mind! If you'd rather work, then work. I guess we should have used protection because I wanted a partner, a spouse, a friend, not someone to help me pay the bills. Maybe you figured I'd be the stay at home dad, and you'd go to work? Because I'm not full time on the force anymore? You're the breadwinner now? Is that what you're thinking? You get up and go to work, and I stay home with the kids and have supper waiting when you come home?"

Gary threw the covers off and got out of the bed. He stumbled in the dark for the doorway and went to the kitchen. He poured a glass of Scotch and sat on the couch. He realized he was starting to tremble. His nerves were shot, and the Scotch wasn't working fast enough. He set the glass on the table and leaned forward. He put his face in his hands and broke down in tears. He found himself sobbing. Gary had to be close to a nervous breakdown before he cried; he didn't cry often. He cried when he saw pictures of Charlottes dead body, while identifying her in the crime scene pictures. He cried when he told Jerry what had happened to Charlotte. And he cried tonight, while sitting alone on the couch in the dark living room.

Kylie came down the hall and saw Laurie watching her grandfather from the hall. She looked at Kylie frightened. Kylie shook her head, put her finger to her lips to indicate Laurie needed to be quiet. She kissed Laurie on her forehead and pointed for Laurie to go back to her own bedroom. Kylie smiled encouragingly at Laurie. Laurie responded with a worried and unsure smile. She went back to her room. Kylie sat down beside Gary and put her arm around his bare shoulders. She pulled him to her. Gary leaned into Kylie and wept.

"Gary, love, whatever is wrong, we'll work it out. I never said I wouldn't be a stay at home mom and wife. I simply said I hadn't put that much thought into it yet. I figured there was time to plan all that. This is the first time I've done this! You can't just make up your mind this is going to be like it was with Charlotte and Jason. And God, Gary! I'm sorry! I'm sorry I haven't been here. I didn't know! They needed help at the hospital. I was trying to be nice. I guess you're right though. I mean, I don't have to do it so much. I can arrange to do it just two or three times a week. How about that? Would that make this any better? Stop crying, Gary. Please? You're worrying me. If this because of something I've done ..." she started. Gary shook his head.

He had to take several breaths and his nose was stopped up now, making breathing difficult. He tried sniffing but coughed instead.

"It's not your fault. I'm a paranoid jilted scared worried old man. It's not your fault. I'm just wanting to make things with us good, better than they were with Charlotte and Jason. I wasn't there like I should have been, Kylie. I saw she had issues, but I kept making excuses for her I should have been around more to see there was something going on. I keep thinking about that one day, that one day I came home and found her almost dead in the bathroom and poor little Jason was ..." Gary couldn't help it. He began to cry again.

"He was sick and undressed, and freezing, and his diaper hadn't been changed since the night before. He was hungry and crying and alone; you know he thought nobody cared about him. I knew. I knew I failed them both miserably then, and I've spent 40 years trying to make it up to him, to both of them. I can't help it. I just wanted something different with us, with me and you. I know it's obnoxious and old fashioned, but I just hoped we'd have something different. I was glad I'm home more because I thought the three of us, four of us now, could really spend a lot of time together. I could make it up to everyone by doing it right his time."

"Gary, baby, you're doing it right by us all *now*. You don't have to keep trying. You are an excellent father and grandfather and I'm sure you'll be a fantastic husband. And now I know that it's so important to you that we do this a certain way. That job isn't more important to me than you and Laurie and the baby are. When the baby gets a little older, like I said, maybe I'll go back to work during the days when it's at school. That's so far away, Gary. Maybe by then, I'll not even want to go back to work! Please stop using us to fix what happened to you, Jason, and Charlotte though. It's not fair to any of us," Kylie added.

Gary looked at her.

"Is that what it is I'm doing?" he asked, looking worried. She nodded. He sighed. He tried to calm down, and he steadied his voice.

"Okay. You're right. That's not okay to do. That's not fair to you, to any of us."

"Thank you. It'll be okay, Gary. We'll just find time to discuss these things, okay?"

"Okay. Alright," Gary agreed. Kylie smiled.

"Just tell yourself it's about us now. Charlotte isn't here."

Gary smiled weakly. He could tell himself that; telling Charlotte that would be a different story. Because Gary was quite sure she was very much so here. In what capacity, he still wasn't exactly sure. But he was sure, she was here.

CHAPTER 30

Tuesday morning, Karen and Roy showed up for breakfast. Karen helped Anne and Tammy with breakfast while they waited for Jason and Lexi to arrive. Faye was exceptionally active this morning, tormenting the cat, playing with the water faucet, playing with the radio, and she had even started the coffee for them.

Nobody bothered acting irritated or frustrated though. They just accepted it; she was here, and she'd always be here. This morning, they had all asked her nicely to please just make herself visible more often, so they at least knew where she was. She decided she'd consider that. It could be fun, she decided. It was already fun being able to torment them when they couldn't see her. But it might be even more fun for them to have to see her all over the place. Then they'd know when she was watching them and that could prove to be even more annoying than being invisible.

Jerry was a little odd this morning. Nobody knew if it was because of his over-active dead wife or if it was because Marilyn was coming to dinner tonight. For some reason, Marilyn being there made him nervous. In one way, he wanted her to spend more time there. In another, he was constantly on edge when she was. He thought, maybe, if she was there more often, he wouldn't be so awkward when she was there.

He came in from the back porch and approached his chair in the kitchen. As he got ready to sit down, his chair pulled itself away from the table for him. He looked at it warily, but the others in the kitchen had seen it and laughed. He sighed and sat down. Will looked at him for a moment; Jerry looked very tired. He'd looked tired to Will for several days. Will sat at the table beside his dad, instead of at the other end of the table where he usually sat. Jerry looked mildly surprised. Will smiled at Jerry, but the look in Jerry's eyes bothered him.

"What's up, Daddy?" Will asked. Jerry just sighed and looked rather suspiciously at his son. He looked at James and Eliza in their highchairs. He looked at Miss Priss hissing at nothing.

"Nothing. Stop it, Faye. I just don't feel good."

"You're still feeling sick?" Will was surprised. Jerry shook his head.

"No. No, not like that. *Stop it Faye! Leave my damn cat alone!*"

Jerry's outburst scared Miss Priss, who ran from the kitchen so fast she didn't even actually go anywhere for the first several seconds, then when she finally got going, she ran directly into the kitchen doorway. She fell over, got up, and left the room quickly. Everyone in the room stopped what they were doing and looked at Jerry. He stood up and left the room wordlessly.

"Faye, girl, I think you done gone a bit too far. Don't mess with the man's cat," Karen advised.

The lights turned off and they all saw an odd thick light near the door, then it was gone. They all saw it, but they didn't laugh or make any snide comments. Tammy, especially, was having mixed emotions about what she'd just witnessed. Anne sighed. Will saw her wipe her eyes.

"Let's just eat, huh? I'll take Jerry his upstairs. It looks like he's having one of his days."

They all sat down to eat, but nobody much felt like eating. Anne had left the room to take the breakfast to Jerry. On the tray, she even put a small blue Fiestaware bowl with scrambled eggs and sausage for Miss Priss. She felt sorry for the fat old cat. She put Jerry's coffee in his insulated cup with a lid because she knew she'd never make up the stairs without spilling it.

Anne called out to Jerry to announce her arrival because she couldn't knock with her hands full. The door wasn't quite shut all the way, so she used her foot to push it open. Jerry sat in his armchair with Miss Priss in his lap. Miss Priss looked very angry, her giant puffy tail switching furiously back and forth; Jerry looked very uncomfortable. He was petting the cat, looking like he felt he had to protect her. Anne set the tray on the occasional table in the middle of the room.

"Here's your breakfast, dear. And here is Miss Priss's breakfast."

Anne set the cat's breakfast on the floor on her placemat and Miss Priss struggled to get out of Jerry's lap. She jumped on the floor with a heavy thud, looked at Anne with a look of superiority, threw her tail straight up in the air, nose up, and marched over to her breakfast. Then, Jerry stood up and dragged himself to the table. He looked like he was being punished.

"What's the matter, Jerry?"

"Marilyn texted me last night; she found a week that would be good for us to go on our trip." He stirred his grits and eggs together.

"Well, that's good."

"No, it's not. She selected the week that Faye died."

"Ohhhh,"

"How? How could she suggest that? How could she not know what that would do to me? How in the hell could she think that that's a good idea? I swear, it's like she doesn't know me at all! It's like she doesn't care."

"Maybe she just didn't think about that part, Jerry," Anne suggested. Jerry looked at her in disgust.

"That's my point! How has she not thought about that?"

"I mean, maybe she was thinking about the other things. Maybe she was just thinking about spending time alone with you. Maybe she was just so excited that she looked for the first week she could go away with you and it just happened to be that week." Anne found herself defending Marilyn Beales. Jerry narrowed his eyes at her.

"You're taking her side?"

"Oh, come on, Jerry. I'm not taking anyone's side. I'm telling you that if I were Marilyn, and you told *me* you were going to take *me* away from this screwed up messed up dysfunctional high- strung crowd, just the two of *us*? *I'd* not be thinking of anything else! I'd be so over the moon I wouldn't be doing anything except finding the first chance we'd have to leave! Your mind is always on Faye, but do you really expect hers to always be? I'm sorry. But this is one time I think you're not being fair. You haven't even talked to her about it, have you? You just got that text message and decided she was a thoughtless, cruel person?

"I'll tell you this; when she was here, when you were sick, she didn't have a clue what she was doing. But she came because she wanted to give you the impression she cared. She wanted to show your family she cared. She may not have shown it exactly right all the time she was here, but she didn't come here because she wanted to be here. She came here to show us that you were important enough to her that she would come here anyway.

"I had to talk her through a whole lot of things. I did it because she wanted to impress you. I did it because she was trying so hard to prove something to us. And I'll say it; I think you're assuming shit and being just plain mean. I hope you'll rethink your opinion. I think you are about to lose something really great, if you don't."

Anne stood up and walked to Jerry. He looked at his plate, looking just as sad as he did before she talked to him. She stood behind him and rubbed his shoulders for a minute, then she put her arms around his neck and leaned forward. She kissed his cheek and whispered in his ear.

"You are amazing, loving, and sweet. You are compassionate, understanding, and strong. Yes, you're strong. I run to you every time I have a crisis for a reason. Please, Jerry, believe me when I say this; as much as I love you, I want you to be happy and fulfilled. I want you to take every chance you have at being happy. I want you to embrace every little thing that makes you feel good. I'd do anything in the world I have to do to make sure you are happy and that's why I have to tell you this; Marilyn is good for you. She's not as good for you as I am. And she's not Faye. But those two things do not mean she isn't good for you. Calm down, baby. You've got this. I promise you; you have got this." Anne kissed his cheek, then his ear, then his forehead, and a sweet kiss on his mouth. She smiled at Jerry and left him alone.

As he sat there alone, he smiled to himself. Anne had said she'd be over the moon if he'd take her away from here. She'd be looking for the first chance to get away with him. If Anne only knew that he'd give his right arm to be able to run away from here with her. Being married to Faye was one thing. Being in a relationship with Marilyn was another. Being in love with Anne was something else altogether. It was a wonderful something else.

Jerry looked at his food and started picking at it. He didn't really want to eat, but he decided he would try since Anne had gone to the trouble to bring it all the way up here to him. He took one bite, and the right corner of his mouth turned down. He kept chewing and tried very, very hard to concentrate on his food. His eyes smarted, but he just blinked quickly several times and took a breath. He chewed again, and then a tear rolled down his nose and dropped to the edge of his plate. He just chewed. Within another minute, Jerry was sitting there, slump shouldered in his chair, eating through tears. The tears came, more and more, and he kept taking deep shaking breaths, and his trembling hand kept trying to bring food to his mouth.

Downstairs was an entire family, laughing, visiting, talking, and eating. Jerry sat alone in his bedroom, their bedroom, weeping in his food. He could say everything they wanted to hear. He could go through the moves, and he could smile through the terrible heart-wrenching times. He could keep doing this; he'd been doing it for years now. And he was about to mark another year.

Jerry didn't want Marilyn. He loved Marilyn, but he wanted someone else. He couldn't have Faye; he knew this. He just wanted things how they had been. He didn't want to have to schedule vacations around Faye's death date. He didn't want to sleep beside her seemingly empty pillow anymore. He didn't want to have to open her cold cream or spray her bottle of Charlie to smell her. He didn't want much at all. He just wanted his wife back. He knew he'd never marry again or be able to introduce someone as his wife. He knew he'd been left with a funny filtered image of his wife, one that was sometimes clear and sometimes cloudy. It was an image that appeared out of nowhere yet left with a swift smear of light in what appeared to be fog. He was left with a voice that was always clear and beautiful as crystal, yet always sounded entirely too far away. He was left with a love he could see and hear but could never hold again.

And this is where Anne came in. Anne, he could hold. He could hear her and see her, and he could hold her. And God, how he loved her! He would do anything in the world for her. He would give his own life for Anne. He would take her wherever she wanted to go, and he would pet her and kiss her and give every ounce of his being to make her happy and take care of her. Then, he realized he did all of that already. She wasn't his wife, not really. But only according to the courts. In his heart, she was his. She had his heart, and she had his name. He'd have never in a million years thought a man could be this in love with his own daughter-in-law. But here it was.

"Jerry and Anne Granger. Jerry and Anne. Hello. I'm Jerry, and this is Anne, my ..." Jerry stopped talking. He thought the word *wife* in his head, but didn't say it out loud. He didn't need to. Faye was there in the room, near the wardrobe. She watched her husband break down in tears into his breakfast. Faye had been watching many things over the past several years. She saw more than she sometimes wanted to. She saw more than she should, and she saw more than the rest of the family would have preferred. She saw something now that changed how she felt about the rest of the things she'd seen.

"Jerry ..." Faye called to Jerry from the wardrobe. He caught his breath at the sudden sound and closed his eyes tight as he recognized the voice. He looked in his plate for a minute before turning to face Faye. She looked at him with a look of utter sadness.

"Hi, Faye," he said with no emotion.

"Oh, Jerry. What have you done? Why did you give that away? Why would you have done something like that? Do you really think that's what I'd have wanted?"

"I don't know what you're talking about." Jerry was genuinely curious.

"Anne. Why did you give her to Will? You love her, Jerry. You are in love with her, so why did you give it all away? I died, Jerry. Not you! You don't love Marilyn; not like you love Anne. You could have married her, honey. I'd have understood! I wouldn't have been angry. You are an idiot, Jerry. Do you see what you've done? You'll spend the rest of your life here, in this house, with the woman you're in love with that you can't have! How in the world do you think this is going to work?"

"I'm married."

"Not like that! Not anymore! And you know you won't marry Marilyn! You would never marry that woman and leave this house! And of course, she's not going to move in here with all these idiot people! What have you done? You could have been happy again, Jerry. Anne makes you so happy already. If you had *married* her ..."

"No! I couldn't have married her. You marry one time. You don't just trade these things in! At least, I don't!"

"But Jerry! Would you have wanted that for me? If you had died would you really expect me to be alone for the rest of my life?"

"I'd haunt you. You wouldn't be ... alone," Jerry said hesitantly. Would he have wanted Faye to move on? Would he have wanted Faye to remarry? Now he was curious.

"Who would you have married, Faye? If I'd gone first?"

"I don't know. Maybe Gary."

"Gary? *Gary?* You'd have married my best friend? What the hell?" he was completely aghast and astounded by this news.

"Well, this is Liberty Creek. No matter who I said, you'd have known them. So, it just stands to reason I'd pick Gary. I know him, and the boys would have ended up brothers! And I mean, he's really cute. I always liked Gary. And he's a man of God ... well, sort of."

"So, you'd have married my *best friend*? Oh, I would have *so* haunted you."

"You wouldn't want me to be happy if you died? You'd want me to be alone?"

"I wouldn't want you alone and sad. But I wouldn't want my *best friend* doing you."

"You know Gary and you know he'd be a good person. I don't like the thought of you and Marilyn but at least I know her. I know she's honest and hard-working and a good person. I know you can count on her. But Anne? I knew nothing about her. That was terrible, not knowing the person you were with. I couldn't protect you anymore. I couldn't do anything to fix it if something went wrong.

"But Jerry you should have done something with that. I wish you hadn't given that up because of me." Faye was distressed and frustrated. It was bad enough being dead, but being this upset and dead was worse. Jerry just looked at her.

"I don't have regrets. I have my whole family. I have my brother back. I have my son home with me. I have Anne here with us. I have two beautiful little babies here with us. And I have you, Karen, and I have Mare ... I guess."

"But you *love* Anne."

"I do love Anne. I'm *in* love with Anne. She reminds me of you. What's done is done. I'll deal with this however I can. I'll be miserable. But I'll be quiet about it. There's no choice here, no options. It just is what it is." Jerry looked sadly at his half-eaten food. He quickly ate the rest of it in just four bites because he didn't want to offend Anne and he certainly didn't want to worry her or Will. If Will saw Jerry's food was only half-eaten, he'd immediately start with the health questions.

Will had been on a very strange kick the last couple of days. He'd been questioning everything Jerry did. Why did Jerry go to the bathroom twice so close to each other? Why did he drink that extra glass of water? Was he feeling dehydrated?

Why did he rub his eyes like that? Why did he have a coughing fit? Was he experiencing trouble breathing? Jerry briefly wondered if Will had perhaps poisoned him and was now waiting anxiously for it to take effect or something.

"Well, love of my life, I'm going downstairs with my plate. Just ... don't worry about me. I'll be okay. I don't have a choice," Jerry told Faye. He didn't smile or anything. He just sighed and winked at her and left the room.

Everyone was still gathered at the kitchen table, which surprised Jerry. Tammy had joined them all and was listening to the odd conversation that was taking place. They were listening to Karen tell a story about Merlene Shaner who had apparently called her that very morning about a pain in her lower stomach.

"I asked her why she was calling me? She said she didn't want to go the doctor unless she had to. The fool. I told her I couldn't tell her what her problem was from way up here on this road. I told her it could be anything. She might have ovarian or cervical cancer; she might have appendicitis; she might just need to go to the toilet. I asked her when her last movement was, and she told me that wasn't it. I told her if she knows so damn much then why was she calling me at 5:30 in the morning asking me why her old belly hurt?" Karen shook her head and ate a bite of biscuit. Will looked at her oddly. Jerry sat down at the head of table, next to Eliza.

"You told her it could be cancer? I'm sure that was a comfort," Jerry said.

He glanced around table and saw Will looking at him worriedly. Jerry looked away.

Karen answered Jerry,

"Well, that's how they found mine! I was having bad pains and I knew it wasn't cramps. I'd had those. These were different. I guess it's best to find it early instead of waiting till folks have to start talking to you about living wills and burial plots." Karen said this so reasonably. Jason joined in now.

"Ug, I hope she doesn't have appendicitis. That'd suck. She isn't in any position to have to get surgery. Wendell doesn't help with anything as it is. Five kids under what? 12 years old? And having to get her appendix removed?"

Caleb followed this conversation with interest.

"What's a *pendis*?" he asked, pronouncing it slowly and clearly.

"A what, Caleb?" Lexi asked distractedly. She was wiping Eliza's chin with a napkin.

"Pendis?"

"I don't know. Where'd you hear it?" Lexi asked. Caleb sighed and looked at his mother like she wasn't really bright.

"Daddy just said it. Miss Merly has to get her pendis moved?"

"Oh, her *appendix*. It's a body part," Roy offered.

"She can have a *body part* moved? Where is it on her body?"

"*Removed*. It means taken away, taken out of her body," Jason corrected.

Anne groaned.

"Really? Is this really breakfast conversation?"

"It's inside your body, between your large intestine and rectum. About here." Jason leaned back in his chair and pointed to his own stomach to show Caleb its location. He clearly didn't care that Anne was opposed to the subject at the breakfast table. Caleb looked at his dad and nodded thoughtfully.

"And I know what a rectum is. I learned that at the stable. It's a butthole."

"Oh, Caleb!" Anne said with disgust while everyone else laughed.

Caleb wasn't done with the morning anatomy lesson.

"Doesn't she need her pendis though?"

"*Appendix*. Well, no. Not really. Lots of people have them removed," Jason answered.

"What's it for then?"

"Oh, good grief. It protects the good germs in your gut. Like, it helps your body recover after you get sick with tummy problems."

"Like throw up and,"

"Caleb! Don't say it!" Anne warned. Jason smiled.

"Yes, like that *other thing*. It's helpful, but apparently, we don't really have to have it to live."

"What about rectums? Do we really need those?"

"Uh, yes we really really do," Jason answered.

"What about brains? Do we need those?" Caleb pressed.

Jason sighed. Will smiled.

"Well, I don't know, Caleb. Seems like an awful lot of folks are running around without them these days." The others laughed. Caleb looked thoughtful still.

"So, if we don't need all our body parts, can we take them out if we want to?"

"Why would you do that?" Will asked.

"I don't know. It's dumb we have them," Caleb reasoned.

Will, always full of entirely too much information, decided to use their breakfast hour to educate Caleb on the world of organ transplants.

"Well, we get extra body parts. They help us out, but they may not always be needed. We have two kidneys, but we only need one. If one quits working, we have a backup. We kind of get spare parts. And it's a good thing. Sometimes someone needs a new kidney or something and someone who has an extra one can donate it to them. If you needed a kidney, see, your mom or dad could give you one of theirs. And they'd still have one, which is all they need."

"So, you can give your body parts to other people?"

"Yes. Body parts are *neat*. A lot of people say, when they die, they want all their body parts donated to other people. The dead people can't use those parts anymore, but someone else who is sick might need them if theirs doesn't work anymore. People have donated their hearts, pancreas, lungs, intestines, livers, eyes, kidneys ... even hands and faces! And some people donate their *whole body* to science for doctors to study." Will told him this with enthusiasm. Anne had long given up trying to get a table appropriate conversation and had gotten up to get Jerry more coffee. Caleb was pondering this information.

"What if I want an *extra* part? Can I buy one?" he asked.

They all stopped eating and looked at Caleb curiously. Karen set her fork down.

"Child, what kind of extra body part are you wanting?"

"Two more arms."

"What for? What would you do with four arms?"

"I'd look like a monster."

"Well, you'd certainly look interesting," Will agreed.

Then, they all heard it. It was a sound that they had not heard in a very long time, in many years to be exact. But there was absolutely no denying what the sound was. They all broke into smiles and found themselves shedding a few happy tears when the sound of Faye Granger laughing filled the kitchen. It was a laugh that was loud, joyous, and full of life and energy. It was Faye's belly laugh that used to be heard on a regular basis in the old house. It was a laugh everyone in the entire house could always hear when Faye was truly tickled by something.

Then, just like in the years before, Faye's laughter made everyone around her start laughing. And as they wiped their eyes, they could see her near the sink. After a moment, she left. Faye went wherever it was she went between hauntings. And Jerry wished for the millionth time, he could go with her.

CHAPTER 31

Tuesday passed uneventfully. The rest of the day was unusually quiet. Roy and Karen went home. Marilyn came to dinner and went home afterward. The whole rest of the week was rather slow, and nobody seemed to have a lot to say to each other. The house was still and sleepy this week.

On Friday, Lexi stayed home because Thursday night Caleb had spilled baby shampoo in the tub and hadn't told anyone. So, when Lexi stepped in the tub Friday morning to take her shower, she slipped in the shampoo and hit her head on the tiled wall. Falling the way that she did, she hurt her left leg and arm badly, in addition to twisting her right wrist when she landed on it. It was swollen and bruised, but she didn't think it required a trip to the ER. Karen came over before going to the Grangers to look at it. She told her to keep an eye on her wrist and head. The knot in the back of Lexi's head didn't seem too bad yet, but Karen told her she needed to stay home and off her feet today. After a few more instructions, Karen went to do her work at the Granger's.

Anne was stressed out because she was making cupcakes for the Spring Festival, which would take place the next day. She was ill with Will for volunteering her; Anne wasn't much of a people person yet. She was comfortable with certain people from town but not comfortable enough with town to host a booth at a big festival. She just kept reminding herself Will would be there at the booth with her.

Gary was stressed out himself. He was one of the organizers of the festival, and people had been calling him all day with questions and last-minute problems. Anne was one of them; she needed to know how many cupcakes she should make because she wanted to make sure there were enough without having to bring home a big pile of them afterward.

Tammy was cleaning the Granger living room when a strange car pulled down the long driveway. She watched it through the window but didn't think much of it; the Grangers had a steady stream of visitors during the day because of the stables. Their car disappeared, and Tammy kept cleaning the living room. A few minutes later she heard someone knock on the wooden frame of the front screen door. Tammy sighed. She went to the door and there she saw someone she didn't recognize. There was a man, who appeared to be late 20s, dressed kind of odd for someone who was looking to talk horses. He looked like he just left his desk job.

"Can I help you?" Tammy asked him through the screen.

The man cleared his throat three times and put his hands together as if he were praying.

"Um, yes, ma'am. I'm looking for Mr. Granger?"

"Well, which one, sug'? There's three of 'em."

"Uhhh, is it Jerry?"

"I wouldn't know. That's why I'm asking you."

"I think he's the one I need to talk to. Yeah."

Tammy looked him up and down, her dust rag in her hand. She looked at him suspiciously. She sighed and opened the screen for him. He awkwardly thanked her and came inside. He stood in the large grand front hall and looked up the wide staircase. Tammy watched him for a moment before she went to find Jerry. He was kinda odd. Tammy made her way to the kitchen, where Anne was cussing about frosting cupcakes.

"Hey Anne. Where's Jerry? He still working?"

"Yeah. What's going on?"

"There's some fella here to see him."

"Send him to the stable," Anne suggested.

Tammy shook her head.

"No, this isn't horse related. I can tell. This fella may even be afraid of horses."

"Oh, well then let's not send out to the stable, I guess. Just call Jerry's phone," Anne told her. So, Tammy looked at the list of numbers on the wall and dialed his number on the cordless phone.

"Hello?" he shouted into the phone. Tammy could hear horses and dogs in the background.

"Quit yelling. There's some dried-up nervous-looking fella here to see you. He looks like somebody made him come here; he doesn't look like he wants to be here at all."

"What's he want? Who is he?"

"Oh shoot, I don't know. It wasn't any of my business. I just let him in because he looked like he was about to cry if he had to keep talking about it."

"Well, in the future, please at least get a name before inviting strange people into my house."

"Oh yeah, he's definitely strange."

"Where's Anne? She didn't talk to him?"

"No. I answered the door, and he wanted to talk to you, not Anne. Are we gonna sit here on the phone all day talking about it, or are you gonna come in here and see what he wants?"

"Oh fine. I'll be right there. Offer him something to drink."

Tammy went back up the hall and back into the living room. The strange man was inspecting the huge pocket door and eight-inch-wide door frame surrounding it. He seemed enamored by it. He was running his hand along it.

"Do you want a drink?" Tammy asked, looking at him.

"Oh, yes, thank you. Some water would be nice," he answered, not looking away from the woodwork. Tammy shrugged.

"Alright. I'll be right back with your water. Jerry will be here in a minute."

Tammy went to the kitchen to fetch the glass of water. As she came out of the kitchen, she met Jerry in the back hall. He was wiping his forehead with a rag.

"It's getting a bit too hot for this early. It's not even middle of April," he told her.

"Do you want some water too?" Tammy asked.

Jerry thanked her but said he was fine for now. They went to the living room and met the man playing with Jerry's door. The man heard Jerry's boots and looked up nervously. He made his praying hands again.

"You must be Mr. Granger."

"I'm one of them, Jerry Granger. It's my understanding we don't know who you are yet?" Jerry pointed out good naturedly, holding his hand out to shake.

The man shook Jerry's hand and looked embarrassed.

"Oh, yes sir. My name is Alex Richardson. I apologize for just showing up here uninvited; the folks in town referred me to your place. You see, I'm a paranormal investigator. I've traveled a good bit to meet you. Sir."

"Let me take a wild guess; you're from Clifton Forge?"

"Oh. Well, yes sir. As a matter of fact, I am. How did you know?"

"Small town, people talk. Have a seat, son."

Jerry sat in his brown leather recliner and Alex sat on the soft leather brown couch. Tammy left them alone. She moved across the hall to clean the library, which also served as an office. Jerry and Alex looked at each other for a moment before Alex started talking.

"Mr. Granger, I've been reading about y'all's place for years. My folks took me on a road trip one weekend when I was a kid, and my mom drove us past this place. I remember thinking how great it was, especially when my folks told me about the, well, stories.

"My parents died years ago, and ever since then, I've been kind of interested in ghosts. See, I'd tell people about things I'd see. And nobody believed me. The older I got I realized it wasn't all in my head. I knew I really was seeing these things. And, well, I decided to start working with it, researching others' stories and experiences. Well, the stories and experiences from this place have always fascinated me the most." Alex finished, looking shyly at Jerry. Jerry sat, his chin slightly lifted and head back. He did this when he was listening carefully to someone.

"How old were you when your folks passed?"

"I was 10. They were killed on the way to a dinner date, in a car wreck. It was their twelfth anniversary. I was home; my grandfather was staying with me so they could go out."

"I am very sorry to hear that. That had to have been difficult for a child your age; well, for a child any age, really," Jerry added, thinking about Will and Jason.

Jerry didn't like paranormal investigators. They always came into his house and acted like they knew more about his ghosts than he did. These ghosts were his. He felt he knew them better than anybody, and for them to try to talk to him like he was the ignorant one who had contacted them always irritated him. He never called any of these jackasses for help. They always called him.

This guy, though, Jerry felt different about. It was likely his sad story, but there seemed to be a trace of sincerity and compassion to his words. Jerry got the impression this young man did what he did because he truly felt a genuine connection to not just ghosts, but to Jerry's house. Jerry didn't think this guy was simply after followers on the internet. He felt this guy actually cared.

"What are you wanting to do, exactly?"

"Just do some tests, observe, nothing that should cause any problems, sir. I just want to see if I can witness any ghosts and … things," Alex replied.

At this, Faye's large wooden rocking chair with the red plaid seat cushion began rocking by itself. Jerry smiled at Alex's reaction. Alex stared at the chair with his mouth open. Jerry nodded toward the chair.

"Alex, that's my wife, Faye. Faye, this is Alex Richardson. He wants to get to know you."

Jerry and Alex visited for another 15 minutes. Jerry then gave him a tour of the house, and then had to give his regrets for cutting the visit short. He had more work to do outside, and he would need to talk to the rest of the family about Alex's interest in the house and what he was wanting to do. He made a promise to contact Alex within the week. They told one another goodbye, and Jerry went outside to get as much work in as he could before five. He only had an hour and knew he wouldn't get everything done he'd wanted to do today. His day was already behind because Ray Barton had called him numerous times accusing the Grangers of trying to steal his horse business. He'd gone so far as to threaten to shoot the Grangers and anyone associated with the Granger's business. He'd called four times already and was obviously quite inebriated when he did so. Jerry had no choice but to finally give them a heads up at the breeding stable. Will was mad about the whole situation and was taking it out on everyone.

As Jerry worked outside, Tammy was finished with her work-day. She lingered for a bit again, sitting in the kitchen with a glass of tea, visiting with Anne and Karen. They heard Marilyn's voice calling from up the hall.

"Where are all y'all? Hello?" she asked as she came to the kitchen doorway. She should have known they'd be in here; she didn't know why she even bothered calling out to them. Marilyn had a large gift bag in her hand. She set it on the buffet.

"Hey, Marilyn. How are you?" Tammy asked. Anne was chewing a bite of pimento cheese sandwich.

"Oh, hey Tammy. I'm good, thanks. How about you? Anne? Um, I guess Jerry is still outside? I brought something for, well, I got something in town and wanted to go ahead and bring it up here today."

"Well that's sweet. Jerry is still working; Ray Barton has apparently been threatening to kill all of us all day. Jerry is mad about it. Will is, too. Some ghost hunter showed up here today, and he took a good two hours of Jerry's time." Anne caught Marilyn up on all the news.

Marilyn looked around. "Well, where's Lexi and the kids?" she asked. This time, Karen answered her.

"Oh, that. Caleb dumped the shampoo over in the tub last night. Lexi went to take her shower this morning, slipped in the shampoo and cracked her ol' head open, sprained things and bruised things. Yeah, she was a beat up old wet mess when I got over there this morning to see about her. Jason didn't want to leave her home alone with the kids until he knew she was okay enough. I told her she could send those kids over here anyway, but she said Caleb didn't act like he felt good. So, I said *fine then; keep them over here with you and your bashed-up self.*

"I called her a couple times to make sure she hadn't fallen over or anything. She seems to be okay, just bitching and moaning, but that just means she's feeling like herself," Karen said with a smirk.

Marilyn smiled at Karen's comment. They all loved Lexi, but she certainly did seem to have one crisis after another. Marilyn set her gift bag on the kitchen table and sat down.

"Well, I guess I'll wait a bit, if that's okay." Marilyn looked around the table at the other three women.

Anne stood up and wordlessly poured Marilyn a glass of tea. Just as she handed the glass to Marilyn, they heard the back-screen door slam shut. Then they heard Jerry using numerous expletives. He came stomping angrily into the kitchen.

"That stupid son of a bitch is this close, *THIS CLOSE*, to being shot in the head! I'm so sick and tired of that damn idiot! Who in the Hell does he think he is? Gonna call me and tell me *I'D* better watch out? Me? Bullshit! He thinks he can intimidate and threaten me? And he thinks I'm not gonna do something about it? Dumb bastard."

Jerry stomped around the kitchen, paying zero attention to those in attendance. He went to the refrigerator and pulled out the sweet tea. Anne looked at Marilyn; she had not been present all day for the numerous times Jerry had come in yelling about Ray Barton.

So, she told Marilyn simply, "Ray Barton."

Anne went to the cabinet and pulled Jerry's favorite glass down. She took the big Mason jar of tea away from Jerry and put it on the counter. He looked at her, his eyes bright and mad. Anne just pointed toward Marilyn. Jerry looked at Marilyn and seemed surprised.

"Well, hello. Did we, were we supposed to get together today?" he asked.

"Oh, no. No, honey. I ordered something in town Monday, and it was already ready for me to pick up today. So, well, I was so excited I wanted to go ahead and bring it today instead of waiting until tomorrow. But I'd like to wait until everyone is in here before I give it to yall."

"Oh, Well, alright, I guess. Give me some sugar. I have to go to the bathroom." Jerry kissed Marilyn on the cheek before excusing himself to the half bath. A moment later, Will came inside and was surprised to see not only Tammy still there but Marilyn there as well. He washed his hands, dried them, then looked at Tammy with a small smile.

"Do you like us so much you want to hang out after the workday?" he asked her.

Tammy shook her head.

"No. I just don't feel like driving all the way back right now. I need to though. I need to get my stuff together for tomorrow still. I still need to press my dress for Sunday. I'm so excited. I got the most darling pair of shoes a couple months ago, and I've just been dying to wear them. Finally, Sunday I can."

"Why couldn't you wear them before?" Will asked with his brow furrowed.

"Oh honey, they're white. I couldn't wear them before Easter. Folks would talk."

"Anne wore some white shoes not long ago though. I knew about the Easter white rule, but I figured y'all weren't doing that anymore since Anne wore them," Will argued.

Again, Tammy shook her head.

"No. If you're talking about those pumps she wears, those are *winter* white. That's not *white*-white. There's a difference. White-white is a linen white. That's summer white. Winter white is sorta with a cream or ivory touch to it. These shoes I got are *summer* white. And you don't wear those before Easter. That's tacky. You know you can't even buy summer white shoes here in town until they start putting the Easter clothes out in stores. You want white shoes after Labor Day or before Easter clothes are put out, you gotta go out of town or do that online. I don't know what would possess someone to do that though. Anyway, I wanna see what Marilyn brought," Tammy finished.

Will looked oddly interested, although slightly confused by Tammy's lesson in identifying and properly wearing winter white and summer white. Anne could tell he'd obsess over this now. From now on, any time Anne wore white shoes, Will would make sure she was wearing the right color white. She sighed. Roy came in to gather Karen up and tell everyone goodbye. He visited with Marilyn and Tammy. Jerry had come back in the kitchen by then and was drinking the tea Anne had made him. Marilyn did a headcount and realized that everyone was there.

"Um, I want to go ahead and give y'all this, now," she said nervously, as she handed the big gift bag to Jerry.

He took it and looked inside. He looked curiously up at her as he set the bag back on the table and pulled something out. He unfolded a large, beautiful cream and deep green throw blanket. He held it for a moment and just looked at it before showing everyone else.

"So, is that winter white?" Will asked Tammy, pointing to the throw. He seemed genuinely curious. He wanted to get this straight.

"No, honey. That's just cream colored. It sure is a pretty color though, with that green." Tammy admired what she could see of the throw.

Marilyn began explaining,

"See, Monday I was downtown and went in Mary's store. She had some pretty pillows in the window. Well, I went inside and saw these throws she was doing. And, well, I decided to get one ..."

As Marilyn paused, Jerry held up the throw for everyone to see. Along the four sides of the beautiful cream throw, was deep green ivy. In the middle of the top and bottom of the throw was a deep green plantation looking house. And in the center of the throw, in matching deep green were the words *Love Lives Here* written in script. Below that, in larger but matching letters it said *Faye.* They all looked at it for what seemed like an eternity to Marilyn. Marilyn filled in the silence.

"See, Mary usually puts *last* names in the middle. But well, I saw these and for some reason, I thought about Faye. I thought maybe she'd like one. You know, maybe it'd look nice hanging over the back of her rocking chair? Maybe, I mean, y'all can put it wherever you want. It's just where I saw it, in my mind, when I thought about getting it."

They all stopped looking at the blanket and looked at Marilyn. Jerry smiled a crooked smile. Tammy wiped her eyes. Jerry handed the blanket to Marilyn.

"It's beautiful, and it's so sweet of you. You're right, I think she would like it. And I agree; it'd look nice on the back of her chair. But I think that you should be the one to put it there. I mean, it's from you, for her. So, here ya' go."

They all went to the living room together. Marilyn placed the blanket over Faye's rocking chair, so that Faye's name was centered on the back of it. They all stood there and just looked at it. The chair began to slowly rock. This brought a smile to everyone's face and tears to Marilyn's eyes. Jerry nodded.

"Yeah, you know? I think Faye likes her blanket."

And Faye did.

Shortly afterward, Roy and Karen went home. Marilyn was invited by Anne to stay and join them for supper. While they ate, nobody spoke much. Jerry thought about Marilyn and Faye and what Anne had told him in the bedroom. Marilyn thought about Faye and her rocking chair with the new blanket. She hoped that the next time she saw Faye, Faye wouldn't have that disgusted, pained look on her face. Maybe the blanket made things okay between them. Anne thought about the next day when she'd have to go help Will run a concessions booth downtown. She wasn't looking forward to it, but she had agreed to do it because, well, because Will had already said she'd do it. Even if he hadn't, she guessed she'd have done it anyway. She liked to make Will happy, and if her playing the part of the happy housewife and mother made him happy, okay. It made both him and Jerry happy, she knew. She also knew, not so deep inside, that it made them happy because she was being Faye. It was an awesome responsibility and overwhelming footsteps to follow in but from the time Anne had arrived, her only desire was to make these stupid old men happy. So, Anne was already more like Faye than she realized.

And Will? Will spent several minutes pondering winter and summer white. He thought about Ray Barton, and he thought about his mom and her new blanket. He also kept thinking about how weird it had been with Lexi and the kids not there today. He'd gotten quite used to having them there Monday through Friday and seeing them on Saturday. This made him think of something.

"So, how's Lex? She gonna be able to make it to the shindig tomorrow?" he asked Anne. Anne shook her head at his use of the word *shindig*. He could be such a dork sometimes.

"I guess so. She felt well enough to call here and whine about Jason today. So, I guess she's feeling okay."

"What did Jason do this time?" Jerry asked with a smile.

"He didn't come and check on her. Caleb was being high maintenance today. Apparently, he stuck Lexi's pantyliners all over Teague. He wrapped them around Buck (Caleb's cat), and when Lexi tried to pull them off Buck, it pulled at his hair and Buck got pissed off and scratched Lexi. You know; typical Lexi problems."

Anne didn't feel like eating. She was tired and that just made thinking about the busy day tomorrow that much more exhausting. They finished up dinner. Jerry told Marilyn he'd pick her up in the morning to take her to the festival. Then after telling everyone *goodnight*, she drove home. Marilyn would be attending the festival just like most every other citizen of Liberty Creek.

Jerry went to sleep where he was again accompanied by his wife. The children went to sleep, accompanied by the soft, comforting noises their rooms made in the night. Will and Anne went to bed, but only Anne slept. Will lay in bed for a long time that night thinking.

Saturday morning, they all got up, had breakfast, and tended to the usual chores. The only interesting thing that happened was Jonathon fell off the roof of the stable. They thought perhaps he had broken a rib, but after a few minutes, he assured them he was fine. Then everyone got ready for the festival.

It was a very pretty day for early April. Jerry was in a better mood than he usually was in April. He took the kids with him in his truck since Will and Anne had to carry food and things in Will's truck. So, Jerry and the kids went to get Marilyn. After a short discussion, they decided to leave the truck at her house and walk downtown to the festival. And even though everyone knew Jerry was their grandfather, they couldn't help but marvel at how much he acted like their father. He handled James just as he had handled Will and he was as wrapped around Eliza's finger as he could have been. It was such a sweet relationship he had with these children. He beamed with so much pride in them, any stranger would have thought they were his.

When they arrived at the town square, they looked for Will and Anne's booth. They found Lexi sitting in a folding chair under the haunted oak tree. She had a big bruise on the side of her face poorly covered with makeup. She had a gauze bandage wrapped around her right wrist. Jerry paused to look at her.

"Baby, you look like hell."

"Thanks. I feel like it. Every muscle in my body hurts. It hurts to stand, to sit, to walk, to do anything. It's like I pulled everything in my body when I fell. Jason tried to help me with makeup because he was worried people would think he beat me. Caleb keeps talking about me just getting new body parts." Lexi groaned as she tried to readjust herself in the chair. Marilyn felt bad for her. It was obvious this wasn't a case of Lexi overreacting.

"Do you want a drink or anything? Something to eat? There's all kinds of stuff here, I know," Marilyn asked. Lexi was touched. Marilyn wasn't usually so nice to her.

"I saw Wyatt with a hotdog and a Coke. It looked good. Yeah, thanks. If you could find a hot dog and Coke, and maybe some cotton candy, it'd be nice," Lexi said pitifully.

Jerry nodded.

"We'll see what we can dig up for you, sweetpea. Don't go running off."

"I couldn't go running anywhere if I wanted to. Even my back hurts."

So, Jerry and Marilyn went and mingled while they found a hotdog, and a cold can of Coke for Lexi. They then went to Will, who was in charge of the cotton candy machine. He seemed to be enjoying himself, although he wasn't incredibly coordinated with the machine. Will had pink, blue, purple and green cotton candy stuck to his clothes and even in his hair and goatee and a stray strand of pink cotton candy in his eyebrow. Every time he made a new cone of it for someone, cotton candy threads would escape and fly about the air around the booth. Some cones were enormous while others were half the size. When he discovered Jerry and Marilyn wanted one for Lexi, he made her one of his enormous ones. This didn't go unnoticed by Anne, but she didn't think much about it.

Roy and Karen made their rounds, and Jason took the kids to the various booths and tables while Lexi ate her picnic lunch alone under the tree. While they did this, Laurie was walking around with Luke and Stacia, which didn't go unnoticed by her overprotective grandfather. Gary and Kylie were at the face painting table with Caleb when Gary looked up and saw Luke run his hand through Laurie's hair while gazing lovingly into her eyes.

"What the hell?" he asked, louder than he intended.

Kylie gasped.

"Gary! Easter festival! Kids! Family event! You're a *preacher* this week!" Kylie was both shocked and mortified. She thought to herself, oh dear, she was already acting like a preacher's wife.

Gary snapped his head back and looked at her with his green eyes on fire. He pointed at Laurie and Luke.

"Look at them! Look at that! Do you see that? What in the world is she thinking? What is *he* thinking? That pervert! Where's Jerry? Where'd Jason go with the baby? They have that child molester *working* for them! Oh, no way is this gonna …" Gary was all set to keep talking but Kylie put her finger to his lips. He stopped but he didn't want to. He was breathing heavily, and his eyes kept darting between Kylie and his granddaughter.

"Gary. Stop. Just stop. Child molester, Gary? Really? We all know Luke. He is not a pedophile. He is only four years older than her. Isn't that the same thing as when you had a crush on Karen as a kid? It is possible to be 15 and attracted to a 19-year-old. I mean, hello! I told you that I had a crush on you when I was 15! And that was a *lot* more than four years difference. He's a nice kid, Gary. They aren't doing anything; they're just hanging out. And heads up, if a girl likes a guy enough, no amount of grounding or threatening is going to keep them apart. If anything, it'll just make them more determined to see each other! Chill out!" Kylie tried to keep her voice down because she didn't think people should see her and the preacher arguing at the Easter festival.

Gary fixed his mouth in a hard line. He was mad about the situation and wanted nothing more than to go hit Luke and lock Laurie in her room for the next three years. But he did neither. His breathing slowed a bit. He didn't want to, but he calmed down.

About 30 minutes later Laurie and Luke found themselves standing right beside Gary and Kylie, and Laurie was certain her grandfather was going to shoot Luke right there at the spoon and egg races. He didn't; Gary even smiled at them, but it looked far from sincere.

Jason saw Laurie and Luke together; he wasn't as bothered by it as his father was. He knew Luke. Yeah, Luke was 19, but he was a good guy, and Jason felt a person's behavior was far more important than their age. It wasn't like Luke was 30. It was just four years, not even quite four years, actually. Jerry and Roy saw them and found humor in the situation because they knew that Gary was purely boiling mad inside.

When Tammy and Carol Raleigh came to work Will and Anne's booth for the second part of the day, Will and Anne went and sat with Lexi for a while. Lexi wasn't enjoying herself at all. Laurie and Luke had come to visit with her for a while earlier. Gary came and sat with her when he got tired of walking around with Kylie. Jason dumped Teague off on her when he started whining and obviously wanted a nap. At some point a big shepherd dog that belonged to the Weavers came to visit for about an hour. Roscoe (the dog) lay down right beside Lexi's chair and after about 10 minutes he fell asleep for a bit. So, Lexi wasn't lonely anyway. She had a constant stream of visitors including one kid about seven years old that walked up to her and asked her if she'd been hit by a garbage truck. Lexi wanted to go home.

Will was such a darling. He walked over to Elderod's Pharmacy and got her some Tylenol. Jason acted put out by her inability to help with the kids; Will, though … Will acted worried about her and made her wish for the millionth time Jason was more like him. Anne was not at all fazed by Will's willingness to run to the pharmacy for Lexi. Anne knew Will was a truly genuinely nice guy who would do most anything for most anyone. She also knew Lexi milked it for all she could. Anne didn't even care, not really. Anne kept her eye on her though. Anne had enough reasons to keep an eye on Lexi; she learned that with Uncle Roy recently. Lexi wasn't bad, or mean, or even particularly devious, but Lexi needed attention here lately, and Anne knew Lexi well enough by now to know Lexi found ways to get it.

The day was a pleasant one for everyone except Lexi. The weather was beautiful, and spring was finally truly in the air. As four o'clock approached, people were closing down the booths and packing up tables and chairs and boxes of various things. The leftover hotdogs and chips and such were packed up and taken to the police dept to feed employees and the five people locked up in the three cells.

Anne had exactly five cupcakes left so she said to give them to those spending the night in jail. Everyone loaded up cars and trucks and went home. Jerry and the kids walked Marilyn home, told her goodbye, and Jerry brought the kids home. The kids fell asleep within five minutes.

While everyone was enjoying the festival downtown, the house sat, waiting. It wasn't empty, it wasn't still. It was simply waiting. Doors opened and closed, curtains moved, and chairs rocked. Toy balls and Matchbox cars rolled across the old oak floors. The radio in the kitchen played classic rock. If anyone living had been present all day, they'd have heard the murmuring of soft voices wafting through the wide halls and large rooms. They'd have perhaps even felt the breathing of the walls as the house watched over all those who were active. Yes, when the living left the house, or even just went to sleep at night, the house was busier than the living realized. This was when those who resided here, often unseen, were most active. This is when they truly came out to wander and play.

In those still quiet evenings, when the grandfather clock in the hall would announce the late-night hours, the house was very much so awake. This is when those who lay low during the rest of the day made their rounds. This was when they wandered without worry and visited. The spirits truly came to life during this time, and the wooden walls and floors took on a life and personality of their own. The handmade bricks and hand-carved mantles and stair railings listened and watched. Everything listened and watched. Every stone and splinter felt and heard everything that went on in this house.

And outside, the rolling hills and graveyards tucked in the thick woods of the Appalachians and the outbuildings on the property were all just as active. As the moon hung over the farms on Teague Road, many souls walked the land. The soil, the trees, and wooden fences were all just as much as alive as the walls of the house were.

Faye was content for the most part, these days. She had learned to let her loved ones know what she wanted. She had learned to show her feelings, and she had learned to laugh aloud. She had learned to touch things, to move things, and to get the attention she desperately wanted. Faye had learned that Marilyn was okay, after all. She was a fast piece with her sappy Kentucky accent and her eight-inch heels, back in the day. She wanted Jerry back then and she couldn't have him. And now, Faye took some pleasure in knowing that whereas Marilyn may be sleeping with Jerry, she still didn't really have him. No, Marilyn wasn't a threat. She was okay now. The house itself had not yet completely accepted Marilyn but Faye had. Faye had nothing to do with the chorus of soft voices Marilyn had heard several times. She had nothing to do with the haunted salt-shaker that night or several other things Marilyn had witnessed. Faye did know, however, that the more comfortable this house became with Marilyn, the more it would let her see and hear. So, if Marilyn thought this was going to get any easier, she was mistaken.

As for Anne, Faye was better understanding this very odd relationship between her husband and their daughter-in-law. Oh, it was unorthodox and taboo, but she did think she was beginning to understand things. Jerry had loved Faye all these years; he'd loved her in a way he had never loved anyone else. And he still felt that love; Faye had no doubt. But Jerry had managed to find room in his heart to also love Anne. It wasn't the exact same way; Jerry and Faye had over 50 years together. That alone had given them something Jerry and Anne didn't have. But Jerry loved the things about Anne that reminded him of Faye. It wasn't a sick relationship. It wasn't disgusting or anything even shameful Faye was seeing now. The man was simply in love for the second time in his life and there was just so much he could do about it.

Faye had begun doing what she could to help Anne out these days. Anne was about to begin reading Faye's second notebook. There were a few times Anne had spoken aloud to Faye, while reading the notebook. Anne was still a little miffed about Faye cleaning up the house, but Anne reminded herself, it was still Faye's house too. And she'd spent many years cleaning this house. If Faye wanted to help Anne and Tammy out with the housework, then fine.

Jerry was not any happier this April than he had been in the last several years before, but he was working on things. There was a difference in getting better and moving on. He knew he'd never truly get better, but he was learning to move on ... or make everyone think he had, he thought. But they all knew. Marilyn had explained the situation that day at lunch; everyone was seeing Jerry's situation just a little clearer. And Jerry would take Marilyn out of town, but he'd simply have to explain to her he would have to wait until May. He decided he'd even tell her why.

When the family came home Saturday night, they ate an early dinner, and everyone went to bed earlier than usual. Anne however got back up; she figured her mind was too busy thinking about Easter plans the next day. So, she went downstairs to get something to drink and just think.

Anne got a glass of tea and sat in her seat at the table. The kitchen faucet turned itself on. Anne sighed and walked over to the sink. As she was about to turn off the water, she looked up in the wide white windowsill at the three blue Mason jars. These were Faye's jars, and they held an assortment of wildflowers, which Anne dutifully kept filled for Faye. Even in the dead of winter, Anne brought Faye flowers from town. When Anne looked at Faye's flowers, she saw the water was almost out. She left the faucet on and filled the jars with water. She replaced the jars and adjusted them just exactly how Faye had left them when Anne first came here. Anne looked at them for several minutes, and although she felt herself begin to smile, she felt tears in her eyes.

After a moment, Anne turned to go back to the table and saw Faye beside the fireplace. Faye just looked at her; it was a curious look. Anne felt Faye wanted something.

"Hi, Mom," Anne said to the woman who stood watching her. She had never referred to Faye as *Mom* before. They both decided they liked it. Faye brushed her hair out of her face and smiled. Anne was at ease now with this woman; yes, she was just a woman. Anne was no longer able to see the differences between Faye and anyone else in this house.

"Anne ..."

"Are you doing okay, now? Is everything okay?"

"It's good." Faye sounded far away, as always, but she smiled.

Anne nodded and looked around for a moment. She looked around the semi-dark farmhouse kitchen, surrounded by Faye's things, and she felt very, very sorry for this woman. Anne recalled something Karen had told her Lexi had done while Anne was sick. So, after a moment Anne decided to make a second glass of tea. She walked to the table and sat the tea across the table next to Jerry's seat. This is where Faye had always sat. Anne then sat down in her own chair. She looked back at Faye who now stood near the sink. Anne patted the table with her hand.

"Come and visit, Mom?" Anne asked. She watched as a blurry thick white light made its way toward the table. Faye's chair pulled back, and the white light seated itself in the chair. After a moment, the light became clearer, although not perfect. The light disappeared and then there was Faye.

It was a turning point for the two women, a significant one. Faye sat with her daughter-in- law and Anne sat with her mother-in-law. They sat visiting in the kitchen, and whereas the conversation was awkward at times, they felt they had begun a whole new chapter in their relationship.

This house sat dark and quiet while the two women got comfortable with one another. But it watched, and it listened, and it was content. Faye had struggled for so long to become a part of the spirit of this house. Faye wanted this house back, her family back. And this house had given her all the time and strength she needed to do that. Was it like others had thought; even Marilyn at one point? Was it something evil, something that possessed people? Or was it love that kept people here and kept them here long enough so that even in death they could learn to feel and experience that love? It was surely love that kept Faye Granger here, running around and picking things up, visiting with her grandchildren, standing by her husband, and doting over her son. And it was love that had won Marilyn over; she loved Jerry enough to spend more time here. And in doing that, she and the house had become better acquainted.

It was love that made Anne take care of this crazy family and their unusual house; she was different from Marilyn though. Anne had walked in through that screen door on the very first day and felt a responsibility to this house; her feeling of responsibility came to the house before it even really came to the men who lived here. These three women were here because of love, pure and simple. They all three loved Jerry, and they all three loved this family. And they all three loved this house. Marilyn had seen that blanket in Mary's store and saw *Love Lives Here*. And that's when she smiled, and she knew. Nothing evil was there, at least not enough to overpower the love present. Love did live there, even among the deceased. It lived not just in the people. This house was not like other houses. This house had a soul and personality and spirit all its own. They all had known that for a while. Now Marilyn saw it too. And next week, Alex Richardson would see it too.

The curtains blew in the windless mountain night, Eliza's doll fell from the couch to the floor, the floorboards creaked beneath invisible feet, and a Tonka truck rolled near the old dishpan of Will's matchbox cars. While Clarissa hummed Green Grow the Lilacs in Eliza's bedroom window, the heavy smell of cigar smoke lingered on the front porch while Officer Johnson looked out over the empty driveway ... the same driveway Clarissa Buchanan watched from Eliza's window tonight, with anticipation, like she did many nights. She stood in Eliza's window waiting for her sweetheart from Tennessee to come back for her ... and he would.

The house settled, sighing, and stretching. The moon hung high in the dark early morning of Easter Sunday. It was a happy house, and it was because despite wars, deaths, plagues, tears, storms, fights, arguments and heartbreak, this house had managed to keep its loved ones close even in death. It had managed to keep the family together, and that's all that mattered. Yes, love lived here. And it was obvious now that it would never die. Because nothing and nobody here ever *really* died. This house would see to that.

To Be Continued